MY SECRET
Submission

J.M. WITT

DEDICATION

To all the Sirs, Masters, Daddies, Doms, and Dommes who've taken that lost sub under their protection so that they might fly free in their embrace.

To all the subs, littles, slaves, and babies who've discovered the wondrous creature that lies within. They deserve to be treasured.

ENSNARED

He was my darkness.
He was my dangerous.
He was my deadly.
He was my devil.
He was my demise.
I was his starlight.
I was his shelter.
I was his salvation.
I was his saint.
I was his sanity.
We were ensnared.

~ J. M. Witt

MY SECRET
Submission

CHAPTER
One

LOST

THERE'S NO LONELIER EXISTENCE than being a stay at home mom and a traveling widow. The bed next to me was almost always empty and when my husband was there, he wasn't present. I was no longer his top priority and hadn't been in a long time. It was like I had a roommate who I screwed occasionally, but other than that I felt as if we were strangers. For longer than I cared to admit, I believed that I'd rather be alone than live with someone and feel this lonely.

I pulled away from the drop-off lane at the airport as relief flooded me. Finally, a much needed break. Don't get me wrong, I loved my husband, but I was accustomed to him traveling and needed the break. *We* needed the break. There'd been so much fighting, so much silence, so little intimacy. He'd even said he was content, that all marriages struggle and I should get over it. It was like he didn't care and just assumed our issues would pass. I didn't know how much longer I could sit and wait. We'd both gone to therapy, together and separately, and it hadn't helped.

The kids were in the back sniffling as we drove away.

"It's going to be fine guys. We'll Skype with Daddy every day." I wasn't even sure that would happen, but I was trying to cheer them up.

I put on a movie and began the drive home. They all had their headphones on and I scrolled through my playlist, anxious to listen to *my* music without Todd groaning about it. I put on *Lost* by Liza Anne. The words were almost all true. I was most certainly lost.

Our marriage wasn't perfect. We had our ups and downs like every couple, but lately it just felt like it was more difficult than it should be. Things hadn't been the same since having our youngest and that was several years ago. I really needed this time alone to reflect without tripping over his underwear. Three weeks without his help with the kids would be the biggest struggle, but I'd manage. I always did.

Friends rarely called and I understood, but it didn't change how I felt. They all had responsibilities of their own and most had a husband who was home every night. Some days I just wanted to shout to the heavens, but even that would be interrupted by one of my motherly duties; I was certain of it!

That night after I put the kids to bed and finished up some editing, I logged into my KinkyFodder account. I'd created it a few months ago—mostly for research purposes—but I had a message waiting and wanted to check it out. It was probably just like all the rest, some ridiculous offer from someone claiming to be a Dom at the tender age of twenty-two. *Not likely kid.* I'd probably just delete the message and log out like I usually did.

I read the message over and over again. Then I checked out his profile. A profile he actually spent some time on. He'd written a short essay about himself. He was a few years older than me, was married, had a family, traveled for business, had desires his wife couldn't understand, etc. He kind of just laid it out there—if he was being honest. He lived in the next big metropolis about an hour from me.

I went back to the message.

What are you looking for?

It was the simplest question, but I couldn't stop re-reading it, over-analyzing it. What was I looking for? Fuck. Did I even know? I had desires, too, that my husband just couldn't quite wrap his mind around. I wanted, no, needed sex more than he did which was beginning to give me a complex, especially when he refused. What grown man doesn't want a wife willing to have a roll in the hay? Unless he was getting it elsewhere, and I didn't want to go down that road again. Now, don't get me wrong. There were times I turned him down, but more often than not it was the other way around.

I had cravings, desires, and a curiosity to explore deeper into BDSM. That curiosity had been there for a very long time and I was trying to come to terms with it. I decided to respond to the message. *Keep it cool Mer.*

Friendship would be primary. Someone to talk to who doesn't think I'm odd! Trying to explain it to my husband, when I feel like he thinks I'm damaged or weird is hard. He just doesn't get it and I can't explain it. I'm a SAHM and he travels a lot. I won't lie; I fantasize about nights away, but not sure if or when that would happen.

I took a deep breath and hit send. I mean, what did I have to lose? It was just an email.

A week passed and I rarely heard from Todd. He called the kids almost every day, but barely spoke to me. It hurt, but was almost easier that way, and it was something I'd grown accustomed to. Just more evidence for me that he wasn't invested in me, in us, like he should be. Friends asked if I thought he was having an affair. I was no stranger to his infidelity; it'd just been a long time.

Two weeks later, Todd got home and the kids were ecstatic to see him. Me, I was just happy to have help with the kids. I was a horrible mom and wife. He'd just gotten home and my first thought was 'how the hell do I get away from them all?' Instead, I hugged him dutifully and put a smile on my face.

I never got a reply to my sent message at KinkyFodder and wasn't sure if I ever would. I didn't have time to worry about that as I had responsibilities to tend to anyway. Besides the kids and Todd, I was on the PTA and planning to run for PTA President. I also moonlighted as a freelance editor for romance novelists and had a desire to write my own novel, but didn't know when I'd find time. I took care of all the bills at home so you could add 'accountant' to my resume, too. God, I just wanted to be able to turn it all off and I had no idea how to do that.

A few months later, Todd and I were in bed. He was finally smacking my ass with a little bit of passion. I moaned as he slid in from behind. Grabbing my hips, he pulled me back and plunged back in.

"Don't stop…"

"I'm not."

"Not that. Smack my ass...harder." It was finally starting to feel good and then he just stopped. I needed more.

My request went unanswered. I played with my clit as his thrusts from behind became more deliberate. He was close and I was just getting warmed up. *Concentrate Mer, find your release.* Closing my eyes I visualized that I was somewhere else, with someone who did what I wanted without me having to ask. The sensations were rising as my whole body tensed. I was going to get off too, goddammit.

"I'm almost there, Todd. Don't stop."

"Come on, Mer. I'm so close."

I wanted to scream at him to 'Stop talking and keep fucking!' Tuning him out, I worked myself harder until my face was buried in the sheets, my orgasm finally taking over. His hands were the only thing holding me up and then he grunted his release behind me. The same old convulsions I was used to consumed him as I gingerly fondled myself, trying to enjoy every last tingle.

He released my hips and I rolled over to my side of the bed. Throwing me a towel from our nightstand drawer, he headed to the bathroom to clean himself up. I wanted more and knew it wouldn't happen, but I was going to try anyway. Climbing in next to me, after putting his underwear on, he kissed me sweetly and rolled over. Circling my arms around him, I tried rousing him for round two.

"Todd, please... Let's do it again." I nibbled on his shoulder as he grunted.

Groggily, he muttered, "I'm going to take a jackhammer to that vagina of yours. Maybe then you'll be satisfied. Shouldn't you be exiting your sexual peak, not entering it?"

Totally annoyed, I pushed away from him and spit out, "You're a dick. Maybe one orgasm is enough for you, but I want more. And if you knew or researched anything about female sexuality, you'd know I'm just reaching it, not exiting it."

I waited a moment and realized he was already drifting off to sleep. *AGHHH.* I should be happy. He got me off. Well, ok, I got myself off. But, shit. I climbed out of bed, threw on some yoga pants and a t-shirt and left the room. Sex with him had always been this way. I needed more to get me turned on, to keep me there, and wanted more when it was over. Todd, not so much. For months I'd been trying to get him to explore further and he was unreceptive, sometimes going as far as making me feel guilty for my cravings.

Sitting on the couch with my laptop, I checked my KinkyFodder account.

Still no reply. I re-read his profile. Spanking, corner time, orgasm denial—uh, no thank you—teasing… The list went on and on, though he didn't list anything that scared me or made me nervous. I slammed my laptop shut, ignoring PTA emails and editorial messages and opted to get caught up on my DVR. Things would get better with Todd. They had to. Didn't they?

Six more months passed. Things were bad at home. I was so unhappy. I'd proposed an open relationship, purchased new toys, a kit so Todd could tie me to the bed. Talking hadn't worked, so maybe new items would. I was trying everything to get him to open up and explore. We were married. Shouldn't I be the one person he'd want to evolve with, grow with sexually?

"What's with the sudden interest in anal?"

Sighing. "I'm just saying I'm interested. In all the years we've been together we've never done it. Why are you opposed to it?"

"I just don't like it."

"You mean the ONE time you did it? This isn't like getting the kids to take a 'like it' bite. You have to try it more than once. And why not with me?" I could barely contain the smile on my face and he wasn't amused.

"I said 'NO' Mer. Drop it."

It was another pointless argument with Todd. I'd had enough of his lackadaisical attitude toward me and our marriage.

"You're a fucking idiot." The kids were outside and I just ripped into him. His chin popped up and he looked to me like I was crazy. "I'm a fucking catch and you're losing me, if you haven't already lost me."

"Meredith, I don't want to lose you."

"Well you have a fucking funny way of showing it. I've been begging and pleading with you for YEARS." He just stared back at me dumbfounded. "Guys hit on me all the time." Ok, not *all* the time. "Any man would be happy to take your place and you're too self-absorbed in your fucking job to notice me. I'm good looking, I work out, I'm fucking funny, and Jesus, I LOVE sex. You're a fucking idiot."

"You're being ridiculous." His voice was calm and flat.

"Am I? If you were invested in me like you claim to be, things wouldn't be so difficult between us."

Staring at me dumbfounded, he nodded. "Maybe you're right."

"About?"

"Marriages go through tough times. It's to be expected."

How could he be so calm? "Yes, they do. But what isn't expected is for me to be the only one putting in some fucking effort."

He set his laptop aside, not saying a word. I wasn't trying to be an egomaniac, but I was confident enough to know I was right. If he stood up, I didn't see it. I was already out the door and heading to my SUV.

"Mom, where are you going?"

Looking to my daughter, I tried smiling through the tears. "I have to run out. I'll be right back. Daddy's inside."

She just nodded, but watched as I pulled out of the drive. What I know now is that was the moment I put up my walls in regards to Todd. I shut down, no longer wanting to be hurt by him. I was tired of all the letdowns and rejection. Yes, all marriages hit rough patches, but this had been going on for years. Anytime he said he would put in more effort, he would—for a few weeks—and then the same old Todd would resurface.

I mean, what was I doing this for? This seemed like insanity. I felt like a hamster in a wheel and wondered when or if things would ever change. And I knew they wouldn't change unless I was that change. But what did that mean? Was I prepared to be a divorced mom, single, really alone...? I just didn't know. The other option was to grin and bear it. I shook my head. I'd been doing that for far too long already. Too many years of waiting for him to show he still wanted me, wanted us, loved me, loved us. It was just too much and deep down I knew too much time had passed.

A few days later, Todd and I were walking on eggshells around each other. Nothing new really. That night I plopped down at my desk and powered up my laptop. Immediately I thought about *him* and the message that he never replied to. Logging into KinkyFodder, I checked his profile. No change. I deleted a few other messages, none of which intrigued me in the least, and then logged off. I had PTA things to deal with and there was always editing to be done.

A few weeks later I was on my computer when my email program alerted me to a new email awaiting me at KinkyFodder. Thinking nothing of it I opened it up and there it was, there *he* was. He'd finally replied and according to the timestamp it was within the last hour. I took notice of where Todd was and spotted him in the other room watching baseball. I was safe.

Sorry - I am not sure I ever responded to your reply. I do not get on here much unless responding to someone's message. Did you find a friend to talk to? I know the feeling of having a spouse that just doesn't get it. Mine is vanilla but at least now understands this is a "real" thing...

Did I find a friend to talk to? What a loaded question. Only girlfriends and we mostly joked about it. No one knew how deep my cravings ran, probably not even myself.

I've talked to my husband, basically demanding more, and it's helped some. We have good days and bad as I'm sure most relationships have. I still feel like a fish out of water most days.

I totally underplayed how bad things were in my relationship. I mean, who tells someone they just met 'Yeah, marriage is in the shitter!'? I vaguely wondered how long I'd wait for a response this time. Several minutes later another email popped up. It was him. Deep breath and I opened it up.

It took me a long time to accept this as "normal" or at least that many share the same interests even if not exactly mainstream. Took me longer to figure out how to make it work in my "normal" life. That, I have found, is a never ending process/learning experience.

Was this dude for real? This was so bizarre and liberating. Someone to really *talk* to about this shit with no judgment. Bring it on!

Yes. Agreed. I hate that word 'normal', always have. Who can say what's normal? Writing and reading are outlets for me, which is good and bad for fantasies! It's nice having someone to talk to who 'gets it'. I wouldn't normally just give out my email, but that's more accessible to me. meredith@meredithedits.com
~Meredith

I must have been out of my mind. But I just didn't care. I needed and deserved to have someone to talk to. And considering it took him almost a year to respond to my first reply, I wanted to make sure he had a way to email me directly, if he wanted to. Months and years of feeling like my desires were wrong and dirty seemed to vanish after a few simple emails. It was now after ten p.m. and Todd had gone to bed. Another email alert popped up.

Is that a corporate/business email? Looks like it. If so – I would be VERY careful with it. Do you have a generic gmail or yahoo email account? If not – I would set one up for discretion and to keep this completely separate from the regular life.

My email is bruisedassets@yahoo.com and it is NOT a corporate account so you can be as free to speak (type) as you would like.

Hope you had a great weekend.

I laughed at his email and knew what he was getting at. How much did I tell him? I sighed and threw caution to the wind.

It is, but it's my business. I'm Meredith Edits. No one else has access to it.

Weekend is ending soon. Kids go to school tomorrow, thank God.

Hope you had a good weekend as well!

I looked to the clock. It was late and I had to get the kids' snacks and lunches ready for the morning. Heading to the kitchen, I did just that and sure enough when I came back to my laptop, another email awaited me.

Lol. Well – that makes it easier and should be discreet. However, it only takes one error of judgement to get some lunatic stalker that requires a lot of admin changes. Been there. NOT fun and it made me very cautious. Luckily it was a while ago. Send me a note and I will respond. Weekend was great. Getting ready to work out before bed.

So clearly he'd been down this road before. It was oddly reassuring. At least one of us wasn't navigating blindly.

TO: bruisedassets@yahoo.com
10:39 PM
Subject: Hey there
I understand the caution. People tend to forget that we're all just people.
I'm looking forward to getting back to my gym routine tomorrow now

that the kids will be back in school.
~Meredith

Sending an additional email through KinkyFodder, I let him know that he had an email waiting from my personal email account.

> **TO: meredith@meredithedits.com**
> **10:44 PM**
> **Subject: Meredith – Re: Hey there**
> *Hello... what do you edit/write? I have a degree in Engineering and Business (double major). I'm one of those unusual engineers that can write and actually find it important.*

I started giggling. This was going to be fun.

> **TO: bruisedassets@yahoo.com**
> **10:47 PM**
> **Subject: Re: Meredith – Re: Hey there**
> *Would you like to take any guesses?!*
> *LOL*

> **TO: meredith@meredithedits.com**
> **10:49 PM**
> **Subject: Re: Meredith – Re: Hey there**
> *Not really... but now you have me wondering... :)*

> **TO: bruisedassets@yahoo.com**
> **10:54 PM**
> **Subject: Re: Meredith – Re: Hey there**
> *I mostly edit adult romance, 18+ highly recommended. I've been toying with the idea of writing my first book, which would be adult as well.*
> *Writing has always been a passion of mine, but I let it slip away. Thinking it's time to get it back.*

> **TO: meredith@meredithedits.com**
> **11:07 PM**
> **Subject: Re: Meredith – Re: Hey there**
> *Ok. Just did some cyber snooping... damn... lol. How long have you been doing that? That has to make the conversations with the husband a lot more interesting... "honey – read the fucking books!!!"*
> *How did you get into that genre?*
> *And that is NOT what I was thinking at all. I was thinking something benign like child books or cooking.*

TO: bruisedassets@yahoo.com
11:26 PM
Subject: Re: Meredith – Re: Hey there

LMAO. Yes, we've had arguments about it because he refuses to read anything I edit, let alone write. Yes, I confess, I'm a dirty bird.

I used to write 'romance' stories as a young girl, I just didn't realize they were 'romance' books then. Everyone presumes I edit children's books and I just laugh and say that the books I edit create children! Must be my innocent looking face.

I picked this genre because, admittedly, I enjoy reading it. The kids, editing, and PTA keep me pretty busy.

The joy of cyber snooping. You probably know way more about me now than you may have wanted to know! LOL

TO: meredith@meredithedits.com
11:37 PM
Subject: Re: Meredith – Re: Hey there

My wife read that series that blew up overnight and had me read a few passages. I didn't read enough to objectively comment, but the buzz in the D/s world was it was ridiculously inaccurate as far as that goes. Granted – most reading it think a sharp smack on the ass is borderline abuse so it may have been pretty over the top and thus adequately salacious.

So – do YOU write what you want?

Maybe if you finish it I will read it if I get a personalized copy... :)

Do the kids know what you edit/write?

TO: bruisedassets@yahoo.com
11:52 PM
Subject: Re: Meredith – Re: Hey there

I'm sure I know what books you're referring to and I like to believe the ones I edit (and plan to write) are better and more accurate. That series actually inspired me to get back to writing, but for different reasons.

People need to live a little. A sharp smack on the ass is always welcome. I would say that I tend to write what I want or what I may be open to.

The kids know, but don't quite comprehend at their young age. Though some of the teachers at the school know and ask for new reading material and I'm happy to oblige. They don't know that I'm thinking of writing my own book.

I had to try to get some sleep or I'd regret it in the morning.

A few hours later, I woke and couldn't resist checking my phone. No email awaited me. I rolled my eyes at myself and flipped to my stomach, forcing myself to sleep.

CHAPTER
Two

R-EVOLVE

I**T WAS THE FIRST DAY OF SCHOOL** and I was running around the house like a chicken with its head cut off. When I sat down at my laptop for a quick check, I found an email awaiting me.

> **TO: meredith@meredithedits.com**
> **7:49 AM**
> **Subject: LOL**
> *I guess I have a different perspective/interest on the motivation due to how we were 'introduced' :) One good thing about that series is that it brought D/s play more out in the open and now it isn't so taboo to talk about. My wife still remains mostly vanilla, but has a much better understanding of my 'kink'.*
> *I just fed the kids and have to get them to school for the first day. After today they will mostly take the bus. My wife works at the hospital and just left for the day. Helps that I work from home, travel some, and can be here when she's not to help with the myriad of events the kids attend.*
> *I think a sharp smack on the ass is just the start... :)*

I decided to quickly respond, liking the fact that we were both busy with similar activities. Was it odd that I didn't find it weird to be talking to a dad who was doing typical 'mom' duties? If anything, it was nice because I felt like it was just another thing we had in common.

> **TO: bruisedassets@yahoo.com**
> **8:14 AM**
> **Subject: Re: LOL**
> LMAO. I'm cracking up. I'm currently running around like a chicken with its head cut off. My kids just finished breakfast and this is the first year they'll all be on the same schedule, the youngest starting kindergarten!
> My husband travels a lot and I enjoy the break.
> Yes, I appreciate the exposure that series brought D/s. People think it's about the money, like only the rich enjoy it. It has nothing to do with status. And there's so much more to it like chemistry and trust, along with needs and wants!
> Talk soon.

He typically worked from home, but did travel as well, though not like Todd did. I wasn't exactly sure what kind of Engineer he was, but had a feeling he was probably in some kind of Sales. I was surrounded by Salesmen; Todd, my father, and *him*.

"Hmph." I still didn't know his name. In due time. We were still just getting to know one another.

Walking the kids into school that morning, I was bombarded with PTA questions. *This was a mistake.* What the hell had I been thinking or smoking? Taking on the role of President, someone should've committed me. I got the kids settled in their classrooms and tried sneaking out of the building.

"Meredith! Just who I was looking for." Her voice pierced my ears and my eyes closed. I took a deep breath, put half a smile on my face and turned to face her. "How are things going? This fundraiser needs to be a success if we're going to get the teachers those smart boards."

Smiling, "It's going well. I'm very aware of what needs to be done, Judith."

Judith was an over-involved parent, but one who refused to serve on the board. She always knew more, was more informed, and knew all the answers about *everything*. In other words, she was a gossipy know it all bitch who loved making my life miserable.

She looked at my jeans and t-shirt, pulled back hair, and I knew she was judging me. She was one of those Stepford Wives type, except she was newly divorced. Didn't work, stayed home—with a fulltime nanny—and looked like she'd ordered all her outfits out of a magazine where purses and shoes cost more than my car payments. To say she took her ex-husband to the cleaners was an understatement.

I didn't give a shit what she thought of me and my clothing choice. Everything about her was always put perfectly in place, including her home. My house was always in the midst of chaos and I was fine with it...to a degree. My house wasn't dirty, it was lived in. And it's not like I'd ever have Judith over for tea. Though the thought of making her uncomfortable with the toys that were always scattered across my floor was amusing to me.

"Well, I should get going." She just pursed her lips and nodded her head in response.

Turning, I made myself walk out the front doors as I rolled my eyes. Once in the sanctuary of my SUV, I cranked the radio and pulled out of the parking lot, making my way to the gym.

As I left the gym some time later, I checked my phone and found an email.

> *TO: meredith@meredithedits.com*
> *10:13 AM*
> *Subject: Re: LOL*
> *Well – it's not the money that prevents me from spanking her... She has submissive tendencies and can take a pretty hard spanking. It's just not her thing – most of the time.*
> *Weekends are packed with family and kids' activities, but I get downtime when traveling. I set my own schedule so I have a lot of flexibility when needed, which helps.*

I didn't hesitate and responded while sitting in my SUV.

> *TO: bruisedassets@yahoo.com*
> *10:39 AM*
> *Subject: Re: LOL*
> *My husband just started spanking. I just can't figure out if he enjoys it or not. I know I do. He's not very take charge in the bedroom, which is what I want/need. I get tired of giving suggestions. He jokes that he's the only one of his friends complaining about his wife's high libido. Grass is always greener.*
> *Just left the gym. Need to head home and shower before picking up the youngest from Kindergarten.*

I got home with just enough time to shower, get some work done, before I had to pick up my youngest—her first day being a half day. When I returned home... another email.

TO: meredith@meredithedits.com
1:04 PM
Subject: Re: LOL
    I understand the dilemma. My wife says the same thing about her peers. They're all sex starved and/or their husbands are lame in bed. She, herself, is one and done. Rarely does she have multiple orgasms. I think she has some sort of Catholic guilt. Why would you deny yourself that?
    Do you have a nice toned ass? I like spanking a nice firm ass. Nice thought heading into lunch and then my own workout.

    TO: bruisedassets@yahoo.com
    1:27 PM
    Subject: Re: LOL
    I'm such a guy in that way. Stressed, tired, happy...I typically want it. Who doesn't want/need that release as often as possible?! LOL. Mine is a one and done guy, but will on rare occasion please me more than once...but it usually requires some form of begging.
    The church guilt I never understood. I, too, am Catholic and still am like, nope. God created sex for a reason. I'm exploiting it, I know.
    I like to think I have a nice ass. I'm not super thin and recently lost weight, but I'll always have booty. I'm also tall, about 5'10" and will never be 'petite'. And all the working out just increases my libido.

TO: meredith@meredithedits.com
1:37 PM
Subject: Re: LOL
    I prefer athletic/toned over skinny as I tend to think most guys do. Especially if talking about spanking. I don't want to worry about breaking some starving waif in half while spanking them. I'm 6'1" and 225, mostly in my legs.
    I am also Catholic, had a staunch Catholic mother who still attends mass almost daily. She does NOT approve of pre-marital sex, let alone my sordid fetishes.

I giggled to myself. Guys tended to exaggerate their height where women didn't. I was tempted to respond with, 'So you're 5'10" too?' I decided not to.

    TO: bruisedassets@yahoo.com
    1:44 PM
    Subject: Re: LOL
    Yes, I'm sure I'm on the prayer list at my mother's church. Me and the porn I read and edit. Wait till she finds out I'm writing it! LOL
    Definitely working on the toning. I need to lift more. Just need to get into a routine. I try to go 5-6 days a week. I'm a slight masochist and enjoy the pain.

I keep waiting for my husband to tie me up and fuck me into next week. I'd like to feel it for a day or three after. No point in denying it...given how we were 'introduced'.

Christ! Did I really just send that? I was in the kitchen when my email pinged again. Deep breath. I sat down at my desk to read and reply.

> *TO: meredith@meredithedits.com*
> *2:21 PM*
> *Subject: Re: LOL*
> *I have no problem providing a spanking that will be felt for several days... :)*

I became flushed as I read his response. This was way too much fun. I crossed my legs, well aware of the throb that had begun.

> *TO: bruisedassets@yahoo.com*
> *2:29 PM*
> *Subject: Re: LOL*
> *And there's the opening. Lips pursed, I sit here smiling. 'A spanking that will be felt for SEVERAL days.'*
> *I've been very bad... ;)*

Pressing my lips together I waited an agonizing ten minutes for his response.

> *TO: meredith@meredithedits.com*
> *2:40 PM*
> *Subject: Re: LOL*
> *It's amazing how something that will/should give an opposite reaction to a smile will bring a smile to one's face. Ahhh...the joy of the D/s dynamic. Thinking about which paddle would be most suited for you...*

I was well aware of the sigh that slipped between my lips. I debated what to say as I typed my response.

> *TO: bruisedassets@yahoo.com*
> *2:48 PM*
> *Subject: Re: LOL*
> *Yes, we're definitely wired differently when the thought of pain brings us pleasure! I can feel the burn...and I've only experienced bare hands.*

I hadn't even had a chance to catch my breath when his reply came through.

TO: meredith@meredithedits.com
2:51 PM
Subject: Re: LOL
Only bare hands...?! Oh, you poor child...there is SO much more. :)
I'm off to run some errands before picking up the kids. Work out will have
to wait until this evening.

TO: bruisedassets@yahoo.com
2:59 PM
Subject: Re: LOL
I know. I'm deprived! :(LOL
Sorry if I kept you from your workout. Well, sorry, not sorry. LOL

Soon it'd be time to meet the other kids at the bus stop. Music filled my office. *R-Evolve* by Thirty Seconds To Mars rang through my ears, soon to be replaced with yelling kids. Of course a few more emails were exchanged as well, nothing of great importance. Our emails were clearly all over the map from talking about work, family, relationships, politics, to extremely sordid and filled with naughty innuendo.

Several days later we were still constantly emailing. Some days we only exchanged a few emails and then there were days where our thread was over thirty a day. But there was rarely a day we didn't exchange an email. Almost every morning I awoke to a message from him and went to bed the same way.

TO: meredith@meredithedits.com
11:55 AM
Subject: Re: Late night...
Good luck with your author's release today. Hope you don't have an early morning, but that's probably the case with the kids.
Not a caffeine drinker? Me either, never tried it as I saw my parents and peers become slaves to it. Guess that is part of my Dominant personality – I like to be in control. :)

TO: bruisedassets@yahoo.com
12:09 PM
Subject: Re: Late night...
I enjoy the occasional coffee, but prefer flavored over black.
I have some control issues, but, well, I submit under the right circumstances. That sounded really bad...LOL

I loved how we teased and flirted in email and seemingly nothing was lost in translation.

> *TO: meredith@meredithedits.com*
> *12:51 PM*
> *Subject: Re: Late night...*
> *I prefer strong, confident women that know what they want and know they like being submissive in the bedroom. I don't want someone that needs to be told what to do or to keep their shit together all day long... :)*

> *TO: bruisedassets@yahoo.com*
> *12:55 PM*
> *Subject: Re: Late night...*
> *Yeah. I don't deal well with being told what to do or what I should conform to. Another stigma people don't get. Just because I enjoy and want to be submissive in the bedroom doesn't mean I'm not strong and confident. I just want and expect the same from my partner...minus the submissive. Well, I don't know. There may be a little bit of a switch in me!*

> *TO: meredith@meredithedits.com*
> *12:59 PM*
> *Subject: Re: Late night...*
> *Too many people associate being submissive with being a 24/7 intellectual doormat. It is annoying but not surprising.*
> *Switch huh...? LOL*

CHAPTER
Three

BLUE BLOOD

A FEW DAYS LATER, AFTER more flirtatious emails and friendly chatter I asked what I'd been curious about from the beginning.

> *TO: bruisedassets@yahoo.com*
> *12:51 PM*
> *Subject: KinkyFodder*
> *So...what made you message me, besides the close proximity? There's no wrong answer. I've been messaged by several people and you're the only one to spike my interest.*

> *TO: meredith@meredithedits.com*
> *2:37 PM*
> *Subject: Re: KinkyFodder*
> *Proximity definitely helped. I was looking in the general area and so many of the profiles from women were screaming for attention or confirmation. I saw the pic of only your eyes and the basic profile that you were married and I thought – I want to get to know what is behind those blue eyes.*
> *I also assumed you were discreet and trying to understand what you wanted and needed.*

> *TO: bruisedassets@yahoo.com*

3:06 PM
Subject: Re: KinkyFodder
I don't really understand the selfie whore complex.
The late nights caught up to me. Just woke from an hour nap.
The eyes. Yes. One thing I'll always admit to loving on myself.
The last few years have been rough at home. I'm changing and evolving and he doesn't understand it. I need more, have asked for it and he can't/won't give it. I thought we'd grow/evolve together and he's adamant that he will not change.

TO: meredith@meredithedits.com
8:27 PM
Subject: Re: Late night...
I agree on changing and evolving. For me we were evolving together and then the ring had some mystical power that stopped evolution in favor of procreation. It comes and goes. She is much more aware now but still doesn't know how to make it work for us both. I have always disassociated sex and love. They certainly can go hand in hand, but for those of us that are wired the way we are – it isn't love – it's carnal. But the professional psychiatrists and psychologists will tell us otherwise...
I think we'll continue to grow as a couple – just not sure it will ever be as fast as I need it to be to feel balanced in the relationship.
So I have found other outlets until if/when that happens... :)

It should've been a red flag, but I was guilty of the same thing. I was looking for an outlet my husband couldn't provide. Truth was I'd contemplated divorce, contemplated staying for the kids, and neither choice seemed like the right one.

TO: bruisedassets@yahoo.com
8:45 PM
Subject: Re: Late night...
Yes. I feel like I wasn't quite sure what I needed until a few years ago. There have been months without intimacy.
I've brought up open relationship and he flipped. My own parents stayed together, unhappily, not getting what they needed from the other.
You're the first person I've talked so candidly with about all of this. Girlfriends don't get it. Dare I say they're too vanilla...

TO: meredith@meredithedits.com
10:23 PM
Subject: Re: Late night...
We live under this false notion that a mate should be everything to the other and it just isn't feasible and rarely attainable. Most of that is propagated by organized religion. However, I also don't believe we should just be fucking everyone. I think people can have deep bonds with multiple partners and still be in love with someone. The problem is those people seem to never meet until later in life after much searching and internal strife by

trying to conform to the norms of society.

Sigh. It was a lot to process. In my head I completely agreed with almost everything he said. It made sense to me. I'd always believed you could care for more than one person. The problem was most people didn't believe that themselves and would never get past the 'one person for life' thing.

A little bit later, after a couple more emails, he finally asked what I was wondering if he'd ever ask, after I had finally inquired to his name.

> *TO: meredith@meredithedits.com*
> *11:07 PM*
> *Subject: Re: So...*
> *Gregor. Sorry, I thought I put that in an earlier email.*
> *How do you envision an ideal first meeting with someone?*

Gregor. It was different and something I wouldn't forget. Not Greg or Gregory, Gregor. Then I scanned his question. First meeting. Was he referring to lunch, drinks, a picnic? I didn't want to presume anything. The butterflies started just like they did all those years ago when the time came to meet someone face to face after days or weeks of online chatting.

> *TO: bruisedassets@yahoo.com*
> *11:18 PM*
> *Subject: Re: So...*
> *Gregor...well, there's no bad name association there. Had you said Mike or Shawn I may have slammed my head on my desk! Lol*
> *Well, I'm no novice to meeting people from online...granted it's been over a decade and it's how I met my husband. Restaurant, store...though I did meet someone once at a hotel. Yes, I was young and crazy once. I need to know I can talk with someone, make eye contact, and vice versa. I did meet a couple men that gave me the heebie jeebies. Warning, I can come off as incredibly shy and have been accused of having RBF. I just like to observe people before I open up.*
> *Not sure if that's what you were looking for.*
> *What about you?*

The next morning I practically had tears rolling down my face upon reading his response.

> *TO: meredith@meredithedits.com*
> *7:00 AM*

Subject: Re: So...

I prefer to meet in a dimly lit, shady motel that rents by the quarter hour where there is plenty of random and non-connecting DNA evidence to confuse the eventual/potential crime scene. No sense in making extra work for myself scrubbing and cleaning.

I wasn't clear on the question. I guess I was taking safety precautions and the getting to know you phase where one is able to confirm the other is not bat-shit crazy as a given and THEN what an encounter will entail. I would want to meet for drinks or lunch and develop some real life rapport. Anyone can be a word maestro behind a keyboard, but I want to know the wit and chemistry translates into real life.

If only a couple guys gave you the heebie jeebies you were batting well above average... :)

This response was going to be fun. Again, no need to hold back.

TO: bruisedassets@yahoo.com
7:18 AM
Subject: Re: So...

Lmao. Yes, totally agree. I'd like to decide if I want your particular body as a skin suit or if I should move on to the next guy.

Lunch or drinks sounds great.

The encounter itself, I mean, where do I begin? I want to be able to get lost in what happens. I haven't been with another person since I got married. You're more practiced and I'd want to know what you need and expect for it to work too. Some days I'm a wham bam girl and others not so much. I'm probably a typical girl in the fact that I need that touch, petting, spanking, kissing to get going...I just totally lost my train of thought. Oh, but I know it's a mental game too. Just the thought of someone not getting winded five minutes into pounding me is a win. :-) Couldn't resist.

The guy I dated right before my hubby was that guy, the one I had and practically did have sex with everywhere. We were animals. I got off with penetration every time. He turned out to have a criminal record beyond other things I couldn't deal with.

I continued about my day. Got the kids to school, went to the gym, came home and showered, did some editing, and handled some PTA business. My laptop pinged and when I opened my email, his response was awaiting me.

TO: meredith@meredithedits.com
2:11 PM
Subject: Re: So...

I can last longer than 5 min and have no criminal record nor have I ever been arrested.

It definitely starts with the mental aspect and goes into the physical.

Lunch might work easier just because my evenings are pretty tight when I am not traveling. I set my own schedule so getting away in the middle of the day is not an issue when I am home. What general area do you live in / have a place in mind to meet?

I won't be online much this weekend. Will be with family and limited access to cell.

I took a big breath and started typing my response. He lived an hour away, or so he said. I didn't even know if he'd know where my po-dunk town was.

> *TO: bruisedassets@yahoo.com*
> *2:37 PM*
> *Subject: Re: So...*
> *Well that's good. Same here, never even had a speeding ticket and the only drug I ever used was an occasional cigarette back in college.*
> *Tuesday and Thursday this coming week are good. I live in Middlebury off interstate 54. I'm willing to meet somewhere in the middle. I'm jittery just thinking about it. (Remember, I'm shy...lol)*
> *I appreciate the heads up about the weekend and understand. Mine will be working all weekend so I'll be pulling my hair out with the kids and self-medicating with sex scenes to edit/write and deadlines to meet! Ok, there may be some chocolate involved and wine once they're in bed!*
> *I attached a picture from the other day. I'll probably be blushing though in person...I'm easily embarrassed, but I can dish it back out too!*

I attached a picture of myself from a few days earlier. That night I went to bed still not getting a response. He said he'd be out of touch so I didn't expect to hear from him until Sunday or Monday. Around three in the morning I was jolted awake by nothing and grabbed my phone. It was on silent, but I had an email from him waiting for me. Smiling, I opened it as Todd lay snoring next to me.

> *TO: meredith@meredithedits.com*
> *1:37 AM*
> *Subject: HOLY SHIT*
> *Just got to hotel about 30 min ago. Got kids back down and now catching up on emails.*
> *Read your email and HOLY FUCKING SHIT...!?! Did your profile on KinkyFodder always read Tipton?!? Was that because Middlebury was too small or to give some wiggle room? Our worlds may have already collided or could certainly collide in the future. George Castanza moment going on. I also live in Middlebury and give almost the exact same directions/references to interstate 54! So - meeting for lunch shouldn't be a chore...lol. I put Anapolis as it was the major city/locale and didn't think Middlebury was even relative to a search.*

I am sure the odds are much lower than they seem right now, but I have never looked anywhere in my backyard.

So - do we still meet or do we leave it as this as to not upset the applecart? Or do we meet and leave it as intellectually connected friends who give the silent smirk if/when we cross paths at a restaurant, school, etc...?

I am still struck by the odds.

I am thinking about you all jittery. I am thinking more about devilishly sending you inappropriate texts while you are two rows away at a future PTA meeting or you making subtle comments while our kids are on the soccer field together.

That could be some interesting fodder for your authors and you if the chocolates and wine aren't getting you through the editing.

My chest constricted and I couldn't breathe. I climbed out of bed, clasping my phone to my upper body, where below, my heart was hammering away. It was so loud I thought for sure its thrumming would wake Todd who laid sound asleep next to me.

Closing the bathroom door, I sat on the edge of the tub and made myself take deep, calming breaths. Scanning the email again, I just couldn't believe it. It couldn't be true, could it? We lived in the same town? We lived in the same town! 'Holy fucking shit' was an understatement. And I'd sent him my picture. FUCK! Then my eyes stared at the words of his question. '*Do we still meet or do we leave it as this...?*'

NO. YES. Wait, what was the question?

It was my first instinct and my gut reaction. There was no way I was walking away now. Besides, we had yet to meet in person and there was a part of me that was convinced he wouldn't be attracted to me and vice versa. I didn't really think about the opposite happening.

I knew I wanted and desired his mind and he had said the same in regards to me. He too had sent a discreet picture, nothing sordid, and nothing that included his face—he was extremely cautious and that was fine with me—but pictures could lie. It wouldn't be the first time someone sent a picture or gave stats that were misleading.

I was completely flustered when I sent my response.

TO: *bruisedassets@yahoo.com*
3:17 AM
Subject: *Re: HOLY SHIT*
OMG. My heart is pounding and I'm pretty sure in a good way. I keep looking at this as worst case the chemistry isn't there and I gain a friend. I

think it's always said Tipton and I did that for the reasons you stated.

I've always been the wallflower type. I also feel like I can't walk away now and don't want to. It could make some things easier and others more difficult being so close.

So, we're a Middlebury Peak family. Maybe you're one of the dads who's smiled knowingly or like 'dat bitch cray cray'. Lol

Ugh. I'm not going to be able to sleep. My heart is still racing.

I don't want to walk away...

Sitting there, I pondered so many things. He'd been so completely discreet, yet informative about his life that I felt even more secure in his confession that we lived in the same town. Had he been dishonest—I believed—about anything he'd told me he would've disappeared or stopped talking to me. Or just not admitted to it.

I told him that the geographical closeness could be wonderful and cause potential problems. I couldn't even process all the possibilities running rampant in my head. *Oh. My. God.* What if our kids *were* in the same school together? What if we'd already met and didn't know it? My rapid breathing and sprinting heart started again.

Dropping my head between my legs, I forced myself to relax. *Shit!* I was the PTA President. *Fuck!* What if he was on the PTA too, or a member, or his wife was? I started laughing and wasn't sure if it was from fear or excitement. I mentally started trying to figure out if I knew any Gregs or Gregors. Nobody came to mind. I glanced at my phone and saw it was close to four a.m. I had to try to get some more sleep, though I knew it was nearly impossible.

He said he'd be out of touch most of the weekend and I had things to tend to and the fundraiser to focus on. There was no point in obsessing about it all now. What was going to happen would happen, if it was supposed to. I wasn't someone who believed everything was predestined, but I did believe things happened for a reason. It was just up to us what path we took when certain choices presented themselves.

He wasn't the only one 'struck by the odds'.

I tossed and turned for a while before getting back to sleep for a short time. When I woke I headed to my office. I scrolled my playlist, knowing what song I was searching for. Her melody sang about someone making her feel again, someone who'd been near her the whole time. Finding it, I played it, the song, *Blue Blood* by Laurel that now had a whole new meaning.

I re-read his email and my initial response. There were a few things I felt I hadn't answered fully and decided to respond again, knowing full well I wouldn't hear back from him for a day or two, most likely. Of course, he'd said that before he sent his reply after one in the morning.

> *TO: bruisedassets@yahoo.com*
> *9:41 AM*
> *Subject: Re: HOLY SHIT*
> *So, I'm replying again when not half asleep (though it eluded me) and adrenaline running rampant in me. Lol*
> *Kramer was my favorite, George and Elaine following closely behind, and I feel like him, just barreling through a door...with myself and others going WTF?! (insert video clip...lol)*
> *Part of me was going to suggest Laredo's because it's one of my favorites, but given the circumstances....well who knows who we'd run into.*
> *My brain is screaming at me 'this shit only happens in books!' or 'I've seen this movie' lol*
> *I'd log on every couple months to KinkyFodder and wonder when and if you'd ever respond back. And, well, being what/who I am, I wasn't about to pursue you figuring it'd happen when and if it was supposed to. I am struck by the odds, too, and filled with relief at the thought of someone being so close who might get me. I can't help but wonder if we have mutual friends and acquaintances.*
> *And, are you insinuating that you want my phone number to send me inappropriate texts? Ask and you shall receive. I found a great meme yesterday that'll make sense here if I could find it again. Something about 'I want to be the reason you turn your phone away from prying eyes'... I serve as the President on the PTA, of course, maybe you already know that? Though I don't know what I was thinking. I can't deal with the Desperate Stepford Housewives. Somedays I feel like I'm going mad.*
> *Thinking about me all jittery...lol (Smiling) Someone likes the idea of me squirming. Mission accomplished.*
> *So. I think you know where I stand based on my first response. I'll wait to hear from you.*
> *Enjoy your family and kids this weekend.*

I sighed. It was done. He knew how I felt and there wasn't much more I could do but wait to see if he responded. I just shook my head. This was crazy. Abso-fucking-lutely crazy. How was this even possible? My picture on KinkyFodder didn't reveal my identity, but the one I'd sent him a few days ago had. Was this a scam? No. There was just no way. My crazy brain started throwing around words like fate, kismet, serendipity...

'Jesus Mer. Take a pill!'

I tilted my neck from side to side, trying to stretch the tight muscles. I busied myself with all the things I needed to be focusing on for the rest of the weekend. Editing, cleaning, kids, running a household, and the dreaded PTA.

CHAPTER
Four

I'M ON FIRE

T HE REST OF THE WEEKEND passed like any other. Nothing too exciting happened and I didn't hear from Gregor. I'd had some inspiration and was working on my book. There had also been lots of editing and PTA work. I needed the distraction and was grateful I had inspiration. After I got the kids to bed Sunday night, I sat back down at my laptop.

> *TO: meredith@meredithedits.com*
> *8:00 PM*
> *Subject: Re: HOLY SHIT*
> *Back and absolutely beat. May not be able to respond in much detail tonight.*
> *We are at the same school. I just can't get over this.*
> *I, too, enjoy Laredo's but may not be the most discreet. Though, we could always use the PTA as an excuse.*
> *Good news is I should be in the office Thursday so lunch may be an option. Isn't curriculum night that night, too?*
> *Hope you had a great weekend.*

My eyes were bulging out of my head. Our kids were at the same school, he has my picture, and I run the PTA. *Jesus Fuck!* It was a big school, but still.

> *TO: bruisedassets@yahoo.com*
> *8:13 PM*
> *Subject: Re: HOLY SHIT*
> *Glad to hear you're back safe. Get some rest. I'll probably be up late working. I've had a smidge of inspiration between chasing kids...*
> *I can't believe we're at the same school. I guess you'll get to send those texts you were thinking about at PTA meetings. You seriously didn't know when you saw my picture? I won't be at curriculum night, not likely anyway.*
> *Thursday is currently open. Maybe going East to start with is best.*
> *My sleep has been restless (eyes glaring at you, Sir) with a wandering mind...*
> *Talk soon.*

I didn't hear anything else during the rest of the night or the next day. I tried to not think about it or let it distract me. I loved and hated how I couldn't get him out of my mind. I restrained myself from scanning the school directory and wondering who he might be. Gregor still didn't ring any bells. Maybe it was a name he made up?

After dinner the next evening I heard back. Todd had taken the kids out for ice cream so I was alone and free to read and respond.

> *TO: meredith@meredithedits.com*
> *6:41 PM*
> *Subject: Re: HOLY SHIT*
> *Staying focused today or letting productivity be derailed by naughty thoughts...? Nevermind. Your productivity IS naughty thoughts. Can't spank you for that one...*

> *TO: bruisedassets@yahoo.com*
> *6:44 PM*
> *Subject: Re: HOLY SHIT*
> *Umm...you can always spank me...*
> *Home alone for a while...*
> *Went to the gym, worked on my manuscript, did some editing, thought dirty thoughts...*
> *You?*

> *TO: meredith@meredithedits.com*
> *6:46 PM*
> *Subject: Re: HOLY SHIT*
> *Out with clients and thinking dirty thoughts... :)*

TO: bruisedassets@yahoo.com
6:51 PM
Subject: Dirty...
Sigh. Something I found that struck a chord with me...and made me laugh...
I attached a picture of a 1950's housewife with word bubbles over her head, not sure you'll be able to view it. They read: I mean, I like him, but... just wish he'd haul me over his lap and spank me.
You'll have to open it to see...
:)
Dirty things everywhere...
Dirty music blaring...
Dirty thoughts running amuck...
About to get clean, in a dirty way, in the shower...

I didn't hear back from him that night. The hardest part was having no one to talk to. Of course there was Tami, but I was still feeling her out with her views on this kind of thing. She was an editing friend and we hit it off right away. Thank God she lived close by. But I wanted someone to talk to more in depth; it was such a delicate situation. And I certainly couldn't talk to any of my mom friends from the school.

SHIT!

Then it dawned on me. What if he's the husband of one of my friends? The name he gave me could've been complete bullshit because maybe he DID know who I was. But how would he explain that later on?

AGH!

I was staring at my email and listening to one of my playlists the next day when his response came through. *I'm on Fire* by Bruce Springsteen was playing. I loved this song, always had, and now it had more meaning to me. It screamed Gregor.

TO: meredith@meredithedits.com
12:12 PM
Subject: Re: Dirty...
Which paddle should I use...?

I dropped my head on my desk. All of them! Giggling to myself, I sent my reply.

TO: bruisedassets@yahoo.com
12:16 PM

Subject: Re: Dirty...
You're the expert...
And I'm seriously having anxiety about the fact that you know who I am.
It's not fair!

TO: meredith@meredithedits.com
12:20 PM
Subject: Re: Dirty...
Not sure I am an expert.
I promise, I didn't know you and we've never interacted...not yet, anyway.
:)

TO: bruisedassets@yahoo.com
12:29 PM
Subject: Re: Dirty...
We can become experts together.

TO: meredith@meredithedits.com
1:12 PM
Subject: Re: Dirty...
You have time to chat on the phone? I have over an hour of windshield
time.
555-2527 Corporate phone. Be discreet with texts or VM! Don't need to
provide any masturbation fodder to the IT department...

Holy crap! He'd given me his number. He wanted to talk on the phone.
BREATHE!

TO: bruisedassets@yahoo.com
1:16 PM
Subject: Re: Dirty...
Yes, I can call now if you like.
555-7478

TO: meredith@meredithedits.com
1:20 PM
Subject: Re: Dirty...
I'll call shortly...

My heart was racing waiting for his call. I didn't even have time to save his number in my phone because I was so nervous. I nearly dropped my phone when it did start ringing.

Taking a deep breath, because the last thing I needed to sound like was a jittery teenager, I answered my phone.

"So he finally asked for my number."

A deep chuckle rang through the phone and was followed by, "How you doing today?"

"I'm good. How are you?"

We talked about our kids, favorite movies, the weather, and everything else in between. We didn't get naughty on the phone which was actually nice. We needed to build a rapport with one another and that's just what we were doing. He had a slight drawl to his voice and I could listen to it all day. We spent about thirty minutes on the phone, not long, but it was sufficient.

We continued exchanging emails the rest of the day and somehow got on the subject of feet and toe sucking. Don't ask!

> *TO: meredith@meredithedits.com*
> *6:30 PM*
> *Subject: Re: Feet...*
> *You definitely don't want my feet in your mouth...*

> *TO: bruisedassets@yahoo.com*
> *6:38 PM*
> *Subject: Re: Feet...*
> *LOL. I don't mind my toes being sucked, not sure about sucking toes.*

> *TO: meredith@meredithedits.com*
> *6:41 PM*
> *Subject: Re: Feet...*
> *I have nasty feet...lol. If you want to suck on them – I don't want to suck anything on you...*

> *TO: bruisedassets@yahoo.com*
> *6:44 PM*
> *Subject: Re: Feet...*
> *I'm not into sucking toes. LOL*
> *No sucking, nothing? Hmm...*

> *TO: meredith@meredithedits.com*
> *6:46 PM*
> *Subject: Re: Feet...*
> *Reread what I wrote...lol. ANY woman that sucks my nasty feet is going to be too nasty for me to want to do anything to them...*
> *I am very orally inclined. Very.*

TO: bruisedassets@yahoo.com
6:49 PM
Subject: Re: Feet...
LMAO. I just snorted. I'm sitting in the dance studio, hiding in the corner with my laptop, and writing dirty things. Not anything to do with sucking toes...
I'm not that kind of nasty. Promise
And thank God. Someone who isn't orally inclined would probably be a hard limit for me. Once one discovers that joy...there's no going back!

TO: meredith@meredithedits.com
7:12 PM
Subject: Re: Feet...
It comes naturally... or so I've been told. :)

Later that night we were still emailing and asking Twenty Questions. We found out that our kids were at different dance studios. One less place to worry about running into him!

TO: meredith@meredithedits.com
10:26 PM
Subject: Re: 20?s...
The girl I lost it to dropped a line on me that worked...lol

TO: bruisedassets@yahoo.com
10:33 PM
Subject: Re: 20?s...
Ah, good ole peer pressure. What was the line?
For me, we planned it out. It was LAME! LOL

TO: meredith@meredithedits.com
10:35 PM
Subject: Re: 20?s...
I will tell you at lunch Thursday.

TO: bruisedassets@yahoo.com
10:37 PM
Subject: Re: 20?s...
Sigh. You're a tease.
I have 'lines' too. Though I haven't used them in years. LOL

TO: meredith@meredithedits.com
10:39 PM
Subject: Re: 20?s...

You like it though...

TO: bruisedassets@yahoo.com
10:42 PM
Subject: Re: 20?s...
Shh. Those are our secrets. I'm supposed to be the tease...

TO: meredith@meredithedits.com
10:44 PM
Subject: Re: 20?s...
Yeah. Times have changed. Blame the feminists. You're fucked!

TO: bruisedassets@yahoo.com
10:45 PM
Subject: Re: 20?s...
LMAO...how to correctly respond to that?
To be fucked or not to be fucked.
That is the question...
You like getting me riled up!

TO: meredith@meredithedits.com
10:48 PM
Subject: Re: 20?s...
Metaphorically. Literally.
I do.

TO: bruisedassets@yahoo.com
10:51 PM
Subject: Re: 20?s...
You like the fact that I won't be able to sleep...again! I'm going to have to drug myself. LOL
Legs are clenched so tight...
Keep talking...LOL

TO: meredith@meredithedits.com
10:54 PM
Subject: Re: 20?s...
Those clenched legs will make anal sex a little more painful, especially with an already swollen bottom...

TO: bruisedassets@yahoo.com
10:57 PM
Subject: Re: 20?s...
So he likes to do it in the butt, or he's probing (pun intended) to see if I do...
I don't mind it...better when done correctly.

TO: meredith@meredithedits.com

10:59 PM
Subject: Re: 20?s...
It goes hand in hand with the ass fetish.

TO: bruisedassets@yahoo.com
11:05 PM
Subject: Re: 20?s...
Probably safe to say my ass is re-virginized. Haven't had it since before my husband. He's not interested no matter what I try. I mean, I have three holes...use them!
Lucky you...

I went to bed that night with a smile on my face. Todd was out of town, as usual. I woke in the middle of the night to find Gregor had sent a response shortly after I'd gone to bed.

TO: meredith@meredithedits.com
1:01 AM
Subject: Re: 20?s...
I prefer three hole access... :)

TO: bruisedassets@yahoo.com
4:26 AM
Subject: Re: 20?s...
Ass up, face down?
Keep sweet talking. LOL
Hope you had a good evening. I finally got some sleep. Another 2 hours before I need to be up.
Talk soon.

I rolled back over and happily went back to sleep. Lunch was a day away and I couldn't wait.

In the morning, I was getting the kids ready for school when my email pinged.

TO: meredith@meredithedits.com
7:49 AM
Subject: Re: 20?s...
Absolutely!

TO: bruisedassets@yahoo.com
7:54 AM
Subject: Re: 20?s...
What a visual to start your day with?! Maybe I should switch out spin for yoga. LOL

TO: meredith@meredithedits.com
8:24 AM
Subject: Re: 20?s...
Maybe I should paddle you right before spin class. Give you 30-45 min of REAL reflection while you toil along.

TO: bruisedassets@yahoo.com
8:30 AM
Subject: Re: 20?s...
Oh, Dear Lord! You gonna meet me in the parking lot. Put on a show for everyone? LOL
You just want my mind on you, branded by your mark. The thought of a tender ass and reliving it every time I sit down. (All smiles, Sir)

TO: meredith@meredithedits.com
8:32 AM
Subject: Re: 20?s...
Doesn't have to be the parking lot. We can find a spot a little more discreet for your discipline. And yes – keeping thoughts on your punishment makes it more effective... :)

"MOM!"

I about jumped out of my skin. I looked at the clock and knew I had to get moving. Gregor would have to wait for a few minutes! Back to life, back to reality.

CHAPTER
Five

IN FOR THE KILL

Wᴴᴇɴ I ɢᴏᴛ ʜᴏᴍᴇ ғʀᴏᴍ the gym, I couldn't resist sitting down to email him.

> *TO: bruisedassets@yahoo.com*
> *11:07 AM*
> *Subject: Lunch tomorrow*
> *So, I was thinking if the weather holds up that we should get takeout. We can sit in a park or in one of our vehicles with no prying ears.*

> *TO: meredith@meredithedits.com*
> *11:37 AM*
> *Subject: Re: Lunch tomorrow*
> *Takeout is fine. Especially if it is nice out.*

> *TO: bruisedassets@yahoo.com*
> *11:41 AM*
> *Subject: Re: Lunch tomorrow*
> *I could use some sun for my fair skin!*

> *TO: meredith@meredithedits.com*
> *11:46 AM*
> *Subject: Re: Lunch tomorrow*

I can provide instant color to your fair skin in certain areas...

> ***TO: bruisedassets@yahoo.com***
> ***11:50 AM***
> ***Subject: Re: Lunch tomorrow***
> *I'm counting on it.*

> ***TO: meredith@meredithedits.com***
> ***11:53 AM***
> ***Subject: Re: Lunch tomorrow***
> *May just have to bend you over one of those picnic tables after lunch and warm it up...*

> ***TO: bruisedassets@yahoo.com***
> ***12:03 PM***
> ***Subject: Re: Lunch tomorrow***
> *(I will NOT dream of picnic tables ALL DAY) Dammit.*
> *I have to take a shower. Errands await.*
> *I'll be going through my wardrobe later...Gotta find the jeans that make my ass look best...LOL*

> ***TO: meredith@meredithedits.com***
> ***12:07 PM***
> ***Subject: Re: Lunch tomorrow***
> *I have to decide which pants make my cock look the best.*

> ***TO: bruisedassets@yahoo.com***
> ***12:09 PM***
> ***Subject: Re: Lunch tomorrow***
> *OMG...(blushing)*
> *Yup, I got nothing. Apparently I'll be taking a cold shower...*

I didn't hear back and begrudgingly went about my day. Surprisingly, I was able to get a lot done. Laundry, bills to pay, house to clean, editing, made a few PTA calls, and worked on my manuscript. It was exciting and scary to be working on my own piece of work.

Shortly before the kids were due to arrive home on the bus, another email popped up.

> ***TO: meredith@meredithedits.com***
> ***3:51 PM***
> ***Subject: Re: Lunch tomorrow***
> *How did the shower work out for ya...?*

Groaning to myself, I typed my response.

TO: bruisedassets@yahoo.com
3:53 PM
Subject: Re: Lunch tomorrow
I behaved, though I didn't want to.

TO: meredith@meredithedits.com
3:59 PM
Subject: Re: Lunch tomorrow
How long do you think you will be in the shower tomorrow...?

TO: bruisedassets@yahoo.com
4:01 PM
Subject: Re: Lunch tomorrow
Before or after we meet?!?!

TO: meredith@meredithedits.com
4:03 PM
Subject: Re: Lunch tomorrow
Both

For the love... The man was going to make me crazy and I was enjoying every second of it.

TO: bruisedassets@yahoo.com
4:09 PM
Subject: Re: Lunch tomorrow
I'm trying to distract myself. Lol
I know myself. The more I get off, the more I want it. I just wished it worked the other way, but keep thinking 'if I abstain I'll be calmer'. Probably not. I'll probably self-implode if you touch me.
I should just shut my mouth and stop talking. Lol
I'm staring at my wardrobe, stomach is already fluttering. Is it Thursday yet?

The kids got home from school and I let them play outside since the weather was so nice. I tried on a few outfits, took some pictures and sent them to a friend. Tami. I'd opened up to her about Gregor a few days prior, unable to keep it all inside anymore. Some may say she was a bad friend because she supported me, but she was my sounding board. She didn't judge me and sometimes that's all we need. Whether we're adults or children, we're going to do what we're going to do and what we feel is right.

After the kids, and most likely his as well, were in bed I got another email.

TO: meredith@meredithedits.com
8:15 PM
Subject: Re: Lunch tomorrow
Ahhh...the butterflies and swirling stomach of apprehension. Tell-tale signs of a very naughty lady who knows she is about to be spanked like a very naughty girl...

Jesus... Should I be so excited? The only guilt I had was that I didn't feel guilty.

TO: bruisedassets@yahoo.com
8:19 PM
Subject: Re: Lunch tomorrow
Just remember I'm still a lady who wants a little bit of wooing...
Don't expect to throw me in the bed of your truck and have your way with me...yet.
Outfit has been selected :)

TO: meredith@meredithedits.com
8:21 PM
Subject: Re: Lunch tomorrow
LOL

TO: bruisedassets@yahoo.com
8:24 PM
Subject: Re: Lunch tomorrow
That's all you got?! LOL?
If you're not careful, I'll go commando...maybe

Who the hell was I kidding? There was no way I was going to go commando!

TO: meredith@meredithedits.com
8:29 PM
Subject: Re: Lunch tomorrow
I don't think the bed of my truck would be conducive.
I wasn't expecting you to just fall at my feet with your breasts exposed and breathlessly whisper 'take me'

TO: bruisedassets@yahoo.com
8:31 PM
Subject: Re: Lunch tomorrow
Lol. Thank fucking God. We can role play that later! :)

TO: meredith@meredithedits.com
8:35 PM
Subject: Re: Lunch tomorrow

I am kind of amused by how much effort went into your outfit for tomorrow. Like you are going to the prom. I will decide what to wear roughly 5 min before walking out of the house assuming I even change...

TO: bruisedassets@yahoo.com
8:41 PM
Subject: Re: Lunch tomorrow
Exactly my point why you men have it so easy. I'm not wearing a dress, though! I'm a jeans and nice top kinda gal. I did paint my fingernails, though...
If you prefer, I can wear pajama pants, a baggy t-shirt, no bra, pull my hair back, and have yesterday's makeup smeared around my eyes. That's hot!

TO: meredith@meredithedits.com
8:46 PM
Subject: Re: Lunch tomorrow
That's fine. I'm going to wear a chaw stained wife beater with gym shorts, dress socks and shoes. After I git dun whoppin yo ass we can git on over to Walmart too and shop for jewelry to show we're serious...

TO: bruisedassets@yahoo.com
8:48 PM
Subject: Re: Lunch tomorrow
LMAO. Now you're speaking my language. We should get matching tattoos first. LOL

I got the kids' lunches and snacks together and got some more laundry done. Todd went to bed that night and didn't even say anything to me. I decided to call Tami.

"Hey. How are you? You ready for tomorrow?"

I exhaled sharply. "Why am I so nervous?"

"Because you like him. At least in email and on the phone."

Groaning, "I know. He's not going to be interested. I don't know why I'm stressing."

"Shut your face, whore. He's going to be interested or he's a fool. I'd fuck you, if I liked beaver."

I started cracking up, "Thanks." I looked at the clock and sighed.

Like she knew, she asked, "Has he emailed?"

"Yes. No. We were joking about shit, but he hasn't responded yet." Yawning, I tried talking and couldn't.

"Girl, go to bed. You need your rest for tomorrow."

"I know. Alright. I'll talk to you tomorrow."

"I want every fucking detail!"

"Yes ma'am! Love you, Tami!"

"Love you more!"

I disconnected the call and put my cell down on my desk. Sitting down, I typed up another quick email.

> *TO: bruisedassets@yahoo.com*
> *10:58 PM*
> *Subject: Bedtime*
> *Not sure how much longer I'm staying up. Pretty whipped. LOL*
> *I should be home in the morning shortly after 9am. We can finalize logistics then. Supposed to be over 80 tomorrow. Beautiful day for shenanigans...*
> *Talk soon...*

> *TO: meredith@meredithedits.com*
> *11:13 PM*
> *Subject: Re: Bedtime*
> *I've been watching the news...And trying to get caught up with emails in between breaks. We can touch base then. Sleep well!*

> *TO: bruisedassets@yahoo.com*
> *11:16 PM*
> *Subject: Re: Bedtime*
> *Get caught up on emails. That ass is mine tomorrow...wait. I think that's your line. Lol*

I crawled into bed and fell asleep quite easily with a smile on my face. Of course, per usual, I woke after four hours of sleep...to an email. Smirking, I read his email and then typed my response on my phone making sure Todd was still asleep.

> *TO: meredith@meredithedits.com*
> *11:46 PM*
> *Subject: Re: Bedtime*
> *And what do you want to do with MY ass...? :)*

> *TO: bruisedassets@yahoo.com*
> *4:16 AM*
> *Subject: Re: Bedtime*
> *I can be a lil grabby... :)*

I rolled back over and passed out for another three hours, actually waking to my alarm blaring. Grabbing my phone, there he was.

TO: meredith@meredithedits.com
7:26 AM
Subject: Re: Bedtime
I thought you were going to bed last night...?

TO: bruisedassets@yahoo.com
7:33 AM
Subject: Re: Bedtime
I did. I always wake up after a few hours of sleep and fight to get back to it.
I'm currently calm, cool, and collected. Got some sleep. Clock is ticking...

TO: meredith@meredithedits.com
7:36 AM
Subject: Re: Bedtime
I'm getting ready to feed the kids and get them off to school.

TO: bruisedassets@yahoo.com
7:38 AM
Subject: Re: Bedtime
Ditto. Though mine appear to still be sleeping which is good and bad.

TO: meredith@meredithedits.com
9:01 AM
Subject: Re: Bedtime
I will probably be wrapped up here around 11 this morning.

TO: bruisedassets@yahoo.com
9:10 AM
Subject: Re: Bedtime
Ok. Kids are at school. Time to shower. Talk soon.

TO: meredith@meredithedits.com
9:46 AM
Subject: Re: Bedtime
Arrggh – so much for working out prior...

TO: bruisedassets@yahoo.com
10:18 AM
Subject: Re: Bedtime
I can wait if you want to work out...

TO: meredith@meredithedits.com
10:21 AM
Subject: Re: Bedtime
I will do it tonight after the kids go to bed. Need to do some yard work after we meet and before they get home from school. Hope to beat the rain

that's supposed to come... :)
I should be ready to leave here by 11. Where do you want to meet? Do you have your best ass jeans on...?

TO: bruisedassets@yahoo.com
10:26 AM
Subject: Re: Bedtime
Ok. I can leave here at 11 too. Casey's, it's about 8 miles over off 54. I can wait in the parking lot then we can order food.
You'll have to be the judge about the jeans...LOL

TO: meredith@meredithedits.com
11:05 AM
Subject: Re: Bedtime
OMW
Red shirt and jeans (with bulge in front). Hat

TO: bruisedassets@yahoo.com
11:08 AM
Subject: Re: Bedtime
Grey top, jeans, black sunglasses....you know what I look like :)

TO: meredith@meredithedits.com
11:13 AM
Subject: Re: Bedtime
Bra size?!

TO: bruisedassets@yahoo.com
11:15 AM
Subject: Re: Bedtime
I'm parked in back...

TO: meredith@meredithedits.com
11:17 AM
Subject: Re: Bedtime
You like it in the back...?

The emails as we drove helped calm my nerves. I purposefully ignored his question about bra size. I thought for sure I might pass out. Sitting, *In for the Kill* by Billie Marten played on my speakers, I waited. I saw a pickup truck pull in. Holding my breath, as it got closer I realized it wasn't him. As the air burst from my lungs, I tried to calm myself. My stomach was in knots and my legs were bouncing.

A few moments passed and another truck pulled in. Pressing my lips together, I hoped it was him and knew for sure it was when he waved at me. At least he was certain of what I looked like. I watched as he parked in the very back of the lot.

There was no going back. I got out of my SUV, took a deep breath, and walked over to his truck. Normally, I wouldn't do that; I'd make him come to me. But, nothing about this situation was 'normal'. The smile he greeted me with should've been my warning. I'm glad I knew how to swim because I was pretty sure I'd just jumped into the deep end.

CHAPTER
Six

ALL THE KING'S HORSES

As I reached his truck I found his window rolled down. Crossing my arms—a nervous habit—I smiled and took him in. He wore glasses, a red polo, and had on a baseball cap. His eyes were blue, but not like mine. They had more grey in them and looking in them made me instantly more nervous and grateful I still wore my sunglasses.

That smile, I couldn't stop staring at it as he asked, "How are you?"

"I'm good. You?"

I knew instantly that I'd never run into him at school, or never paid him any attention. Of course, it's not like I was actively looking for someone. And had I been looking, I wouldn't have picked him out of a lineup to be the guy I was chatting with in email. He was good looking, just not someone my eyes would've lingered on. My eyes typically drifted to taller, more rugged looking men. He didn't fit my mold, not that Todd did either. It was neither here nor there. I'd learned long ago that drop dead looks on a guy was rarely a good thing. And that didn't mean Gregor wasn't good looking, he was.

He got out of his truck and we started walking toward the entrance to Casey's.

"You still want to do takeout?"

Nodding, "Yes. It's gorgeous out." Hesitating, I asked, "If that's good with you?"

"That's fine."

With my arms still crossed, we walked side by side. When we reached the door he held it open for me and I thanked him. Pushing my sunglasses to the top of my head, I grabbed a menu and looked it over, though I already knew what I was going to get. Handing it over to him, his eyes caught mine and flutters danced in my stomach.

Smiling, "Your eyes are breathtaking. Your picture doesn't do them justice."

I felt the blush creep up my face as I smiled shyly and thanked him. "Thank you."

Still smiling, he looked over the menu. The waitress behind the counter looked at us and asked if we were ready to order. Gregor motioned me forward to order first. Pulling out my wallet—because I didn't have any expectations—I opened it up and he stopped me.

"No, no. I got it."

"Thank you."

We waited about fifteen minutes for our food to be made and stood by the entrance chatting. Then it dawned on me that he'd never quite clarified if he'd seen me at the school or not.

"So, did you know who I was or not?"

Confessing, "No. I've seen you a couple times since you sent me your picture, but I didn't want to muddle the waters any."

Grinning, "So you've been stalking me."

He belly laughed, "Hardly. Unless you like that kind of thing?"

I snickered and was going to say something when the waitress walked over and handed us our food. He carried the bag and headed toward the door. There was a little old lady in front of us and he made sure to get the door for her and me both. He caught her eye and I pressed my lips together, amused by her reaction to him. Her eyes traveled up and down his figure and then she looked back to me and grinned.

"Well, I could use someone like him around."

Smiling, I admitted, "Couldn't we all." Another man walked through the door and she observed him closely too. "Life's too short. Go and get him."

She cackled as Gregor stood by, amused at our interaction. "Oh, honey...back in my day..." I wasn't sure if she was talking to me or Gregor. She winked at him, nodded in my direction and headed toward her car. I couldn't help but wonder what she wanted to say, if anything. Did she suspect?

He walked me to my vehicle and handed me the food asking, "Where to?"

"Follow me. There's a park nearby. Shouldn't draw suspicion."

"Ok." I watched as he walked away, the smile still plastered on his face as he climbed in his truck.

Taking a deep breath, I pulled out of the lot to the park down the road. Once I'd parked, I stepped out with our food as we headed to a bench and sat down. I was already immensely comfortable with him, but unsure of anything else.

We started eating and began talking about our lives in a bit more candid way. We got on the subject of spanking as punishment when we were kids. I admitted that spanking was something my parents did on occasion.

"Did you feel like they were being mean or using it as an act of love?"

Tilting my head, "I don't think it was something they did to be outright mean. It was to teach me a lesson, so out of love I guess."

I laughed at a memory that came to me and he looked to me and asked, "What?"

Shaking my head I recounted the memory for him.

"I was four or five and I'd done something wrong. Don't ask me what it was, but my dad had a friend over and it was time for me to go to bed. But not before my mom made sure to tell him I had a spanking or two coming my way.

"He pulled me over his knee, in front of his friend, and pulled my underwear down. When he was done, I had tears rolling down my face, but I was a defiant little shit." Looking to Gregor I smiled wickedly, "I'd never admit that it hurt. I looked to him and said, "That didn't hurt" as I wiped the tears away."

Gregor's eyes were almost gawking at me as he tried to contain his laughter. He was failing miserably at it. "What did the friend do?"

"If I remember correctly, he looked at my dad with this expression that said 'Oh, shit. Got a live one here.'

"Probably should've been a warning to my parents then and there that spanking wasn't necessarily going to work with me."

Then he started belly laughing and I joined him.

"I kept up that same attitude growing up until the spankings stopped. Never mattered how hard I got spanked or how many tears rolled down my cheeks, I'd respond the same way. 'That didn't hurt.' I think my dad gave up. I guess you could say I have daddy issues of some sort."

We continued to laugh over this for several minutes. Looking back, I realize how turned on he was by my response, though I didn't quite understand it then. To him—I was just assuming, of course—I was this little girl, now a woman, who'd never back down from a spanking. For someone into spanking, I was a dream come true. I just didn't know it then.

What was supposed to be an hour long lunch to get to know each other turned into several hours. We sat in the sun expressing desires and exposing secrets. I had long since turned to face him while we talked, his back remaining against the bench.

I had revealed things to Gregor that Todd didn't even know about me. Secret cravings, secret needs, and the secret betrayals of my past. Gregor held more of my secrets in the palm of his hand than I did. He had the potential to destroy everything I'd built, but I trusted him not to.

Things grew quiet and as I looked at him he complimented me once more. "Seriously, your eyes are stunning."

I just shook my head. "Thank you." I took a breath, gathering the courage to ask what I didn't want to but needed to know. "So, I need to know if I'm 'Thursday' girl. I need to know if I'm just one of many you're playing with. Safety, etc."

"There hasn't been anyone in a long time."

Relieved, I simply said, "Ok."

"So are your parents still together?"

I shook my head. "Well, technically, but my mom passed away several years ago. I don't really know if they were ever really happy. Maybe they stayed together for us, my sister and me. I don't know. My dad remarried a couple years after."

He listened intently as I continued discussing their marriage from my perspective. Then he began doing the same in regards to his parents' marriage.

"Mine stayed together, are still together, but I often wonder if my dad has someone else. My mother is a miserable woman and I hope my dad has someone, somewhere, that makes him happy."

"Have you asked him?"

He just shook his head. "No."

"Maybe you should."

"I'm not sure I really want to know. Validation isn't necessarily a good thing."

"I get that. I know that my parents had affairs, or at least they both accused each other of it. For me it's simple, if you're not getting what you need, crave, and desire at home, you're going to find it somewhere else." He nodded his agreement. "I'm not saying its right, but it is what it is."

"It's almost impossible to find one person to meet all your needs, especially when most of us get married so young. We're still discovering ourselves and odds are if you do find that person to meet all those carnal needs, as well as others, it happens later in life."

Everything he said made sense. It wasn't pretty or accepted by society, but it was the truth. When I got married I had no idea that the cravings and needs I now had would come to be. And I certainly didn't know that Todd wouldn't be open to exploring them.

"I wanted to tell you that you have my complete trust." I looked to his face as his eyes narrowed on mine, like he wondered where I was going with this. "Given the circumstances, you could've ceased all contact with me once I revealed that we live in the same town. Had you been lying about anything detrimental, well, we wouldn't be sitting here now." He just stared at me as I nodded, "Thank you."

He just shrugged and added, "I still can't get over the odds of it all."

Smiling, I agreed. "It's a small, small world."

We sat quiet for a moment before he asked, "So, what are you looking for?"

That was a loaded question and brought me back to the present. Sighing, I was honest with him. "I'm not looking to break up anyone's marriage. I guess what I feel guilty about is that I don't feel guilty."

"I get that. It's a process that took me a long time to grasp."

"I have needs, desires, and right now he's not willing to go there with me."

"I want us to agree to a few things." I nodded. "Don't disappear on me. If things need to end, we do it like adults. I've had a couple just vanish on me and I have no idea what happened to them."

"No, I agree and appreciate that. I'm a big girl. Just be honest."

"Do you have a safe word?"

Smiling, "Yes."

"What is it?"

"You'll laugh."

Shaking his head and smiling, he persisted, "I still need to know. What is it?"

"Unicorn."

Laughing, "Ok. Unicorn it is." He took a deep breath. "And no falling in love. If either of us starts falling, we need to walk away."

"Agree. I'm not looking to fall in love."

He quietly observed me for a moment and nodded his head. His hand stretched out across the back of the bench toward me. "So, what do you need from me today?"

Such a simple question and I became completely tongue-tied. "I, umm..."

I wasn't trying to play coy, but I felt like an idiot. What did I need from him? I didn't have a fucking clue. Where did we go next? He had yet to touch me, which I respected. The conversation flowed between us with ease, but was there physical chemistry? Would I recoil if he touched me? I didn't know, I had no idea, and I sure as hell wasn't about to make the first move.

As if he sensed my wariness, his hand reached out and grasped me just above my knee. *Jesus, fuck!* The heat of his hand seared me and I immediately had a puddle in my panties. If I was struggling with words before, they were impossible now.

He repeated his question, his stern voice catching my attention, "What do you need from me? We're running out of time."

"Umm," looking around, we weren't anywhere that would give us shelter from prying eyes. "I'm so new to this..." I reached my hand out and ran my fingers over his forearm as he gently massaged my leg.

"Your body language is telling me you're comfortable."

"I am."

"You open to a sample?" Dumbstruck, I nodded as he directed, "Follow me."

Like a fucking giddy kid headed to the candy store, I jumped off the bench and gathered my things. We got in our separate vehicles and I followed him back toward our side of town. Driving down back roads I wasn't entirely familiar with, my heart wouldn't stop pounding as I followed him. After a few minutes, we finally found a secluded spot where no one seemed to be at.

I parked and waited as he cleared some things from the back seat of his quad cab. "Come here."

Holy shit. Here we go. He was chewing gum and I took that as a good sign. He moved into the back seat and I climbed in with him. Closing the door behind me, he then sat down in the middle of the bench, his minty breath filling the small space between us, and pulled me over his knee with ease.

Rubbing light circles over my back and legs, his deep voice soothed my fears. "Relax. Just over the clothes. Should be enough to give you a taste of what's to come."

"Oh, ok." My body was tense, my confidence wavering.

He continued to run his hands over my clothes and I began to relax against him; his thigh was under my ribcage and I was well aware my jean clad ass was at his disposal. I'd seen the small paddle on the seat when I climbed in and wasn't concerned in the least. That was a mistake!

Music played softly in the background and as I tried to figure out what song it was, the first smack of his hand came down on my ass and he didn't stop there.

I felt myself slip away straightaway, the tension rolling off my shoulders in waves. The only sound I could hear was his hand whacking my ass. Yes, this is what I've been craving. Nothing else existed in that moment except us.

"Meredith?"

How long had he been saying my name? Shit! Barely lifting my head, I responded groggily, "What, yes?"

"How's that feel?"

Sighing, I confessed, "Good, really good."

I didn't try to get up as he ran soothing circles over my butt once more and started in with that small paddle. He was relentless and I loved every second of it. And holy shit did that little paddle hold a punch. Adrenaline was pumping through me, yet I was eerily calm.

"Come here." The spanking ceased as he helped me to my knees. Staring into my eyes, he scanned them carefully and smiled. "Jesus. You're already in another place."

I didn't know what to say because I wasn't entirely sure what he meant. The only thing I could feel was the sting on my ass and the feel of his hands holding me. Cupping my face, he whispered something I didn't quite catch and ran his hands to the back of my head. My head lobbed to the side as my eyes closed. I was complete putty.

"I have to see." My eyes popped open as he asked, "Can I?"

"Yes." I didn't even know exactly what he was asking and I didn't care. The answer would still be 'yes'.

He unbuttoned my pants and pushed them down my hips before draping me back across his lap. I buried my face in the seat as his hands moved over me once again. One hand reached under me and squeezed my breast through my shirt as the other moved over the back of my panties. I wanted his hands on every part of me. Gently, he pulled my panties down and moved his hands over my new marks that I was eager to see. I didn't have any idea what they'd look like, but I wanted more.

He paddled me some more and teased me. Almost as if he was unsure, his finger ever so lightly traced down the crease of my ass and over my folds.

"You're soaked."

Tell me something I don't know, Einstein. And I knew he could tell more from seeing than touching. I was slightly embarrassed at his telling of my body's confession, but it just fueled my desire.

I moaned, wanting more, needing more, and then just as quick he pulled me back to my knees. Unable to control myself I grabbed his face and pressed my lips to his. He indulged me for a moment and then separated us. I felt like an idiot. Maybe I shouldn't have kissed him? I'd never been so aggressive before. He pulled my underwear and pants back up and helped situate me.

"Come on. Time to get back to our regular lives." He opened the door and I climbed down. He walked me to my SUV and kissed me quickly. "I'll talk to you soon." That big grin was back on his face and he smacked my ass before I climbed into the driver's seat.

Smiling, I nodded and said, "Ok. Talk soon."

I pulled away with a smile plastered on my face. *All the King's Horses* by of Karmina came on the radio. The words were like another smack on the ass. What just happened had really happened and I was floating on a crazy high.

I got home with some time to spare before I needed to pick up the kids at the bus stop. Running to the bathroom, I dropped my pants and examined my ass. My breath caught as I traced the barrage of red and purple welts. Squeezing gently, my clit pulsed as the pain seared me, and I smiled. I pulled my pants back up and left the bathroom. Before I went to get the kids, my phone chimed to a new email.

> *TO: meredith@meredithedits.com*
> *4:17 PM*
> *Subject: Re: Bedtime*
> *Glad we finally got to meet! Sorry we had to be brief. Talk later! :)*

I wasn't sure a four hour lunch was considered brief, but I'd play along with it. I didn't respond until later when I got home.

> *TO: bruisedassets@yahoo.com*
> *4:47 PM*
> *Subject: Re: Bedtime*
> *Me too. It's refreshing to be so candid with someone. I'm a fucking horny mess after that spanking. I'll be around later tonight. I know you have a packed schedule today. Talk soon.*

CHAPTER
Seven

BLUE EYES BLIND

The rest of my evening went as it usually did. Homework, dinner, bathing kids, and putting them to bed. Todd even made a comment that caught me a little off guard since I thought he was being his typical self, aloof and paying me no mind.

"You're glowing. Looks like you got some sun today." It was an unexpected compliment.

My stomach dropped, like a bowling ball was placed in it. "Yes. I went for a run and forgot the sunscreen." What I really wanted to say was, 'Thanks. After a proper spanking from Sir I *should* be glowing.' But I refrained, though I'm sure the expression that would've appeared would have been priceless.

Later that night after falling asleep on the couch for a few, I couldn't contain my horniness and decided to cozy up to Todd in bed. Leaning in his ear, I whispered, "Get me off, please. I'll be quick."

And I was. He didn't hesitate in my request to just finger me. I mean, I was making it incredibly easy for him. It was what it was and I didn't even have to remove my clothes. I just wanted, *no needed*, to get off. I know how that sounds, but I wasn't the first woman—or man—to do it and I wouldn't be the last. One man had made me incredibly horny and the other was available to ease it. I had to take advantage; Todd wasn't always willing to get close to me anymore.

After that and since I'd gotten a nap on the couch, I couldn't sleep so I headed to my office. I sat there daydreaming about Gregor and our time together that day. *Blue Eyes Blind* by ZZ Ward was on repeat as I thought about his blue eyes, so different from my own.

Around midnight as I was getting ready to shut down for the night, I got a response from Gregor.

> *TO: meredith@meredithedits.com*
> *11:56 PM*
> *Subject: Re: Bedtime*
> *Ahhh – love reading about a horny mess... :) Tell me more. In explicit detail.*
> *Ended up being a late night. Still not finished with work. I finally got pissed and shut it down.*
> *I forgot that I volunteered for a field trip tomorrow so I won't be around. Then we're attending an end of summer party Saturday so I probably won't have a lot of time during the day.*

We hadn't discussed seeing each other again, but clearly he was thinking about it. I took that as a good sign as I started typing my reply.

> *TO: bruisedassets@yahoo.com*
> *12:04 AM*
> *Subject: Re: Bedtime*
> *Yes. I fell asleep on the couch after putting the kids in bed and woke close to ten. That never happens. I'm sporting a wicked sunburn, which is my own fault. I know better.*
> *I drove home in a fog and floated on that high for several hours, panties clinging to me. I'm still throbbing and wet and I made (maybe that's a strong word...lol) my hubby get me off. I couldn't help but think about how you'd do it. I want more...*
> *I'm sitting here wondering what you thought, if I got you as excited as you got me... So much better when someone has walked inside your head and understands little intricacies I'm still learning about myself.*
> *I'm about to pass out, but will talk soon.*

As I crawled into bed, another email popped up on my phone.

> *TO: meredith@meredithedits.com*
> *12:07 AM*

Subject: Re: Bedtime
I assumed you felt my erection while bent over my knee... :)

TO: bruisedassets@yahoo.com
12:09 AM
Subject: Re: Bedtime
You seemed pretty happy. I may have been in a lil bubble of my own. I think a gun could've gone off and I may not have blinked. I promise I'm more attentive when time allows...

TO: meredith@meredithedits.com
12:11 AM
Subject: Re: Bedtime
You were just fine... :)
It certainly wasn't conducive to expansive play but I knew how much you needed to just feel the intensity and I wanted you to at least have that...

I was never going to get to sleep. I started my reply.

TO: bruisedassets@yahoo.com
12:14 AM
Subject: Re: Bedtime
Thank you. I just, yeah, wow. And I know that's just the tip of the iceberg. Feeling myself slip away in your lap, to another place, was definitely intense.

TO: meredith@meredithedits.com
12:16 AM
Subject: Re: Bedtime
I assume it was very dark in the room when you made him take you...?
You were definitely marked.

Giggling quietly, as to not wake Todd, I let my fingers swipe away on my phone.

TO: bruisedassets@yahoo.com
12:18 AM
Subject: Re: Bedtime
Lol. I requested a fingering and left my pajamas on. I'm most certainly marked!

I made myself put the phone down. I drifted off to sleep with a smile on my face, ass throbbing pleasantly, and it only intensified the more I thought about it. What had I gotten myself into? I thought about it and didn't care. I was at a point where I didn't want to have regrets. Now that I'd had a small taste, I was ready for the buffet. I wanted to experience all of it NOW.

When I woke a few hours later, my sunburn the only pain I felt, I couldn't resist the temptation to check my phone. I set it on the bathroom counter as I applied some burn cream to my sunburn. He'd responded right after my latest email and I pressed my lips together as I waited for the email to load.

TO: meredith@meredithedits.com
12:25 AM
Subject: Re: Bedtime
You needed a good tongue lashing afterwards...
I was wondering what you tasted like. And how much was running down your leg. And what thoughts would be dancing around your head tomorrow as you struggled to sit still.

TO: bruisedassets@yahoo.com
3:28 AM
Subject: Re: Bedtime
Sitting still isn't too difficult cuz I just go back to the truck and relive it every time...
I'm told I'm pretty sweet...

I knew that I was blushing at my brazenness and didn't care. He enjoyed it and I liked this side of myself, where I didn't have to worry about being judged for speaking my mind, dirty or not.

Setting the phone down on my nightstand, I climbed back into bed, rolled to my side and ran my hands over my ass cheeks. I could feel where the skin was still raised and taut from his paddle and closed my eyes, reveling in the slight discomfort.

Stretching out in bed a few hours later, I turned my alarm off and picked up my phone. *Whoa!* It was an incredibly long email, longer than any he'd sent before. In a split second I wondered what it could possibly be about. Me, his wife, work, family life... They were all possibilities. Then I wondered what his wife really knew, if anything. Pushing the thought aside, nerves rattled me as I began to scan the email.

Wow. He'd opened up a whole new part of his world to me, his work world, in greater detail. I felt honored that he was comfortable enough to speak to me about it. He was struggling with things at work and so was the company.

Paragraph after paragraph greeted me as I scrolled through it on my phone. He was definitely a rare breed based on what he was telling me about with his work experience, customers, etc. I had some time before the kids would be up and getting ready for school so I headed to my laptop. After I read it a second time, I started my reply.

> *TO: bruisedassets@yahoo.com*
> *7:17 AM*
> *Subject: Re: Bedtime*
> *I think I understand the work/customer thing. My husband really struggled leaving his former employer because he was the one that many customers insisted on having on their projects since they knew he'd take care of it. He has a very diplomatic, no bullshit side to him which is typically respected in ANY industry.*
> *You seem to be another rare breed (clearly). I hope that things work out in a positive way for you, I'm sure they will. You didn't get where you are today without doing a few things right!*
> *I was up applying some burn cream to my sunburn. It's helping.*
> *And, my brain was whirling, going to naughty places. It's very rare for me to get 6hr or even 4hr straight of sleep. My brain is always on and it's hard for me to unplug. I've been toying with a storyline and writing my own book for several months and this field research is taking me there. Now, don't think that's why I'm pursuing this. I'm not. This is for me. If it rubs off in my writing, that's just a bonus!*
> *It looks like he'll be out of town later next week for a short trip w/ longer stints beginning shortly after. I need the time for writing and field research. ;-)*
> *I hope you have a great day and weekend. I know you're super busy. Every time I let my mind drift away to that place, my body becomes one entire heartbeat. It's amazing and infuriating. Lol. Until next time...*

As my day got started and the kids trickled down the stairs, the youngest had the tell-tale signs of not feeling well. Mom problem 404. I administered some medication and got the others ready for school. Once they were on the bus and my youngest was resting, I headed to my office. I took a deep breath and sat down on my tender cheeks. I may have even wiggled from side to side to elicit every single painful nerve into awareness. An email awaited.

> *TO: meredith@meredithedits.com*
> *8:59 AM*
> *Subject: Re: Bedtime*
> *Does your bottom need a reminder...? :)*

My clit pulsed and ass stung—like he'd administered a fresh smack—just at the thought of a reminder.

> *TO: bruisedassets@yahoo.com*

9:17 AM
Subject: Re: Bedtime
OMG. If I could have your hands on my ass again right now, I'd be there in a heartbeat. Goosebumps just thinking about it...
But, mom duty calls. Sick kid at home.

TO: meredith@meredithedits.com
9:20 AM
Subject: Re: Bedtime
Might be a little traumatic for them... :) seeing mommy get her ass beat in such a way. Of course – seeing your naked bottom being spanked and paddled won't be near as traumatic as seeing you forced down to your knees and having my swollen cock stuffed into that mouth of yours while you stare up at me with the gorgeous blue eyes with a look that says there is NO PLACE you would rather be at that moment (even Italy...)
But I digress...
I'll be at the school most of the day volunteering after we return from the field trip, kids have extracurricular activities tonight. Supposed to rain this morning. Didn't get to the grass yesterday due to an issue that came across my desk – I mean lap.

Christ almighty. I dropped my head onto my arms as they rested on my desk. Gregor had remembered my mention of Italy. It was someplace I'd gone in college and had yet to return, but desperately wanted to. I knew what I'd be doing at naptime... Masturbating. If my child decided to nap, too. I tried to gather my thoughts and took a deep breath. Staring at the white screen and chewing on my lip, I started my reply.

TO: bruisedassets@yahoo.com
9:27 AM
Subject: Re: Bedtime
Yes, hence why I can't. I'm sure I'll be napping when/if she does.
MY fields were more important to tend to yesterday. Lol. And this issue of mine of almost always being wet is getting worse and worse. Wonder why? I'm currently a puddle of want. Maybe I should have you examine it more closely, before OR after I get on my knees...
I'm available during the day next week on Wed and Thurs. Though I have an appt on Tue. OMG...I'm laughing and wondering if my marks will be gone by Tue. My massage therapist will certainly be wondering and curious since she knows what I edit and read!

There! That should leave him speechless... Maybe. There was no delay in his response. Shit!

TO: meredith@meredithedits.com
9:31 AM
Subject: Re: Bedtime
After your knees you will have to wash your face. I am thinking about how those sweet little lips and gorgeous eyes will look with cum splattered all around them. Very distracting thought.
You may go through several pairs of panties today.
Next week I'm out of town M-W, might get back Wed morning. Could be a nice welcome back stop...

I just couldn't. Couldn't focus. Couldn't breathe. Couldn't cap the desire. Couldn't stop wanting more. Of him. Motherfucker wanted to play, he should know by now that I was game!

TO: bruisedassets@yahoo.com
9:33 AM
Subject: Pulse
Sigh. Just thinking about things to come and my heart rate quickens knowing of the pain and pleasure to be had.
And YOU won't have to wash your face after you're done with me. I'll eagerly kiss every drop of myself from your lips...
I may go through several batteries too...
I'll keep Wednesday open...

I also included another attachment. Just words, words that had never been more accurate in that moment. 'She loved how his words disturbed the rhythm of her pulse.' Surely that email would shut him up. I had shit to do. And it did. I didn't hear back from him until later in the afternoon.

TO: meredith@meredithedits.com
3:34 PM
Subject: Re: Pulse
It will be on more than just my lips...
Again, I asked myself, 'What the hell had I gotten myself into?'

TO: bruisedassets@yahoo.com
3:38 PM
Subject: Re: Pulse
How did I know that'd be your response...?
To truly enjoy pussy, one must devour it...
Lord almighty, I prayed he knew how to devour it.

TO: meredith@meredithedits.com
3:40 PM

Subject: Re: Pulse
Front to back. Back to front.

FUCK!

TO: bruisedassets@yahoo.com
3:42 PM
Subject: Re: Pulse
You'll have to let me know if Gregor is the name you want falling from my lips when I'm pleading with you for more...

TO: meredith@meredithedits.com
3:43 PM
Subject: Re: Pulse
You are assuming you will have enough breath to even plead...

TO: bruisedassets@yahoo.com
3:45 PM
Subject: Re: Pulse
Umm <thud> I'm on my knees waiting...

Then he was quiet. Clearly he liked the thought of me on my knees and waiting. I shouldn't have been surprised.

CHAPTER
Eight

GIRL CRUSH

I WAS OUT RUNNING ERRANDS that night after dinner when Tami called.

"What up biotch?"

Laughing, I replied, "Oh you know. Same ole, same ole. You?"

"Uh, I call bullshit. You better fucking spill the details."

"Oh, my God!" I'd forgotten to call Tami yesterday and couldn't believe she'd refrained from calling me until now.

"Bitch, you're lucky I saw you online or I would've called the troops to find your ass. Making me wait over a day... Was it bad?"

Giggling, "No. It was anything but bad."

"I fucking knew it!" She paused and waited for me to say something. Where did I even begin? "Meredith! Tell me!"

"Ok, ok. We chatted...for hours."

She interrupted me, "Is he hot?"

Sighing, "If you saw him walking down the street you probably wouldn't look twice. But, fuck. He's in my head, Tami. Without even trying, he's in it. I've never been so open and candid with someone."

"That's good. Honesty is really important if you're going to take this to a true D/s level."

"I know. I told him I trust him, but he's guarded."

"Why is he guarded?"

I sat in the parking lot of my local grocery store after loading my groceries and continued filling Tami in.

"Apparently he had a bad experience a while back. The chick went psycho."

"Do you think he's hiding something?"

I scrunched my eyes and lips and groaned, "No, not like you may think. He needs to know he can trust me. I can wait for him to open up, if he chooses to do so. I asked him if I was 'Thursday girl' and he said there hasn't been anyone in a long time." I paused and added, "I believe him. We're too intertwined with one another as it is for him to risk lying to me. We could both fuck up each other's worlds if we wanted."

Chortling, "Ain't that the fucking truth. I can't believe you two are in the same fucking town AND the same school. Jesus. You two are crazy."

Sighing, I agreed. "I know. I just..."

"What is it?"

"I don't see this ending anytime soon. Like, I don't know. This won't be over quick."

"Christ Meredith. I get it, I do. Just be careful."

"I didn't have sex with him!"

She was laughing, "Well, if you did I'd expect you to tell me. And that's not what I meant. Be careful with your heart."

"We agreed to no emotions, no falling in love."

"Good! Now...if you didn't have sex, what did you do?!"

"Ok, I have to get home, but I'll give you the cliff notes." I took a big breath and just went to the good stuff. "He spanked me in the backseat of his truck."

"WHAT?"

"Tami, I had no idea. I've never experienced anything like that. I totally zoned out."

"Bitch, it's called subspace."

I groaned, "I don't know if it was subspace, but I was fucking out of it. Couldn't hear anything or feel anything but him. He stopped a few minutes in and made me look at him. He said something like 'you're already somewhere else' and then he resumed, but with my pants and underwear down."

"Holy shit!" I smiled because I could almost see her jumping up and down with excitement.

"I'm never going to get enough."

"Yeah. That's the hard part. Has he mentioned seeing you again?"

"He's alluded to it."

"Ha! That's good!" She said something I didn't catch to someone else and then said, "I need to go. We should get together Monday."

"I can probably do dinner."

"Perfect. Ok. Talk to you later."

I got home and put the groceries away. Todd helped carry them in and put them away and then he went back to the couch and me to my office. I had yet to get a response from Gregor about me waiting on my knees, but knew it had to be coming.

Sure enough, a few minutes later, an email popped up.

TO: meredith@meredithedits.com
8:43 PM
Subject: Re: Pulse
Maybe you should seductively deep throat a banana and send me a pic of you in action (or otherwise phallic like object).

And so the requests for naughty pictures began. Was I allowed to make requests too? My paranoia creeped in as I started thinking about the possible repercussions of such a picture. Who was I kidding? The picture was already out there, but with girlfriends.

TO: bruisedassets@yahoo.com
8:51 PM
Subject: Re: Pulse
While I'll admit there's a picture out there somewhere of me and a 'phallic' vegetable from a girl's night in...I'm not sending it. Let's just say my friends were shocked!

That should shut him up! *PING!* Fuck!

TO: meredith@meredithedits.com
8:53 PM
Subject: Re: Pulse
And why not...?

Asshole!

TO: bruisedassets@yahoo.com
8:57 PM
Subject: Re: Pulse
I'd have to find it. It's from several years ago and I was still carrying a lot of baby weight. Not saying I'm an expert deep throat, but I can take a lot. I'll look for it after the hubby is in bed. He hasn't even seen that pic. Lol
If I was really naughty I'd suggest meeting me on the corner at midnight so I could prove it to you in person...

Yup. I was a whore.

TO: meredith@meredithedits.com
8:59 PM
Subject: Re: Pulse
:) Feel free to deep throat something else and send it to me – favorite dildo or otherwise
At this rate – I'm not going to make it to 10...lol

I could feel the sub and Domme in me fighting with one another. Part of me wanted to send it, knowing it'd please him and part of me was like 'Fuck him!' I wouldn't degrade myself to do such things. Sighing. Yes, yes I would. Shit!

TO: bruisedassets@yahoo.com
9:07 PM
Subject: Re: Pulse

LOL. I understand. It's been a lot of late nights for us both. I'll work on the picture when I'm alone. My ass already misses you...

I got up and headed to my room and found my current dildo of choice and placed it in the bathroom for easy access later. Heading back to my desk, another email.

TO: *meredith@meredithedits.com*
9:19 PM
Subject: Re: Pulse
Would love to give you a good night spanking...
How were we ever going to get anything done, ever?!

TO: *bruisedassets@yahoo.com*
9:23 PM
Subject: Re: Pulse
Would love to get one... I keep squeezing my marks and instant tingles. What have you done to me? Lol.

I didn't wait long, again just a few short minutes.

TO: *meredith@meredithedits.com*
9:28 PM
Subject: Re: Pulse
Did you take pics so you have the visual reminders...?
I simply gave you something you have needed for a long time. And amazingly – only a small piece of what is to come.

Closing my eyes, I replayed it for myself again. Crossing my legs to try to subdue the throb, it only increased. Why hadn't I taken pictures of my ass? It's not like I was going to create a scrapbook, at least not a paper copy. I giggled at the thought and started my reply.

TO: *bruisedassets@yahoo.com*

9:33 PM

Subject: Calm

I did not, but I keep looking at them and touching them.

Sigh. I'm like a kid at Disney. I want to try everything NOW. Told you, I lack patience. But I am a fast and eager learner, always have been.

I think that's something that struck (no pun intended...lol) me last night. What I've been craving is indeed what I've been needing. I can't wait for what's to come. I feel like this calm has settled over me, knowing I have an outlet now.

Todd went to bed and I checked the laundry before returning to my office. Again, he'd gone to bed not seeking any type of physical contact with me; dismissing me as usual.

TO: meredith@meredithedits.com

9:45 PM

Subject: Re: Calm

I promise I won't be the storm that precedes the calm. At least not a bad one... :)

Good night. I keep drifting off. That is my sign.

Sweet dreams of spankings and denied orgasms.

TO: bruisedassets@yahoo.com

9:51 PM

Subject: Re: Calm

Get some rest. And I hope your dreams are filled with naughtiness, too.

TO: meredith@meredithedits.com

9:53 PM

Subject: Re: Calm

It's weird knowing I could run out and get milk and squeeze in a sound spanking or a BJ without even being noticed...

TO: bruisedassets@yahoo.com

9:55 PM

Subject: Re: Calm

Yes. Agreed. The good and bad of close quarters... I mean...it could always be both...

TO: meredith@meredithedits.com
9:58 PM
Subject: Re: Calm

I have that party tomorrow and will have to run out and pick up some things in the morning and I keep thinking – hmmm...

TO: bruisedassets@yahoo.com
9:59 PM
Subject: Re: Calm

Sigh...he's working tomorrow. I'm a desperate housewife... But, if you need to take bottles back tomorrow night...

TO: meredith@meredithedits.com
10:02 PM
Subject: Re: Calm

It will be a late night tomorrow unless you have some way to blend into the group... :)
Maybe Sunday night...

TO: bruisedassets@yahoo.com
10:04 PM
Subject: Re: Calm

Lol...I'm a wallflower and don't blend in unless I'm with friends.
I may need to make a milk run Sunday night... :)
I thought you were going to sleep... Or are you too busy visualizing me milking your cock?

TO: meredith@meredithedits.com
10:07 PM
Subject: Re: Calm

No. As soon as I laid down – mind started racing. So I started going over financial news.
And thinking about how quick I could get out for a drive by sucking.

TO: bruisedassets@yahoo.com
10:10 PM
Subject: Re: Calm
Good to know we enjoy torturing each other.
I should get to work on that picture...

I didn't hear anything for the rest of the night. I finished more laundry and then I sent him two pictures. You can use your imagination as to the scandalous nature of the images I sent of me deep throating my vibrator.

TO: bruisedassets@yahoo.com
11:36 PM
Subject: Ask and you shall receive...
Is that what you had in mind...?

In the morning I still hadn't heard from him. God! What if he hated the pictures I sent? I knew I shouldn't have done it. I hopped in the shower and when I got out I had an email waiting. The nerves were getting to me as I opened it up.

TO: meredith@meredithedits.com
8:08 AM
Subject: Re: Ask and you shall receive...
Uh huh... :) nice to wake up to...
Finally fell asleep and stayed asleep – other than the storms. Now need to finish getting ready to head to this party.

I took a deep breath. He seemed pleased.

TO: bruisedassets@yahoo.com
8:19 AM
Subject: Re: Ask and you shall receive...
Glad to hear you got some rest. Just got out of the shower. Hoping to get some work and cleaning done. We'll see how the kids behave.

TO: meredith@meredithedits.com
8:22 AM
Subject: Re: Ask and you shall receive...
Hang a big paddle on the wall and tell them mom is serious...

TO: bruisedassets@yahoo.com
8:29 AM
Subject: Re: Ask and you shall receive...
Kids, mommy has been very very bad...I'll be right back.
Not exactly how I picture it. Lol.

TO: meredith@meredithedits.com
8:32 AM
Subject: Re: Ask and you shall receive...
I meant the paddle would be for THEM if they don't behave...LOL

I was laughing as I typed my response. Clearly, I knew what he meant. I just enjoyed the teasing and bantering.

TO: bruisedassets@yahoo.com
8:35 AM
Subject: Re: Ask and you shall receive...
I know that, silly.

TO: meredith@meredithedits.com
8:38 AM
Subject: Re: Ask and you shall receive...
:)
Ok. I'm headed to the store...
With visions of sore, bouncing bottoms and deep throated cocks swimming around in my head.

TO: bruisedassets@yahoo.com
8:39 AM

Subject: Re: Ask and you shall receive...
I'll be here envisioning my next spanking...

I waited a few and no response came. It was to be expected. He had things to do and I so did I. The kids were at the neighbors' playing when an email popped up a couple of hours later.

TO: meredith@meredithedits.com
11:06 AM
Subject: Re: Ask and you shall receive...
Heading to get snacks to bring – want to meet on the side of the road to get your bottom warmed back up...? :)
I cannot believe how humid it is... ugghh. Sweating my ass off and it's only 75

TO: bruisedassets@yahoo.com
11:09 AM
Subject: Re: Ask and you shall receive...
You have no idea how badly I want that. Chastising myself for doing too much talking and not enough fondling at lunch.
He's working a short day. Should be home by 5pm. Not a short fucking day.

TO: meredith@meredithedits.com
11:10 AM
Subject: Re: Ask and you shall receive...
It's important to build rapport and trust. Even though you feel like you need to make up for the last 20-30 years of 'lost' time you still have PLENTY of time to get it all in... :)

TO: bruisedassets@yahoo.com
11:13 AM
Subject: Re: Ask and you shall receive...
Looking forward to it. And I agree. It would be nothing without the trust and rapport.
And I can't stop thinking about you being all sweaty. Well played, Sir...

His reply didn't come for about thirty minutes and as usual, left me breathless.

> *TO: meredith@meredithedits.com*
> *11:42 AM*
> *Subject: Re: Ask and you shall receive...*
> *I can't wait to hear you gasp as I slide my well lubricated, swollen cock into your sore, burning ass the first time...*

I mean, how did I respond? Shit!

> *TO: bruisedassets@yahoo.com*
> *11:46 AM*
> *Subject: Re: Ask and you shall receive...*
> *I can't wait for you to hear all my gasps for the first time...and look forward to making you gasp, too.*

And again, silence. An hour later I emailed him a quote from my book I was working on.

> *TO: bruisedassets@yahoo.com*
> *12:56 PM*
> *Subject: Handiwork*
> *Writing...thanks for the inspiration...*
> *"I want to be owned by you in ways I didn't know possible...until now."*
> *I've also attached a picture of my ass. 46 hours post spanking. Enjoy your party...*

We had a cookout with the neighbors while the kids played that night. It was nice to have the distraction. That night Todd was heading to bed and I was back at my laptop not expecting an email, but eagerly hoping for one. I got my wish.

> *TO: meredith@meredithedits.com*
> *11:07 PM*
> *Subject: Re: Handiwork*
> *Beautiful!!!*

Party went well. Just got home after several hours of karaoke...

I had music playing and scrolled through my playlist of inappropriate songs given our situation.

TO: *bruisedassets@yahoo.com*
11:09 PM
Subject: Re: Handiwork
Hmmm...I should've come and sung Girl Crush by Little Big Town and left! Lol.

TO: *meredith@meredithedits.com*
11:12 PM
Subject: Re: Handiwork
You might have been able to hear us from there... :)

He ignored the song reference, but maybe he wasn't familiar with it or playing coy. Didn't really matter.

TO: *bruisedassets@yahoo.com*
11:15 PM
Subject: Re: Handiwork
I've been busy writing, editing, listening to music, and trying to drown out my kids. It turned out to be a beautiful evening for you, though!

TO: *meredith@meredithedits.com*
11:16 PM
Subject: Re: Handiwork
Did the words flow free...?

TO: *bruisedassets@yahoo.com*
11:19 PM
Subject: Re: Handiwork
Yes and no. I'm in the middle of a sex scene...getting distracted by thoughts of crew cab pickup trucks.

TO: meredith@meredithedits.com
11:21 PM
Subject: Re: Handiwork
Any way to integrate those distractions...?

TO: bruisedassets@yahoo.com
11:23 PM
Subject: Re: Handiwork
LMAO...well, you tell me...

I sent him a scene and was nervous to share that part of me. Though it was a part of me I knew he appreciated. I didn't hear from him until morning. I imagined him passed out in bed from too much drinking and sun because I didn't want to imagine him doing anything else.

CHAPTER
Nine

FINGERPRINTS

I WOKE UP TO AN EMAIL awaiting me.

> *TO: meredith@meredithedits.com*
> *7:08 AM*
> *Subject: Re: Handiwork*
> *I see the scene didn't read "he drug her into the back seat of his crew cab after he cleared away the piles of his normal life and realized it really needed to be cleaned"...probably not as enticing to the intended audience.*
>
> *Woke up an hour ago. Sleep didn't come back a callin'. I think the allergies/ sinus issues that have been around since the weather broke awhile back have finally rooted and are not going away any time soon without pharmaceutical intervention. Argh. Trip to the clinic is in my future. Hoowah!*
>
> *If my head did not feel like a snot balloon - I would probably be masturbating to the sight of your well-marked ass and your thoughts about it still bouncing around in your head that you have shared.*

> *TO: bruisedassets@yahoo.com*
> *7:48 AM*
> *Subject: Re: Handiwork*
> *You make it sound like you forced me. I was more than willing to be dragged in there.*

I've had to take medication the past two nights and feel better this am.

The thought of you masturbating to images and thoughts of me makes me wet. I wish I was there to help ease the ache of both your heads. :)

TO: meredith@meredithedits.com
7:58 AM
Subject: Re: Handiwork

I didn't mean in the Kentucky sense like I drug you by the hair kicking and screaming... :) There certainly wasn't a physical or intellectual struggle that I noticed. Of course – I did have a tad bit of bias... :)

How many times a day have you looked at the marks over the last several days? How wet does it make you seeing the marks and watching them evolve?

His fingerprints and paddle marks were all over my ass, and I wanted them on my entire body. I should've been concerned with the fingerprints he was leaving on me internally. Reminding me of a song, I put it on and soaked in the words. *Fingerprints* by Kita Klane helped take me back to the truck as I typed my reply.

TO: bruisedassets@yahoo.com
8:12 AM
Subject: Re: Handiwork

Am I supposed to be keeping track? Countless. My panties are forever soaked and I find excuses to go to the bathroom, lock the door, and look.

I'd gladly get on all fours and crawl back to you just to be on your lap again...

TO: meredith@meredithedits.com
8:36 AM
Subject: Re: Handiwork

That could be dangerous crawling across 154 unless you crawl fast.

TO: bruisedassets@yahoo.com
8:49 AM
Subject: Re: Handiwork

LOL. Sigh. You like the idea of me on all fours and you know it. I was thinking of a more private setting...

TO: meredith@meredithedits.com
9:15 AM
Subject: Re: Handiwork

I think I will thoroughly enjoy you in many forms of movement and positions. :) Heading to the clinic. My kids will be with me so unfortunately there won't be any last minute blo n gos or spank n wanks.

TO: bruisedassets@yahoo.com
9:29 AM

Subject: Re: Handiwork

LOL. Hopefully they get you what you need medicinally. Looks like another day here where I'm sitting with legs clenched, trying to get people motivated to clean their shit.

I look forward to our secret liaisons, blo n gos or spank n wanks...just a few things to enjoy...

I wonder how long I can hold out before taking my pleasure into my own hands. Friday around noon and counting...

The kids were restless and I was trying to get work done. Todd picked up on it and decided to take the kids out. I was grateful and started working on the latest book I was editing. A couple hours passed when another email from Gregor came in.

TO: meredith@meredithedits.com
11:31 AM
Subject: Re: Handiwork

Doc put me on antibiotics – was pretty sure I needed them. Actually a nurse practitioner and very cute and peppy. She had the active eyes – definitely some spunk behind them. Of course I already had spanking planted firmly on my mind going in.

Maybe I can give you a pre-bed spanking on my way home tonight if you have to go out for milk or anything... :)

TO: bruisedassets@yahoo.com
11:37 AM
Subject: Home Alone

Sigh...He took the kids out.

Glad you got the meds you need. I will need to run out for fruit, etc. at some point. Hubby was making googly eyes at me earlier...

Panties soaked, I'll channel you into my writing. Must remember to shower whilst alone so that I don't expose the secrets written on my ass...

TO: meredith@meredithedits.com
11:39 AM
Subject: Re: Home Alone

If I give you a reminder tonight – you will be showering alone for the next week and will have some tough questions with your upcoming appt.

I would like to take those soaked panties off and stuff them in your mouth while recoloring that bottom of yours.

TO: bruisedassets@yahoo.com
11:45 AM
Subject: Re: Home Alone

Sigh. The pleasure alone I'd get in spin class tomorrow morning with a tender ass.

Not really a doc appt, massage and she knows what I'm into...kind of. I'll just tell her the truth; consensual spanking. If anything it'll brighten her day! She's a dirty old broad.

I just can't even think about it without turning limp, becoming flush, and my pulse racing. I may have to appease the hubby with bjs so that my ass remains in your hands...

What time are you thinking?

TO: meredith@meredithedits.com
11:49 AM
Subject: Re: Home Alone
Tell her you were just doing research and it was very well received. Give her some fodder to take home with her.
Sometime between 830 and 9pm.

TO: bruisedassets@yahoo.com
11:52 AM
Subject: Re: Home Alone
Or I could tell her I fell down some stairs. Think she'd believe me? LOL. I could always go have a 'drink' with a friend...after appeasing him.

TO: meredith@meredithedits.com
12:01 PM
Subject: Re: Home Alone
You going to come see me with a mouthful of cum...? LOL
Good grief! I was cracking up.

TO: bruisedassets@yahoo.com
12:05 PM
Subject: Re: Home Alone
LMAO. Umm, no. I'll already be out and about if the girlfriends are up for an impromptu dinner. His cum will long be washed down my throat. :) If he decides to let me swallow...

TO: meredith@meredithedits.com
12:08 PM
Subject: Re: Home Alone
I enjoy a mix. Definitely swallowing at times. Facials are great after a spanking session that ends with the obligatory BJ while kneeling before me and looking up with those bright, blue eyes. Coming on tits or splattering a load on the lower back or ass after a pounding from behind is always nice as well. Or when I know I have a rather large load waiting – getting a slow, deliberate HJ while kissing and then having you blow the load on my chest while you watch up close and personal is always a turn on.

What are some of your favorites?

Here we go again. My heart was palpitating and I couldn't breathe. I wanted to run to the bedroom and masturbate like never before. But I didn't. Instead I attempted my reply.

TO: bruisedassets@yahoo.com
12:15 PM
Subject: Re: Home Alone
(Clenches legs) He's never given me a facial. He's a lil too tidy with his cum. Lol.

I'm not opposed to any of them. The kissing and HJ sounds the most appealing, but that's because I LOVE kissing. To hear every lil moan and breath that closely while I nibble your lip, and vice versa, is a huge turn on for me, with roaming hands. Lovers forget how important touching and kissing is. It's not all about the fucking, just enhances the fucking when done properly. I'm not opposed to the face fucking either...

TO: meredith@meredithedits.com
12:28 PM
Subject: Re: Home Alone
Maybe I will have to send you home with a mouthful and let the taste linger along with the throbbing pussy and burning bottom...

How much to tell or confess? What was the fucking point of holding back?

TO: bruisedassets@yahoo.com
12:38 PM
Subject: Re: Home Alone
I'm not the girl who loves to swallow, but I do it. I was also the girl at the private Christian high school who had other girls seeking my advice. LOL. I'm sure it helped put a smile on the faces of a few guys who had girls with terrible gag reflexes. I promised the girls if they just went a little deeper, it'd just pour down their throats and wouldn't be as bad as they thought it would be. There's a story idea. Sex therapist on a Christian college (high school might be too taboo) campus. LMAO.

And all I know is I want my next orgasm to be yours to do with as you see fit...

TO: meredith@meredithedits.com
12:47 PM
Subject: Re: Home Alone
Hmmm... Maybe I should make you hold it in your mouth for a little while as you look me deep in the eye. Make sure you get the full effect and it hits every taste bud so I can be sure it will linger. Then let you swallow and send you on your way...

I will make you wait and beg for that next orgasm. I will be sure there is plenty of built up pressure and tension that I can tease and manipulate for my own desire and amusement until I am ready to watch you release it. Then I will thoroughly enjoy and soak in every sight, sound, and touch as your body takes over and wretches in release...

> **TO: bruisedassets@yahoo.com**
> **12:49 PM**
> **Subject: Re: Home Alone**
> *If you're not careful, I'm going to come in my chair... I'm not opposed to begging.*

> **TO: meredith@meredithedits.com**
> **12:52 PM**
> **Subject: Re: Home Alone**
> *You are NOT to come until instructed to do so – understood?*
> *At son's game. TTYL*

Groaning, I smiled. And so this was what orgasm denial was? Let the games begin. I waited on my reply and rushed to the shower. The kids and Todd would be home soon so my window was closing.

> **TO: bruisedassets@yahoo.com**
> **1:49 PM**
> **Subject: Re: Home Alone**
> *Showered and shaved. I behaved and will continue to do so.*
> *Have a good game.*
> *Talk soon...*

I managed to set up dinner plans with a friend who actually lived nearby, but we hadn't seen each other in several months. Though things at home were bad, Todd had given me 'the eyes' early in the day and I knew what he wanted. I surprised him, and blew him in the privacy of our bedroom as the kids played outside. I told him I didn't expect anything in return and had to run to meet Elaine for dinner. In all honesty, I was saving my orgasm for Gregor. I got his email as I pulled into the restaurant parking lot to meet her.

> **TO: meredith@meredithedits.com**
> **5:52 PM**
> **Subject: Re: Home Alone**
> *They don't keep score at this age. However we played pretty well and posted more outs than the other team.*
> *Keeping your hands off that pussy...? Behaving?*

> **TO: bruisedassets@yahoo.com**
> **5:59 PM**

Subject: Re: Home Alone
Way to go!
It's very slippery, I don't have to touch it to know.
I'm behaving!
Meeting a girlfriend for dinner and drinks. Then I'm all yours.

TO: meredith@meredithedits.com
6:02 PM
Subject: Re: Home Alone
Heading out shortly to play. You do realize if we meet that I will be a hot sweaty mess from playing...? I don't shower there. Hope dinner goes well!

TO: bruisedassets@yahoo.com
6:06 PM
Subject: Re: Home Alone
I already said I was thinking about you hot n sweaty.
We're at Angelo's to have pizza!

TO: meredith@meredithedits.com
6:12 PM
Subject: Re: Home Alone
That's where we used to go after playing when they kept late hours.
I won't have my phone with me while playing. Think of a place to meet.
I'll be in touch.

I saw Elaine pull in and put my phone away. I had almost two hours to chat with her and pretend I wasn't waiting for someone else's call. She complained about and praised her husband. Typical for any wife. I was guilty of it myself. We shared a lot of laughs, too.

As we were paying the bill, my phone alerted me to a text. Not his typical mode of communication, if it was him.

It was indeed Gregor seeing if I was free and if I'd thought of somewhere to meet. I texted back that I was wrapping up. I said my goodbyes to Elaine and sped out of the parking lot as I sent an email. He'd warned me to be cautious with texts so I emailed instead.

TO: bruisedassets@yahoo.com
8:06 PM
Subject: Re: Home Alone
Are those dirt roads patrolled at night?

TO: meredith@meredithedits.com
8:12 PM

Subject: Re: Home Alone
Yes. I have a thought. Meet me at Middlebury bank. You can follow. I should be there in 10-15 min.

TO: bruisedassets@yahoo.com
8:16 PM
Subject: Re: Home Alone
Ok. I'm about 10 mins out.

I was giddy as the blood pumped through my veins. As I approached the bank I saw his truck sitting in the parking lot. Pulling into the lot, I rolled my window down and was greeted with his big grin. The grin that made me horny and nervous that first day and still had the same effect on me.

"How you doing?" That voice. Its deep vibrato played along my spine like a xylophone.

"Good, you?"

He just smiled. "Follow me. It's not far."

I nodded as he pulled away and I followed closely. I knew most of these dirt roads, but I didn't know the secret hiding spots—if there were any—never having a reason before. Apparently he did or he was just shooting in the dark. A few minutes later he pulled into a dark alcove. As our headlights hit the area, I saw picnic tables under a gazebo and no other cars were there. Pulling up and away from his truck, I climbed out of my SUV, leaving my phone and purse inside. I didn't need the distraction.

My eyes quickly adjusted to the darkness. Yes, I had great night vision, always had. He sat on a picnic bench with his back against the table, legs jutting out. There was a long wooden paddle resting on the table and had I not been so excited, I may have shit my pants at the sheer size of it. It was close to three feet long, probably a few inches wide and around an inch thick.

I sat down next to him and he pulled me closer. I realized I was shaking. A mixture of the slight night chill and my nerves. As I crossed my legs his hand went around my back. I couldn't stop smiling as the butterflies swirled in my stomach. Turning toward me, he nestled his hand between my legs, pulling me a little bit closer.

"You ok?"

Nodding, I closed my eyes.

"You're nervous." It was a statement, not a question.

As my eyes opened I saw his smile. "Of course I'm nervous. I haven't kissed another man in over a decade until I kissed you." He just looked at me, his hand squeezing my thigh. "And I want to do it again."

CHAPTER
Ten

POISON

I watched as he removed his glasses and turned his baseball cap around so that the brim was facing backward.

"If anyone stops, we're just talking. I'm helping a friend through a hard time."

Smiling, I nodded my agreement. Though in my head I thought, 'you're the one with the 'hard' time.'

With one hand still around my back, his other removed itself from my thighs and came up and slowly stroked my neck. My hands were clenched in my lap and I instantly began to relax at the feel of his skin on mine. The heat from the pad of his thumb eased me even more as it ran along my jaw. Looking into his eyes calmed me, the moonlight just making them that much more seductive.

My breathing was becoming erratic at the anticipation. I was acutely aware that he was taking in my every breath, sound, and cue, garnering my reaction to him. Smiling, he cupped my neck with both hands and ran his fingers over my skin and then he pressed his lips to mine.

Our kiss from the day we met had been sweet and quick. This wasn't that kind of kiss. This was all consuming. It started slowly but grew harder and more fevered.

My hands finally reached for him, unable to resist touching him. Gripping his hoodie, just above his waist, my hands dug into the soft material. His thumb traced down my throat and I couldn't contain the moan that escaped me. Pulling on my hair he divided our mouths as I protested, my lips desperate for more of him.

"There it is; that moan I've been waiting for."

His words just turned me on more as I dug my fingernails into him and yanked him back to me. The smallest groan escaped him as he kissed me again. I couldn't get close enough to him. I wanted to straddle him, lay across his lap, have him press me down against the table... So many choices and I couldn't decide.

Without thought, I swung my leg closest to him over the bench. He didn't hesitate in pulling my other leg across his lap, pressing his erection into my thigh. Our kiss was getting out of control and I didn't want it any other way. Tongues dueling, teeth biting, lips sucking. His hand cupped me through my jeans as I cried out.

"Oh, God." I pressed my hips closer as his hand dug into me further.

I dropped my head to his shoulder and he began kissing my neck and sucking on my ears as my hips rocked against his hand. As good as his lips felt on my neck, I needed them on my mouth again. And that's just what he did.

Lifting my head, he dug his hands into my hair and attacked my mouth. I'd never had a man's tongue so deep in my mouth and I had a brief thought that 'this, this is what kissing was meant to be like.' Had I ever truly been kissed before now?

If he fucked liked he kissed, I was in deep shit. The man kissed like there was no tomorrow. In all my years no one had ever kissed me the way he did. He held my face, pulled my hair, and manipulated me for his use. Sucking and biting on my lips and tongue, causing moans from me that even I hadn't heard before. It was like he wanted me to have a small taste of what fucking would be like with him to see if I could handle it. Lord, I wanted to handle it.

Growling, his words traveled through me. "Is my naughty girl ready for her punishment?"

He pushed my leg from his lap and before I knew what was happening, we were standing in front of the table. His hand darted under my shirt and released my breast. He began pinching my nipple and massaging my breast. Soft moans fell from my lips. I'd always thought my breasts were practically numb, but they weren't numb to Gregor.

His mouth lowered as he pushed my shirt aside and sucked vigorously on my nipple. Panting, I confessed, "You're making a liar out of me."

Lifting his head, he questioned me. "How's that?"

Smiling, I told him. "My breasts aren't sensitive. At least that's what I thought until just now."

Still twirling the throbbing bud between his fingers, he smiled. "Just needed the right buttons pushed." I giggled and then moaned as his mouth took my breast into his mouth once more.

"Oh!" He'd scraped his teeth around my nipple and I wondered if he'd marked it as well.

Then he pulled my shirt back down and steadied me. "Drop your pants and panties." He motioned to where he wanted me, ordering, "Bend over and get that ass in the air."

I was slightly embarrassed, but did as I was instructed to do. My pants dropped to my ankles, along with my soaked panties, and then I climbed on the table. Knees spread and resting on the seat, my forearms did the same on the tabletop.

"Higher, I want your knees on the table."

Jesus! I did as he said. His hands began to move over my exposed flesh, tingles moving through my entire body.

His breath in my ear surprised me because of how fast he moved out from behind me. "You're going to count with me. Make sure I can hear you and that you don't miss a single stroke or we start again. Is that understood?"

His humid breath against my ear and neck nearly had me convulsing.

He raised his voice and repeated the question. "Is that understood?"

Panicked, because I realized I'd agreed, but hadn't verbalized it, I consented, "Yes!"

"What was that?"

"YES!"

Gripping my hair, he yanked back and demanded, "Yes, what?"

Shit. I was an idiot. "Yes, Sir!"

"Good girl." Releasing my hair, he continued running his hand over my hips and ass. "Now," he picked up the paddle which had been sitting on the table under my torso, "you're going to pick how many strokes." *WHAT?!* Back in my ear, he added, "And if you pick too few," he paused for effect, "I'll *double* the number I pick."

My brain started racing. What number did he already have picked? I had no idea what kind of damage that paddle would do to me, but I knew it could be significant. And, I was most certainly curious. How many strokes was too few? FUCK! But I wasn't a wimp either. I'd signed up for this and I was going to fucking take it like a champ.

His voice jolted me as he spit out, "I'm waiting. You don't want me to pick."

Panting, "Fifteen."

He was back in my ear confirming, "Fifteen?"

"Yes, Sir. Fifteen, Sir."

A small chuckle escaped him. He was pleased with my number and maybe surprised. I could feel the smile of his lips against my neck. "You're a good girl. I'll break it up into two parts. Don't forget to count." He kissed my neck and then he was gone.

Smack!

"One!" Fuck, ok. That hurt, but it wasn't...

Smack!

"Two!" Oh, hell. Maybe...

Smack!

"Three!" Fuck me. That fucking hurts. Oh, but that feels good. His hand was running over my ass and just as quick he stopped.

Smack!

"Four!" Was I allowed to beg for mercy?

Smack!

"Five!" My voice was already cracking. I gripped my hands around the edge of the table, digging my nails in.

Smack!

"Six!" Suck it up, Meredith. Live a little.

SMACK!

"Seven!" Shit, I might fucking cry. No, I will NOT cry. He said he'd break it into two parts right?

His hands and lips started moving over my ass and my body slacked and moaned with desire. Then his fingers trailed over my pussy and then abandoned my soaking lips just as quick. That must have been what he meant by breaking it up into two.

Smack!

I almost forgot where we were at when I remembered and cried out, "Eight!"

Smack!

"Nine!" My hands had moved to grip my hair. My eyes were watering as I pressed them against my arm.

Smack!

"Ten!" Now I knew what hazing was like.

Smack!

"Eleven." My voice was wavering and he knew it. Hot lips trailed over my ass once again. And just as I'd start to moan...

Smack!

"Twelve." It was barely a whisper.

"I can't hear you."

"Twelve!"

"Good girl, but that earned you another strike."

I started shaking my head in refusal, but I cried out in agreement, "Yes, Sir!"

Smack!

"Thirteen!" Tears were trickling out and I no longer cared. The next three smacks were the closest in succession. Maybe he wanted it over, too.

Smack!

"Fourteen!"

Smack!

"Fifteen!"

Smack!

"Sixteen!"

The sound of the wood paddle dropping to the table sent relief flooding through me. I felt him behind me as his hands gripped my hips. Hot lips pressed against the small of my back and continued to move over every inch of my ass along with his tongue. As my ass throbbed and ached with every touch from him, it just increased the already overwhelming desire I had. This was the true meaning of pleasure and pain and I knew I was already addicted.

Oh, my God. What was that? It took a minute to register what I was feeling. His silk tongue was licking me from front to back. *All* the way back. Sweet mercy. My hips pressed into him without thought. His mouth moved as his teeth gently scraped over my fresh marks and then a finger slipped inside my pussy.

"Oh, God!"

"You are NOT to come, do you understand?"

"Yes, Sir." I sighed as he continued his sweet torture. "Please don't stop."

That earned me a chuckle right before his mouth started moving over me again. Fingers in my pussy and thumb circling my clit, his tongue prodded my anus. Holy hell it felt good. Before I knew it I had fingers in both holes as he pumped me until I didn't think I could take any more!

Holy shit, I was going to come if I didn't regain control. Slamming my hand on the table, my ass still in the air, I gripped the edge and began cursing.

I gasped and the force of that gasp startled me. "Fuck!" I clenched around his fingers as he continued fucking me. I couldn't come, but I wanted to so bad.

He slowed before pulling his fingers out of me. Teasing, soft kisses fell upon my cheeks once more. I didn't want it to be over. We weren't done were we? Then I felt his hands on me as he pulled me from the table. Jesus, I could barely stand. Bending down in front of me, he slid my panties and pants back up my legs. I took both waistbands from him and situated myself.

Before I could question anything, or do anything, his hands were in my hair again. Kissing me, I let him lead the kiss. Christ, I could drown in him. My legs were trembling as I held onto him for support. He pivoted his body and sat down on the seat of the picnic table. I was leaning over him, still kissing him.

Hand still in my hair he whispered, "On your knees." He continued to kiss me as I began to lower my body.

Guiding me to my knees, in between his, the kiss broken, I kept my eyes down and placed my hands in my lap. His own gently cupped my face and tilted my chin upward.

"Look at me." I did as he asked as our eyes met in the dark of the cool summer night. "Fucking beautiful." His eyes continued to devour mine and then he asked, "Are you ready for my cock?"

Maybe a little too eagerly, I sighed, "Yes."

He untied his running shorts and out popped his beautiful cock. I reached for him as his hands fell into my hair and held me back.

"Is this what you want?" One hand left my hair as he gripped his cock. I nodded as he added, "No hands. I'm going to fuck that beautiful face."

I gulped as he lowered my head, hand tangled in my long, dark locks. I let my tongue lavish him from root to tip so that he understood how much I craved him. Slowly, I took him in my mouth and let him press into me further as his hips flexed upward. A deep moan filled the night air and I sucked him harder in response.

"You like that sweaty cock?"

Pulling off him just enough so he could hear me, I replied, "Yes, Sir." Then I resumed my task.

I could feel him pulse against my tongue, hands still in my hair. He pushed my long dark hair to the side and angled us so that he could see me sucking him.

"Jesus. Who taught you how to do that? Or are you just a natural?"

Giggling, I let him pop out from between my lips. I'd been asked this before. I wasn't one to brag, but I knew how to suck a cock. "Nobody taught me. Just a natural I guess." I shrugged my shoulders and made eye contact with him as I slid my lips around him once more.

A small chuckle left his mouth which was turned up in a grin. Then he moaned again, pressing up into my waiting mouth deeper. My hands moved up to his hips as he began to fuck my mouth once more. I thought for sure he'd spill his load before he pried me off him, but he didn't. Uncaring of the mess my saliva had made, he attacked my mouth with his once again.

Hands in my hair, stroking my cheeks, he praised me. "You're a natural and so obedient. I'm going to thoroughly enjoy you."

Smiling, I gazed into his eyes and coyly whispered my gratitude. "Thank you, Sir."

"But I have to go." I understood, but I was visibly disappointed. "We have plenty of time, but now I need to get home."

"I know, so do I."

He pulled us to our feet, which was a struggle for me. Quickly, he knelt down and rubbed my legs helping to bring them back to life. The fact that he knew my legs were aching and tended to them spoke volumes to me.

"I have homework for you."

Homework? Ummm..."Ok."

"I want you to go home and bring yourself to orgasm three times in a row, but don't come. Then you're going to email me in explicit detail your thoughts and what you were doing each time. When I finally allow you to come, I want you a quivering mess, ready to explode."

Shocked at his demand and turned on, I groaned. He smiled wickedly as I conceded. "Yes, Sir."

"You know how to get out of here?" I nodded. "Drive safe. I'll talk to you soon." He kissed me quickly and then smacked my ass one more time before pushing me toward my vehicle.

I climbed into my SUV completely afloat. I found myself questioning what had happened once again. My heart was racing, my cheeks were flush, my panties— Jesus—I probably could have rung them out like a dishrag. We pulled out of the alcove at the same time and headed in different directions.

Hitting shuffle on my playlist, *Poison* by Vaults came on. Yup, I'd definitely been poisoned. I decided to drive around for a few, certain I probably looked like a two bit hooker with flushed cheeks and swollen lips. Then I started shaking. *What the hell?* Like uncontrollable shaking.

Without hesitation, I called Tami. Thank God she answered.

"What's up?"

"I just saw him. Oh, my God. I can't stop shaking."

"Oh, Jesus. You're crashing. He's supposed to be doing aftercare."

"We were short on time. I was fine when we parted." Then I started crying. "Why am I crying?"

"Jesus, Mer. Are you driving? Pull over and relax." I did as she suggested and took some deep breaths. "Are you sure you're up for this?"

Choking out between sobs, "Well I'm not walking away now!"

She sighed. "Was it good? Do I want to know?"

I laughed, "Yes and yes!"

I told her what happened and felt immensely better afterward. I was still a little shaky, but nothing I couldn't handle. She also told me she'd been asked to cover someone's shift tomorrow night. I knew she needed the money, so we canceled our dinner plans.

I drove around some more before heading home. All the lights appeared to be off which meant Todd was probably in bed. Once there I checked myself in the rearview mirror. My eyes were a little puffy and my lips felt worse than they looked. Opening the door as quietly as possible, I heard nothing, confirming Todd was already in bed. Thank fuck.

It'd been over an hour since Gregor and I parted ways. I knew I needed to email him so he didn't worry. Would he worry?

> *TO: bruisedassets@yahoo.com*
> *11:16 PM*
> *Subject: Fucking Hell*
> *The adrenaline rush is going to take some getting used to. Can't stop trembling. Thank you, Sir.*

CHAPTER
Eleven

SECRET

TO: meredith@meredithedits.com
11:21 PM
Subject: Re: Fucking Hell
Thank you for allowing me to do so... :)

TO: bruisedassets@yahoo.com
11:23 PM
Subject: Re: Fucking Hell
As you wish, Sir

I had homework to complete and wasn't sure where to begin. I'd never done anything like what he'd requested so I was walking blindly. I tiptoed into the bathroom and changed into my pajamas. I examined my ass and my jaw dropped.

Shit!

I might be showering alone for more than a week. My hands ran over the strokes he'd painted on my skin and I smiled. My clit throbbed and since I had the required comfortable clothing on, it was time to get to work. Todd was snoring away and I headed back to my office. An email awaited me.

> *TO: meredith@meredithedits.com*
> *11:58 PM*
> *Subject: Re: Fucking Hell*
> *Finished my work. Very tired.*
> *Going to drift off to sleep while slowly stroking my cock thinking about the way your lips felt wrapped around it...*
> *Good night*

Ugh. I was disappointed he was going to sleep, but I let it be. I knew he had to be exhausted. Scrolling through my playlist, I selected Angel Snow's song *Secret*. Secrets were surrounding me. It should be my new middle name.

I would do my homework and make sure he woke to a pleasant email, my assignment completed. I made sure the kids' lunches and snacks were packed for school the next day, threw in a load of the never-ending laundry, and then sat at my desk and stared at my laptop.

I had an assignment to do and it wasn't going to complete itself. I was still shaky, horny, and wide awake. It was getting late and I knew I needed to stop delaying the inevitable.

> *TO: bruisedassets@yahoo.com*
> *12:23 PM*
> *Subject: My favorite number*
> *How'd you know 3 is my favorite number?*
> *Sitting at my desk, pants undone, my fingers running circles over my slick clit. Thoughts of my chest pressed against the picnic table as you marked me and owned me. My head starts spinning, a telltale sign that I'm about to come...*
> *Dipping inside, imagining the pleasure your finger in my ass brought me. Was that the shocker? I loved it. Dreaming of your cock filling me in both places. Legs begin to tremble, ass clenches...must stop*
> *Thinking of the cold night air on my ass, your hot cock in my mouth, your searing tongue on my clit. On my knees in front of you, I felt safer than I have in so very long, to be myself, exposed to you wholly. Breasts awakened when I thought them numb. Hand is shaking as I continue playing with my clit. Adrenaline is still pumping through me fiercely. My body cramping with the need to come. Stopping, breathless, heart racing...*
> *I hope that's what you meant. My body is trembling again. I'm going to bed before someone finds me in a puddle on the floor.*

I stared at the email, embarrassed to send it, but knowing I had to. After what we'd done under that gazebo, what did it matter now? My head was heavy and my body ached. I needed to rest. I sent the email, shut down my laptop, and crawled into bed.

The next morning I showered and got dressed. My ass was a wonderland of reds and purples that I couldn't stop touching. When I checked my phone, I had email. He'd altered the subject and like an idiot, I didn't think anything of it.

> TO: meredith@meredithedits.com
> 7:38 AM
> **Subject: Re: My favorite number – Assignment #1**
> *I can't claim to have known 3 was your favorite #... :)*
> *Yes – that is what I was looking for.*
> *Today you will do the same except three times and report back accordingly.*
> *I'm thinking about the puddle on the floor.*
> *Have a great day!*

WHAT! Ugh! I shouldn't have told him three was my favorite number. Of course, had I said five or six I'd be in more agony. I typed up my reply.

> TO: bruisedassets@yahoo.com
> 7:42 AM
> **Subject: Re: My favorite number – Assignment #1**
> *I hope you got sleep and that the meds are starting to make you feel better. I drifted in and out of sleep all night, waking each time with a pulsing clit.*
> *Hope you have a great day, as well.*

I went about my morning. Got the kids on the bus and then headed to the gym. When I left class I had an email eagerly awaiting me.

> TO: meredith@meredithedits.com
> 10:06 AM
> **Subject: Re: My favorite number – Assignment #1**
> *How does the bottom look today...?*

I smiled and typed my reply.

> TO: bruisedassets@yahoo.com
> 10:32 AM
> **Subject: Re: My favorite number – Assignment #1**
> *Just leaving the gym and headed to the grocery store. Send a picture soon...*

I didn't hear back right away. Groceries were put away and I was debating about eating lunch or to shower first when my phone gave off that familiar alert. I also still had three assignments to complete and the day was half gone.

> *TO: meredith@meredithedits.com*
> *12:09 PM*
> *Subject: Re: My favorite number – Assignment #1*
> *Looking forward to it and reading about how the workout went with that sore bottom...*

> *TO: bruisedassets@yahoo.com*
> *12:14 PM*
> *Subject: Re: My favorite number – Assignment #1*
> *Just got home and put the groceries away, need to eat lunch.*
> *The paddle bruises from last night are definitely different in feel and color compared to Thursday's spanking. More tender in a different way. I'll admit that the majority of the time on the bike I was lost in thought, bent over the picnic table. Then I went and lifted weights and my arms are jello.*
> *I'll send pictures in a few...*
> *Hope you're having a good day.*

I decided there was no point in delaying the picture taking. Heading into the bedroom with my phone, I dropped trough and took a picture of my ass. Ok, I may have taken several before I found one I approved of. Staring at the picture, I scanned the marks that stared back at me in the picture. Purples, reds, pinks, and greys all stared back at me. Yup, significant was an understatement to that paddles power.

> *TO: bruisedassets@yahoo.com*
> *12:29 PM*
> *Subject: Re: My favorite number – Assignment #1*
> *Here's your picture. On to assignment #1 for today...*

Since I was running short on time, I dove into assignment #1 before it was time to shower. Assignment #2 would probably happen *in* the shower. Ok, I was going to accomplish this. Get it girl!

> *TO: bruisedassets@yahoo.com*
> *1:17 PM*
> *Subject: #1*
> *My brain is complete mush. Collapsing in bed I grab my vibrator and run it over my panties. Almost immediately my hips are arching, seeking a*

deeper connection. Goosebumps travel my body and my vision blurs...I want to come so bad. But I don't.

Deep breaths and then I pull my panties down and use the same vibrator to circle my clit. All I can feel is your hand on my neck kissing me, demanding I not come. You got me so close last night and I wonder if you even know how close. Trembling, I stop just as the moans are ready to consume me.

Running my hand over my still tender nipple while pressing the vibrator in slowly, just the tip. My breasts so tender that my legs start to shake when I tweak my nipple. It's red and raw and I can't stop touching it. I want you inside me. Every inch as I clench around you so tight. Thighs are shaking with near release, so I stop...

I wasn't waiting long for my reply. Good to know he was paying attention, or at least had his phone handy.

> **TO: meredith@meredithedits.com**
> **1:27 PM**
> **Subject: Re: #1**
> *My cock is now rock hard. And will soon be oozing precum.*

> **TO: bruisedassets@yahoo.com**
> **1:29 PM**
> **Subject: Re: #1**
> *If I was there I'd gladly lick it away.*
> *Any favorite moments from last night that you care to divulge?*

I answered some work and PTA emails while I waited for his response.

> **TO: meredith@meredithedits.com**
> **1:47 PM**
> **Subject: Re: #1**
> *Maybe you can tonight... I'm heading out of town after dinner... :)*
> *Where are you Thursday morning? I may be staying in Casper Wednesday night, trip's been extended. I could check out late...*
> *There were MANY parts that resonated. However, the gasp you made when you just about came and had to hold back stuck out profusely in my mind... :)*
> *So yes, I DID know how close you were and how difficult it was.*

So many things started swirling in my brain. Tonight. Thursday morning. 'I could check out late'. Closing my eyes, I knew I wanted complete privacy with him like nothing else. Casper was over an hour away. I started my email back to him.

TO: bruisedassets@yahoo.com
1:58 PM
Subject: Re: #1
    I can see about getting away tonight for a few but can't guarantee. I could leave here Thursday am around 8. Not sure how late they'll let you check out. We both need to be back to get our kids off the bus. I'm still waiting to hear about his travel schedule.
    I think there was probably some cussing following or preceding that gasp. Christ, make the throbbing stop.

I didn't wait to see how quickly he'd respond. I had to take a shower and planned to complete assignment #2 for the day while in there. It was one of the hardest things I'd ever done—driving myself to the brink to only deny myself. In my robe, I sat down and read his reply before typing my own response.

TO: meredith@meredithedits.com
2:18 PM
Subject: Re: #1
    Thursday checkout would be 1, but I would need to leave by noon. If you left at 9 you should be there by 10:30. We can play it by ear.
    Tonight I would just quickly rewarm that bottom and send you back home with the throbbing worse.

I knew instantly that I was going to get out tonight if it was the last thing I did. And I would make Thursday work somehow.

TO: bruisedassets@yahoo.com
2:39 PM
Subject: #2
    In the shower, water running down my body. My nipple so tender. Pulling the shower head down, I let the water run over my clit and I'm almost immediately doubled over with the pleasure of it. But it can't happen.
    Shaking my head, not sure I can do this again. I let the water beat over me again. Deep breaths, slow circles...dropping the shower head and grasping my knees I let the almost orgasm fade away again.
    Tears filling my eyes, I have to do it again. I let the water tickle my lips and entrance, avoiding my clit. But my clit needs the attention. My arms are shaking and I let the shower head work its magic once more. Gasping, moaning, I drop the shower head again, shaking my head as a few tears fall from my eyes.
    I'm warning you, I may cry when you finally allow me to come...
    A lot can happen in an hour and a half... I'd get there as soon as I could Thursday.

I didn't get a response right away and needed to get dressed. I worked for about an hour before it was time to get the kids off the bus. We started in on homework and Todd called to say he'd be late. I fed the kids dinner and still no email from Gregor had come through. I had no idea if I'd be able to see him tonight. I snuck in a quick email to him.

> *TO: bruisedassets@yahoo.com*
> *5:54 PM*
> *Subject: Tonight*
> *I won't be able to leave here until 7/7:30pm tonight. I understand if you'll already be on the road.*
> *I'd almost prefer to come up late Wed night and do the walk of shame... but I'd also be playing with fire.*
> *I keep hearing your whispered words about me being a 'natural'. Sigh.*

I was cleaning the kitchen and asking the kids what they wanted packed for lunch the next day when my phone alerted me to another email.

> *TO: meredith@meredithedits.com*
> *6:28 PM*
> *Subject: Re: Tonight*
> *I won't be ready to leave until after that.*
> *As far as Wednesday evening – FAMILY AND HOME FIRST!! I will be a stickler on that. This should complement your life – not add strife (except the part where you are denied orgasms). While I would love to have you in the evening for a couple of hours where we could have a couple of drinks and take our time – it is NOT worth it.*
> *I will let you know what my ETD is.*

I was relieved to find out he hadn't left yet and I knew he was right about Wednesday evening, Thursday morning. I couldn't help but feel like I needed his touch like I needed my next breath, but I had to get a grip.

> *TO: bruisedassets@yahoo.com*
> *6:34 PM*
> *Subject: Re: Tonight*
> *Nope. I agree which is why I made the 'fire' comment. Of course, I may enjoy being told what to do, too. Lol*
> *I need to run to the bank to deposit a check at some point. Thursday is still open for me.*
> *I'll wait to hear from you.*

Todd got home shortly after and reheated his dinner, totally ignoring me. He was playing with the kids and I was trying to get some work done. He was putting the kids to bed when an email from Gregor came through. Todd and I had drifted apart. I'd begged and pleaded with him and he just didn't seem to care. Deep down I knew that we were over.

> *TO: meredith@meredithedits.com*
> *7:58 PM*
> *Subject: Re: Tonight*
> *Probably leave in the next 15 mins.*
>
> *TO: bruisedassets@yahoo.com*
> *7:59 PM*
> *Subject: Re: Tonight*
> *Same spot? Somewhere else?*
>
> *TO: meredith@meredithedits.com*
> *8:05 PM*
> *Subject: Re: Tonight*
> *Same.*

I told Todd I had to run to the bank and the store. He didn't question me. I hopped in my car and drove the few minutes to where Gregor awaited. His truck was there and he was stepping down from the driver's seat as I parked. I walked toward him and he yanked me close and kissed me.

"How are you?"

Smiling, "I'm good. You?" His hands moved to my ass and squeezed. I groaned at the ache and the pleasure. "Umph...shit."

He smiled and then pulled me under the gazebo as we sat down at the same table we had the night before. We chatted for a few minutes about Todd and my sex life—or lack thereof—like it was the most normal conversation for us to be having. He rarely talked about his sex life, just random comments about his wife and her lacking libido.

It was in that moment that I realized how long I'd felt alone. Talking to another adult—a male one at that—with similar interests, desires, and frustrations was gratifying in a way I couldn't explain. Finally, a connection had been made. Though we were meeting in the dark, in a secluded location, I felt like I was finally out of the shadows and the sun was shining down on me.

Then he kissed me and there was no hesitation as we began to play, my legs draped over his. My walls of apprehension were crumbling faster than I thought they would, knowing how touchy feely I was allowed to be with him. His hands dove into my hair, tilting my head to where he wanted it so he could kiss me fully as I melted into him. His attention the night before to my left breast was resumed. His hand worked expertly to free my nipple as he began palming my breast, applying just enough pressure to make me moan.

Groaning in response to my hand squeezing his erection through his jeans, he separated our mouths and worked down my neck. I didn't bother trying to contain my moans and gasps, knowing they only fueled him on. And, we all knew I was so horny I thought I might explode. Like he could hear my thoughts, he whispered a reminder in my ear as he palmed me through my pants.

"Don't come."

Whimpering, I obeyed. "Yes, Sir. Oh!"

Who was this Adonis? Who taught him how to make women melt like this? What the hell was wrong with his wife? If I had this at my disposal I'd be utilizing it to my fullest advantage. I cupped his balls and felt his cock jump in response as he pinched my nipple harder in return.

"Fuck!" It was a good 'fuck' and he knew it.

"Back on the table, on your knees."

As I stood, he undid my pants and yanked them to my knees along with my panties. This time my knees were on the seat. Closing my eyes, I took deep calming breaths. I saw no paddle and wondered if he would use just his hand. The sound of metal clanking rang in my ears, but I didn't think much of it until I heard one of the most magical sounds I'd ever heard.

WHIRRR.

My breath caught and I know I gasped... Loudly. The sound of his belt being pulled free from the loops of his jeans and flying through the night air had me panting with desire. I can still stop and think about that sound and my body instantly responds.

His hand gently moved over my cheeks as he warned me. "This is going to hurt."

CHAPTER
Twelve

SHAPED LIKE A GUN

MY HEAD GREW HEAVY AS MY chest felt light. I immediately stuck my ass a little further in the air as my torso relaxed against the table. He made me wait as his fingers fondled me and then his mouth. I was beginning to drip, could feel it as the cool night air blew against my exposed skin and just enhanced the feeling of my arousal running down my thigh.

"Such a naughty little slut. You're dripping for me."

His teeth nibbled on one of the many marks that colored my ass as I moaned. The heat of his body faded away and as I tried to relax, the first strike of his belt came down on my ass. I may have moaned in pleasure at the sting that vibrated through my ass cheeks.

"Count!"

"Yes, Sir. One!"

He took small breaks, but it didn't end until I'd whimpered out, "Twenty." Tears rolled down my cheeks as I heard him buckling his belt once more. It was over...for now. I wiped the tears away, ashamed, not wanting him to see them.

His hands ran over my skin. They were warm and soothed my rewarmed bottom. Slowly, my body stopped trembling from pain, the pain turning into desire. His fingers stroked me and fucked me slowly, deliberately, until I was pleading with him.

"Please, Sir. I want to come."

He pulled me from the table and dressed me as he talked softly to me and gave me further instruction. "Not yet."

I wanted to kick and scream; throw a temper tantrum. But I was quickly dissuaded by his next comment. Always. His words seemed to have this effect on me.

"Show me how bad you want to come like the obedient slut you are." He was unzipping his pants and I wasted no time.

Dropping to my knees in front of him, the gravel digging into the tops of my feet, I sucked him into my mouth. His hands clung to my head and ran through my hair sending new sensations through my body as he began to pulse in my mouth.

"Fuck. Squeeze my ass."

My hands moved from his hips to his ass and squeezed as he'd ordered me. His groans became more and more prevalent as he fucked my mouth. I wondered if he'd allow himself release this time or not. Then I knew he was going to grant himself the relief when his body stiffened. He spurt down my throat and I recognized instantly that he tasted sweet, sweeter than any other man I'd sucked off. I continued to run my lips and tongue over him until he pried me off him.

He was still semi-erect as he pulled me to my feet, kissing me deeply. Then I watched him wipe the final drop off his tip and then lift his finger to my mouth. I greedily sucked it into my mouth as a massive grin stretched across his face. He tucked himself back into his pants and pulled me close.

"I should start carrying a mat for you." He was acknowledging the gravel as he then bent down and cleaned off my knees.

Giggling, I remembered and said, "I have a yoga mat in the back of my car. I would've dug it out had I known."

Pulling me close, he whispered against my lips. "I should go. I have a two hour drive."

"Ok."

"And you have homework to complete." I nodded. "I want you to go home and offer your husband what you just did for me." I searched his eyes, surprised at the request. "Ok?"

Unsure, but knowing I'd obey, I acknowledged him. "Yes, Sir."

Kissing me, then slapping my ass, he said his goodbye. "I'll see you Thursday. Don't forget your homework!"

"Yes, Sir. Drive safe. Email me when you get there."

Shaking his head in amusement, he said, "Yes, Mom."

I got in my vehicle and he waited to make sure I was heading out and then followed suit. We both waved as we pulled down the road in opposite directions. I pulled into the bank parking lot and made my deposit. Sitting in a parking spot after, I sat and reflected, while waiting for my swollen lips to calm.

From the moment we found out how close our real lives were—and possibly already intertwined—I knew I couldn't turn away from him. Most people probably would've freaked, but it was the opposite for me. This shit didn't just happen. Did it? There was a reason for it, had to be. Maybe I was walking into the lion's den, but I was prepared to be eaten alive. That was the point, wasn't it?

After a short drive, the trembling done with, I headed home. Todd was in his recliner when I walked in. Following my instructions from Gregor, I crawled into Todd's lap. He seemed a little apprehensive and questioned my motives.

"What's gotten into you?"

Sighing in annoyance, I pulled back. "Nothing. I crawl in your lap all the time and this is always your reaction."

And it was true. Crawling in his lap was something I did often and nine times out of ten I was refused. I shouldn't have been surprised. He pulled me close and kissed me. I tried not to think about how lame his kisses were when compared to Gregor's. Todd's kisses lacked passion.

Passion.

Gregor was overflowing with it.

Trying to push Gregor out of my head, I kissed Todd back and let my hands roam. I moved closer and could feel his erection through his pants. I knew I couldn't get naked in front of him so I started to unzip his pants and maneuver my way down. Then, abruptly he stopped me.

"I'm not in the mood. I have a big day tomorrow."

I glanced down at his obvious erection and then back to his face. "Umm..."

"Meredith."

Putting my hands up in defense, I yielded. "Ok."

I climbed off his lap and headed to the bathroom. Closing and locking the door, I tried to calm my emotions. I would never understand that man and maybe I wasn't supposed to. Fighting the tears, I took another deep breath and decided to distract myself with Gregor's marks.

Dropping my pants, I examined my ass. I giggled at the thought of it looking like a crime scene. Then I lifted my shirt and examined my breast once I freed it from my bra. Shit! My breast was clearly marked, too. I shook my head and replaced my clothing. I used the restroom and headed back to my office, Todd paying no mind to me.

> *TO: bruisedassets@yahoo.com*
> *10:22 PM*
> *Subject: OMG*
> *So, I think you want me on my knees with you and at home, fully clothed.*
> *My nipple is marked. Lol. Something to add to the keep hidden list.*

I knew he was still driving and didn't know if he'd respond tonight or not. Turning on some music, *Shaped Like a Gun* by Tailor taunted me about my relationship with Todd. I got caught up on emails and dove into some work. Shortly after eleven, Todd already in bed, I got an email from Gregor.

> *TO: meredith@meredithedits.com*
> *11:18 PM*
> *Subject: Re: OMG*
> *Just got to the hotel. Took a while longer than it should have.*
> *How bad is the nipple? Is it obvious...? Not marking my territory, but you can't really get a proper spanking without some marks.*
> *As soon as I got into the room I felt wiped.*
> *Of course – thoughts are elsewhere... :)*

> *TO: bruisedassets@yahoo.com*
> *11:23 PM*
> *Subject: Re: OMG*
> *Compared to the other – it's obvious. We'll see how it looks in the am.*
> *So, I crawled into his lap tonight and while he was turned on, he refused me. Said he has a big day at work tomorrow. I'm sure you understand how hard that rejection is for me.*
> *On another note... best cock n cum I've tasted, probably ever. I was also lacking on protein intake today. So, thanks for that. :)*

I laughed as I re-read it once I sent it. I was horrible, we were horrible, but it was so much fun.

> TO: meredith@meredithedits.com
> 11:35 PM
> Subject: Re: OMG
> *You tried and offered your talents – you can't force him to accept... :)*
> *Thank you for the compliment. Diet and exercise has a major influence on taste and I have been told that before. I have nothing to compare it to though so I will have to take your word for it... :)*

I groaned and rolled my eyes at the remark about him hearing it before. I knew I wasn't the only girl he'd blown his load in, but that didn't mean I wanted the reminder. Slightly annoyed, though I knew it was ridiculous, I started on my last homework assignment for the day.

> TO: bruisedassets@yahoo.com
> 12:08 AM
> Subject: #3
> *Sitting at my desk, slow music playing softly. Needing to drift away to where someone wants and craves my touch like I do his. Sweat pants and panties pushed aside as I slowly stroke myself. Bottom is extremely tender, every movement sending little bursts of pain through me. I imagine I'm sprawled out on that picnic table as you devour me. My clit so hard as my legs flex... I pull my hand away and try to relax.*
> *I want to lie in your lap as you stroke and pull on my hair, turn the world off as we turn each other on. My head feels heavy as my legs start shaking again. Growing wetter and wetter, I envision you behind me, on top of me, beside me. Dip a finger in and twirl, seeking that gasp-worthy touch. It hurts to clench my ass, so I do it over and over as the tingles travel through my abdomen. Panting, I stop before it's too late.*
> *Bite my ears, neck, shoulders, ass, make me beg. So easily I get distracted when your hands and mouth are on me, that I grow still and lose focus. I think about the tears that fell from my eyes with the last few lashes, my legs trembling. Then your hands caressing, lips sucking, tongue licking, teeth biting. So much all at once and yet, not enough. Clenching around my own fingers, palming my clit. Imagining me begging you to make me come and you giving me permission to do so. Thighs flexed, I must stop...*

I waited a few minutes to see if I'd get a response. When I didn't, I decided to shut it down for the night. I needed to sleep. I slept more soundly than I had in several days. When I woke, Todd was gone and I was practically humping my body pillow. I figured 'what the hell' and moved on to my first assignment for the day. When I was done, I grabbed my phone and sent the email, noting he'd never responded to the one from the night before.

> *TO: bruisedassets@yahoo.com*
> *7:14 AM*
> *Subject: Day 2, #1*
> *I wake up throbbing and find myself open and wet. Sliding two fingers inside, my back arches and I grip my headboard with my free hand. Softly gasping, I circle my clit and notice the feel of my back sweating. So warm, I circle faster until my vision gets clouded and stop.*
> *I can't touch my breasts without thinking of you. My clit is thrumming away, begging for release. Licking my fingers, I start again. Vigorously, I seek orgasm until my feet lose all feeling and I stop, forcing it to cease.*
> *Rolling over, my ass in the air, I bury my face in the pillow. Frustration doesn't begin to describe it. Humping my hand, I squeeze my breasts and imagine you behind me. My core is tight, my body stiffening as I climb the cliff again. I feel myself dripping, my body aching for more. Clenching my legs, I let my ass fall back down and pant into the pillow, more dripping, more need, more want....must wait.*

I was still catching my breath when his reply came through.

> *TO: meredith@meredithedits.com*
> *7:16 AM*
> *Subject: Re: Day 2, #1*
> *One down. Two to go.*
> *How good it will feel when it is finally granted.*

Agh! He was infuriating!

> *TO: bruisedassets@yahoo.com*
> *7:18 AM*
> *Subject: Re: Day 2, #1*
> *Hmmm.*
> *I may sleep for days once it happens or just want more and more. Who am I kidding? It'll be both.*

I was making breakfast for the kids when his response came through.

> *TO: meredith@meredithedits.com*
> *8:06 AM*
> *Subject: Re: Day 2, #1*
> *:) That sentiment goes both ways...*

Knowing that he felt that way just made the want, throb, burn, and ache for him even worse.

> *TO: bruisedassets@yahoo.com*
> *8:10 AM*
> *Subject: Re: Day 2, #1*
> *Sigh...you're not helping the drip, drip, drip confessing you want more of me. :) Should be another great workout today, a total blur!*

> *TO: meredith@meredithedits.com*
> *8:11 AM*
> *Subject: Re: Day 2, #1*
> *I need to bury my face deep into that soaking pussy and feel that first, emphatic release.*

Jesus Christ! Put the phone down, Meredith. I was certain he had the power to make me disintegrate on the spot. And that's what I did. He could wait like he so often made me do!

CHAPTER
Thirteen

PULL ME UNDER

Ⓘ WENT ABOUT MY MORNING. After the gym, I made a few phone calls, and then jumped in the shower. It was time for assignment number two. After I got dressed, I sat down at my laptop and recounted the three torturous events with music playing. *Pull Me Under* by Adria was on and I had a fleeting thought and wrote it down, saving it for just the right moment. 'I want to drown in my submission to you'.

> **TO: bruisedassets@yahoo.com**
> **11:50 AM**
> **Subject: Day 2, #2**
> *Shower time again. Slowly I let the water tickle my hands before letting the water circle over my clit. Slow and steady, deep breaths. Turn the heat of the water up slightly and close my eyes as it warms me. Legs start to tremble and hips buck. I'm afraid to go any further.*
>
> *Start again, turning the heat up again. Push myself to the edge of the cliff as I lean against the shower wall. My body screaming at me to give in. I make bigger circles with the water and as the first jolt of my climax tries to hit me, I pull the water away. My body so frustrated, like there's this weight on my shoulders I can't get rid of.*
>
> *Trying something different, I spray my clit from behind and enjoy the*

new sensations. Breathing is erratic as my hips push back. Squeezing my breasts, that ache desperately, the first wave creeps up again as my legs tense, walls clamping down. I pull the water away as tears fill my eyes again in utter frustration. I may have screamed out in frustrated denial...

I grabbed a bite to eat and headed to my massage appointment. Standing in the room to undress, I almost left my underwear on, but after two years of seeing the same therapist and always going naked, I decided to have no shame. I climbed on the table as usual and waited for Maude to come in.

"How are you, Meredith?" Opening my eyes, I glanced at her and told her I was good. "Any areas of concern?"

Chuckling, I said, "Yes and no. Just the usual."

"Ok, sweetie."

I was practically asleep, facedown, when her hands traveled under the towel and over my hips and I flinched. I heard her gasp and I immediately tried to cover for myself. "Sorry. It's, umm, sensitive."

She knew something was up, "Honey, what happened?"

Shit! "So, I'm not sure how to say this. It was a consensual spanking...field research."

"Well, honey, you only live once. I hope whoever it is, that he—or she—has the marks to match." I belly laughed at that as she added, "This is nothing. The things I've seen in my day. Your secret is safe with me."

When I got home, exhausted didn't begin to describe how I felt. I had a couple hours before the kids would be home. Fuck it. I set my alarm and lay down in bed. I didn't hear from Gregor until later that night.

TO: meredith@meredithedits.com
7:08 PM
Subject: Re: Day 2, #2
Assignment #3 should be relatively quick based on that report...

TO: bruisedassets@yahoo.com
7:11 PM
Subject: Re: Day 2, #2
Should be interesting. I'm being summoned to bed. I'm sure I'll be attempting to turn the tables on him to avoid ass exposure. Lol.
I crashed hard for an hour this afternoon. Much needed sleep. Hope you had a productive day.
My massage appt was quite interesting. She basically encouraged me on

and said 'you only live once'. Though, she did wonder if whoever is bruising
my ass has the marks to match mine. Lol

Over an hour later Todd pulled me from my office chair and took me to the
bedroom. The kids were in bed and as he walked about the room I started thinking.
I wasn't sure how I was going to play things, but I knew I couldn't let him see me
naked. He walked back over to me. Taking control, I pushed him onto the bed.

We fooled around for a little while and then—unsure how—things went to
shit and he climbed under the covers. I walked to his side of the bed and leaned
over him.

"I'm exhausted, Mer." He must have caught the quick scowl that I knew I made.
"I know, I'm sorry." He kissed me and then released me as he rolled over.

I just shook my head and left the room. I didn't have the time, patience, or need
for his games. Not when Gregor's were so much more fun. And, I found an email
waiting for me.

> *TO: meredith@meredithedits.com*
> *8:32 PM*
> *Subject: Re: Day 2, #2*
> *How did the summons go...?*
> *Tell her to mind her own ass... :)*

> *TO: bruisedassets@yahoo.com*
> *9:11 PM*
> *Subject: Re: Day 2, #2*
> *He's the oddest man ever. He summoned me, then turned me down, then*
> *kissed me... Apparently we're still in negotiations?*
> *LOL...it was an interesting convo for sure!*

> *TO: meredith@meredithedits.com*
> *9:22 PM*
> *Subject: Re: Day 2, #2*
> *Try surrounding him with strippers and blow...*

I busted up laughing and quickly grew quiet, praying I hadn't woken anyone.

> *TO: bruisedassets@yahoo.com*
> *9:26 PM*
> *Subject: Re: Day 2, #2*
> *Seriously! Lol. He probably would've gotten me off, had I asked, but I'm*
> *not ok with just pussy eating. At least you get me...*

TO: meredith@meredithedits.com
9:31 PM
Subject: Re: Day 2, #2
I get you, but we share the same wiring harness from the factory...

TO: bruisedassets@yahoo.com
9:33 PM
Subject: Re: Day 2, #2
Yes, that factory really makes things interesting and a hell of a lot more fun!
Us and our different wiring are just sitting here, eating popcorn, wondering when the fucking will begin. Please? Can we just screw? :)

TO: meredith@meredithedits.com
9:44 PM
Subject: Re: Day 2, #2
I'm 2 hours away right now. In the hotel bar having a glass of whisky and doing email while catching up on the stock market and wondering if the blonde working on the laptop across from me is looking at me or through me while working like I am...

What the hell? I immediately saw red.

TO: bruisedassets@yahoo.com
9:46 PM
Subject: Re: Day 2, #2
LOL...I wasn't offering to drive 2 hours right now, though it's tempting.
Someone has a thing for blondes? I'm not sure how I'm supposed to respond to this...

TO: meredith@meredithedits.com
9:49 PM
Subject: Re: Day 2, #2
Lol...I didn't say I had a thing for them. She just HAPPENS to be blonde. Not to worry. Looks like a hipster douchebag is distracting her at the moment...

I may have growled in annoyance, though not sure if with him or myself.

TO: bruisedassets@yahoo.com
9:52 PM
Subject: Re: Day 2, #2
Lol. Well it's none of my business except that you're being safe. Should I distract you???

I waited an hour for a response. I will neither confirm nor deny that my mind may have thought crazy thoughts about burning that blonde bitch alive. Jealousy, hurt, anger...you name it, I felt it. But I knew I had no right to.

> *TO: meredith@meredithedits.com*
> *11:09 PM*
> *Subject: Re: Day 2, #2*
> *Please... :)*
> *I'm getting ready to head up to my room and stroke myself to sleep while thinking about how good your lips feel wrapped around my swollen cock while tweaking your nipples and NOT allowing you release...*

> *TO: bruisedassets@yahoo.com*
> *11:12 PM*
> *Subject: Re: Day 2, #2*
> *I'm getting ready for task #3 today. I hope you know how implicitly I trust you with my safety, desires, wants, and needs. Thank you for listening tonight, Sir...and all the other nights. I think you already know I'll be drifting off to sleep thinking of you in me, on me, etc.*

I was glad I said it. I knew he wasn't careless, but it needed to be said. By the time I finished my third assignment, packed lunches, and did some laundry it was after midnight when I finally sent the email.

> *TO: bruisedassets@yahoo.com*
> *12:21 AM*
> *Subject: Day 2, #3*
> *Touching myself, the dull ache constantly reminding me of you. Whenever I think about Monday night, all I hear is your belt pulling through the loops of your jeans in the night air. You're opening up a whole new world for me and I crave to please you knowing you'll reward me. The pulsing is stronger and stronger as I cup myself through my sweats. The weight on my chest is heavy, like I can't breathe. I'm always wet. Your touch over the past few days consuming my thoughts. Putting my hand in my panties I circle my clit thinking of your teeth on my neck. Small tremors build as I lay back then sit up tall, pressing myself into my hand and the chair...gasping in response*
> *He grabbed my ass a few times tonight and I was immediately bent over your lap or the picnic table as the painful pleasure surged through me. Tension rolls off my shoulders and down my back if I sit just the right way. Constantly repositioning myself so I can feel you again. Wetter and wetter, I'm so tired, horny, desperate...I think if I thought about you long enough, I could come without a single touch. Pressing my clit, my thighs clench and I let it ebb away*
> *I'm wet from front to back because of you. I could almost picture myself writhing on the floor in need. My legs go numb as I circle my clit*

again. The pressure is becoming so intense. My legs spread wider, my face feels overheated. My body trying to deny me, waiting for your touch, your command. Fighting with myself as I circle my clit harder. Ass clenches, hips raise, eyes grow heavy with the release about to come. I stop, dropping my head back as I suck my fingers clean.

I was about to head to bed when my email pinged. He was still up!

> **TO: meredith@meredithedits.com**
> **12:23 AM**
> **Subject: Re: Day 2, #3**
> *Technically the last two assignment #3's have been late. Both after midnight. You on CST...?*
> *I am turned on immensely by the thought you could come without even touching yourself. It will make providing your eventual release that much more tantalizing...*

Shit! I should've known he'd be ridiculously strict. Fuck me!

> **TO: bruisedassets@yahoo.com**
> **12:27 AM**
> **Subject: Re: Day 2, #3**
> *I'm going to start banging my head on my desk. Lol. I'm a night owl, trying to schedule tasks around everyone in my house! I won't be late tomorrow (today)! I have an early morning on Thursday. :)*
> *Only your words have gotten such a reaction from me. When you put your hand on my leg at lunch...I thought I was going to burst into flames. Mental connection is a big part of it, but the heat that surged through me had me tongue tied. Not sure if you noticed... :)*

I sat and within minutes another email popped up. There were no words, just a picture of his dick, fully erect. Well then! I ran to the bathroom and took a fresh picture of my bruised ass and included it in my response to his dick pic.

> **TO: bruisedassets@yahoo.com**
> **12:37 AM**
> **Subject: Re: Day 2, #3**
> *Well I guess we know what I'm dreaming of tonight. Some more of your handiwork.*

I didn't hear anymore from him and needed to get some sleep. In the early hours, I woke, Todd already gone. Drenched in sweat, I knew I'd been dreaming of Gregor. I started in on my homework, typing the three almost releases on my phone, my breathing still heavy.

> **TO: bruisedassets@yahoo.com**
> **7:20 AM**
> **Subject: Day 3, #1**
> *I wake from a dead sleep. My body is sweating like never before, that dull throb ever present. My satin jammies are soaked. I know I've been dreaming of you and the things you can do for me. My hips rise, seeking my hand. I run my hand over my soft, smooth lips, my clit poking through. My legs and hips unable to be still. I want, no need, you so bad. My eyes close as my womb clenches...must stop*
>
> *I pull my body pillow close, needing something to hold onto. I feel almost delusional and I'm scared my body will shut down on me Thursday from all the angst. My fingers slide right in and my body grips them tight. Flicking my clit back and forth, I want to scream your name. Sweet torture as my hips writhe...*
>
> *My heart is racing, my back is still soaked, everything is soaked. I want that gasp, that moan, the pleasure from your cock sliding into me for the first time. I want to be the one to get you off. Punish me with your dark cravings. Words have never come so easy for me. Licking my fingers, I circle vigorously. From my thighs to my chest I'm in a euphoric state. My head is so heavy. Panting, my body begging me to go all the way. When my legs clench, I stop.*

And in typical Gregor fashion, I waited. The kids were in the throes of morning rituals when my phone alerted me to a new email.

> **TO: meredith@meredithedits.com**
> **8:20 AM**
> **Subject: Re: Day 3, #1**
> *The words are definitely flowing. I expect more to be flowing as it gets nearer.*
>
> *Only 5 assignments more to go until the final.*
>
> *Will you continue to behave? Or will self-discipline erode and require terse punishment? Will you be rewarded with that sweet release? Or will you be whipped with a belt and required to start over for disobedience?*
>
> *Enjoy your morning workout. :)*
> *Gregor*

Five! No, he couldn't mean... Shit! And why did he sign the email? He never did that. I just ignored it.

> **TO: bruisedassets@yahoo.com**

8:26 AM
Subject: Re: Day 3, #1
5? Are you giving me 3 to do tomorrow BEFORE I see you?
I'm very obedient. If you wanted a rule breaker, that's not me. Lol.

TO: meredith@meredithedits.com
8:27 AM
Subject: Re: Day 3, #1
Tomorrow is a day. You will have to get busy a little earlier.
You are very obedient. :)
Mother, shit, fuck... I groaned loudly as I started my reply.

TO: bruisedassets@yahoo.com
8:29 AM
Subject: Re: Day 3, #1
Groaning. Yes, Sir.

We exchanged several more emails throughout the morning. He gave me the name of the hotel where he'd be at so I could plan my drive accordingly. After lunch, I moved on to assignment two for the day.

TO: bruisedassets@yahoo.com
12:49 PM
Subject: Day 3, #2
Taking off every article of clothing hurts after that workout, my entire body preferring the ache you bring. I step in the shower and immediately begin. I imagine what you'll do to me tomorrow, hard and slow, hard and fast. Shivers run up my spine as the water refuels the release my body needs. The shower head spraying my clit, my other hand holds my head as I lay it on the shower wall. I imagine your hands slowly dragging over my freshly spanked bottom, squeezing my breasts, licking my pussy, taking what's yours, and my thighs clench as my chest begins to heave.

It comes quicker and quicker each time so I try to draw it out. My legs are trembling and I pray I don't collapse. Biting my lip as soft groans fall from my lips, I'm panting your name. Remembering how you take control of our kiss and how it makes me melt, your hands in my hair. Trying to think about things that'll make me not want to come so quickly, but my body has other things in mind. My hips rock back and forth seeking more pressure from the water and just when I think I might come, I pull the water away, breathless, trying to compose myself.

How am I going to do this 4 more times in 18hrs? I can do it, it's worth it. I spray from behind again, imagining you pressed against me. Please distract me. I want to thoroughly enjoy it. Time is of the essence, enjoy it, savor it. I squeeze my breasts as goosebumps cover my body in the steaming shower. My back is arched, my knees bent as my thighs convulse, my clit beating so hard as my nipples pucker again. If I go any further I'll ruin it all...so I stop, panting my disdain.

CHAPTER
Fourteen

BEAUTIFUL UNDONE

TO: bruisedassets@yahoo.com
2:16 PM
Subject: Day 3, #3
Sitting at my desk with a never used toy, a vibrating tongue ring now wrapped around my fingers. Oh how it tickles. How can I be so numb and turned on all at once? I think about it around your tongue as you tease me. My ass clenches, my thighs are shaking, toes curled as I apply direct pressure to my clit. I want to be fucked into submission, your wish my command. I want to suck your cock when time isn't such an issue and run my nails over your ass and thighs. I want to make you squirm like you do to me. I want to feel him jump in my hands as I stroke him. I circle the tiny vibrating bullet faster, harder, until the only thing left to do is stop, before I break all the rules.

I want to lay down on your lap, bury my face in the sheets while you do with me as you see fit. I think about what an amazing kisser you are and imagine those kisses on my neck, ears, back, ass, thighs, pussy. I feel my juices flow more as I slide my fingers in and out. I grab the little ring again and start playing with my clit. I can feel the moment my eyes glaze over, lost in the surges building me up. Everything is tense, but my body can't do it, won't do it until you say I can. It's sweet misery. I keep circling, playing with fire, wondering what will break the spell. I pull my fingers away, my head spinning from being so near release once again.

I want to cry, sleep, and screw for days. My brain is entranced with everything that's already happened and can't fathom what's to come. I drove by our spot today on the way to the gym and the vibration of the road made me ache and sent chills down my spine. Hell, I'm noticing the vibration of everything. My blender, my toothbrush, the washer…I'm ridiculous and desperate. I push my fingers in and out imagining no vibration, just the slickness of our bodies. My bruised ass is longing for more and doesn't ache like I want it to, like you make it. I'm a goner for spanking. So I stroke and fuck myself imagining you spanking me and fucking me at the same time. My legs lose feeling as I drop my head back, panting, eyes rolling back…how will I ever get enough? My thighs grip tight around my hand and I force myself to slow before I come all over my chair.

TO: meredith@meredithedits.com
2:27 PM
Subject: Re: Day 3, #3
You are going to be a mess when you finally get here tomorrow… :)
Make sure you stay FOCUSED on the road. I want you here in one piece…

His words annoyed me and made me sigh. He *wanted* me a mess and we both knew it. And was I really supposed to believe he was concerned for my safety? I mean, I know he didn't wish me harm, not that kind anyway. Ugh. I was overthinking again. He had me completely undone.

I carried on with my day and managed to get away in the evening for a long overdue pedicure. Sitting down in the chair, as it began to massage my back, I sighed. My phone gave that all too familiar tone and I checked my email.

TO: meredith@meredithedits.com
6:27 PM
Subject: Re: Day 3, #3
You are required to do your last assignment within an hour of seeing me tomorrow morning. I want to ensure that clit is ready to explode when I touch it.

Closing my eyes, I did the math in my head. I was going to have to find a fucking rest stop or something. It was over an hour drive and he knew that.

TO: bruisedassets@yahoo.com
6:30 PM
Subject: A lil peace
Guess I'll be pulling into a rest stop…
You're distracting me. I just sat down for a pedicure and now my panties

are wet thanks to you...

> **TO: meredith@meredithedits.com**
> **6:31 PM**
> **Subject: Re: A lil peace**
> *I didn't make them wet...*

> **TO: bruisedassets@yahoo.com**
> **6:33 PM**
> **Subject: Re: A lil peace**
> *Didn't you?!?!*

> **TO: meredith@meredithedits.com**
> **6:37 PM**
> **Subject: Re: A lil peace**
> *I wasn't there. Did you spill something on them?*

> **TO: bruisedassets@yahoo.com**
> **6:40 PM**
> **Subject: Re: A lil peace**
> *You don't have to be here to be in my head... It's a dirty, dirty place to be...*

> **TO: meredith@meredithedits.com**
> **6:44 PM**
> **Subject: Re: A lil peace**
> *:)*
> *Is your ETA still 9:30am?*

> **TO: bruisedassets@yahoo.com**
> **6:46 PM**
> **Subject: Re: A lil peace**
> *At the latest.*

> **TO: meredith@meredithedits.com**
> **6:47 PM**
> **Subject: Re: A lil peace**
> *One stroke of the belt for every minute late.*

I smiled thinking 'Yes please!' Agh! What was wrong with me?

> **TO: bruisedassets@yahoo.com**
> **6:49 PM**
> **Subject: Re: A lil peace**
> *OMG. I will not admit to giggling, Sir...*
> *What do I get if I'm early?!?!*

Now that I'd sent it, I wasn't sure I wanted the answer.

> *TO: meredith@meredithedits.com*
> *6:52 PM*
> *Subject: Re: A lil peace*
> *Extra time with Sir.*

How could I argue with that?

> *TO: bruisedassets@yahoo.com*
> *6:54 PM*
> *Subject: Re: A lil peace*
> *Perfection...*

The rest of the night went like it typically did. I packed snacks and lunches while Todd and I ignored each other. After getting some work done, and once Todd had gone to bed, I emailed Gregor.

> *TO: bruisedassets@yahoo.com*
> *10:54 PM*
> *Subject: tonight...*
> *Hope you're having a good evening. I pray I can sleep tonight. I'm exhausted, but lately that doesn't mean anything.*
> *My bottom looks like a crime scene attempted to take place there. Lmao. Should be even better tomorrow.*

> *TO: meredith@meredithedits.com*
> *10:59 PM*
> *Subject: Re: tonight...*
> *Crime scene is going to be compromised tomorrow...*

I had a hilarious thought as I began laughing. I loved bantering with him as we egged each other on.

> *TO: bruisedassets@yahoo.com*
> *11:02 PM*
> *Subject: Re: tonight...*
> *Can't stop laughing; big smile. Drip, drip, pulse, pulse...*

> *TO: meredith@meredithedits.com*
> *11:03 PM*
> *Subject: Re: tonight...*
> *Lmao...*

People are looking at me as I am laughing at my phone at the bar...

> **TO: bruisedassets@yahoo.com**
> **11:06 PM**
> **Subject: Re: tonight...**
> *Lol. Glad I can make you laugh about the carnage about to occur tomorrow. At least we get it and appreciate it. Maid service might be traumatized walking down the hall though...lol.*
> *We could really fuck with them and arrange the pillows and blankets to look like a body has been wrapped up...*

He didn't respond right away like he had been. I was answering some PTA emails when his response finally came back.

> **TO: meredith@meredithedits.com**
> **11:39 PM**
> **Subject: Re: tonight...**
> *Bring some ketchup and balloons.*
> *Just got back to my room (315)*
> *I'm going to sleep. Have to get my rest. Need to discipline a very naughty girl tomorrow...*

> **TO: bruisedassets@yahoo.com**
> **11:41 PM**
> **Subject: Re: tonight...**
> *LOL*
> *Noted*
> *Get some rest. Your naughty girl will be tired, but enthusiastic and obedient...*

> **TO: meredith@meredithedits.com**
> **11:46 PM**
> **Subject: Re: tonight...**
> *Will do. You as well.*
> *Let me know when you leave in the am. Drive safe!!*
> *And make sure those lips are well rested as well... :)*

I waited until midnight and proceeded with assignment number one for the day. Gregor had given me permission to count it for Thursday even though he'd chastised me for sending ones after midnight from previous days.

> **TO: bruisedassets@yahoo.com**
> **12:23 AM**
> **Subject: Day 4, #1**

My heartrate keeps increasing, along with the throb of my clit as the hours tick down. I can't stop thinking about it without getting all tingly. Thoughts about how you'll use me for your pleasure run through my mind. Just the softest touch to my bud and she perks up. The second I become deliberate in my task my ass and hips buck. Circling harder, my face grows flush as I imagine your tongue fucking me, the same way it fucks my mouth when kissing me. My chest is beginning to heave as I try to quiet my grunting. My eyes are heavy as I circle on. My stomach begins to contract and my vision shifts....must stop

Pants are in the way; so I discard them so I can spread my legs wider. I want to feel you rub your dick all over my clit, teasing, taunting... Feel your hot cum burst on me, it's a lovely feeling that I want to feel with you. My knees are shaking as I writhe on my hand in the chair. Ass up, face down, just do it already. And that mouth of yours bringing pleasure to places never touched by another tongue and I need more. My clit is so swollen, trying to convince me to finish. Wetter and wetter I can hear my fingers slide all around. The feeling of fullness swells inside me and just before I'm about to give in, I pull my hand away as goosebumps run over my neck...

My head is spinning, my clit beating to its own drum. I can feel my heart hammer against my chest as my nipples rub against my t-shirt. I squeeze them hard trying to replicate your touch, but it's an impossible task. My hands are shaking and I'm desperate for the morning to come. My thighs are now tingling as I spin sweet circles over my clit. Deep breaths as I control myself. Gripping the edge of my desk with my free hand as my lips part with every sigh. My body is utterly confused by my denial. My back is arched and walls contract, needing something to grab on to, needing you to fill them. I can't hang on much longer, but I tease myself a little more. Just when it's about to consume me, I stop, my body screaming in protest...

I collapsed in bed and woke a sweaty mess once more. Todd was gone. Grabbing my phone, I started in on task two.

TO: bruisedassets@yahoo.com
6:26 AM
Subject: Day 4, #2
I wake again covered in sweat, heart racing as my body is clenching tight to my body pillow. I can feel the moisture pooling between my legs and my hand finds my aching clit. It feels so good and I can barely hold still to enjoy it. Sliding a finger inside, my breath hitches causing me to moan and I hear you say 'there's that moan'. My hips rock up and down eager for more. I need release so bad. My legs clamp down on my hand just before I pull away.

I let my hands roam my body. I can feel my heart pounding in my head and I ache for that to stop, knowing the calm an orgasm will bring me. My back is hot, it's almost unbearable. How many hours are left? My fingers fondle my clit as my head thrashes. It's not fun anymore, it's torture, and I'd rather you be the one torturing me. My whole womb is throbbing for more.

I dip my fingers in, reveling in the fullness as my hips reach up for more contact. Head is spinning and I can hardly concentrate. Must stop.

I wonder how you'll greet me. What will happen first? I'm nervous, excited, relieved today is finally here. My head is still throbbing to the same rhythm as my clit. I'm so locked in my head making sure I don't come. Licking my fingers, I groan as I circle my clit again. I imagine you on top of me, the only thing I can hear and feel is you as you encourage me on. Please let me lose myself again. My brain is like a rerun of our time together, remembering each of your first touches. I'm so close, yet so far. Circling faster, my back lifts off the bed as my legs flex. I'm so close and stop myself, nearly a blubbering mess again, my eyes damp with frustration.

I jumped out of bed and hurried to the shower. I needed to shave and make sure I was ready for Gregor. Praying the kids would behave if they woke early, I climbed in under the hot water. After, I dressed running around, scrambling to get everyone out the door in time. I wanted to get there early if at all possible.

Dropping the kids off at latch-key, I sent Gregor a quick email and got on the freeway. I'd created a playlist of songs that reminded me of him and me, whether it was the lyrics, the rhythm, or something else. *Beautiful Undone* by Laura Doggett rang through the truck. It was a hauntingly beautiful song that had me thinking of nothing but him since the first time I'd heard it a few days earlier. His beautiful blue eyes, how they penetrated into the deepest parts of me, and how I'd let him inside my mind. And soon, I'd let him inside even more of me.

Once I was halfway there I started looking for a rest stop. I had to complete my final assignment and time was escaping me. Pulling into the next remote rest stop, I pulled off to the end of the parking lot and prayed no one would suspect. Thank God for skirts!

TO: bruisedassets@yahoo.com
8:43 AM
Subject: Day 4, #3

My body is riddled with anxiety. Flutters keep running through me at the thought of what's to come. It's hard to breathe, adrenaline already pumping. Palming my clit, I struggle with what I want. I'm wet and needy as I circle my clit while being discreet. My hands are cold sending a whole new sensation through me. Breathe, relax, let it happen, the contractions begin and I stop.

Fuck! I'm so annoyed. I want to be there already. I keep pressing down into the seat, but what I need isn't here. I wish I was more calm and collected, but I'm fucking impatient. I dip my fingers in and out over and over again. My hips wiggle about, ass tensing. My touch will never feel like yours does. I love how you touch me like you own me. More shudders, heart pounding, please just a lil longer. I pull my fingers away and lick them clean.

I'm exhausted, yet feel so alive. Heat is blasting making it difficult to concentrate. I can't be late, but the thought of the belt... Slouching down further, I press into my hand. Thighs shake again, my nipple throbs, ass tingles... it's like my body knows what's coming and won't respond to me like I need it to. It only wants you. Licking, fucking, sucking, spanking. I mentally curse you while trying to control my breathing. One surge nearly undoes me so I stop...

I got back on the freeway, music blaring, and was soon going toward the exit. I only had minutes to spare before being late. Assignment number three took too much of my time.

CHAPTER
Fifteen

UNTIL WE GO DOWN

I PULLED INTO THE PARKING lot of his hotel. Quickly, I emailed him to let him know I'd arrived. He told me to come on up, after telling me how to navigate to the elevators. I had no idea what to expect. I mean, ok, I knew what I was there for, but this was new for me. I looked at myself in the mirror and then looked to the clock, I had seven minutes.

Ruelle was singing her song *Until We Go Down*. Closing my eyes, I took a deep breath. I contemplated so much in those few seconds. It was decided. Gregor was my Eden; beautiful and forbidden... And I wasn't walking away.

I climbed out of my SUV. We only had a few hours and I wanted to enjoy every second. Sunglasses on, I strolled through the lobby and right to the elevator. My heart started hammering in my chest. *Please let the elevator be empty.* I stepped in to the vacant space and selected his floor fearing I might hyperventilate.

Jesus, Mer. Get a grip.

It wasn't like I hadn't met with him in private on several occasions, I was very attracted to him, and I trusted him. That much I knew. The elevator doors opened and I took a deep breath. Walking to his door, I pushed it open as he'd directed and spotted him immediately.

He was lounging—fucking lounging—while I'm ready to drop dead of a heart attack. Legs propped up on the desk, phone in hand, hat and glasses in place, and a shit-eating grin on his face. *Fucker*. I hated how calm he appeared when all I could feel was my heart about to burst in my chest.

He rose to his feet, still smiling, and closed the distance between us as the door latched shut. I walked into the room while he locked all the bolts on the door. I dropped my purse and bag to the floor, and before I was done he was pulling me to him.

"You ok?"

I blew out a breath and admitted, "My heart is racing."

I could hear the smile in his voice when he responded, "I know." He kissed me and then whispered, "Now relax."

Closing my eyes, I focused on his hands. He turned me away from him and placed his hand over my pounding heart where it remained as he pressed his body against mine. Instantly I was calmer. His hands then ran over my shoulders, arms, side, and hips. His touch had this magical power over me as my heart immediately slowed some and I felt the tension begin to ease.

Walking me to the corner, he placed me where he wanted me, my arms above my head as my hands clasped my forearms.

"Don't move."

I closed my eyes and focused on getting my breathing under control. His hands gently trailed over my clothes and then I heard him wandering about the room. I listened to him move around, not daring to look. Then he was pulling me to the couch and placed me over his lap. His hands trailed over my maxi skirt, down my legs, and over my hips.

Noting the thin material of my skirt, he stated the obvious while running his hand over my round cheeks. "Not very much protection here."

Grinning, I replied, "I figured easier access was more important, Sir." I smiled in response to his chuckle.

Pulling the skirt over my hips, his hands gently trailed over the black lace panties I wore. I'd picked them to wear specifically for him, hoping he'd like them, though I knew they wouldn't be on long. Immediately I sighed as his hands traced over the lace covering my ass. His hand dipped between my legs as I exhaled at the feel of him cupping me. Then his fingers pulled the lace panties into my crease, exposing my cheeks to him. He examined his marks with soft kisses and gentle caresses.

I momentarily thought that there was no way three hours would be long enough. Then his hand came down on my ass, like he knew I was distracted. The warmth spread through me, though I was already dripping with my arousal. I could lay on his lap for hours while he did what he wanted to me. There was a serenity, a peace, there across his knees, and it was something that I'd only known with him.

Setting me back on my feet, he returned me to the corner, placed my arms where he wanted them and left me to my thoughts. I was already feeling dizzy with want. I knew when he was behind me again, like he was a part of me. And I waited, not daring to move.

The warmth of his breath drifted into my ear, "You smell good."

"Thank you, Sir."

His hand gripped my hair as his other squeezed my ass. Then with the most fluid of movements, my panties were removed and the bottom of my skirt was tucked into the waistband, fully exposing my bruised cheeks. With his hands, he spread my legs further apart. It was then I realized the TV was on. I knew it was strictly to help mask the noises that would soon be coming from his room.

He spanked me, fondled me, teased me, and then repeated it. Moving me to another corner in the room, near the bed, my throat was becoming parched and as if on cue he handed me a bottle of water. I took a few sips and handed the bottle back to him. Kneeling behind me, he slipped off my shoes, and then my skirt. He took care to fold my skirt and placed it on the windowsill. Next was my shirt and bra and I watched as he folded them as well. For the first time in over a decade I stood entirely naked in front of a man who wasn't my husband. And oddly, I felt more comfortable in front of Gregor than I did Todd.

Bending me over the edge of the bed, his fingers entered me as he reminded me, "You know not to come until I give you permission, yes?"

"Yes, Sir." Oh my, God. How long was he going to torture me? I wasn't sure I wanted to know.

He teased, taunted, licked, poked, prodded, sucked, and finger-fucked every part of my pussy and ass. Sweat was rolling down my back and my body was trembling from it all. I was enjoying it, but the control it took *not* to come was killing me.

Several minutes later, I thought I might begin begging for release when he maneuvered me and I was greeted with his erection poking through his jeans. *Something to distract me.* I happily took him in my mouth, licking the sweet pre-cum from his tip.

"You're my obedient little submissive who does exactly as she's told and what's expected of her." I soaked up his words and moaned in response.

Holding my head, he fucked my face. I squeezed his ass through his jeans wishing my hands were on his bare skin. I craved to feel him. I lavished my tongue around him, sucking and squeezing. Jerking himself away, as if he couldn't take much more, he placed me over the bed again on all fours, and I stayed put. Wondering what paddle he'd use next, I ran my hands through my hair as I let the coolness of the comforter soothe my flushed face. I heard the removal of his clothes and then what I'd realize soon after was the tear of a wrapper.

Gripping my hips, he plunged deep inside me before I could let my mind question the reality of it. "Ohhh..."

There was no need for him to work in slowly, I was more than wet enough for both of us.

He didn't relent and I was grateful. I moaned, groaned, writhed, and convulsed as he tormented me. Maybe torment was the wrong word. I was more than enjoying his torture. His hands reached up and gripped my shoulders, pulling me back harder against him. Christ, I didn't want this to ever stop. Then he flipped me over and knelt down in front of me. Smiling at me, he hooked two fingers up inside me as another entered my ass. I couldn't help the desperate moan of pleasure that left my mouth as I pressed into him and let my eyes close.

"Do you want to come?"

YES! "Yes, Sir."

"Your punishment is over. This is all about your pleasure now."

Hallelujah. His mouth joined his fingers, greedily lapping at my clit. Holy fucking shit. Now part of me didn't want to come. It was too good and I wanted it to last. Lifting my eyes and watching a man do what Gregor was doing was always a trigger for me. It was made better by the fact that he clearly loved what he was doing... And I loved watching him do it.

Panting, "Oh, God. Please don't stop."

Words I didn't want to say, but was accustomed to saying, had slipped from my mouth. *He* was different. He wouldn't stop. What the hell was he doing with his fingers? Christ. It was amazing. You can't teach that, can you?

"Come for me!"

I took a deep breath, relaxing and tensing all at the same time. Sounds I didn't recognize as my own began filling the room. And he wasn't stopping. He threw me a pillow, but didn't miss a beat. I screamed into the pillow as one orgasm and then another flooded me. Two fucking orgasms, right in a row. What the fuck? I didn't know it was possible to have two so close together.

When he did stop, I just lay there trying to catch my breath and get my vision back. I heard water running and knew he was washing his hands. I didn't know what to do. Was it over? Should I get dressed and leave? I felt as he climbed the bed and lay down.

"Come here."

I looked to him and was pleasantly surprised to see his arms outstretched, welcoming me. Sated and smiling, I crawled to him and curled into his arms. His hands roamed my body causing more tremors to escape me. Kissing my face and lips, I was in complete awe of him. We talked and cuddled for a while before things became heated again.

I was rubbing his back, while straddling his ass. His hand reached back to tease my greedy clit. Dropping my head, I kissed and bit at the flesh of his neck and shoulders. It wasn't long till he took control. Flipping me to my back, he lifted my hips in the air and started licking at me again.

Sweet Jesus. There was no way I could go through this again. Nope, yes I could. He was so strong and it was then I realized just how strong. The only part of my body that remained on the bed were my shoulders and head. He held me like I was a ragdoll and brought me to the brink once more. Then a few minutes later he did it again. I was nearly in tears from the power of my fourth orgasm in under two hours.

"Come on. Take a shower with me."

Remembering he had a business meeting, I snickered before saying, "What? Don't want to go to your business meeting smelling like pussy."

Laughing, "Yeah, might not be the best impression."

I took his offered hand. He pulled me to my feet and guided me to the shower noticing he still had a hard on and had yet to come. That was unacceptable.

While in the shower I stroked him as we made out. We weren't leaving that shower until he got his release. We teased and touched for a while and I knew when he was close. His head dropped to my shoulder and his breathing changed. *Please, come for me, Gregor.* I didn't say it, but nibbled on his neck, stroked his cock, and squeezed his ass.

His moans echoed in my ear as his arms braced the wall behind me. I was elated and continued stroking him. As he spurted in my hand, I expected him to beg me to stop. Again, I reminded myself that Gregor was a different man with different reactions. Cupping my face, he kissed me slowly, tenderly as the sensations of his orgasm slowly faded.

We got dressed and with a smile on my face he kissed me goodbye after I thanked him. I left his room and had to try to control the smile that was plastered on my face. Getting in my SUV, I dropped my head back and took a few deep breaths. Spotting his truck, I momentarily stared. I smiled, remembering that first encounter, and then pulled away.

A few minutes later I sat in a drive thru famished and needing food for the drive home. My phone chimed with a new email. It was him.

> **TO: meredith@meredithedits.com**
> **12:36 PM**
> **Subject: Re: Day 4, #3**
> *Was the homework worth it...? :)*
> *Stay focused on the road while you rewind the tapes to view over and over...*
> *BTW – I will be out of touch this weekend. Didn't want you to think I was abandoning you post spanking... :)*

Was he dense? I giggled knowing he was being sarcastic. Would any woman say four orgasms in just over two hours wasn't worth it? It was going to suck not emailing him—more so not hearing back from him—but I understood.

> **TO: bruisedassets@yahoo.com**
> **12:39 PM**
> **Subject: Re: Day 4, #3**
> *I appreciate it. I'm sure I'll be out of touch as well. Jam packed weekend myself.*
> *Homework was definitely worth it.*
> *Thank you again. You have no idea how much I enjoyed myself. I'm floating on cloud nine. Talk soon.*

I didn't get a reply.

The drive home had been emotional in a good way. I listened to music, smiled a lot, and squirmed in my seat. I couldn't stop my fingers from drifting to my mouth—lips kiss swollen—and running across them and then my fingers would drift down my neck where his hand had been. How I wish I could recreate that enraptured feeling of his hand around my throat. I wondered if he'd collar me at some point, knowing I'd let him.

I got home and put all of my belongings away before I forgot. Sitting at my desk, I contemplated a quick nap and decided to do just that. He was in meetings anyway. When I awoke, I had an email waiting.

> *TO: meredith@meredithedits.com*
> *2:28 PM*
> *Subject: Re: Day 4, #3*
> *I probably have a much better idea of how much you needed that than you could understand right now.*
> *If we don't chat prior – have a great weekend and stay on that cloud as long as possible.*
> *Meeting went well. No remarks about smelling like pussy. :)*

> *TO: bruisedassets@yahoo.com*
> *3:36 PM*
> *Subject: Re: Day 4, #3*
> *LOL. Glad to hear your meeting went well.*
> *I totally crashed and just woke up. I feel amazing. I only hope that it was as needed for you as it was for me. I want you happy with the arrangement too.*
> *I wish more people got it.*

Silence greeted me until the next morning. And it was ok because I was distracted with writing. Poetry. I hadn't written poetry in ages—if you could call what I was writing poetry.

CHAPTER
Sixteen

RAISE THE DEAD

I'D WRITTEN INTO THE LATE hours of the night before sleeping. Part of me wanted to share my poetry with Gregor, but I was scared to death. Sharing my writing was different; the poetry seemed more intimate. How many parts of myself was I going to share with him?

Stepping out of the shower that morning, I began my routine of drying off and applying my body cream. Glancing in the mirror, I did a double take and examined my shoulder. Small bruises had appeared overnight. *WTF?* Then I giggled as I remembered how and the exact moment it had happened.

I'd been on my knees with Gregor behind me. Gripping my shoulders, he rammed into me harder and harder.

Sighing, I basked in the perfection that yesterday had been and having the bruises to remind me just made it that much better. I headed to my office and sat down, gingerly.

I felt like someone—Gregor—had breathed new life into me. Putting it on repeat, I listened to *Raise the Dead* by Rachel Rabin as I read the first poem I'd written from the night before.

Thoughts of pleasure
Thoughts of pain
Now one in the same
Quiet my mind
Awaken my soul
Of you, I crave more
My submission
Your demand
Your wish
My command

There was nothing more exhilarating than finally feeling like I'd been set free. He'd broken me out of the self-made prison that I didn't even know I was confined to. He made me feel again, live again, love life again. And it wasn't necessarily what we were doing. It was in finally owning what I was, what I craved, what I needed... He just happened to be the one giving it to me. It was as if his demons swallowed my own, silencing them when he was near. I would never be able to thank him and hoped he knew how grateful I was.

I'd found something special. Never had I let down my walls like I had with him. I'd rarely been able to orgasm with a man the first time, let alone the second time. It'd only happened one other time and it wasn't with Todd. Gregor changed all of that, times four. Maybe it was all the tension and build-up, but I suspected it was something more primal, carnal. And that I felt safe enough with him to just be me and to get lost in the moment.

TO: meredith@meredithedits.com
8:52 AM
Subject: Re: Day 4, #3
How is your bottom this morning and the not so subtle reminders...?
Most will not 'get it' due to lack of wiring and/or lack of initiative. That's
ok though.

TO: bruisedassets@yahoo.com
9:18 AM
Subject: Re: Day 4, #3
Good morning, Sir.
It's one massive bruise that makes me sigh when I touch it. I'm applying
the cream you suggested, hoping it helps. I'm learning that I bruise quite

easily, which is good and bad. I have bruises on my shoulders, which made me giggle when I saw them. I slept better than I have in weeks. Thank you for that. Though, I may have woken with some vertigo, like you were still there behind me—pounding away—taking what was gladly given.

Hope you're having a great day and walking around with the same smile I have...

I didn't hear anything until later in the afternoon. I'd spent most of the day writing and losing track of time. When the alert came, I was surprised at how much time had passed.

> **TO: meredith@meredithedits.com**
> **2:19 PM**
> **Subject: Re: Day 4, #3**
> *Damn, I need blown! I am trying to work out before we leave this evening and this keeps getting in the way...*

Shaking my head, I opened the pic he'd sent of him at full mast.

> **TO: bruisedassets@yahoo.com**
> **2:25 PM**
> **Subject: Re: Day 4, #3**
> *Do I get to take credit for that hard-on?*
> *Sigh. I'm giggling like a school girl. We're going to get into lots of good trouble together.*
> *I'll be out and about later tonight, 6pm. When do you leave!? Clearly I'm focused on one thing and not the fact that you're headed out of town. (stomps foot, pouting)*
> *And, if it's any consolation...I'm tender, but have been wet ALL DAY.*

> **TO: meredith@meredithedits.com**
> **2:30 PM**
> **Subject: Re: Day 4, #3**
> *We better be WELL on our way by the time you're out tonight.*
> *If you want to stop by for a drive by sucking I will leave the door open. :)*

He was teasing me and I knew it.

> **TO: bruisedassets@yahoo.com**
> **2:36 PM**
> **Subject: Re: Day 4, #3**
> *While I'd always be up for a drive by sucking, we both know you don't want me in your house... You're the devil, Sir!*

TO: meredith@meredithedits.com
2:40 PM
Subject: Re: Day 4, #3
Don't confuse desire with prudence... :)

TO: bruisedassets@yahoo.com
2:41 PM
Subject: Re: Day 4, #3
I know...
I may need to go take a quick 'nap' now that I'm all full of desire...

And that's just what I did. Scurrying off to the bedroom, like the naughty slut I was, I grabbed my vibrator and quickly sought my release.

TO: bruisedassets@yahoo.com
3:06 PM
Subject: Re: Day 4, #3
Well that was quick and fun. Thank you. I enjoyed getting off as the video clips from yesterday replayed through my mind.
Maybe she'll give you road head?!

He ignored the remark about road head and simply agreed that the reruns were fun. I couldn't refrain from emailing him my depraved thoughts.

TO: bruisedassets@yahoo.com
3:12 PM
Subject: Re: Day 4, #3
They're definitely fun. Especially the episode of your face buried in my pussy, on your knees with almost my entire body lifted off the bed.

And, immediately a reply!

TO: meredith@meredithedits.com
3:14 PM
Subject: Re: Day 4, #3
Instant erection...
Send me a pic of your properly spanked bottom...bent over.

Sighing, I did as he asked.

TO: meredith@meredithedits.com
4:40 PM

Subject: Re: You're testing my coordination...lol
I was speaking with the principal when your email came through. Made
me smile...

Jesus Christ. I was friends with said principal. Kind of hard not to be when
you're the PTA President. And Judith and the principal were chummy. *Agh.*

TO: bruisedassets@yahoo.com
4:43 PM
Subject: Re: You're testing my coordination...lol
Agh! I assume you're being discreet. I work with these people!

TO: meredith@meredithedits.com
4:48 PM
Subject: Re: You're testing my coordination...lol
Your face isn't in the picture. Do they have reason to recognize your ass?

TO: bruisedassets@yahoo.com
4:49 PM
Subject: Re: You're testing my coordination...lol
Aren't you supposed to be on the road? Lol :)

I carried on with my evening, had dinner with some PTA moms and left as
soon as I could. Nothing exciting happened when I got home either. I was on my
laptop working, Todd watching TV—oblivious to me typing away on my laptop,
when an email from Gregor came through.

TO: meredith@meredithedits.com
10:48 PM
Subject: Re: You're testing my coordination...lol
Just made it. I'll be mountain biking in the morning, though some guys
tried persuading me to play golf. The weather is just too beautiful, I'd rather
be on my bike.

I sent him a response, nothing noteworthy, and got back to work. Though, in
the morning I did email him. I knew I probably wouldn't hear back, but I wanted
him to know I was thinking about him.

TO: bruisedassets@yahoo.com
8:58 AM
Subject: Good morning
I woke up dripping...thinking about being bent over, moaning with every

lash you grant me...

No response came until later in the evening and it was a pleasant surprise. Attached was a beautiful picture of the horizon. He must've taken it while he was out biking and I smiled knowing he was sharing a part of his getaway with me.

> **TO: meredith@meredithedits.com**
> **6:48 PM**
> **Subject: Re: Good morning**
> *Biking was great, though the trails have seen better days. At least the weather and the views were phenomenal.*

That night Tami and I went out for an impromptu dinner. I took a picture of me holding a shot glass and sent it to him.

> **TO: bruisedassets@yahoo.com**
> **10:18 PM**
> **Subject: Good morning**
> *Cheers! Fireball!*

Tami and I enjoyed our evening. We didn't get shitfaced, but we were close. Thank God we'd driven back to my house before we were too intoxicated to do so. Todd had gone to bed shortly after we got home, not up to dealing with our antics. My phone chimed and she and I both giggled, knowing it was probably Gregor.

> **TO: meredith@meredithedits.com**
> **12:13 PM**
> **Subject: Re: Good morning**
> *Looks like someone is going to be hurting in the morning... :)*

I will admit that I had to type my reply numerous times before my fingers cooperated. Yup, I was definitely tipsy.

> **TO: bruisedassets@yahoo.com**
> **12:18 PM**
> **Subject: Good morning**
> *Maybe, but not the kind of hurting I prefer...*

I didn't hear from him until Sunday evening, a couple hours after I sent an email wishing him a safe drive home. His emails were a bit short and he seemed stressed. Not that I could really gather that from an email. My own weekend could have been better. Todd and I had been fighting all day, more like all weekend. All I'd wanted to do was call Gregor, but it wasn't an option and I knew I'd be overstepping.

I'd spent a lot of time reflecting on my marriage with Todd. I had believed for so long that without Todd I'd be lost. Now I feared if I stayed I'd be stuck where I didn't want to be. I was damned if I did and damned if I didn't. Part of me knew I had to leave, but I didn't know if I could muster up the strength to do it. This was when over-analyzing things became torture. The only guilt I felt was because I didn't feel any in regards to the choices I'd made with Gregor. Faced with the choices again, I would do it over and over every time.

Taking Gregor out of the equation, I knew that my problems with Todd had been around much longer than either of us cared to admit. Todd was a good man and had provided for me better than I could've hoped, but he'd become a poison to me and only I had the cure. I wanted to feel for him what I once had, but part of me knew it was almost impossible. Too much time, too much hurt, too much waiting, and too many words had been said that we couldn't take back.

Todd had once begged and pleaded with me to stay, to give him a second chance. But that was the thing... I'd continued to give him so many second chances to try with me. I was sick of pleading with him to see me, love me, and to really be with me, all to no avail. Someone had said, 'But he's a great father and provider' and I agreed, but neither of those had anything to do with him being a good husband. Not in my eyes.

Maybe I'd regret leaving him, but I worried more that I'd end up resenting him if I stayed. My heart needed to be rescued and I was the only one who could do that. I was drowning in a life that I no longer wanted and I knew I'd rather be all alone than continue to live a façade. Life was too short to live it unhappy. The question now, 'Would I really go through with it?'

That evening, as if he sensed something, Todd sat down to talk to me. Observing him over the top of my laptop, I waited. He clearly wanted to talk, though I didn't know exactly what about.

Sighing, "I think we need to talk, Mer."

"Yes, we probably do." I'd already shut myself off emotionally, or so I thought.

"I'm not sure what we're doing anymore. Things just aren't right here," he motioned between us, "and I don't know how to fix it."

I leaned back in my chair. "They haven't been right for a *long* time."

"You never say 'I love you' first. How do you think that makes me feel?"

Those three little words had become stagnant, mundane, and heartless. It was like a standard greeting. 'Hello', 'Goodbye', 'I love you'... It was all the same; something expected so you just said it. But as I thought about the feelings that should reside behind that statement I grew sad. The emotions weren't there. I tried remembering when I last really felt it and I couldn't remember.

When had it stopped? I loved him, but was I willing to lay down my life for his? Then so many other questions surfaced in my mind. Did I try to get it back, could I get it back, and did I want it back? The gears in my brain began churning so fast that I couldn't keep up. Closing my eyes, I massaged my temples, trying to calm myself.

It was a question that I had no idea how to answer. He was right. I didn't say it first, just responded with it when he said it to me. Now what?

I remained silent.

He nodded. "I expected you to leave a long time ago."

My eyes bulged and my mouth hung open, it was as if he punched me in the gut. "Do you *want* me to leave? I've pleaded with you to try with me and we get nowhere. If you're expecting me to leave, should I assume you haven't been trying to work on us like I asked?"

Shrugging his shoulders, "I guess so."

We were both calm and neither of us raised our voice. But now I didn't know what to say or do. "So, now what, Todd?" I said to myself I wanted out. This was my opening. Why wasn't I taking it?

"I guess we have some things to think about and decisions to make."

"Yeah, I guess we do. I need more in the bedroom from you. If you can't give that to me..."

He scrubbed his hands over his face. "I just, I'm not comfortable with anything like what you want." He was referring to my requests in the bedroom and we both knew it.

"So, I'm just supposed to be content at not getting what I need?"

"Jesus, Mer. I don't know. This is a lot to process. I don't want to end our marriage."

"But you just admitted you're doing nothing to nurture it either." We sat and stared at each other. "Do you love me?" He started to speak and I stopped him. "Stop, like *love* me? Passionate, want to climb the Grand Canyon and rip my clothes off love me? If there was still passion here, it wouldn't be so hard between us. Everything feels so labored." I lost my train of thought. Nothing seemed labored with Gregor.

"I don't know. I know I love you, but..."

"Exactly." I ran my hands through my hair.

"I'm so worried I'm going to come home one day and you and the kids will be gone."

I laughed, I couldn't help it. "Where do you think we'd go, Todd? If anything, you'll come home to the locks being changed."

He glared at me, "That's not funny." It kind of was because he knew I'd do it, had done it before when I'd found out about his infidelity when we were dating.

"I'm not going anywhere. That doesn't mean I'm not already gone, though."

He studied me for a long moment before getting up and heading to the bedroom. I released a huge breath. What had just happened? It was the opening I needed to leave or to start the process. But one didn't just throw away years together after a five minute conversation. Did they? *FUCK!*

There was this overwhelming sadness and happiness all at once. The sadness was because I finally realized my husband would never do the things I needed him to or make me feel the way Gregor did. Happiness because I'd found someone who could make years of fantasies come true. Gregor made me feel and experience things I never thought I would.

Then I panicked. If I ended things with Todd, Gregor might take that the wrong way and end things with us. I started pulling open the drawers of my desk. Candy, chocolate, and salty snacks all greeted me, but it wasn't what I wanted. I wanted a cigarette. I rarely smoked them, like maybe at the bar with Tami, but never around Todd—or Gregor. But I fucking wanted one NOW.

My chest was tight and my eyes burning. Todd had closed the bedroom door, probably going to bed. I went to the half bath and splashed some cold water on my face. The faint *ping* from my phone sent relief and exhilaration through me.

Gregor.

It's like he knew when I needed to hear from him without knowing it.

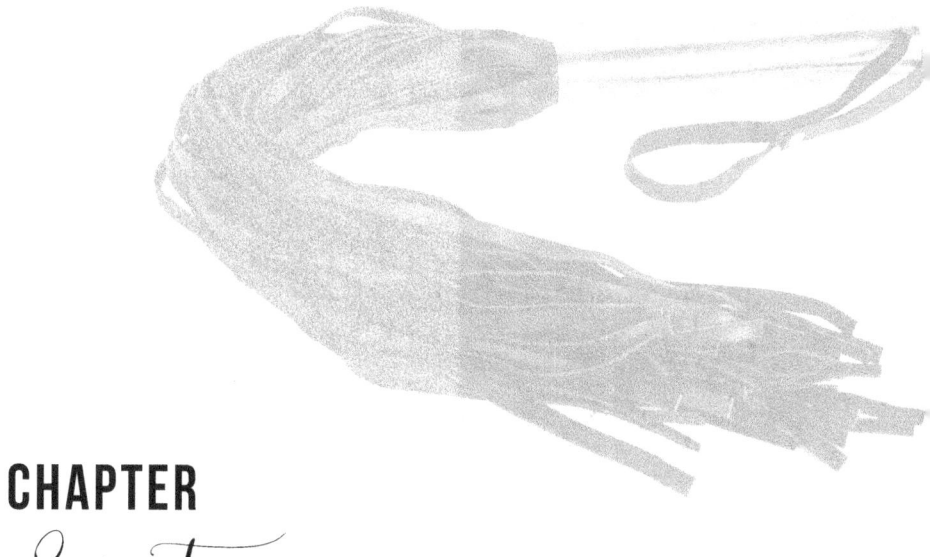

CHAPTER
Seventeen

PIECES

NEEDING MUSIC TO DISTRACT ME, I sat down at my desk. *Pieces* by Rob Thomas came on shortly after. I stared at my laptop. A laptop that had a picture of the kids and I, Todd wasn't present, on the desktop. I listened to the song more than once as tears fell down my cheeks. I needed to stop doubting myself and whether or not I could make it on my own. I knew that was my biggest fear, supporting me and my kids.

I'd sent Gregor an email before my talk with Todd, about sending dirty emails to one another. I smiled at his response asking, 'How dirty?' I started my reply.

> *TO: bruisedassets@yahoo.com*
> *10:18 PM*
> *Subject: Re: Hola*
> *Lol. I may need a few minutes to compose myself. Todd and I just had the most serious talk we've probably had ever. Months and years of issues finally came to a head. Some of his comments surprised me, some didn't.*

> *TO: meredith@meredithedits.com*
> *10:31 PM*
> *Subject: Re: Hola*

Keep it balanced, non-defensive, and constructive. Hard to do but much harder in the long run if you don't. Hope it went well and continues to be productive! :)

Ugh. I'm not sure if any of that happened, but I know we weren't screaming at one another.

> **TO: bruisedassets@yahoo.com**
> **10:35 PM**
> **Subject: Re: Hola**
> *It was the nicest either of us has been in a long time. We have some decisions to make. He's not comfortable with what I need, but also admitted he's been waiting for me to file for months. He knows I'm unhappy and he is too. I'm trying to let it all sink in.*

> **TO: meredith@meredithedits.com**
> **10:51 PM**
> **Subject: Re: Hola**
> *That is a lot for you to take in. For both of you. If you love him and want to be with him – tell him that. Tell him as long as you keep talking – you can figure something out that works for both. It may not be perfect – but it will be a start.*
> *Something I came to accept is the idealistic nature of the perfect mate is very tough to come by. Not impossible, but one risks passing their whole life by trying to find something that may not exist.*
> *If two can accept that they can't be everything to each other and TRULY be ok with that – they stop trying to live up to the impossible ideal and the pressure that comes with it. Instead, they can focus on the positives and accentuate those. I am not quite there yet with her but we are slowly getting closer.*

It was oddly reassuring that he, too, was still working on things with his wife. For as long as he'd been married and in the lifestyle, they were still together. I didn't know how things would ultimately end with Todd and me, but Gregor gave me a sliver of hope about the future.

> **TO: bruisedassets@yahoo.com**
> **10:58 PM**
> **Subject: Re: Hola**
> *I do love him, it's the whole 'being in love'... I'm so baffled and kind of angry with some of his responses. He did seemingly agree that if he felt passionate about me and us that things would be better.*
> *I'm torn to two extremes; just try to ignore it and keep the peace because we've built so much and just giving up...*

I need to try to get some sleep. Hope you can do the same. Sweet dreams of naughty things...

I just couldn't think straight anymore and just wanted my bed. I just wanted to be held, by anyone. Crawling into bed, I tried curling up to Todd, but he was unreceptive. I knew he felt it, his breathing indicated he was awake, but had absolutely no reaction to my touch. Tensing at my touch might have been easier for me to handle versus the nothing I got. In the morning, Todd left for work and once I heard the front door close, I grabbed my phone. Gregor had been up late or really early.

TO: meredith@meredithedits.com
3:09 AM
Subject: Hope you are sleeping...
I've existed between those two extremes and it was a very rough, dark period. It is very hard to make a decision when alternatives both run counter to one's true self.

If you want to talk tomorrow (today) – let me know. It won't solve anything (obviously) but it helps just having that outlet that understands and has been there.

Hope you are sleeping... :)

TO: bruisedassets@yahoo.com
6:32 AM
Subject: Re: Hope you are sleeping...
I would love to chat with you/see you but don't want to cause any grief. I can talk to my friends but only so much because they wouldn't understand this.

I tried crawling into bed and cuddling with him, desperate for some kind of consoling. I of course know better. It didn't happen. I'm a very physical creature, he's not.

I hope you got some rest. You're up late/early. You have no idea how grateful I am for you...for many reasons.

Talk soon.

Now that he'd brought it up, I wanted to sit and talk with him very badly. I had so many questions for him, not that asking them—or him answering them—would do anything to help my situation. As I got the kids breakfast, a reply came back from him.

TO: meredith@meredithedits.com
8:02 AM

Subject: Re: Hope you are sleeping...
I probably won't be able to meet but should be able to call later. Once the kids are at school I'm going to try to lie down. I was up much of the night with work stuff.

Just because he may not reciprocate the physical touch does not necessarily mean you aren't getting through. If you want/need to snuggle – do so. It doesn't have to be overly overt. Sometimes we just need some consistency and repetition before we feel like it isn't a test. I know it seems odd and it may not be the case but trying it won't hurt.

TO: bruisedassets@yahoo.com
8:12 AM
Subject: Re: Hope you are sleeping...
Ok. I should be home working most of the day.
I plan to keep talking to him. He always kisses me goodbye in the morning. Needless to say that didn't happen this morning.
Thank you again.
Of course, the thought of being bent over your knee and my mind silenced sounds good too. I hope you're able to get some rest.

I went about my morning, trying desperately to turn both Todd and Gregor off. I never got a phone call from Gregor, but he'd emailed.

TO: meredith@meredithedits.com
1:52 PM
Subject: Re: Hope you are sleeping...
Today has been another cluster. I will try you before school ends.

If he called, my phone didn't get it. I knew how quickly his days could go from fine to chaotic, just as anyone's could. He also never brought up calling me. I wanted to overanalyze it, but I wasn't going to allow myself. I had enough on my plate to worry about.

Later in the week, emails continuing to fly between Gregor and me, he sent me a picture of a hay bale. We'd both chaperoned field trips to the same orchard but on different days. Many emails flew between us about whips, switches, bales of hay, etc. His next email threw me for a loop.

TO: meredith@meredithedits.com
1:01 PM
Subject: Re: Hot, sweaty mess...
Go to your concert next week a day early. I'll be in the vicinity. I would be there late, but you could make it worthwhile...

I'd brought up Tami and me going to a concert a couple of hours away. We'd planned to do some shopping and relaxing beforehand. The wheels in my head started accelerating quickly.

TO: bruisedassets@yahoo.com
1:12 PM
Subject: Re: Hot, sweaty mess...
How do I explain going a day early?!?!

I immediately called Tami. She had to work the night before but was going to see if she could switch with someone.

"Don't worry. If I can't switch you should still go. I can meet you the next day for the concert."

"Are you sure?"

"Yes! Make this happen. I know you want to spend the night with him."

She was right. I did want to spend the night with him. I needed more than the couple hours we had in Casper.

TO: bruisedassets@yahoo.com
1:31 PM
Subject: Concert
It's worked out. I'll be there a night early. :)

I was so excited and wondering how to contain my excitement. I didn't hear back for a few hours, after the kids were home.

TO: meredith@meredithedits.com
4:36 PM
Subject: Re: Concert
I should arrive shortly after ten p.m. I'll call to book the room.

TO: bruisedassets@yahoo.com
4:39 PM
Subject: Re: Concert
Guess I'll need to find something to keep me occupied until then. I'm sure I can time it to arrive around the same time.
So, does that mean I get to wake up with a dick in me the next morning?! Lol.

TO: meredith@meredithedits.com
4:46 PM

Subject: Re: Concert
I better be waking up with my cock in your mouth...

TO: bruisedassets@yahoo.com
4:51 PM
Subject: Re: Concert
That can most certainly be arranged...

Todd surprised me later that night when we were in bed. We were fooling around, trying to make things work, when he asked if he could tie me to the bed.

"Umm...ok." He grabbed some of his ties, which I tried to not laugh about all the clichés involved there.

We had some laughs, had sex—my bruises from Gregor gone—but nothing to write home about. I was struggling to take him seriously. It was just so not Todd.

TO: bruisedassets@yahoo.com
8:33 AM
Subject: Silk ties?
I got tied to the bed last night...lol. I'm having a hard time taking him seriously, but we had some laughs.
Not long till I'm in the hands of a professional...

TO: meredith@meredithedits.com
8:42 AM
Subject: Re: Silk ties?
Laugh and enjoy the learning and experimenting together, but don't compare or criticize. He is way out of his comfort zone and most men will simply not do that. Get the real thing elsewhere discreetly and securely but nurture what you have with him and see where it goes. Unlikely, but he might surprise you. You might surprise yourself. Might find a certain Dominant side and he might be a nice fit for it and strengthen your relationship/sex life while you are being properly fucked and used elsewhere. Lecture over.
I'm still picturing hay bales (from different angles)... :)

TO: bruisedassets@yahoo.com
8:47 AM
Subject: Silk ties?
Yes. Agreed. It'll be something different for us and maybe I'll find MY dominant side somewhere in the mix. Hehe.
Thank you for all you do; mentor, friendship, proper use and fucking... etc.
I can almost feel the hay poking and scratching my delicate skin as you spank me. :)

TO: meredith@meredithedits.com

8:55 AM
Subject: Re: Silk ties?
He might be the more natural or most submissive of the two of you. You may find that taking control allows both of you to get more of what you need. That is coming on VERY little information, but it could be if he is looking for you to assert control and vice versa. Maybe he needs his bottom paddled. Who knows? But take the time to explore together and find out. And keep in mind that it is the journey that should be enjoyed – not the end. You know the end with me due to a complete understanding of the roles and communication. But you still revel in the journey. You two have your own journey that will be different and the destination isn't known yet.
You want something else poked...

TO: bruisedassets@yahoo.com
9:13 AM
Subject: Silk ties?
I love your 'lectures'. Don't stop
I always want to be poked...

Later in the day he sent another email. He was at a local sports equipment store and was sending me pictures of various sized paddles. Ping pong, tennis, if it held the shape, he sent the picture. I was cracking up and playing right into his hand.

TO: bruisedassets@yahoo.com
12:36 PM
Subject: Re: Spanking?
For the love...I'm now squirming in my seat...wet of course.
Sorry. Maybe what I should say is, 'Thank you, Sir. May I have another?'
:)

TO: meredith@meredithedits.com
3:29 PM
Subject: Re: Spanking?
Found this at a garage sale for $1. I thought it could be refurbished and repurposed... :)

I opened the picture and my mouth fell open. The wooden paddle was more than twice the size of his hand and I had no idea what sport it was used for, nor did I care. He'd placed his hand next to the paddle so that the size wasn't lost on me. I was excited and nervous at the thought of him wielding that paddle against my ass.

TO: bruisedassets@yahoo.com
3:35 PM
Subject: Re: Spanking?

Jesus...Hemp oil will help refurbish that. :)

TO: meredith@meredithedits.com
4:29 PM
Subject: Re: Spanking?
Our spot has been overrun by hunters training their dogs this weekend...

'Our spot'. I loved that he called it that, because it would never be anything but that to me. It would always be our secret place.

TO: bruisedassets@yahoo.com
4:33 PM
Subject: Re: Spanking?
Bastards...I miss our spot.

TO: meredith@meredithedits.com
4:34 PM
Subject: Re: Spanking?
I need your ass staring back at me from across my lap...

TO: bruisedassets@yahoo.com
4:37 PM
Subject: Re: Spanking?
Tingles...When and where? I know you're swamped, but I'm around.

He didn't respond until later that night when I was headed home after being out and about shopping, enjoying some alone time.

TO: meredith@meredithedits.com
8:37 PM
Subject: Re: Spanking?
I'm tired. Did you stock up on your Jolly Ranchers?

TO: bruisedassets@yahoo.com
8:39 PM
Subject: Jolly Ranchers
FUCK. No! Guess I'll need to make a run for some more...

TO: meredith@meredithedits.com
8:41 PM
Subject: Re: Jolly Ranchers
Suck. Suck. Suck.

TO: bruisedassets@yahoo.com
8:44 PM

Subject: Re: Jolly Ranchers
Pineapple. Pineapple. Pineapple...I want Sir...

TO: meredith@meredithedits.com
8:49 PM
Subject: Re: Jolly Ranchers
Pineapple is good to make the taste of cum more pleasing... :)

TO: bruisedassets@yahoo.com
8:53 PM
Subject: Re: Jolly Ranchers
Yes, and the flavor I'm currently sucking...
And then came another message, dick pic attached, at full staff!

TO: bruisedassets@yahoo.com
9:04 PM
Subject: Re: Slightly salty and sweet Maximus
That should be with me...in me, on me, over me...

TO: meredith@meredithedits.com
9:08 PM
Subject: Re: Slightly salty and sweet Maximus
Spraying you...

I was in my driveway, dying. Laughing, horny, squirming in my seat. I wanted him so badly.

TO: bruisedassets@yahoo.com
9:12 PM
Subject: Re: Slightly salty and sweet Maximus
If that's what Sir wants, that's what Sir gets...
Sir enjoys torturing me with things I have to wait (impatiently) for.
I waited, and waited, and waited.

TO: meredith@meredithedits.com
11:38 PM
Subject: Re: Slightly salty and sweet Maximus
And now it's time for sleep...

AGH! What the hell had he been doing for over two hours? Nevermind! I didn't want to know, not really. I tried focusing on work, but it was difficult to do, especially with songs playing that constantly reminded me of him.

TO: bruisedassets@yahoo.com

11:40 PM
Subject: Re: Slightly salty and sweet Maximus
Goodnight, Sir. Hope you get some rest.
That ass is mine in a few days! Lol

I went to bed like I'd done for the last several weeks; Gregor on my mind. My dreams were filled with him and my body ached for him. In the morning my phone chimed to alert me of an email. Hiding in bed a little longer, Todd dealing with the kids, I opened it.

TO: meredith@meredithedits.com
8:21 AM
Subject: Re: Slightly salty and sweet Maximus
Had to force myself to sleep/go back to sleep. I don't sleep a lot but with the sinus issues – it is generally sleep related. Body telling me to slow down and rest.
Yeah...? What do you plan on doing to my ass...? :)

TO: bruisedassets@yahoo.com
8:22 AM
Subject: Re: Slightly salty and sweet Maximus
You're the teacher... :) I'm a willing student. But I'll definitely be smacking it and squeezing it.
Now get some rest...or talk dirty to me...

TO: meredith@meredithedits.com
8:25 AM
Subject: Re: Slightly salty and sweet Maximus
LOL
Making French toast, yard work, work emails, kids have sports... Not a lot in the schedule for rest...

TO: bruisedassets@yahoo.com
8:28 AM
Subject: Re: Slightly salty and sweet Maximus
Sigh...That sounds delicious. I'll be right over. Lol. I'll eat that toast off you...
Have a good day.
Get your work done! I'll reward you later! Lol.

TO: meredith@meredithedits.com
8:31 AM
Subject: Re: Slightly salty and sweet Maximus
I could poke a hole through the middle of the French toast and serve it hanging...

TO: bruisedassets@yahoo.com
8:33 AM
Subject: Re: Slightly salty and sweet Maximus
You're an evil man...I like it and I'd devour it, them, both...

I didn't hear anything the rest of the day. Per usual, I spent my Sunday preparing for the week and daydreaming of my night away with Sir. Laundry, cleaning, editing, and the kids filled my day. Later that evening as Todd put the kids to bed, I emailed Gregor once more.

TO: bruisedassets@yahoo.com
8:43 PM
Subject: Sore ass...
Sigh...I miss sitting on a sore ass...
You know this is your fault. I need to be manhandled... :)

TO: meredith@meredithedits.com
8:47 PM
Subject: Re: Sore ass...
I will let you know if she sends me out for something forgotten and try to restore that feeling appropriately.
Of course I know...
Ugh. We both knew that given the hour, it wasn't likely to happen.

TO: bruisedassets@yahoo.com
8:50 PM
Subject: Re: Sore ass...
Grumbles, legs clenched, deep breaths, focus on work. DAMMIT!

Putting on my headphones, I focused on work. A couple hours later he sent his goodnight email.

TO: meredith@meredithedits.com
11:09 PM
Subject: Re: Sore ass...
How's work going? I will be heading to bed shortly. Need the rest. TTYT.
Hope you find something soon to quell the never ending moistness.

TO: bruisedassets@yahoo.com
11:13 PM
Subject: Re: Sore ass...
It's going.
Any requests for drinks, snacks, or otherwise that I can bring?
I don't know that my moistness will ever be quelled, just momentarily satiated...
Talk soon.

CHAPTER
Eighteen

HYPNOTIC

TO: meredith@meredithedits.com
7:13 AM
Subject: Re: Sore ass...
Special requests for snacks...? Only one thing I will be thinking about eating...

And that's one way to start your Monday! Thinking about him going down on me was one way to make sure I'd be horny all day long. I was still half asleep when I responded to his email.

TO: bruisedassets@yahoo.com
7:21 AM
Subject: Re: Sore ass...
I woke to thoughts of our night to come consuming me. I look forward to being your late night meal. To stretch out naked next to you while we indulge in one another...sigh.
I ache...
I look forward to giving you a full body massage somewhere in the mix.
I'm not fully awake. Stop muddling my brain so early in the morning!

TO: meredith@meredithedits.com
7:23 AM
Subject: Re: Sore ass...
Wake up faster...

TO: bruisedassets@yahoo.com
7:26 AM
Subject: Re: Sore ass...
Little hard to do when I'm dreaming of being under the covers with you...
:)

Putting my phone down, I got up and got dressed. I had to get the kids to school and then I was headed to the gym. And, because I could never let sleeping dogs lie, I emailed him before walking into the gym while sitting in my car.

TO: bruisedassets@yahoo.com
9:19 AM
Subject: Gym time.
I'll be imagining a sore ass today in class...

I wasn't expecting his immediate response.

TO: meredith@meredithedits.com
9:20 AM
Subject: Re: Gym time.
I could give you one prior...
Asshat! No he couldn't!

TO: bruisedassets@yahoo.com
9:22 AM
Subject: Re: Gym time.
Better hurry. Class starts in less than 10 mins. Lol.

TO: meredith@meredithedits.com
9:23 AM
Subject: Re: Gym time.
Damn – guess you will just have to imagine it...

TO: bruisedassets@yahoo.com
9:25 AM
Subject: Re: Gym time.
Maybe tomorrow...
I walked into the gym, emails still coming through.

TO: meredith@meredithedits.com

9:27 AM
Subject: Re: Gym time.
You going to play the nurse and see me before my appt..?

TO: bruisedassets@yahoo.com
9:29 AM
Subject: Re: Gym time.
Lol...depends on time. I can always play nurse after, too.

Putting my phone on silent, I jumped on my bike. An email awaited me when class was over. We emailed the whole drive home, me using my talk to text feature.

TO: meredith@meredithedits.com
10:11 AM
Subject: Re: Gym time.
Lol

TO: bruisedassets@yahoo.com
10:35 AM
Subject: Re: Gym time.
I could have you turn your head and cough! Lol

TO: meredith@meredithedits.com
10:43 AM
Subject: Re: Gym time.
You going to give me a prostate exam/massage in the process...?

TO: bruisedassets@yahoo.com
10:51 AM
Subject: Re: Gym time.
Guess you'll have to find out...

TO: meredith@meredithedits.com
10:53 AM
Subject: Re: Gym time.
Interestingly, 'kiss my ass' to your response has a completely different meaning...

TO: bruisedassets@yahoo.com
10:51 AM
Subject: Re: Gym time.
Bend over! I'll bite it, too.

TO: meredith@meredithedits.com
10:51 AM
Subject: Re: Gym time.
Do you lick and kiss with your teeth...?

TO: bruisedassets@yahoo.com
10:53 AM
Subject: Re: Gym time.
Lol. Sometimes...you should know that!
Bite, lick, suck, kiss...
Drip, drip, drip...

TO: meredith@meredithedits.com
10:58 AM
Subject: Re: Gym time.
I can't hide marks as well as you. Especially for bite marks...lol

I decided to keep him waiting and jumped in the shower.

TO: bruisedassets@yahoo.com
11:36 AM
Subject: Re: Gym time.
*I don't have to bite that hard...lol. Though the thought of marking you is
a turn on. But I'll behave... You just have to keep me in line...*

I was editing when another email came in. Immediately, I was groaning in
approval to his demand.

TO: meredith@meredithedits.com
11:58 AM
Subject: Re: Gym time.
*We will work something out for tomorrow. Better get your orgasms in
today – tomorrow is 3 days prior and thus you will be refraining...*
*Headed to my dentist appt. May have to employ boner suppression
techniques with all the thoughts swirling around my head...*

I headed up to the school. PTA duties awaited me. When I pulled in to the
school parking lot, I sent one last email.

TO: bruisedassets@yahoo.com
1:16 PM
Subject: I wonder...
How's the boner suppression going?
*Does Sir have a preference between lace, cotton, satin...or he doesn't
care because it's just going to end up on the floor regardless?*

I spotted Judith's massive SUV and cringed. Taking a few deep breaths, I headed into the school. She must've been in one of the classrooms because I didn't see her. Busying myself with the tasks at hand, I got more done than I expected.

Sitting down, I pulled my phone out of my pocket. I had a few minutes before classes were dismissed. Just when I thought no email awaited, my phone pinged. He'd just emailed.

> TO: meredith@meredithedits.com
> 3:51 PM
> Subject: Re: I wonder...
> The hygienist was much more approving today. She told me I had an overactive tongue...is that code? Or does she know...? :) Lol
> I haven't really thought about it prior. Let me consider.

I knew I didn't have time to respond fully, so it'd have to wait, but not before I sent a quick response.

> TO: bruisedassets@yahoo.com
> 3:56 PM
> Subject: Re: I wonder...
> OMG. I'm laughing my face off. Oral fixation, too, huh? Snort, giggle...
> I'll look forward to your answer since I have a bit of everything.

Still laughing, I walked out of the office the PTA had allocated as theirs, and walked right into him. My phone fell from my hands at the force we hit one another. Clearly I wasn't the only one distracted.

His strong hands steadied me before releasing me. My skin burned with desire for him and I could feel the flush already creeping up my face. The way he smiled at me made me nervous, like a giddy teenager. I couldn't stand to look at it for too long, knowing it could make me lose all sense. His smile confessed that he knew my secrets and desires and that he was going to use them to his advantage.

He bent over and picked up my phone before handing it back to me. Tilting his head at me, his deep voice startled me, "You ok?"

Smiling nervously, I lied, "I'm fine. You?" I looked around, anxious about anyone who might see us talking.

"Relax. We're just two parents talking about our kids." His voice was calm and collected when I was a jittery mess. I felt like you could tell just by looking at me that I was melting into a puddle right there in front of him.

Then he took a step back from me, since we were practically embracing one another. I let out a breath and nodded my head.

A father I recognized walked our way and stretched his hand out to Gregor. "Hey *William*."

Will? What the hell? I missed the rest of their exchange as I racked my brain. I *know* he told me his name was Gregor. There was never a mention to Will or William. Gregor observed me and could tell I was growing agitated. Dismissing him, the other father scurried away as the school bell rang. Soon kids were swarming the halls, oblivious to us.

"I need to get my kids. I'll email you."

Oh, hell no. He wasn't getting off that easy. "Gregor, wait!" His eyes smiled at me. He knew exactly what was coming.

"Yes?"

"I'm confused. Is your name Gregor or William?" I tried calming the anger in my voice, but he caught it.

I was pursing my lips at him when he pulled me back into my office and closed the door, leaving it slightly ajar.

"It's my middle name. The name I've gone by my entire life, the name I prefer."

Confused, I asked, "William or Gregor?"

Grinning, "Gregor. William is on all my legal documents, et cetera. So some people still call me William."

I narrowed my eyes at him. I was annoyed. "So, what the hell am I supposed to call you in public?"

Smirking, he replied, "Sir works just fine."

I exhaled a chuckle and shook my head at him. "I'm sure that'd go over *really* well. Seriously, I have Gregor programmed in my head and now to find out it's not what *everyone* calls you." His eyes scanned my face like it was no big deal, making it hard to be annoyed with him. "You're making this difficult on me!"

"Difficult looks good on you." He pulled me close and shut me up with his kiss. Before I could even register what he'd just done, he was out of the room and vanished down the hall of kids.

"MOTHERF..."

"Mom! We're ready!"

Immediately I was back in mom mode as my kids swarmed around me. "Perfect!

Let's get out of here!"

I couldn't stop thinking about the name issue. As I sat at my desk that night it was still at the forefront of my thoughts. I mean, I guess it wasn't really an issue. He'd given me the name he preferred to be called from the beginning. Of course, this begged the question if he *did* know who I was from the start of things. Gregor would be safer to tell me because he was probably listed in the parent registry as William. I couldn't resist. I pulled out the school directory and found no Gregors listed as parents, but there were several William's.

AGH!

It was pointless. It was just a name. But that over thinking bitch in the back of my head kept nagging me. 'But what if there's more?'

More what? I clearly knew there was more, what this was, and what I'd gotten myself into. He was just someone I borrowed on occasion, just as he borrowed me. What did his name matter? And just like the song, *Hypnotic* by Zella Day, he had me, and I wasn't about to walk away. Name or not.

No emails had been exchanged since I got his earlier response. Maybe he was waiting on me to reply. I decided that the name thing didn't bother me and I wasn't going to bring it up again. And the truth was, I'd call him anything he wanted me to; except Todd.

Looking over his last email, I started my response.

> *TO: bruisedassets@yahoo.com*
> *8:16 PM*
> *Subject: I wonder...*
> I'm surprised no other woman has asked this before. Bad subs! You're supposed to want to please your Sir in ALL manners! :)

> *TO: meredith@meredithedits.com*
> *8:21 PM*
> *Subject: Re: I wonder...*
> I don't think I leave them on long enough to appreciate. I do like the feel of satin and the shimmer. If I am going to be slowly grinded on with them on – satin is definitely the way to go.

Why did I insist on playing this game with him? I'd never win. Editing was calling to me, but writing won out. A while later, I yawned and realized the house was quiet and it was after eleven p.m. No email. Well, I was going to send one anyway.

TO: bruisedassets@yahoo.com
11:23 PM
Subject: Night
Headed to bed soon. Hope you had a good evening...
Talk soon.

TO: meredith@meredithedits.com
11:26 PM
Subject: Re: Night
Worked out, cleaned, showered, worked on some reports for work...
You going to be over my knee tomorrow...?

YES! I couldn't wait! Immediately my mood was improved.

TO: bruisedassets@yahoo.com
11:28 PM
Subject: Re: Night
I would love to be over your knee!

TO: meredith@meredithedits.com
11:33 PM
Subject: Re: Night
Good. Let me see how I can work around my schedule...

TO: bruisedassets@yahoo.com
11:35 PM
Subject: Re: Night
My day is open. Haven't stopped thinking about your hands on my ass all night...

TO: meredith@meredithedits.com
11:39 PM
Subject: Re: Night
It'll be a small window of time. But it shouldn't take long to warm that bottom up and make sure you are in the right frame of mind for our night away.

There was nothing left to say. He said he'd see me, wanted to, and he knew I was ready, willing, and able. I went to bed with a smile on my face.

A few emails were exchanged the next morning. I was meeting him after lunch at our spot. And our spot was compromised when I pulled in. At the same time my phone rang and it was him.

"Hey. Go south. There's another picnic area on the east side of the road. It's empty."

"Ok." I knew where he referred and headed that way.

I pulled in a few minutes later and he was getting out of his truck. Parking away from him, I got out and headed his way. Besides the run in at the school the day before, I hadn't seen him since Casper. Flutters danced, my arms were crossed due to the nerves, and I couldn't stop smiling at him. He was grinning from ear to ear.

Once I was within arm's reach, he yanked me to him, smothering my lips with his. Unfolding my arms, I grabbed onto the waist of his jeans as he pressed me against the side of his truck. His erection highly evident as he grinded against me. His hands moved to my ass and pulled me closer. Moaning, I sucked his lower lip between my teeth before releasing it.

Pulling back, he cupped my face, "God, I missed you, missed those eyes." He observed me another moment knowing full well I was already drunk on him. "I love those eyes."

Why did he have to use that word? No hearts and flowers, Gregor! But I kept my mouth shut.

"Turn around."

The door was open and I let him bend me over the seat, noticing the 'significant damage' paddle as he pulled it off the seat. Stretching my arms out in front, across the seats, I relaxed, the seat caressing my face. Smiling as he pulled my skirt up, his hands ran up the bare flesh of my legs as he spread them wider. I bit my lip and grinned, waiting for the exact moment he noticed. The breeze drifted over my bare ass and I heard the soft groan that he let escape.

His hands caressed my ass tenderly as my eyes closed. "Commando, huh?"

"I knew we were short on time."

"Mmm." His hand gripped my hair as he sneered, "You're my naughty little slut."

"Yes, Sir."

Tucking my skirt up and over my ass, the strokes from his paddle began. He wasn't as harsh as he'd been that first time with that paddle. But it was enough to make me cringe, my eyes water, and get me dripping. He fondled me and fingered me, just driving me more insane.

"Do. Not. Come."

Breathlessly, "Yes, Sir." His fingers resumed their movement over me, in me. "Shit!" I clenched tightly around his fingers, fighting the release.

Just as quickly, my skirt was replaced and he was pulling me off the seat and turning me toward him. Wiping at my eyes, knowing my makeup was running, I watched as he placed the paddle back on the seat.

"Come here."

Cupping my face between his hands, he kissed me slowly. His hands roamed down my body, soothing me and further igniting my desire for him. The kiss quickly became fierce as I reached my hand down between his legs and molded the palm of my hand against his cock.

"I'm really looking forward to having you all night to myself."

Sighing and continuing to fondle him, I cooed, "Me too, Sir."

"I still can't get over how content you look after a spanking." He kissed my temple then whispered, "Love those eyes." And then kissed the other temple.

I couldn't even speak and if I could I didn't know what I'd say. He continued kissing my face and neck as I started to fiddle with his zipper. "I know what you want."

Unzipping his pants, he freed himself. Sitting on the steps of his truck, I took him in my mouth. I couldn't get enough of him. And the more he moaned, groaned, and pulled on my hair, the more I bestowed my talents on him. I knew he was close and again, he denied me.

Like a kid with an ice cream cone on a hot summer day, he snatched the delicious treat away from me.

"Not today."

I looked up at him, hoping my eyes could convince him otherwise. Instead, he stroked all the pre-cum out of his shaft and onto his finger. He offered it to me and I happily took it. Now he was the kid with the treat, the smile on his face the only proof I needed. He then pulled me to my feet and put his hands on the truck on either side of my head.

He was still chewing his gum and I smiled as he leaned in to kiss me. My fingers played with the material of his shirt as I pulled him closer to me.

"I have to go." Sighing, his lips still against mine, I dropped my head to his shoulder. His arms wrapped around me and I did the same. Holding each other, he added, "Hop in."

"Ok."

Pulling us apart, he gently pushed me into the backseat, but not before smacking my ass. He climbed into the driver's seat and then drove toward my vehicle. It really wasn't necessary, but it was a sweet gesture.

"You ok to drive home?"

Smiling, "Yes. Thank you. It was good to see you. I'll see you Thursday."

Motioning me closer, I leaned between the front and back seats. His thumb on my chin, he kissed me once more. "If I can wait. I may need you tonight. I'll email you."

"Ok."

Climbing out, he made sure I got in my vehicle before driving off. Pulling out of the lot, I felt my swollen lips, still pulsing from our kissing and my cock sucking. Glancing in the mirror I saw they definitely looked the way they felt.

> *TO: bruisedassets@yahoo.com*
> *2:14 PM*
> *Subject: Re: Night*
> *Have I mentioned that I love how swollen and used my lips look after seeing you...?*
> I finished the drive home and an email popped up as I pulled in the drive.

> *TO: meredith@meredithedits.com*
> *2:17 PM*
> *Subject: Re: Night*
> *No but it makes me think of how swollen I am right now and how I shouldn't be for what I'm getting ready to do.*
> *Thinking about those deep eyes right now and that well spanked ass...and that certainly isn't helping the erection suppression.*

> *TO: bruisedassets@yahoo.com*
> *2:22 PM*
> *Subject: Re: Night*
> *I'd tell you to think about butt things, but, well...lol*
> *I think I should go commando more often.*

> *TO: meredith@meredithedits.com*
> *2:26 PM*
> *Subject: Re: Night*
> *Commando suits you (and me...)*
> *TTYL. Nurse is pointing at me...*

> *TO: bruisedassets@yahoo.com*
> *2:28 PM*
> *Subject: Re: Night*
> *Enjoy your pokes knowing better ones are coming...*

I spent the next hour or so working and was headed to the bus stop when his email came through.

> *TO: meredith@meredithedits.com*
> *4:01 PM*
> *Subject: Re: Night*
> *Good news! Dr. said I'm healthy enough to have sex. No blue pill needed...*

> *TO: bruisedassets@yahoo.com*
> *4:04 PM*
> *Subject: Re: Night*
> *I could've told you both that! Lol.*
> *My ass hurts, but not enough. What is wrong with me? I want to drown in my submission to you. I want your next release to be mine, as mine will be yours. Remembering that acquaintances have commented on how 'happy' I look lately and asking what my secret is. I can't make this shit up. So close yet so far...*

I didn't hear back until later that night, clearly seeing him before he was leaving town wasn't happening. One more day.

> *TO: meredith@meredithedits.com*
> *11:21 PM*
> *Subject: Re: Night*
> *Nice read after finishing a workout... :)*
> *I'm going to stroke myself to sleep tonight. I'm not going to come – but certainly will be thinking about how quick it will come when you're with me and how much you will revel in bringing it...*

> *TO: bruisedassets@yahoo.com*
> *11:26 PM*
> *Subject: Re: Night*
> *I hope you sleep well. I'm sure it'll be another night of me waking up sweaty and clutching my pillows. Please travel safe. Every time I squeeze my marks, chills run up my spine. Thank you for that.*

> *TO: meredith@meredithedits.com*
> *11:29 PM*
> *Subject: Re: Night*
> *I look forward to sending those chills up and down your entire body...*
> *If you have time before we meet – might want to do a little shopping for a nice Cat o Nine tails or other suitable flogger. And don't go cheap... :)*

CHAPTER
Nineteen

UNDER THE INFLUENCE

A FLOGGER! NOW MY MIND WAS racing as I opened my internet browser. I wasn't even sure where to begin looking. I typed in 'flogger' and was pleasantly surprised with dozens of choices. After looking at them, I knew more of what I wanted. I didn't want something small or flimsy looking. 'Don't go cheap' was also in the forefront.

> *TO: bruisedassets@yahoo.com*
> *11:38 PM*
> *Subject: Flog her...*
> *Sigh...I'm already squirming...and I love the smell of leather. You're trouble...*
> *I'm thinking about this one...though I'm not sure it would be delivered here in time.*

I included a link to the one that sparked my interest the most. Knowing my window was closing to have it delivered on time, I placed the order before he responded. And there was no telling if he'd respond in five minutes or in the morning.

> *TO: meredith@meredithedits.com*

11:43 PM
Subject: Re: Flog her...
Smell of fresh leather is intoxicating.
Have it delivered to your hotel under your name. Pick it up there.
I am reading paddle reviews and about ready to come...

TO: bruisedassets@yahoo.com
11:38 PM
Subject: Re: Flog her...
I thought about that. Too late. Fingers crossed my guy shows up at his usual time. Save that cum for me, Sir...please.
Do I make you nervous yet or do I excite you?!? Lol. You may very well have opened Pandora's Box with me...

And as I mentioned earlier, I didn't hear from him until morning.

TO: meredith@meredithedits.com
7:27 AM
Subject: Re: Flog her...
I fell asleep thinking about how you would respond to the flogger. I think you will fall in love with that implement.
I almost came several times. Was very tired and very, very hard.

I got caught up with the kids, PTA stuff, and then had class at the gym. After a hard workout, I emailed him, knowing he was probably already on the road.

TO: bruisedassets@yahoo.com
10:36 AM
Subject: Safe travels
Just left the gym. I may need a massage, too. Drive safe.
Thinking of our time to come...

TO: meredith@meredithedits.com
10:39 AM
Subject: Re: Safe travels
Had an appt cancel. I'm not leaving till this evening.

TO: bruisedassets@yahoo.com
10:48 AM
Subject: Re: Safe travels
Ok. Does that change things for tomorrow? Just let me know. Just got home...

TO: meredith@meredithedits.com
10:51 AM

Subject: Re: Safe travels
No – tomorrow shouldn't change.
How's your bottom? Need a quick warm up...?

Did he really think I'd ever turn him down if I could help it?

TO: bruisedassets@yahoo.com
10:55 AM
Subject: Re: Safe travels
You're addicting, Sir and I'd love a warm up...

I had an appointment to get my hair cut and needed to shower. When I got out, I had an email from Gregor.

TO: meredith@meredithedits.com
11:11 AM
Subject: Re: Safe travels
I'm not leaving till after dinner so I might be able to warm you up before I leave town...
I'll message you tonight either way.

I finished getting ready and headed to my hair appointment. Talking to Tami on the way there, she decided to come over early in the morning to help me pack and keep me distracted before we left town in the morning. I had to run to the store and did that an hour before I expected Gregor to contact me. Thank goodness everything I bought was non-perishable. I emailed him as I had a funny thought.

TO: bruisedassets@yahoo.com
7:58 PM
Subject: Re: Safe travels
We should come up with a code word for our spot for texting.
I.e.: Rodeo then the time. Lol.

TO: meredith@meredithedits.com
8:03 PM
Subject: Re: Safe travels
Lol. I should be wrapped up here in a couple minutes.

I waited patiently... Ten agonizing minutes later he replied.

TO: meredith@meredithedits.com

8:15 PM
Subject: Re: Safe travels
Just wrapped up. Rodeo in ten minutes?
Just a quick spanking?

TO: bruisedassets@yahoo.com
8:17 PM
Subject: Re: Safe travels
OMW

Again, he arrived before I did. Parking, I hopped out of my car and strolled over to him. As he so often did, he yanked me close and kissed me with a smile on his face. Grabbing my tender ass, he set my marks on fire, sending ripples of pain through my ass as I whimpered.

"Get on the table." I spotted that fucking paddle that I loved to detest in his hand as I walked to the table.

Staring at him, I stood in front of the table and dropped my pants before taking my position.

I'd sent him a picture of my ass earlier in the day and he'd remarked that is was obvious he'd focused his attention on my right cheek. Caressing the marks that were now exposed to him in the moonlight, I cooed.

The spanking was quick. The tongue lashing wasn't. Long enough to get me thoroughly wet, and just when I was about to come he would stop. Then he'd paddle me again, then lick and finger me again. He did this multiple times. I was begging to come and each time he denied me.

Pulling away from me, he then climbed the table and laid on top of my back. The weight of him calmed me, yet imprisoned me.

Yanking my hair, he snarled in my ear. "Tomorrow I plan to be buried to the hilt in that ass."

"Yes, Sir." I was barely able to speak I was so turned on.

"Get dressed." Just as quick he was off me and helping me to my feet.

Sitting on the bench, his eyes met mine in the darkness and I knew what he wanted of me. I didn't know how to explain it. He could get me to drop to my knees with the simple touch of his hand, whisper from his mouth, or gaze of his eyes. Eyes that were a deep blue, darker than my own, and had a power over me that I willingly succumbed to.

Kneeling in front of him, eyes downcast, I awaited his instructions.

"Get to work."

Lifting my eyes, his cock awaited me. I eagerly got to work. And again, he denied himself his release. Pulling my mouth off his cock and up to his face, he stopped short of kissing me. The feeling of his hand around my throat and lightly squeezing didn't scare me. He didn't do it to choke me, he did it as an act of possession, ownership. The only thing it did to me was turn me on more. Closing my eyes, I waited.

"You're a good girl."

"Thank you, Sir."

Then he kissed me. His kisses never disappointed me, always taking and giving more. When I was ready to pounce on him, he ended it. I was putty in his hands, something I was growing accustomed to.

"I have to go. Drive safe tomorrow."

My face buried in his neck as he hugged me. My emotions were threatening to come to a head in his arms, "You, too. Let me know when you get there."

"Will do. Can you pick up condoms?"

"Yes. Anything else?"

"Drinks in the room would be nice." I mumbled my ok. "You're tired."

Shrugging, "Maybe."

"Get some rest tonight. You'll need it."

"Yes, Sir."

I wasn't back on main roads when his email popped up.

> *TO: meredith@meredithedits.com*
> *9:13 PM*
> *Subject: Re: Safe travels*
> *So...keep me entertained on my drive...*

Giggling, I emailed him once I pulled in the drive.

> *TO: bruisedassets@yahoo.com*
> *9:17 PM*
> *Subject: Re: Safe travels*
> *My legs are a wreck after the gym today. I can barely walk the stairs without wobbling. And after those paddlings tonight...sigh.*
> *But the payoff in both arenas is well worth it.*
> *I was so close so many times tonight...thank you for that...*
> *Thinking about velvet lined cuffs...*

TO: meredith@meredithedits.com
9:24 PM
Subject: Re: Safe travels
Maybe you should stop tomorrow and get some.

TO: bruisedassets@yahoo.com
9:27 PM
Subject: Re: Safe travels
I'm gonna go broke buying us gear...

I ended up emailing him before I heard if he'd arrived. I was tired and knew I needed sleep.

TO: bruisedassets@yahoo.com
11:03 PM
Subject: Until tomorrow...
I've debated staying up in preparation for the late night tomorrow or go to sleep.
I'm opting for sleep.
Hope you get some rest and that tomorrow is a good day for you. I'll be riddled with anxiety all day.
Sweet dreams...my ass is super sore...

As I crawled into bed a few minutes later, his response awaited me.

TO: meredith@meredithedits.com
11:14 PM
Subject: Re: Until tomorrow...
Just pulled into the hotel. Have to check in.

I dozed off before I could respond. When I woke, I was deliriously happy. Today was the day. I just had to make it through till this afternoon when Tami and I could hit the road.

TO: meredith@meredithedits.com
7:34 AM
Subject: Re: Until tomorrow...
I crashed as soon as I hit the bed. Didn't even plug the phone in. Looking forward to tonight.

TO: bruisedassets@yahoo.com
8:39 AM

Subject: Supplies

I was wondering if that's what happened to you. I'm glad you got some rest. I know we both needed it! :)

You mentioned condoms and drinks. Anything special?

Brain was a lil muddled last night when you mentioned it. :)

TO: meredith@meredithedits.com
8:34 AM
Subject: Re: Supplies

I will try to stop earlier but if you are getting something – a small bottle of bourbon and coke would be nice.

Make sure your pussy and ass are both very well prepared to be tongue fucked.

Constant firmness in my pants this morning...

"Mom!" I slammed my laptop shut. "We have to go!"

"Yes, sorry." I jumped up from my desk. "Let's go!"

When I got home, I sent my reply just as I saw Tami pull in the drive.

TO: bruisedassets@yahoo.com
9:24 AM
Subject: Re: Supplies

I'll get some bourbon.

Planning to shower and prep at my hotel before heading to yours. I'll be very prepared...

Constant throbbing and wetness in mine...

Do I get to play music tonight? Music is one of my drugs...you'd be another... :)

I heard Tami come in as I hit send. She sat down across from me and glared at me.

"You whore!"

We both started cracking up. I nodded and accepted the title she'd bestowed upon me. We spent the morning cleaning, packing, bullshitting, and checking the porch for deliveries. Todd was supposed to be home around the same time the kids got off the bus and then Tami and I would make the two hour drive south.

Around one in the afternoon, my doorbell rang. I jumped off the couch and ran to the door. My delivery guy was walking away and a box sat in front of my door. Snatching it off the porch, I ran to the bedroom where Tami followed. Opening it up, it was encased in plastic, and heavier than I'd imagined it would be.

The smell was evident through the plastic and we couldn't resist opening it. Tami took a big sniff, "Ahhh. That smells so good."

I swiped it back and inhaled several times, until I was slightly dizzy. "I have to tell him it came!"

> *TO: bruisedassets@yahoo.com*
> *1:34 PM*
> *Subject: Special delivery*
> *Something just arrived on my doorstep...*
> *I may have squealed...*
> *:)*

> *TO: meredith@meredithedits.com*
> *1:41 PM*
> *Subject: Re: Special delivery*
> *Take a pic*

Tami took a couple pictures of me holding the flogger and we sent them on to Gregor.

> *TO: bruisedassets@yahoo.com*
> *1:58 PM*
> *Subject: Re: Special delivery*
> *It smells delicious...*

The rest of the day had moments of crawling and flying by. Finally, we were on the road around dinner time.

> *TO: bruisedassets@yahoo.com*
> *5:52 PM*
> *Subject: Leaving*
> *Just hit the road. Tami and I are making a few stops, then I'll be preparing!*

He simply responded with a smiley emoticon.

"So, you know I hate you right?" I caught the sarcastic tone in her voice.

Looking to her and then back to the road, I tried to contain my excitement. "I'm sorry."

"No you're not. It's ok. I get it."

"Thank you. Really. I think I would've already gone insane if I didn't have you."

Chuckling, "They can put us in the same padded cell."

"Yes, yes they can."

"Are things any better with Todd?"

I shrugged my shoulders. "Maybe because I'm not constantly begging him for attention, since I'm getting it elsewhere."

"He hasn't noticed or asked questions?"

I just shook my head. "Oblivious as usual."

After a few minutes of silence, she asked, "You hungry?"

I thought about it and giggled. "Yes, but I need to be careful about what I eat." She eyed me, knowing what I meant, but I explained further. "Nervous stomach and I don't want to get all gassy."

"Yeah. Might kill the mood." She pulled something out of her purse. "Here. This should help." She handed me a packet of gas relief. "Now pick somewhere. I'm starving."

"You're always prepared."

Scoffing, "I can't believe he asked *you* to pick up the condoms."

Shrugging my shoulders, "I don't mind. If he had a slew of them already on hand I'd be more concerned."

"True. And it's not just a man's world anymore."

"Exactly. And we need to find a sex toy shop. I want cuffs!"

"Oh, Jesus. Ok!"

We stopped for fast food and got back on the road. Music blaring, *Under the Influence* by Elle King playing, we both sang along. Tami dramatically pointed at me during several parts of the song. We listened to it a few times before we let the next song in my playlist come on.

We were over half way there when Tami asked, "So, still no emotions?"

My eyes got big as I responded, "What do you mean?"

"You both agreed to no emotions. How's that working out?"

I decided to tell her about the things he'd said the last couple days. "He told me he missed me when I saw him and that he loved my eyes the other day. Over and over. He said no falling, his rules."

"He's falling."

I just shook my head because if he was, it wasn't how she thought it was—or how I was, though I still denied it. "I can't even process that right now, Tami."

"Damn." She huffed, "But, Dude, NO! You can have *some* emotions but no, no, no, no deep shit. Intense and fun, nothing else!"

"We clearly have a connection. Right now I'm fine with it being strictly sexual. I'm happier than I've been in a long time. I have an outlet."

"But?"

"But if he falls, I'm done for."

"I know you are. That's why I'm worried. Y'all are already teetering. He needs to reel it back in."

"I'm just saying, the odds of me finding this kind of thing again, someone who makes me feel the way I do when I'm around him...I mean, my own husband has never made me feel like this. Even if it is just carnal...I can't expect to find it again. Can I?" She didn't speak as I glanced out the window at the scenery passing by. I whispered not even sure she could hear me, "And that's what scares me most."

I was quiet for a few minutes, the silence uneasy. I wasn't sure who needed to reel it back in, we probably both needed to.

I replied without looking at her, "He's killing me...slowly."

"And not with his song either."

Laughing, I confessed, "I'm not really sure what to expect tonight." She narrowed her eyes at me. Clarifying, "I mean, I *know* what to expect. I just, it's all night."

"And the problem...?"

I laughed. "I don't know." I shifted in my seat and grimaced, "Shit."

She knew why I grimaced, I'd shown her my ass. "I don't want to hear it. Stupid whore."

I snickered. She meant it in the nicest way. She, too, was a submissive, but hadn't been in a fulfilling relationship in a long time. "You should put yourself back out there."

She shook her head. "I don't know. I'm content right now. I'll just live vicariously through you."

"I love you, Tami."

"I know. Love you, too." She was playing on her phone and said, "Next exit has a toy shop."

"Perfect!"

CHAPTER
Twenty

I FEEL A SIN COMIN' ON

W<small>E WALKED INTO THE SHOP, BOTH</small> making inappropriate remarks and laughing.

"Can I help you?" The kid behind the counter didn't look old enough to drink, let alone be able to help two grown ass women pick out sex toys.

"Restraints, cuffs?" He pointed to the other end of the store. As Tami headed that way I said, while pointing to Tami, "Bitch is getting tied up tonight. Whether she likes it or not!"

The clerk blushed and turned to the door as a couple walked in.

Tami was beet red and chided me, "I'm going to choke you."

"Well, just promise you'll stop when I start turning blue."

"Goddammit, Meredith!" I was nearly bent over with laughter.

We found the wall and the selection was pathetic. There was only one kit that caught my eye. They were white silk lined wrist and ankle cuffs. White wasn't my first choice, but they'd do the job. Pulling them off the wall, I examined them more closely.

"Yup. These should do."

"Anything else Madame?" Smiling at Tami, I shook my head.

We checked out and got back in my car. Hitting a liquor store, we picked up a few more items. I got myself some wine coolers, a bottle of bourbon and coke for Gregor, and Tami got a couple bottles of wine.

Standing in line at the hotel, several couples wandered around and I couldn't help but wonder about their individual situations. The deeper into the lifestyle I dove, the more I wondered about the secret desires of those around me and the more I understood. How many of my friends, family, coworkers, acquaintances had secret affairs and longings that no one knew about? The man smiling at his phone in line at the grocery store; was he smiling at a text from a secret lover or from his wife? The possibilities were endless, just like my imagination. The problem was that everyone had an opinion and believed theirs was the only opinion that mattered.

"Meredith!"

Tami elbowed me and I realized the hotel clerk was waiting for me. "Sorry." I pulled out my ID and credit card and handed it over.

Once we had our keys, we headed to the elevator.

"What were you thinking about back there?"

Alone in the elevator, I told her. "Just wondering how many of the couples that we saw downstairs are really having affairs."

Her mouth almost fell open as she thought about it. "You're one twisted bitch."

Shrugging my shoulders, "Well, I mean. Come on. You know I'm right."

"No, you are. I just. Yeah."

"I'm not saying it's my business, I just. This whole thing has really opened my eyes to so many possibilities. People deserve to be happy without the judgement from everyone else."

The elevator opened up to our floor and we walked the hall to our room. Upon approval, we started getting settled into the room when my email pinged.

"Whore!" Tami then laughed as I sat down and eagerly opened my email on my phone.

TO: meredith@meredithedits.com
8:23 PM
Subject: Re: Leaving
Make it to the hotel...?

"He's seeing if we made it yet."

She rolled her eyes. "Aww, how sweet." I smiled at her and she spit out, "Fuck you and your no emotions."

"He's just checking on me."

"Yup. Clearly displaying he doesn't care."

"Stop over-analyzing everything, Tami. That's my job!"

"No shit!"

> *TO: bruisedassets@yahoo.com*
> *8:26 PM*
> *Subject: Re: Leaving*
> *Yes. Just got in. Made a few stops.*
> *Condoms: check*
> *Restraints: check*
> *Bourbon: check*
> *Hopping in the shower soon. You ready?!*

I set my phone down and started organizing my things. Dumping my shower stuff in the bath, I picked out my clothes and Tami was digging in the cooler. My phone chimed.

> *TO: meredith@meredithedits.com*
> *8:35 PM*
> *Subject: Re: Leaving*
> *I have well over two hours to go. Keep that pussy well lubricated...*

"Jesus Christ..."

Tami glared at me, "Shut your whore mouth. I don't want to know what that filthy man had to say." I started belly laughing. "Wait, yes I do. Tell me!" I told her and she fell back on the bed. "Lucky bitch!"

> TO: bruisedassets@yahoo.com
> 8:39 PM
> Subject: Re: Leaving
> *Throbbing and wet all day...*
> *Just thinking about last night makes me tremble...*
> *Getting in shower.*

I put my phone down and Tami put a song on from her phone.

As the words hit me, I shook my head at her. "Bitch."

"Well, if the shoe, collar, restraint fits..."

I started laughing as we danced around the room to *I Feel A Sin Comin' On* by Pistol Annies. We decided to take a picture of all my goodies. Laying out my bra and panties, the flogger, and the restraints, I took the picture and sent it to him. I didn't type any message, just sent the pic.

"Ok. I have to get ready." Grabbing my clothes, I scurried to the bathroom and turned on the shower.

Climbing in the water, I let the warmth run over me. My heart was already racing. A few calming breaths and I was a bit more relaxed. I washed my hair and then took my time shaving, making sure to leave no unwanted hair. After, I applied my shower scrub which left my skin extra silky. Washing my face was the last thing I did before stepping out. Drying off, I double checked my shave job and then applied lotion all over my body.

Stepping into the nude and black satin panties, I then clasped the matching bra on to my body. Looking at myself in the mirror, I was more confident than I had been in a long time. The scar here and a sag there no longer bothered me. At least not when I was with Gregor. I wondered why I responded to him the way I did.

His touch could do what no one else's ever had. It sent me hurtling over the edge into a euphoric state that even my dreams couldn't match. When I looked in the mirror I saw someone new, someone coming to bloom in her own. There was a renewed excitement in my eyes that had been gone a long time. The hardest part was finding the balance between home and work life and my stolen moments of submissiveness with my Sir.

Tracing my hands over where his had been and would soon be again, I was trying to seek the same sensations he'd created. It was impossible. I couldn't get over how potent his touch was. He made me feel again; every nerve came alive under his gaze, under his touch. It had all started with the mental connection we formed and getting to know one another intellectually before we physically discovered each other. Because I had let Gregor walk around inside my head, he knew my mind, therefore he knew what my body needed. At least that's how I explained it all to myself.

Slipping on my maxi skirt, I stepped out of the bathroom. Tami was reading in bed and whistled at me walking about the room in just my bra and skirt. Ignoring her, I grabbed my phone. No email or text from him yet. I pulled on a thin sweater and did a spin for Tami.

"You should slut it up more."

Smiling, "Well, I thought about it, but I didn't want to leave one hotel and walk into another looking like a call girl."

"True."

"I'll slut it up when I get to him." Ducking, the pillow she threw bounced off the wall and landed at my feet. I threw it back and rushed into the bathroom to do my hair and makeup.

"Whore!"

Calling back, "I know, I know!"

I began the tedious process of drying and then straightening my hair before tending to my makeup. I didn't wear a lot, just playing up my eyes. The deep eyes he loved to admire. When I was happy with the result, I looked at the time. I had at least thirty minutes to go. I repacked my shower stuff and got the rest of my things together.

Sitting on the bed, Tami and I stared at one another.

"Why am I so nervous?"

"Because you like him."

"Shut the hell up."

"You shut up. You're hot. You've already done this with him. No need to be nervous."

Sighing, I knew she was right. "I know. Agh! I hate waiting."

"Impatient much?"

"Yes!"

We sat there a bit longer. I was constantly refreshing my email when a new one finally popped up. He was responding to the email with the picture.

> TO: meredith@meredithedits.com
> 10:12 PM
> Subject: Re: Mmmm
> I'm 15 minutes from hotel.

> TO: bruisedassets@yahoo.com
> 10:14 PM
> Subject: Re: Mmmm
> Should I head on out or wait for word.

I sat and waited. I was growing nervous.

"Relax."

"I'm trying!"

PING!

> **TO: meredith@meredithedits.com**
> **10:25 PM**
> **Subject: Re: Mmmm**
> *Head on down. Room 410. Push the door open and make yourself at home. I will probably be in the shower when you arrive.*

"It's go time!"

She hugged me and told me to text her when I got there. I gave her the hotel information and the room number. Grabbing my bags, grinning from ear to ear, I made the walk to my car. It was quite possibly the longest walk in history, like that last walk for a prisoner on death row. Except I wasn't headed to my death, not that I knew of. Giggling, I knew Gregor wouldn't kill me, not intentionally. Maybe metaphorically, but not physically.

Getting in my car, I checked my email one more time before heading out of the lot. I missed the entrance to the freeway, but my GPS was on top of it. It was probably going to take me longer than needed, but I tried to remain calm. Though, I got stopped at almost every stoplight and groaned every time.

"Mother fuck! Turn green!"

Fifteen minutes later, I pulled up to his hotel. I spotted his truck immediately and almost parked next to him, but decided against it. Putting my car in park, I texted Tami to let her know I'd arrived. Looking in the mirror one last time, I approved of my appearance. Refreshing my email, nothing new had arrived. Getting out of my car, I grabbed my bag and my purse and headed toward the entrance.

I was so paranoid the front desk attendant would stop me and scold me. Then I realized I didn't look suspicious and I needed to relax. Strolling past the front desk, I headed toward the elevators. They were empty and I hit '4'.

His room was by the elevator and I almost passed it by. Taking a deep breath, I pushed open the door. Almost complete darkness greeted me. The TV was on, but no lights. The sound of the shower to my right filled my ears as I heard the water and the sounds of it hitting his body. I caught the door before it slammed shut and turned the lock upon its closure.

I walked further into the hotel room, relief filling me at finally being there with him. I set my things down and laid out our drinks. He did in fact have a fridge and I placed our drinks inside. I slowly wandered the room, almost feeling like a trespasser. There was a good sized living area with a couch and immediately I envisioned myself sprawled across his lap as he spanked me.

Shaking the thought away, I grabbed my bag and began unpacking. Placing the condoms, lube, massage oil, and restraints on the desk. I left the flogger in my bag. Then I panicked for a second and wondered if he'd expect me kneeling when he exited the shower. Remembering his email telling me to 'make yourself at home' I knew had he wanted something else he would've stated so.

That's when my eyes drifted to the king-size bed and lingered there. On display at the end of the bed were a few different paddles including the small one from the day we met and the 'significant damage' paddle. His belt was also on display. My mouth opened and my breath caught at the sight of it all, turning me on immensely.

I walked over to them and let my fingers trace over their different textures. Wooden paddles of all different thickness and shape and his leather belt. Everything was spaced out to perfection, except for one vacant spot. Why was there a vacant spot?

The flogger!

Rushing back to my bag, I pulled it out I placed it on the bed where he'd left a space for it. Standing back, I took in the sight once more. I had a fleeting thought to take a picture, but decided against it. *I should've taken the damn picture.* That image would always be firmly embossed on me.

The flogger was still what captured my attention and I couldn't resist picking it up, its weight still surprising me. I let my fingers tangle in its tassels, a chill running up my spine in response. Lifting the tassels to my nose, I inhaled deeply. Placing the flogger back down on the bed, I stepped away from it.

I leaned against the wall and waited for him to exit the shower. Remembering I hadn't silenced my phone, I did that before setting it back down on the desk. The water was still running so I turned my eyes to the television. Some movie I hadn't seen, but it was clearly a suspense movie. Not sure how long I'd want that on. It didn't necessarily set the mood.

I started pacing. His suitcase met my eyes as I spotted it tucked away in the corner. I ignored it and walked to the window. His room overlooked the parking lot and our vehicles. The water stopped. Turning, I quickly walked back to where I'd been standing, between the bathroom and the bed.

A few minutes later he walked out in a t-shirt and a towel around his waist. My arms were crossed as he made a beeline for me. I could clearly see the outline of his dick through the towel. He was happy to see me.

Hands on my hips, he pulled me close. "How was the drive?" He kissed me.

"Good. You?" I kissed him back, my hands wrapping around his biceps.

"Long." He kissed me again and then murmured, "You smell good."

Kissing him back, a smile on my lips, I thanked him. Slow sweet kisses were exchanged as his hands roamed my hips and ass. My panties were soaked and I could feel his cock bob against me. When it started to get heated, he pulled his lips from mine.

"Did you get ice?"

I was an idiot. "No, I can go get some." We walked toward the fridge and I grabbed the ice bucket. Before I left the room, I informed him, "Flogger's on the bed."

Smiling, his eyes moved to the bed. I left the room and headed to the ice machine. When I returned, having forgotten to leave it cracked, I knocked softly. Opening the door, he let me in and I locked it once I walked in, putting the ice back by the fridge. I got out my wine cooler and he poured himself a bourbon and coke.

Taking a sip of his drink, he then kissed me. I'd never had it myself and knew I'd made yet another new discovery. Holy hell. He tasted good with bourbon on his lips. He caught on immediately and teased me.

"Like the taste of that do you?"

Setting my own bottle down, I admitted, "Yes." I pulled his mouth back to mine and licked his lips and tongue until the flavor of the bourbon was gone.

He took another sip, set the glass down on the nightstand and tugged me to him. We quickly became frenzied. His hands yanked my skirt down my hips and then his hands pushed under my sweater, burning everything they touched. Looking down, that fucking towel was still secure around his waist. Like he knew what I was about to do, he handed me my bottle and motioned me to the bed.

"Get up there."

CHAPTER
Twenty-One

DESIRE

H E SAT DOWN AT THE HEAD OF the bed as I walked around and climbed in next to him. Did he want to watch the movie? I wasn't sure. Sitting next to him, he pulled me to him. His full lips teased my own as his hand brushed my cheek and stroked down my neck. He didn't want to watch the movie. Thank God!

We had all night, but everything started happening so quickly. My sweater was yanked off my body as his hands and mouth began exploring every part of me. Yes, this is what I'd been craving. Hours together to let the desire consume us, giving us time to explore.

The movie started getting loud and violent. Grabbing the remote he said, "Not quite setting the tone. Do you want to put your music on?"

I smiled and got up to get my phone off the desk as he muted the television, leaving it on as its light cast shadows over our bodies.

"I know you probably aren't a fan of most of my stuff, but, well..."

"You mentioned a particular song that made you think naughty thoughts."

Pressing my lips together, I nodded. I knew exactly what song he was referring to. Pulling up my 'Gregor' playlist, I scrolled through and found *Desire* by Meg

Myers.

"It's naughty." The strong thrums of the piano immediately soaked into me. I loved this song.

"Good. Now get back here."

On our knees facing each other, we began again. He was listening to the words of the song and smiled sardonically at me.

"This song *is* dirty."

"Told you it was naughty."

"You're my dirty little slut."

"Yes, Sir, I am."

One thing was clear. Gregor had the key that unlocked rooms to my soul I didn't know existed. Now that I'd found those rooms, all I wanted to do was stay and explore every nook and cranny with him. I knew I was a fool to think one night like this would be enough to explore said rooms.

Leaning over him as he lay on his back, he unclasped my bra. Molding both my breasts—one with his mouth, the other with his hand—became his next mission. Rolling me to my back, he worked his way lower once my breasts had both been marked by his mouth. Burying his face between my legs, I moaned like a whore. I lifted my hips in response to his fingers on the waistband of my panties as he yanked them off. Lifting my head, our eyes met as he stuffed my panties in my mouth.

Falling back, my moans were subdued by the material now in my mouth. I started to protest when I felt the absence of his body, but he returned to me just as quick. Dragging the flogger up my body, he placed the handle between my breasts once the tassels covered my face. My sight was obscured and the smell of fresh leather and my own arousal overtook me.

He started to devour me like never before. I couldn't stop my body from thrashing. He was just too good at this. The sound of two of the paddles hitting each other and then the floor stilled me. *Oh, shit.*

He placed them back on the bed and scolded me. "If it happens again, you'll be punished. Understood?" I nodded and then he returned to his task, my pussy. "Do you want to come?"

Panties still in my mouth, I moaned my response.

"Too bad. Not yet."

I groaned and swore I heard him chuckle. He was fucking evil and I loved it.

Removing the flogger from my chest and pulling my panties from my mouth, he rolled me over. His hand came down hard on my ass. My fingers clutched the sheets above my head as I lifted my hips, seeking out another smack.

His hands grabbed my hips and yanked me to my knees. "Get that ass over here." He smacked me again as he gave his order. "Don't. Move."

Panting, I obeyed. "Yes, Sir."

The paddle came down on my ass, the 'significant damage' one. He only smacked me with it a few times before his teeth were biting at my marks, his marks. His breath moved lower as he tongued my clit and then moved to my anus.

"Oh, God."

His thumb pressed down on my clit and remained there, unmoving. He did this often and it was sweet torture. My clit would begin pulsing quicker and quicker and I knew he felt it respond to his touch. I squirmed and his other hand immediately smacked my ass.

"I told you to hold still."

"Sorry, Sir."

I was sure my knuckles were white from gripping the sheets, but I didn't dare look. Removing his hands from my body, I heard the tear of a wrapper. Slowly, he slid into my pussy as well as sliding a finger into my already lubricated ass. My chest was heaving against the bed as he continued sliding in and out of me, slowly picking up his pace.

This agony went on for several minutes. A few songs had already started and ended and I knew I'd never listen to them the same way again. Pulling on my hair, he raised me up to my knees, my back flush against his chest. His strong arms encased me as he fucked me with a renewed ferocity.

Held prisoner by him, unable to move, I surrendered to him. Dropping my head back against his shoulder, I knew he had me. When his fingers touched my clit I about jumped out of his arms, but he held strong.

"Please, Sir..."

Lips and teeth moved over my neck, just making it that much more intense. "No."

The sound of his body slapping against mine, his breath on my neck, his utter possession of my being and my soul had me totally spellbound. My thighs ached and trembled as I concentrated on the feel of him, arms holding me, and I didn't want him to ever let go.

The fullness of his presence inside me vanished and then the desertion of his arms left me shaking. Then the familiar sound of his voice penetrated my ears.

"Up on all fours."

Placing my hands on the bed, I assumed the position. My thighs screamed at me and my arms shook. Strands of material drifted over my back, tickling my flesh, as my neck tilted in response. It only took a moment to realize it was the flogger. His free hand moved over my back, like he knew I needed him to calm me. It didn't take long for the shaking to subside. His hand then left me and the flogger followed.

Silence. Besides the music, I was lost in absolute stillness. I concentrated on my breathing and then it began.

The sound of the flogger flying through the air was the next thing I heard. The smell of leather infiltrated my senses before it hit my skin. My body trembled in anticipation. The first strike came down and I smiled as my head instantly became lightheaded. Tension rolled off me in waves with every blow. He teased me with it, unleashed fury with it, and when he was done I yearned for more. I could feel the tingles from my thighs to my shoulder blades and everywhere in between.

I was panting when he finished. Pulling on my hair, he whispered my silent confession in my ear, "I knew you'd fall in love with the flogger."

And he was right. I decided then and there that I was willing to be flogged every day for the rest of my life if it brought that kind of euphoric feeling to me. The question was if it was the tool, the wielder, or the combination of the two? And that was a question I didn't care to answer.

"Roll over."

I did as he instructed while he knelt on the floor between my legs. My right leg wrapped around his side as he pulled my hips to the edge of the bed. He began kissing and sucking on my inner thigh, my back arching in response. His fingers slid into me once again as he slowly moved them inside me.

"Gregor..." It was barely a whisper as I was near tears. My need for him was overwhelming, almost unbearable.

Lifting my left leg, he removed his fingers from me to slap my ass swiftly. My hips lifted higher, seeking him out. My left foot found his propped up thigh and mounted it there as his fingers entered me again and this time his mouth joined the exploit.

His other hand reached up and squeezed my breasts before moving back down to my sore ass. Squeezing my marks, his tongue and fingers did what they did best. I was fighting to hold back, the palms of my hands pressing into my eyes.

"You want to come for me?"

"Yes, Sir... Please."

"Permission granted. Come for me."

The demands of my Sir were like a song, a melody, and only my soul could sing along. And that deep velvet voice of his was the sweetest song I'd ever heard. I wondered which of us was the song, whom was the instrument, and who played whom better? I smiled at the thought and then pushed it away.

Never would I have believed that I could hold back an orgasm until instructed to let it go. I was now a believer, only partially convinced the first time he'd done it in Casper. But don't get me wrong. I didn't come the second he granted permission, but I was pretty damn close. And I loved that he had that power over me. Or loved that I was able to give him that power, knowing he'd reward me.

Knowing I could now let go, I did just that. But not immediately. I had to savor it, too. I let my body move against his face and hand, seeking the greatest pleasure I could from it. Watching him was what did it. Lifting my eyes, I saw the sweat trickling over his forehead as he ate me. His eyes met mine and nearly undid me. His hand found mine as our fingers intertwined. My free hand took the place where his had been, pushing down just above my pubic bone.

"Sir!"

He knew I was there. Pushing my hips against him harder, his fingers became more precise, his tongue even more diligent, our clasped hands squeezed tightly, and then I threw my head back and let my body take over. It was one of the longest orgasms I think I'd ever had. It wouldn't stop and neither did he. Not until I was completely limp, panting, nearly crying, yet smiling.

Once he separated himself from me, he leaned over my face and kissed me. Then he walked to the bathroom and I didn't take my eyes off his ass until it vanished behind the door. I looked to the clock and just over an hour had passed by. *Jesus! Only an hour! We still had plenty of time.*

Sitting up, my throat was parched. Walking on very shaky legs, I moved to the nightstand where my drink sat. I took a long swig and waited for him to return. When he did, I headed to the bathroom. When I climbed back in the bed, he was sprawled out in the middle of it.

Arms open, I laid my head on his shoulder as he stroked my face and kissed me. I draped my leg over his hip and cozied up to him. Letting our hands roam, we kissed slowly, taking our time exploring one another. It still surprised me how quickly my body began responding to him again. But he didn't rush things.

I enjoyed touching him in ways I hadn't been able to up until that night. We had time and privacy and nothing but desire to quench our thirst. Turning toward me, he wedged his thigh between mine. My breath caught as his lips trailed my neck and I pressed myself against his thigh. Moaning, I nibbled on his skin and felt his dick jump in response.

Letting my hand roam, I teased him with my fingers. Tracing them up and down his shaft, over his balls, and on the sensitive skin of his thighs. His eyes were closed, but his lips smiled in response. When I circled my hand around him, he gently pushed my head away from his mouth. I knew what he wanted and I was eager to give it to him. But, that didn't mean I wasn't going to tease him on my way there.

Climbing on top of him, I pressed my chest against his as I kissed his neck and began moving lower. Finding his nipple, I teased it with my tongue as I felt his hips flex upward.

Taunting him, I moved my mouth back up to his ear and asked, "What something, Sir?"

"You know what I want. Suck my cock."

Smiling, I replied sweetly, "Yes, Sir."

Moving quicker than before, I trailed kisses down his solid chest and abs. His dick jumped in response to my breath blowing over him. Licking him from root to tip, I cupped his balls while doing so. I took my time and enjoyed every second of pleasuring him. His moans grew louder the deeper I took him and the closer he got. I loved hearing him respond to my touch.

His hands pulled my hair out of the way so that he could see me. Raising my eyes to his, he fucked my mouth and then lowered his head back to the pillow as his release took him over. Hands still in my hair, I sucked every last sweet drop from him, swallowing it down. When I was done licking him clean he pulled my mouth up to his.

My hair was a wreck and as we both tried getting it out of our faces I offered,

"I can put it up."

He shook his head, "No, I like it down."

He stroked my face as he said it, tucking my hair behind my ears. I smiled at his words as he in turn smiled once more before kissing me. Leaning over him, I let his tongue explore my mouth as my body ached for him, my moans betraying me. I didn't want to be greedy, but I was eager for more.

I was on my knees next to him when his fingers pressed into me. My legs clenched and my lips stopped moving against his. Gripping the back of my head, he kissed me deeper, that tongue of his fucking my mouth so I had no choice but to kiss him back.

Whimpering, my hips started rocking against his hand as he swallowed my cries. Fingers dug into his chest and shoulder as my arms used him for support. He removed his hand and slapped my ass before his hand resumed manipulating my clit.

"You ready to come again?"

How did he do that? When I didn't respond—still grinding against his hand—he pulled back and studied my face. I tried to play it cool, but his smile ruined it for me. The blush crept up my cheeks as I nodded. I couldn't hide what I wanted, what I felt, what I needed from him. Especially not when I was in his arms.

"Get up here." He rolled to his back and I wasn't quite sure what he was asking. "Pussy. Face. Now!"

"Oh, Jesus."

Tilting his head, he asked, "What was that?"

Holding my laughter, but smiling, I replied, "Yes, Sir."

"That's right. Now fuck my face like a good little slut."

CHAPTER
Twenty-Two

TOGETHER

I'D FANTASIZED ABOUT THIS VERY thing. Todd never let me do it so it was something I wanted that much more. Gregor was clearly game. Sprawled on his back, I placed a knee on each side of his head. Grabbing my hips, he pulled me down to his mouth. I was tense and he knew it.

Slapping my ass, he ordered, "I said to fuck my face."

Smiling, I blushed and began moving my hips. Why was there no goddamned headboard to hold onto? With one hand on the wall and the other grabbing his hair, I sought a deeper connection. His hand was groping my ass as his other spread me further apart.

"Oh, God."

It didn't take long for me to get lost in the sensations. After several minutes, my thighs were quivering and I couldn't take much more, but I wasn't ready to come either.

"I want your cock, Sir."

Looking up at me, he just shook his head, denying my request. He became more aggressive with his mouth and I nearly bucked off his face. Growling, he pulled me back down. Leaning back, I braced my hands on his thighs. He must have sensed me losing control because he lifted his legs and braced his thighs against my shoulders. It was the support I needed as I continued to grind into his face.

"Oh, yes. Right there."

My chest was heaving, hell, my whole body was. Searching, my hand found his erection and stroked him. I wanted to ride him and the very thought of it sent me over the edge. It wasn't as intense of an orgasm, but it definitely was one, one that left you feeling good, but needing more.

I trembled against his mouth, catching my breath before climbing down. But I didn't remove myself from his body, just moved lower. Kissing his lips, I enjoyed tasting myself on him. Wedging his dick between us, I wiggled against him.

"Someone wants more."

"Yes, please. I want to ride you, Sir."

Smiling, he held my face as he kissed me deeper. Then pulling his mouth from mine he whispered, "Get a condom." Smiling, I did as instructed and rolled the condom down his length.

Straddling him once more, he slid right in and sent shivers up my spine as he did. I had to kiss him and lowered my mouth to his. The sensual beat of *Together* by The xx began playing as my body felt every note inside me, like a possession. Gregor's hands were strong and they reminded every part of me, which he could reach, with their tight hold. Around my hips, over my ass, up my back, down my arms...his hands claimed me.

Looking down at him, in between kisses, I asked what I knew would never come to be. "How will I ever get enough of you?"

Grinning, and running his hands over my breasts, he thrust up into me harder and growled, "I'm here now. Take everything you can."

I think my breath left me because his kiss revived me. Then I said what I wasn't sure I should've said, before I thought about what I was actually confessing. I panicked briefly by the look that flashed in his eyes, but his response was perfect.

"I want to be owned by you, Sir."

Clasping his hands with mine, he stole another part of me when he declared, "Tonight, I do own you. You're mine."

In that moment, things changed for me. I didn't know it then, but I know it now. It was that moment, with that song playing, hands clasped, as were our bodies; 'I do own you. You're mine.' Those tiny phrases ripped into me and seared themselves onto my soul. And the collar—though invisible—was then clasped tight around my neck.

I know that what he meant with his words was just for that night, but my instinct—or the stupid girl inside me—believed that it was much more than just tonight he was referring to.

My next orgasm flooded through me with our hands still clasped, but behind my back, as he sucked and marked my breasts. Whimpering in his ear, now chest to chest, he continued to thrust up in me until I was entirely limp. My vision was almost gone. The only thing I could feel was us. Sweat covered bodies clinging to one another with nothing but trembling breaths between us.

When our hands reluctantly released one another, I circled my arms under his shoulders as he held me close. Lifting, I moaned in protest and he shushed me. All he did was sit up far enough to pull the covers over us. Still joined as one, he held me under the covers, kissing my neck and running his hands over my slackened body.

We didn't sleep, but lay that way as several songs serenaded us. Soft, slow kisses were exchanged while lazy hands twirled over each other's bodies as if knowing we were both deprived of this kind of intimacy. It was intimacy that you only read about or saw in the movies. Now I knew that in order to write something so moving, someone had to first be moved.

Kissing my forehead, he peeled our bodies apart and climbed out of bed. I quickly checked my phone and there were no missed calls or texts. Again, we traded spots in the bathroom and when I returned to the bedroom he was face down in the middle of the bed.

Unable to resist, I smacked his ass and watched the smile spread across his face.

Leaning down, I softly asked, "Ready for that massage, Sir?"

He nodded.

Grabbing my massage oils, I straddled his back and got to work. As my hands dug into the flesh of his neck and shoulders, I could feel him sink further into the mattress. We talked and talked some more as I rubbed him down from neck to feet and back up again.

"Want me to do your front?" I knew he caught the innuendo in my voice and rolled over to his back.

"Yes." His eyes scanned my body that was now covered with a skimpy nightie.

I started with his hand and worked my way up his arm, then moved to his other side and repeated my task. Straddling him, I felt his dick grow larger as I pretended to ignore it. Rubbing his chest, I worked my way lower, moving to straddle his thighs. His erection ever present, I massaged his thighs before devoting my attention to his cock.

Sucking his balls into my mouth, I was pleased with his reaction. Soft growls of approval came from deep within him as I dropped kisses along his shaft before taking him in my mouth. It wasn't long before he let go and spilled down my throat. What I loved about him was he enjoyed the torture I bestowed upon him. Licking, sucking, and stroking to my heart's content, working every last drop out of him.

Pulling me up his body and then kissing me feverishly, he asked if I was ready for more.

"Yes, Sir."

"What do want? The choice is yours. Paddle, belt, flogger..." Staring at him, I was momentarily taken aback that I got to choose. Arching a brow, he smirked, "Better hurry. You don't want me to pick."

"Flogger!"

"Thought so." Kissing me, he then moved off the bed. "Get on your stomach."

The flogger whistled through the air before landing on my back, then my ass, and my thighs were next. I felt the bed dip as he climbed over me. The tails began tickling my shoulders as I shuddered in response. The kisses he trailed down my back were just as potent as the flogger slapping against me. I needed them both equally. I loved handing control over to him, knowing he wouldn't disappoint.

Feeling him move to the end of the bed, he asserted his demand. "Get on all fours."

I assumed the position, ass in the air, back perched like a tabletop, eyes closed, and head relaxed. He spread my legs further apart as excitement filled me once more. The flogging continued, but it wasn't long before another tear of a condom occurred.

Collapsing on the bed, he kissed my shoulders and my cheek as we caught our breath. It was nearly five in the morning. Music still filled the room, along with the sordid secrets our bodies had told one another.

A while later, after having to pry myself from his arms, I had whispered, "I'll be right back," and he hesitantly released me.

Upon climbing back in bed, his hands were immediately on me, pulling me close. He wrapped his arms around me like I was the most precious thing to him. His breath on my neck, a leg tangled between mine, his fingers knotted with mine, and I felt him drift off to sleep. His warmth surrounded me, seeped in, and burrowed itself in my bones. And I realized I'd been cold for far too long.

Then I wondered who needed whom more in that moment. Did he need someone to hold onto as much as I needed to be held? The answer was simple and complicated. A man like Gregor didn't hold onto something or someone he didn't want, didn't need. And I wasn't someone who'd let just anyone hold me. We needed each other equally.

Several more times he brought me to orgasm and a couple of times I was on the brink of tears from the sheer power of it all. He tapped into pent up emotions and desires I was still trying to comprehend. He came four times that night. Even in my twenties I never met a man who could do that. Whatever he had, they should bottle it and sell it. It'd make a fortune on the black market.

The passion that consumed us that fateful night was the last thing I expected. For the short couple of hours that we tried to sleep, we were entwined in one another, unable to stop touching each other, stop pleasuring each other. He stroked and kissed every inch of my face and I in turn did the same. The intimacy was unexpected, but everything I needed. Someone was one hundred percent in the moment and into me.

In the morning, after taking me again, he sang *I'm on Fire* to me as I sucked him off once more. Lord have mercy, I may have come unhinged, though I tried to conceal it. His voice was velvet and gravel rolled into one. It was dirty and sexy listening to him sing that song as I did what I did to him. I mean, how many times had that blasted song come on when I was reading an email from him or typing my response? And I'd told him as much. I knew one thing...

If he's the Devil, I'm his advocate.

We lay around like an ordinary couple, knowing we were anything but. He was propped up against the headboard checking work email on his phone. Laying perpendicular, my head was on his chest as we talked and laughed.

Looking down at me as his fingers swept idly across his phone, he apologized. "Sorry. Some things at work I need to handle."

"You're fine. Do what you need to."

He took care of what he needed to and then sat in front of me. Legs around his waist, I began massaging his neck, shoulders, and back. My music had been turned off as we started talking about some of his musical likes. Putting music on from his phone, he started singing along. I wasn't familiar with the song, but that didn't matter. He had my full attention. I could listen to him sing all day...and night.

The morning was slipping away from us and I knew it'd be over soon. He called the front desk to confirm his checkout time. Once he was off the phone, he pulled some protein bars from his bag and handed me one. We sat a while longer, still touching, talking, and laughing.

"Shower with me."

Heading to the shower, we bathed under the warm water, kissing and stroking one another. This was it. He had to leave once we were dressed and so did I. Holding me close, his hands drifted over my slick body as I did the same. He was aroused so lowering myself, I took his release from him there on my knees as the water fell upon us.

When I was done, he helped me to my feet and we shared a long and passionate kiss. It was a kiss where our lips whispered silent goodbyes to one another. I was deliciously happy and already aching to be with him again. Once we were cleaned, he turned the water off and handed me a towel before wrapping another around his waist.

We got dressed as we shared smiles across the room, smiles of adoration. Packing our bags, we double checked that we had everything.

"Ready?"

NO! I nodded and softly said, "Yes. I'm ready."

Walking to the elevator, maid service smiled at us as the woman inquired to our stay. I couldn't help but wonder if she'd heard the morning flogging and cries of ecstasy that had come from our room earlier.

"Did you have a nice stay?" She smiled brightly at us as I nodded.

"We did. Thank you." His eyes met mine discreetly as I pressed my lips together, trying to contain my amusement.

Stepping into the elevator, the doors closed and I let the laugh fall from my lips. He smiled knowingly as the heat in my body was reflected in my face. He walked me to my car and hugged me. Kissing me quickly, he wished me a good weekend.

"Be good tonight and this weekend. I'll talk to you soon."

"Will do. Thank you. I had a great time."

"Me too. You know how to get back to your hotel?"

"Yes. I'll be fine."

"Ok."

Slapping my ass, I climbed into my car after placing my bags in the back seat and watched as he made his way to his truck. Plugging in my phone, I turned it off silent and texted Tami to let her know I was on my way. She replied back right away asking for coffee and I was happy to oblige.

When I looked back up, his truck was gone. Pulling up my email, I wanted to send him my customary 'thank you' message. I was too late. My phone *pinged* and there a new email from him awaited.

> *TO: meredith@meredithedits.com*
> *12:07 PM*
> *Subject: Re: Mmmm*
> *Are you glowing...?*

> *TO: bruisedassets@yahoo.com*
> *12:09 PM*
> *Subject: Sigh*
> *Music from last night playing...*
> *I'll never listen to them the same way again...*
> *I'm still in awe at how my body responds to your words, touch, look...*
> *Until next time the reels will play over and over.*
> *So, yes. I'm glowing.*

I didn't hear back from him and that was ok. I knew he had a busy day ahead of him and so did I. Listening to music, mostly from the night before, I started to become emotional. It was hard to focus as the songs filled me with memories. His touch, his voice, his eyes... Making it hard to breathe and my body felt weighed down by it all. I put it off as pure exhaustion hitting me. We'd only slept a few short hours and for me, it was restless. With all the playing and fucking, it was perfectly normal for me to feel whipped. Pun intended.

Stopping for coffee and a few other things, I made it back to my hotel. The closer and closer I got to my hotel room, and to Tami, the more my emotions inched to the surface. It was like a war began inside of me. I felt irrational at being emotional.

Walking in the door, I set down the coffee and my bags, avoiding eye contact with her. I could feel her quietly observing me, waiting patiently.

Finally, she asked, "Well, how was it?" Looking to her, my eyes betrayed me. Her expression quickly changed from delight to concern. "Meredith, what happened? Are you ok?"

"No, I'm fine. It was amazing." I was well aware of my voice cracking.

She placed the palm of each hand on both sides of her forehead and glared at me. "Jesus Christ. What did you do?"

Shaking my head to clear the tears that were about to spill, I knew where she was going with this and I denied it. "I didn't do anything."

"Yes you did. You fell."

It was like a punch to the gut. What the hell was she talking about? "What! I did not."

CHAPTER
Twenty-Three

RESCUE MY HEART

"**Y**ES, YOU DID." SHE GROANED, "You're breaking the rules. No emotions, Meredith."

I was in denial and spit out, "Fuck you. I did not fall."

I sat down on the vacant bed and stared at her. And like the good friend she was, she waited. She got up and grabbed her coffee and handed me mine. Why I'd gotten myself one was beyond me. I needed to sleep, not caffeinate myself.

Looking at my hands as I played with the coffee cup, I whimpered, "It was amazing. So passionate. I wasn't expecting that." I let the tears fall without wiping them away. "I don't know what happened, I...it just." I sighed. "He's amazing."

"You've said amazing like seven times." She rolled her eyes, trying to get me to smile.

"Well, it was."

"Has he emailed?"

"Yes." Smiling, "He asked if I was glowing."

"Well, you're clearly glowing, but you just got yourself in too deep. Tell me what happened."

"I have to put on music for you to get the full gravity of it all." She understood my attachment to music, had it herself, and agreed.

I started with *Rescue My Heart* by Liz Longley, one song that had played as Gregor and I had lain face to face slowly kissing. I started recounting my night to her from the beginning. I explained in great detail the hand holding, the constant touching, the kissing, and the lack of punishment. He'd paddled me, but not like he had upon previous meetings. The night was full of pleasure and forbidden desires.

"He wouldn't let go of me, Tami. I had to plead with him to go to the bathroom and the second I returned to the bed he was on me again." We both sighed. "And I loved it. I've never felt so desired in my life."

"Definitely sounds like a very passionate night. Did you sleep?"

"He did, for a couple hours. I drifted in and out."

"He trusts you if he was able to sleep."

I laughed, "You're forgetting I was in his vice hold while he slept. Even if I wanted to snoop, I wouldn't have been able to."

"I can't believe you didn't snoop through his things. You had your chance when he was in the shower."

I shook my head. "Why? There's no need. I trust him. Maybe blindly, but I trust him. And I want him to feel the same way about me." I giggled and she pinched her brows together. "There probably wasn't anything 'personal' at my disposal anyway. His wallet and anything else, were probably in the bathroom with him or in his truck." She looked at me slightly baffled. "You don't know him like I do. He's smart and guarded. It's fine."

She shook her head. "If you're fine with it."

"There's nothing to not be fine about." I was getting annoyed because it was making me question him and I didn't want to think about him hiding anything from me. She picked up on it after my long silence.

"I'm sorry. I wasn't trying to make you doubt him. I just know that I wouldn't have had the self-control."

"It's ok. I know it's a lot to comprehend."

We sat in silence, aside from the music playing. Even after having had my coffee, I was yawning and lay back. The reels played over and over in my head. I must have dozed off. When I woke, the room was dark and Tami was gone. I found a note on the bed that said she would be back shortly. She hadn't put down a time, but I looked to the clock to see it was almost four p.m. I'd slept for a couple hours.

No email awaited me.

Going through my bags, I grabbed a change of clothes and headed to the bathroom to shower. Stripping down, I examined my ass in the mirror. The bruises from earlier in the week were changing from beautiful reds and purples to ugly greens and greys. There were a couple of faint red marks from the night before and I traced my fingers over them carefully. It sent shockwaves of remembrance through every nerve in my body. Shaking away the tremor, I turned on the water and stepped into the shower.

What I experienced with him was so much more than I ever expected and possibly more than I was prepared to deal with. As the water pelted down on me, I let the emotions from my night with Gregor run through my mind once again. The tears began to fall as I wrapped my arms around myself. My hands moved to squeeze the marks on my ass and I knew I was at a crossroads. Let go of one of them. Let go of both of them. Keep them both and pray I could find balance. And how did I do any of that and still choose myself? Getting angry with myself and my tears, I forced them to stop.

We'd made a plan and I'd agreed to that plan. The thing that tripped us up— well, tripped me up—were the unexpected emotions. Emotions will fuck up the most beautiful thing every time or make it more exquisite. I was pretty sure my emotions would fuck it up. I had to turn them off, make it stop, keep them at bay because there was no chance I was walking away from him. And if he knew about my emotions, there was a good chance he'd walk away.

It was simple. I DID NOT AND HAD NOT FALLEN. I refused to admit it. This was just for fun, a release we couldn't get elsewhere. Nothing else. The only other thing I knew for sure was this: I had no intention of walking away from him.

"Bitch! Hurry up, I need to pee."

Tami was back. Thank God because I needed the distraction! "Almost done!"

I rubbed my ass with the cream Gregor had recommended and quickly dressed. Jeans and a t-shirt, just my style. Opening the door, Tami barged in as I left the room, quickly trading spots with me. Walking about the room, we started planning our night.

"So, do you want to grab something for dinner?"

Yelling back from the bathroom, "Yes. I'm not hungry, but will be soon enough."

She washed her hands and stepped back into the room as I towel dried my hair. "You feeling better?"

Shrugging my shoulders, "The sleep helped. It is what it is. I can only take it one day at a time right now."

"Have you heard from him?"

Shaking my head, "Not since he emailed after we left. It's only been a few hours." Sighing, I said, "I want to have fun tonight. Tonight is for us! Let's get fucked up! Thank goodness we can walk to the concert."

"Yeah, we just have to make sure we don't get arrested for disorderly conduct or public intoxication."

I laughed and looked at her knowingly. She rolled her eyes at me as I laughed, "We both know it won't be me getting intoxicated."

"Shut your mouth, whore. I can hold my liquor better than you can."

"Yes. With that we can agree!"

Late that night, or early the next morning, we stumbled into our hotel room. The concert had been great and well worth the trip. Of course, Gregor made it that much better. I was definitely tipsy and Tami was drunk. We managed to get into our jammies and climbed into our separate beds.

Scrolling my phone, I huffed and Tami picked up on it. "No email?"

"No."

"Don't you fucking email him. Let him email you."

Groaning, I knew she was right. I dropped the phone next to me on the night stand and put some music on. Tami and I chatted for a bit before we both passed out. Several hours later I woke remembering his breath on my neck, hand on my hip as he slid his hand down lower. I let myself drift into the memory.

Waking warm, relaxed, and in his arms was a wonderful feeling. Realizing I must've fallen asleep, this was the best way to be woken up. Morning sex, there was nothing better. The only thing left to complete that glorious feeling was to be joined as one with him, needing him deep inside me once again. Having him so thirsty for me first thing in the morning, after fucking all night, was the best high. His urgency only increased my need.

He yanked off my nightie and then my panties, wasting no time. My release found me quickly as his hands held my hips against his face. Then grabbing a condom, he put it on and fucked me only the way he could. Sweaty and sated, he kissed me as he covered me with his body before rolling to his side and taking me with him. Nuzzling into him, his hands traveled my body as I drifted off to sleep once again.

A lone tear fell from my eye and to the pillow below my head at the memory. There was a good chance he was going to break my heart, and I was going to let him. Hell, maybe I'd break his.

Before that first spanking, I was so nervous and then it was like this switch had been flipped by Gregor. I became the brave confident girl I used to be, but with a little more edge. I would get through this. I had to.

I drifted back to sleep for a while longer, waking to the alarm on my phone. Tami groaned and threw the pillow over her head. I took that as my opening and claimed the bathroom. About an hour later we were dragging our asses to my car.

"Coffee. Food. Stat!"

Laughing, I agreed. "For sure!"

We spent the drive home much like we spent the drive out of town. Listening to music, singing along, chatting, bitching, and sharing lots of laughs. As we got closer to home, we stopped for gas and a smoke break for Tami.

Checking my phone, I set it down abruptly while we leaned against my car. Still no email and it wasn't like Todd was checking in on me either. And had he been, I probably would've been just as annoyed as I was that Gregor wasn't checking in on me. It was messed up, I know.

Flashing her cigarette at me she offered one to me. "You sure you don't want one?"

Sighing, "Fuck it. Hand me one."

Laughing, she teased, "You'll be sorry."

"Probably."

I was fucking floating on a high from that cigarette and needed a couple minutes before I felt ok to drive. The nice thing about not being a frequent smoker was still getting that nicotine high any time I indulged. I never was a fully committed smoker, never smoking more than four to five a day when I was committed. Clearly, I was quite the addict.

Ugh. Addict.

Just thinking about him had me 'jonesing'. He should've come with a warning label. Something to the effect, 'Danger, may cause addiction once consumed. Proceed with caution. You can't have just one.'

Closing my eyes I realized how much my lips craved his kiss and it'd only been a day. He'd breathed fire into me. Not life; fucking fire. The thought of him was like a spark igniting and when I was with him, I was ablaze. Now I worried about the backdraft, wondering if and when it'd blow my life apart. If it hadn't already.

We pulled into my drive. Tami didn't bother coming in and I couldn't blame her. Maybe she sensed the black cloud overhead even before I did. Climbing in her car, she waved before driving off. She put her thumb and pinky up to her head and mouthed 'call me'. I nodded. Taking a deep breath, I walked into the house.

Home.

I loved this house. Loved it the minute I walked into it the day we were looking at houses. It could've been a little bigger, but we made due. Over the years I'd slowly made it what I wanted it to be with my paint choices, décor, and everything in between.

"How was the concert?" Turning to Todd, he smiled at me half assed, but didn't move to hug me or show me that he missed me.

"Good. It was really good. Thank you."

"You and Tami have some good girl bonding?"

Laughing, "Yes. We always do."

Then I heard the trample of their feet as they ran down the stairs. "Mommy!"

Crouching down, I hugged my kids as they squeezed their little arms around me. "Were you good for Daddy?"

They all nodded with excitement as Todd confirmed that they'd been good. "That makes mommy very happy."

They followed me into the bedroom as I put my suitcase on the bed. "Hey guys, let's go outside. Give mommy a few minutes to get unpacked." Todd escorted the kids out of the room and then outside.

Once I was sure they had left, I quickly pulled my bag of goodies—flogger included—from my suitcase and hid it accordingly.

About an hour later, my phone *pinged*. Heart racing, I pulled up his email. He was responding to the one Tami didn't know I'd sent the night before.

> TO: meredith@meredithedits.com
> 4:07 PM
> **Subject: Re: Good night**
> *Apparently I caught some stomach bug. Hoping you didn't get it. I've been down since shortly after I got home yesterday. Barely moved today.*

Hope you had a good time at the concert.

TO: bruisedassets@yahoo.com
4:13 PM
Subject: Re: Good night
I'm so sorry. I will admit I was growing worried about you and figured
something was going on. I'm fine, but I'll be doubling up on my vitamins! Lol
Concert was great!

Knowing he was sick, it came as no surprise that he hadn't been responding. Todd and I spent the rest of the evening getting laundry caught up and the house cleaned. He was leaving on Monday for a three week city to city training stint. One less thing to worry about. Couldn't fight with Todd if he wasn't here to fight with.

The next morning, before I hopped in the shower, I got an email.

TO: meredith@meredithedits.com
9:06 AM
Subject: Re: Good night
Much better today, but still going to take it easy.
Hope you had a good welcome home...while keeping your ass hidden.

TO: bruisedassets@yahoo.com
9:14 AM
Subject: Re: Good night
I'm glad to hear you're feeling a little better. It was a good evening,
nothing too exciting. I did crash early because I let myself get dehydrated
and may have had too much to drink Friday night with Tami. Lol I'm much
better this morning.
He leaves tomorrow for his 3wk tour. I have to skip the gym and drop him
at the airport. It started an argument. Shoudn't have, but it did.
Hope to talk/see you soon. Feel better.

The next morning I dropped Todd off at the airport. It was probably one of our coldest goodbyes in a long time. I needed Gregor; his humor, his calming presence, his distraction.

TO: bruisedassets@yahoo.com
11:44 AM
Subject: Re: Good night
Driving home from the airport. Ball of stress. Enjoy your day.
When I was almost home, his response popped up.

TO: meredith@meredithedits.com

12:15 PM
Subject: Re: Good night
Stress from...? Having the kids for the next 3-4 weeks?
Pulling in the drive, I typed my response before going inside.

TO: bruisedassets@yahoo.com
12:24 PM
Subject: Re: Good night
   Sigh. That I'm horny (shocking, I know). He critiqued my driving the whole time and I wanted to punch him in the face. He didn't kiss me goodbye (probably sensing I wanted to punch him in the face).
   Maybe I just need my ass beaten till I smile. Lol

I will admit that I spent the day moping around. Gregor was quiet all day and I just couldn't focus on editing, writing, or PTA stuff. I sat down at my laptop that night, having just put the kids to bed, and an email popped up from Gregor.

TO: meredith@meredithedits.com
8:15 PM
Subject: Re: Good night
   If like me, those that spend a lot of time driving can be critical, but it's because of all the accidents we see happen. It's hard preparing for a long trip and remaining 'normal' while going through the mental checklist of shit to get done.
   But I will still beat your ass for you... :)

Then I did what I didn't think I could. I emailed Gregor and told him that I had almost cried with him a couple times after a paddling, but that I wouldn't allow myself to do so.

TO: bruisedassets@yahoo.com
8:24 PM
Subject: Re: Good night
   I get it. Just hard to not feel like he's complacent with me. He was rubbing my neck last night and when I asked him to do it harder, he immediately clammed up and said he didn't want to hurt me. You'd think I asked for an ass whooping like you give. Lol
   I think you need to make me cry. I've been close a couple of times, but then I lock up.

It was the closing to the email and then I hit send. I didn't know how or if he'd respond, but I knew one thing; I wouldn't be the one to bring it up again. The ball was in his court.

CHAPTER
Twenty-Four

ALL I WANT

H<small>E DIDN'T RESPOND TO THE</small> email, not sure if I expected him to or not. I didn't see him that week, but we still emailed every day. What was hardest for me was having the free time—which wasn't often—and not being able to see him. Forcing myself to stop obsessing, I cleaned my house and did what any strong woman did. I got shit done.

Later in the week the flirtatious emails continued; a welcome remedy to my alone time. I knew that he was still fighting illness, but that did nothing to curb my salacious desire for him.

> *TO: bruisedassets@yahoo.com*
> *6:24 PM*
> *Subject: Libido ON*
> *Jesus fuck...I hate you... :)*
> *I need my hair pulled, throat held, nipples pinched, ass beat...*
> *DAMMIT!*

After the kids were in bed, I was working when he finally responded.

TO: meredith@meredithedits.com
10:10 PM
Subject: Re: Libido ON
Oh no...the Jesus fuck has been invoked...
:)

Giggling, I replied, wondering how I got him to come out and play...with me. I also included a picture with different words on it; Love me, spank me, whip me, hold me, fuck me, kiss me, bite me. And 'HARDER' at its center.

TO: bruisedassets@yahoo.com
10:12 PM
Subject: Re: Libido ON
Lmao. Yup. Game on!
Friend sent me the pic. She knows me well...

It was a couple of hours before he responded. I was in bed and asleep for a couple hours when I woke to a response that he'd sent an hour earlier.

TO: meredith@meredithedits.com
12:39 AM
Subject: Re: Libido ON
Lol. The universal modifier...'HARDER'
I think my lack of libido may be tied to everything leaving an aftertaste like a roll full of dirty pennies.
Heading to bed. Good night! :)

I scanned his email and had to re-read it. Then I started laughing at myself as I replied.

TO: bruisedassets@yahoo.com
1:36 AM
Subject: Re: Libido ON
Yuck. The metal taste. Of course, I originally read 'dirty panties'...lol
I crashed at 1130 and just woke up all hot n sweaty. Your fault! I fell asleep thinking about waking with your hand on my hip from Friday morning...and then all the rest...
Hope you're sleeping.

Later that day after a doctor's appointment and various errands, I was laughing my ass off at an email from him. Somehow a conversation had ensued between some children at the school during drop-off about how 'punishment' was horrible. He'd mentioned in the email that had I been there, I wouldn't have been able to keep a straight face. And he was right.

> **TO: bruisedassets@yahoo.com**
> **1:43 PM**
> **Subject: Re: Libido ON**
> *OMG...lol. I NEED to be punished, Sir. I ache for it...*
> *I can't stop giggling. I would've had to leave the room, especially had you been there, too.*

Around dinner time I got my reply.

> **TO: meredith@meredithedits.com**
> **5:08 PM**
> **Subject: Re: Libido ON**
> *I was smirking thinking about you being on the other side of the room and trying to keep it together...*

> **TO: bruisedassets@yahoo.com**
> **5:16 PM**
> **Subject: Re: Libido ON**
> *You know me so well...lol*
> *Garbage out, homework done, house cleaned. Now for dinner. Is it bedtime yet? One week almost done...*

> **TO: meredith@meredithedits.com**
> **5:37 PM**
> **Subject: Re: Libido ON**
> *I need a long massage.*

> **TO: bruisedassets@yahoo.com**
> **5:39 PM**
> **Subject: Re: Libido ON**
> *One of mine?! I still want one from you...*
> *You're going to drive me to drink. I suddenly have a craving for whisky... need to taste you on my lips again!*

> **TO: meredith@meredithedits.com**
> **6:13 PM**
> **Subject: Re: Libido ON**
> *Mmmm...whisky lips.*
> *I need a BJ.*

> **TO: bruisedassets@yahoo.com**
> **6:19 PM**
> **Subject: Re: Libido ON**
> *I need something to suck on...needed to suck on you yesterday... :)*

But it'll have to wait until next week when I'm kid free once again.

> **TO:** *meredith@meredithedits.com*
> **6:23 PM**
> **Subject:** *Re: Libido ON*
> *Headed out of town later next week for the rare business trip and will be gone through the weekend.*
> Ugh. Well, I was going to put in my request.

> **TO:** *bruisedassets@yahoo.com*
> **6:26 PM**
> **Subject:** *Re: Libido ON*
> *I'm formally putting in a request for a marked ass before you leave. Lol :)*

> **TO:** *meredith@meredithedits.com*
> **6:29 PM**
> **Subject:** *Re: Libido ON*
> *Noted. I will have my assistant put that on the calendar accordingly...*
> *May send you home in cum soaked panties after the spanking. Make you sit in my warm, sticky mess and preserve the feeling.*

I dropped my head to my desk when I got the response. How was he still able to leave me nearly speechless?

> **TO:** *bruisedassets@yahoo.com*
> **8:13 PM**
> **Subject:** *Re: Libido ON*
> *Promise?!*

> **TO:** *meredith@meredithedits.com*
> **8:24 PM**
> **Subject:** *Re: Libido ON*
> *Won't promise but certainly will keep it on the top of my mind...*
> *I rather like thinking about you squirming from a sore bottom and feeling all squishy at the same time from my cum and your juices.*

> **TO:** *bruisedassets@yahoo.com*
> **8:27 PM**
> **Subject:** *Re: Libido ON*
> *Sigh. You're killing me.*
> *Juices are already flowing...*
> *And playlist is on random. What should come on? I'm on fire. Jesus fuck...*

That night I fell asleep to Daniella Mason's *All I Want.* It too, was another song that had played from our night away and as I listened to it the video reels played over and over.

The emails continued all weekend and into Monday. I worked all day and late into the nights as I listened to my dark songs and the words were flowing, poetry included. I worked and re-worked the poem I was working on and after I was satisfied, I sent it to him.

> **TO: bruisedassets@yahoo.com**
> **12:50 PM**
> **Subject: Re: Sinful Sunday**
> *I'm blushing and over-heated. This just flew off my fingertips...*
> *My secret, my desire, my passion*
> *Deep inside where only you can go*
> *Harder, rougher, unleash your beast*
> *I want it all, everything you got*
> *I'll meet every thrust, every kiss*
> *With more vigor than before*
> *Can you handle me?*
> *Do you want all of me?*
> *I'm yours for the taking*
> *Spank me, flog me, fuck me*
> *Punish me like only you can*
> *Pleasure resides in your weapon*
> *Caress the welts with your tongue*
> *Then do it again...*

I didn't get a response until the evening.

> **TO: meredith@meredithedits.com**
> **6:20 PM**
> **Subject: Re: Sinful Sunday**
> *:) Glad to see your fingertips are electric*

> **TO: bruisedassets@yahoo.com**
> **6:24 PM**
> **Subject: Re: Sinful Sunday**
> *Can't help but think dirty thoughts...you've corrupted me...lol. Ok, so we both know I was already corrupted.*

> **TO: meredith@meredithedits.com**
> **6:27 PM**
> **Subject: Re: Sinful Sunday**
> *I may have introduced your corrupted mind to reality, but I can't be responsible for any more than that... :)*

Let me know when you are through with your workout tomorrow. We may have to rodeo briefly... :)

TO: bruisedassets@yahoo.com
6:30 PM
Subject: Re: Sinful Sunday
Will do. I'll email you when I get home and then I'll need to shower.
I look forward to the rodeo. :)
Maybe I'll bring you a cherry jolly rancher tomorrow...of course I may already be sucking on it. :)

He didn't respond until late in the night.

TO: meredith@meredithedits.com
12:27 AM
Subject: Re: Sinful Sunday
I will give you a break to suck on something else...

TO: bruisedassets@yahoo.com
12:32 AM
Subject: Re: Sinful Sunday
I might enjoy this...maybe I'll bring a few, really draw it out and enjoy it.
My bruises are gone and I frowned when I noticed.
Just crawled into bed. Bad habit picked back up from younger days... music playing as I drift off to sleep. Get some rest, Sir. I'll be dreaming of jolly ranchers and Maximus. Giggle...

TO: meredith@meredithedits.com
12:37 AM
Subject: Re: Sinful Sunday
Did those bad habits include being paddled and giving BJs in the middle of the day...?
BJ queen sounds more regal... :)

Smiling, I decided to tease him some more.

TO: bruisedassets@yahoo.com
12:41 AM
Subject: Re: Sinful Sunday
LOL. I'll accept that title!
How is Maximus? Eager, needy, throbbing?

TO: meredith@meredithedits.com
12:43 AM
Subject: Re: Sinful Sunday
Going to be throbbing shortly. Going to stroke and tease him before I

fall asleep.

When I woke in the morning I sent him a simple message.

> *TO: bruisedassets@yahoo.com*
> *7:22 AM*
> *Subject: Re: Sinful Sunday*
> *Good morning...*

He didn't respond, but I tried to not overthink it. When I got home from the gym, I emailed him again.

> *TO: bruisedassets@yahoo.com*
> *10:57 AM*
> *Subject: Home*
> *Just got home. Jumping in the shower.*
> *So many choices...red panties, black panties, lace panties, no panties...*
> *Sigh.*

When I got out of the shower, an email awaited. Pervert. I knew the mention of panties would get him to respond.

> *TO: meredith@meredithedits.com*
> *11:24 AM*
> *Subject: Re: Home*
> *:)*
> *Finishing some reports and then I will be ready to meet.*

> *TO: bruisedassets@yahoo.com*
> *11:33 AM*
> *Subject: Re: Home*
> *I'll be waiting... :)*

And I waited, and waited, and waited some more.

> *TO: meredith@meredithedits.com*
> *12:43 PM*
> *Subject: Re: Home*
> *Almost finished.*

He was trying to give me an anxiety attack.

TO: bruisedassets@yahoo.com
12:45 PM
Subject: Re: Home
Ok...

Thirty minutes later I got a text that Rodeo 1 was compromised and to head to Rodeo 2. Scrambling to my car, I headed out. Parking away from him like he'd taught me to do, I got out of my SUV and began the walk over to him.

Wasting no time, he pulled me to him. Hip to hip, his erection jumped against me as I circled my arms around his ribcage and let him kiss me.

"You smell good." His lips moved over my neck and to my ear as I trembled under them.

How had I survived almost two weeks without his touch? I wanted to feel this every day and maybe that's why it felt so amazing because every day just wasn't possible. I lost myself in his kiss and embrace. I loved how tight he held me, letting me know who owned me in the short moments I was with him.

"You ready to be punished?" It was a soft whisper against my ear and I nodded. "Turn around."

I did as he directed and leaned into the backseat of his truck. His hands slowly moved up my legs, lifting my skirt as he went. Closing my eyes, my lips forming a soft smile, I reveled in his touch. Stiff fingers moved over my lips and parted them as he coated his fingers, causing a small moan to escape me. He moved closer.

The feeling of his erection pressed against me was one of the most gratifying feelings. I loved the proof of what I did to him. He moved against my hip while working his hands over my now exposed flesh. I couldn't stop myself from wiggling against his cock so that I could feel more of him. And when he grabbed my hips, seeking more pressure, I knew it was the same for him, too.

"You've never cried in front of me."

His words hit me hard, maybe harder than his paddle ever had. Proof that he'd read the email with my request to cry now out in the open. Apparently he was just biding his time, waiting for the right moment. This wasn't the first time he'd proven to me that he paid attention more than I thought he did.

"No, Sir."

"You're going to now."

"Yes, Sir."

How was he going to do that? I tried to relax, but this was a side to myself I hadn't shown him. Hell, Todd had never seen me fully cry. I wasn't one to break down and sob. All I knew was the quiet ugly cry; chin trembling, hot tears rolling down cold cheeks kind of cry. On rare occasion I'd let a few sobs break free in the shower knowing that my secret was safe under the disguise of the water.

His hands moved over my ass that no longer bore his marks. My ass was a blank canvas ready for the colorful strokes of his hand, flogger, paddle, and belt. He chose the 'significant damage' paddle, or as he called it, the 'punishment paddle'.

The paddling began and it was meant to hurt, meant to make me cry. Pressing my lips together, the prideful Meredith surfaced telling me that I better not cry. Then I heard my father telling me to 'suck it up, Meredith. No crying.' I fought with wanting to let go, but not wanting to feel so vulnerable. Or maybe it was that I wasn't sure I could handle it if he proved he could.

I lost count after twenty strikes. He did it. He got me to break down. Tears fell freely, my shoulders were trembling. Pulling me up, he turned me back to face him and crushed his arms around me as I cried. Then I panicked and tried to stop the tears. And he felt it.

"You're still tense. You're not letting it all out."

Bending me over again, the paddle bit out against my skin once more. I was scared to death to *really* cry in front of him. I listened to him as he coaxed me, paddled me, and assured me I could cry in front of him. It was then I knew I was safe with him, in every way.

Burying my face in my hands, my back began to shake with more force. My sobs tore through me in the backseat of his truck. He struck me with the paddle a few more times before he ceased.

Hauling me back up to him, he wrapped his arms around me once again. I clung to him as if my life was connected to his and in that moment it was. My sobs were only muffled by his shirt. One hand ran over my back while the other rubbed at my neck and ran through my hair.

"Get it out. It's ok." His voice was gentle and reassuring.

Continuing to cry, I tried to ignore the fact that I sounded like someone who needed medical intervention. Growing up I was taught—as I'm sure many women were—that crying was a weakness and something to keep private. And admittedly,

I was a sensitive soul and cried easier than most. But I rarely broke down.

Gregor broke me down.

I took in a jagged breath. "Everything is such a mess. I've made a mess of everything."

Squeezing me tighter, "You're going through a lot of changes. And there are just more to come. You'll get through it, Mer. It was a long process for me. You'll get through it, we'll get through it."

I cried for a while as he soothed me. Soon all I wanted to do was sleep, but the situation didn't allow for it. We held each other and all I wanted was to steal a few hours with him and stay in his arms. But we had responsibilities to tend to.

"If you need to cry, vent, whatever...know I'm here for you."

There were so many places my over analytical brain could take that statement. But I needed to stop. Afraid what else I might say if I continued crying. So instead, I deflected.

"I wasn't sure if you'd read that email." I looked in his eyes, his arms still holding me, caressing me, "But you just keep proving over and over that you read everything I send you and you hear me. Thank you."

He just smiled and kissed me again. It was soft, yet possessive. "There are still more tears in there, but it's a start."

He was right. He knew me better than I knew myself. When I was with him he seemed to uncover parts of me yet undiscovered. It was like being found while getting lost. Wiping my tears, he kissed me softly as his hands moved under my sweater.

Soon we were both clawing at one another, touching, stroking, and trying to get closer. I undid his belt and my fingers itched to yank it loose of its confines. I smiled and wondered what he'd do if I pulled it free, handed it to him, and bent over. Topping from the bottom, it's what I did on occasion. Or at least I tried. I knew him well enough to guess he probably would've laughed, but whether he would have belted me; that I didn't know.

He freed his cock for me and I dropped down to claim him with my mouth. He stroked my face the entire time, letting me control the movements. When it was over, him not allowing his release, but his taste still lingering, he hauled me to my feet and kissed me.

Then our caresses became sweet and gentle. His head on my shoulder, just like mine was on his, I rubbed his back as best I could. I didn't want to leave and knew it was coming soon. We were both very relaxed and it made it that much better. And worse.

We kissed for a few minutes before he said, "That should give you plenty to think about the next few days while I'm gone."

Dropping my head to his shoulder I groaned. "Be safe. I'll miss you."

Cupping my face, he smiled at me and kissed me gently. "You ok to drive home?"

"Yes. It's not far."

We exchanged one last hug and then we went our separate ways. He was leaving the next day and wouldn't be home until Monday. He warned me he'd be out of touch, but he'd said that before and still found ways to reach out. I guess I'd have to wait and see.

CHAPTER
Twenty-Five

I FORGET WHERE WE WERE

I GOT HOME AND SAT AT MY DESK thinking about what'd just occurred. I think I was slightly in shock. Turning on my music, *I Forget Where We Were* by Ben Howard caught my eye. Another song from our night away and I hit play.

Sitting there, I stared at my email. I wanted to email him, but my thoughts were scattered. What did one say after taking a beating like that? I smiled. Yes, I'd asked for it and had consented to it. I did feel better, but was still really emotional.

I was beginning to understand how potent he was, how addictive. It was the only word I could use to describe him: an addiction and there was no remedy. He had what I wanted, what I needed, what I craved, knew it, and gave it willingly. And in doing so, he got the same thing in return. Every part of my being benefited from him. I could ask for more and know he'd give it. There was no shame or guilt in what we had; just primal, carnal, and unequivocal need.

TO: bruisedassets@yahoo.com
2:47 PM
Subject: Thank you
It was great seeing you and tasting you again. I hope you have a safe trip.
Thank you again for listening and doing what you do. Nobody's ever just

held me and let me cry like that, yes, even the husband.
  Hopefully I can give you another massage soon.
  Talk soon...

His response was almost immediate.

  TO: meredith@meredithedits.com
  2:49 PM
  Subject: Re: Thank you
  I have a pre-cum trail all the way down my boxers... :)
  Sometimes a good cry goes a long way. I wasn't always this communicative
or able to deal with such things. It was a long process. :)

  TO: bruisedassets@yahoo.com
  2:57 PM
  Subject: Thank you
  Sorry, not sorry... :)
  I had to change my skirt for the same reason...
  I really do feel better. One day at a time, that's for sure.
  Well, I'm grateful to be on the other side of the long process! :)

I had yet to hear from him when I crawled into bed that night. Rolling over
after two in the morning, I saw my phone flashing that familiar color letting me
know I had email.

  TO: meredith@meredithedits.com
  12:04 AM
  Subject: Re: Thank you
  Get the spots cleaned up...? :)
  Finally packed. Too much shit kept piling up today and one rather
welcomed interruption...
  Smiling, I typed my reply.

  TO: bruisedassets@yahoo.com
  2:30 AM
  Subject: Re: Thank you
  Lol. Yes. Though I left another in bed...
  I'm glad you took the time to get away. It was great to see you and you're
also a welcome interruption. :)
  I did get some writing done, too.

When I got back from dropping the kids off at the bus stop the next morning,
I had an email.

TO: meredith@mereldithedits.com
8:48 AM
Subject: Re: Thank you
I hope you have an inspired next couple of days of writing.
:)

TO: bruisedassets@yahoo.com
9:11 AM
Subject: Re: Thank you
I'm being bad and skipping the gym. My back is killing me this morning. It felt fine yesterday, but this morning...No go. Heading to the shower to turn my bathroom into a sauna. Hoping it helps.
I'll see you in my dreams...until your return.
:)

He was gone. I didn't hear from him for days. I won't lie. It sucked. Every morning I hoped to find a surprise email and was let down. Hope was a great thing...sometimes. Other times, hope was a fucking asshole.

The days passed, but I couldn't say like they normally did. I had a new normal now, one that included Gregor. I wanted to email him every detail about my day, but didn't want to be a nuisance either. I did my best to keep it to one email per day. Just my way of letting him know he was missed.

TO: bruisedassets@yahoo.com
9:11 AM
Subject: Daydreaming...Day 2
Just thinking about you and how relaxed you were when I was running my hands all over you...
I look forward to doing it again...

With Todd and Gregor both out of town, it became very evident to me who I missed. Gregor was who I wanted to see most, and who was returning first. I couldn't stop thinking about him and the things I wanted to do with him, have him do to me. I loved staring in his eyes, whether we were talking or kissing, though he still made me nervous and undid me with his gaze.

I wanted my wrists bound while he ran the soft leather of the flogger over my body, and I imagined the sensations it would cause. Back arching, breasts thrust in the air, and legs clenched as my shoulders shook with the shiver running through me. I imagined being face to face with him with my cuffed wrists around his back or clutching the headboard. He never let up, always giving me more. Each time was better than the last.

Closing my eyes, I squirmed in my seat as the ache from my bruises was nearly gone. And while he gave me more and more, I too wanted to give him more. I wanted, no needed, to fulfill his desires as well. Anytime I got him to moan in pleasure, or sigh, I felt like a queen. I wanted him to claim every part of my body, use me for his pleasure knowing it would also bring me my own. It was like the stars finally aligned and unleashed me from my confines, but bound me to his.

Only a day or two left, depending on how you looked at it. The writing and poetry continuing to flow. I emailed him.

> *TO: bruisedassets@yahoo.com*
> *4:49 PM*
> *Subject: Triggers...Day 4*
> *I was standing in line at the store today, waiting to checkout. Observing those around me, the gentleman in front of me was smiling at his phone. I thought of us. He was responding, text or email, I'm not sure. But immediately my mind drifted to you, my Sir, and a poem started rattling off in my head. I was completely distracted checking out and rushed to my car after. I grabbed my phone and started typing a message to myself. Here's the finished product.*
> *He invades my thoughts when I least expect it*
> *A word, a sound, a song, a look from a stranger*
> *The only trigger needed to make me think of him*
> *That's when the flutters begin to build again*
> *I need his touch, long for his embrace, crave his kiss*
> *Goosebumps trail my flesh at the thought of him*
> *The pulsing begins and I start to ache for him*
> *Only he will satiate my appetite; blessing and curse*
> *Never have I had such a craving, yet been so sated*
> *He brings me peace, pleasure, and pain*
> *My thoughts are tangled up in him and our story*
> *He's my muse, my devil, my deliverance*

The next afternoon I was cleaning house and finishing laundry when my phone pinged. I may have run to my desk to pull his email up on my laptop.

> *TO: meredith@meredithedits.com*
> *2:34 PM*
> *Subject: Re: Triggers...Day 4*
> *I have emerged! Heading home. Hope you had a productive weekend after the rough start... :)*

He was referring to another email I'd sent after a rough day with the kids.

> *TO: bruisedassets@yahoo.com*
> *2:45 PM*
> *Subject: Re: Triggers...Day 4*
> *Ah...he's alive!*
> *Writing was productive as I'm sure you read below.*
> *Talk soon...*

I kept it brief, not wanting to overload him. Later the next morning he emailed again and had me laughing.

> *TO: meredith@meredithedits.com*
> *11:18 AM*
> *Subject: Re: Triggers...Day 4*
> *I hate coming back from long trips to a loaded SPAM folder...*
> *According to my SPAM I have major ED issues, a small penis, and I'm overweight, yet there are still HUNDREDS of gorgeous, horny housewives that are just dying to fuck me.*

> *TO: bruisedassets@yahoo.com*
> *11:23 AM*
> *Subject: Re: Triggers...Day 4*
> *Lol. Well I keep getting offers on KinkyFodder from other 'Sirs' and emails for Russian housewives. Apparently I need a wife and another Dom. LOL.*
> *However, I AM dying to fuck you...if that counts and I'm technically a housewife. Gorgeous, depends on the day! Lol*

I didn't get a response until later in the evening. He was headed out of town again and I probably wouldn't see him until the next week, if I was lucky. Todd would be home Friday, after three weeks. The kids were ecstatic to see him. I didn't know what I was.

> *TO: bruisedassets@yahoo.com*
> *12:33 AM*
> *Subject: Midnight inspiration*
> *Will you use me up or fill my cup*
> *Take everything I give and empty me out*
> *You give me more but will it be enough*
> *Sinking into you but don't let me drown*
> *Wielder of paddles and master of pleasure*
> *My scars are hidden but your eyes see*

Chew me up and let me inside you
Show me your secrets and your rock bottom
In the dark of night you're my midnight lover
Imprinted on me but will you forget me
Lay me down and love me with your pain
Any way you want but I'll never run away

TO: meredith@meredithedits.com
12:35 AM
Subject: Re: Midnight inspiration
I need a long massage. Just got to my hotel.

TO: bruisedassets@yahoo.com
12:37 AM
Subject: Re: Midnight inspiration
I'd love nothing more than to give you one...
I'll be around when you get back...but you can't mark me until next week.

I went to bed and it happened yet again. Bolted awake by nothing, I checked my phone as his email came through.

TO: meredith@meredithedits.com
1:35 AM
Subject: Re: Midnight inspiration
HTF am I going to mark you if you're giving me a massage...?
I'm getting ready to jerk off to thoughts of you rubbing my chest and back. I will probably fall asleep long before I come.

TO: bruisedassets@yahoo.com
1:37 AM
Subject: Re: Midnight inspiration
I'm cracking up at your response about marking me. You're creative and I'm sure you'd find a way!
Wish I was there so I could stroke maximus for you.
Now all I can think about is rubbing and stroking you. So tempted to call you and let you whisper me back to sleep, telling me what other images you think about involving me and you...
Sweet dreams, Sir...

When I got out of the gym the next morning I had a response waiting for me.

TO: meredith@meredithedits.com
9:49 AM
Subject: Re: Midnight inspiration

I was asleep shortly after. Cum soaked towel on my chest... :)
Put a massage table in your office.

If only it was that easy! I typed my reply.

> **TO: bruisedassets@yahoo.com**
> **10:37 AM**
> **Subject: Re: Midnight inspiration**
> *What was that about prudence and desire?! Sigh. You can sit between my legs in the back of your truck while I work my magic. God, I want my hands on you and vice versa...*
> *I'm so fucking horny...*
> *Devil...*
> *It's your fault...*

I was finalizing some details for the upcoming PTA fundraiser when his email came in.

> **TO: meredith@meredithedits.com**
> **2:34 PM**
> **Subject: Re: Midnight inspiration**
> *Side business for you. That way it won't look out of the ordinary when I come over for a massage and THEN paddle you...*

> **TO: bruisedassets@yahoo.com**
> **2:37 PM**
> **Subject: Re: Midnight inspiration**
> *LMAO. You're killing me. I take it you enjoy my massages. :)*
> *My desk is big enough...just need to clear off my laptop...dirty, dirty thoughts...*

I snorted at his reply.

> **TO: meredith@meredithedits.com**
> **2:42 PM**
> **Subject: Re: Midnight inspiration**
> *Might be big enough, but hardly will create the illusion of a viable massage business... :)*

> **TO: bruisedassets@yahoo.com**
> **2:45 PM**
> **Subject: Re: Midnight inspiration**
> *LOL. Sigh.*
> *So, when am I giving you that massage?! :)*

TO: meredith@meredithedits.com
2:49 PM
Subject: Re: Midnight inspiration
Tomorrow won't work. Conference calls, training, kids, etc. With not enough time in between for a proper massage...

I got swamped with emails, phone calls, kids, and everything else and wasn't able to reply right away.

TO: bruisedassets@yahoo.com
4:49 PM
Subject: a bit of writing...
I'm around next week...you have my contact info. Lol
Little more poetry...
Fade into him and let us begin
Our consenting cat and mouse game
The sting of his belt
The whip of his flogger
The smack of his paddle
The caress of his hand
Their signature now adorns me
Molding my skin and mending my soul
His fingers tickle them
His teeth taunt them
His tongue soothes them
His lips kiss them
Time passes and they vanish
The craving for more a persistent yearning
I want the welts
I need the pain
I want the bruises
I need the reminder
That he is real and I'm alive
And for a moment he was mine

His response came after the kids were in bed. My mission partially accomplished...distracting him.

TO: meredith@meredithedits.com
8:09 PM
Subject: Re: a bit of writing...
I'm working out while watching political news. Sweaty. Muscles hard. Heavy breathing. Mind is in three places.
Politics
Fitness

Flogging you.

I enjoyed this game way too much.

> **TO: bruisedassets@yahoo.com**
> **8:11 PM**
> **Subject: Re: a bit of writing...**
> *You're seriously killing me...I'm a horny hormonal mess. I need your kind of pain...*
> *Was sitting here daydreaming about our night away...sleeping (barely) next to you, kissing you, riding you, massaging you, biting you, licking you, sucking you...*

This was the part of the game I hated. I didn't hear back until the morning.

> **TO: meredith@meredithedits.com**
> **6:53 AM**
> **Subject: Re: a bit of writing...**
> *What did that lead to...? :)*

> **TO: bruisedassets@yahoo.com**
> **7:01 AM**
> **Subject: Re: a bit of writing...**
> *Taking matters into my own hands at bedtime, but I'm still aching...*
> *Turned on some music, then ran my fingers over my neck, chest, stomach, imagining it was your hands I was feeling. Dreaming of the flogger dragging over my body and lashing out. Cupping myself the way you do. My clit pulsing away, dying for your touch. The way you lick, caress, fondle, tease, fuck. It didn't take long, but it wasn't enough. I want it to be controlled and delivered by you...*

I got the kids to school, headed to the gym and got home to shower. I had a ton of errands to run and I knew he was busy all day as well. I was finally able to respond later in the day to his mid-morning email and then had to finish up a few more things around the house before the kids got home.

> **TO: meredith@meredithedits.com**
> **10:53 AM**
> **Subject: Re: a bit of writing...**
> *Just finished with some BS conference call.*
> *Thinking other things at this point... :)*

> **TO: bruisedassets@yahoo.com**

2:25 PM
Subject: I want to be flogged
Keep thinking about leather floggers and my Sir.
Hope you're having a good day.

The emails continued as they always did over the next couple days. Todd was coming home and my nerves were shot. We hadn't talked much while he was gone and I didn't know what to expect. The only thing I did know was that he'd be home long enough to fuck with our routine, theirs mostly. He liked to let them stay up late. I'd learned early on my kids thrived on their routine, strict as it was, it made us all happier. Getting the kids back on track Monday would be a pain in the ass.

TO: meredith@meredithedits.com
10:53 AM
Subject: Re: I want to be flogged
Saw you at parent teacher conferences. How'd it go? All glowing reports here.
This day started as a clusterfuck and hasn't improved much since...
Do you need a stern paddling to destress and refocus...? :)

TO: bruisedassets@yahoo.com
11:17 AM
Subject: Yes, Sir. May I have another...?
Sounds like we both need some us time.
Hope your day improves. Of course you saw me at conferences. Stalker!
My bruises from last week are fully gone. I need more, but it'll have to wait.
Need your hands in my hair, on my neck, and all over my ass... :)

Again, he was silent until that night. Todd was now home, but had already gone to bed. We'd barely talked, him just admitting he was exhausted and needed sleep.

TO: meredith@meredithedits.com
10:02 PM
Subject: Re: I want to be flogged
You should see if you can get away for a night before the Holidays...

The Holidays were over two months away. What happened to one day at a time? I was slightly panicked, yet exhilarated at the thought of him planning so far ahead. I fell just a little further down the rabbit hole.

Two months.

I had a feeling he had no intention of letting me go and I knew that I felt the same way.

CHAPTER
Twenty-Six

FALLING

TO: bruisedassets@yahoo.com
10:11 PM
Subject: Mistletoe
Give me a window. I'll see what I can do... :)
You going to kiss me and flog me under the mistletoe?!

I went to bed that night listening to music, many songs and artists I'd never heard of. And that is typically how I found some of my favorite songs. I loved my Top 40, but new and unexposed indie artists were the ones with the songs that really pulled at my heartstrings.

TO: meredith@meredithedits.com
7:51 AM
Subject: Re: Mistletoe
If there is mistletoe in a hotel – it will probably be in the lobby... :)

Laughing, I began.

TO: bruisedassets@yahoo.com

7:56 AM
Subject: Re: Mistletoe
Well that could be some added excitement for the other guests. Lol.
Give me dates and I'll see what I can work out with the schedules. He'll be home, which makes some things more difficult than others...

When his reply came, he had me laughing again, never missing a beat.

TO: meredith@meredithedits.com
9:55 AM
Subject: Re: Mistletoe
I will be forecasting the rest of the year next week and will let you know.
A little lobby BDSM extravaganza for the guests...? Guess it depends on how the GM of the property bends... :)
May have to buy a red flogger for the holiday season.

Now he had my head spinning. The thought of a red flogger was sexy as hell. Good thing I had Todd and the kids to distract me for most of the day. There was a barrage of things to get done before he left again on Monday.

I had a few moments of privacy in the afternoon and finally responded to his email.

TO: bruisedassets@yahoo.com
1:36 PM
Subject: Re: Mistletoe
Sounds good. Makes me all tingly just thinking about it...night away, flogger, you...sigh.
Should I find myself a Santa hat, maybe some bells?! Maybe I can sit on Santa's lap...
Craving you...

More errands, more work around the house, more arguments with Todd...

TO: meredith@meredithedits.com
4:43 PM
Subject: Re: Mistletoe
You going to sit on Santa's lap and tell him how naughty you were and see if you can get a rise out of him...?

TO: bruisedassets@yahoo.com
4:48 PM
Subject: Re: Mistletoe
I'm sure I could get a rise out of him. Lol

Can't stop thinking about our video reels... to the point shivers run up my spine... :)

I went to bed alone that night. Todd on the couch watching TV, Gregor probably at home. Music sung me to sleep, where I slept peacefully most of the night.

TO: meredith@meredithedits.com
8:00 AM
Subject: Re: Mistletoe
Which video did you pick out last night...?

He asked. It was only right to tell him.

TO: bruisedassets@yahoo.com
8:07 AM
Subject: A girl has needs...
I was thinking about me riding you, kissing you, hands clasped with yours...how I feel found with you while getting lost with you...
And what happens when you dream about Sir all night? Your husband gets attacked in the morning whether he likes it or not. Lol
Happy Sunday...

I stayed in bed as long as I could before getting up to shower. When I was getting dressed, after showering, an email came through.

TO: meredith@meredithedits.com
9:50 AM
Subject: Re: A girl has needs...
So did he end up liking it...? :)
No such luck here...lol

TO: bruisedassets@yahoo.com
10:06 AM
Subject: Re: A girl has needs...
Lol. He made a comment about me liking morning sex. (Shaking my head) He knows this. It didn't go as well as it could have.
I'd love to ease your tension... :) Most of my dreams consisted of anal play with you. Sigh...your needs and wants are now my own...
Time to make my grocery list.

I did my grocery shopping while Todd took the kids to the movies. They needed their dad and I was happy for the break. Though Todd not taking the thought or initiative to go out with *me* alone would never stop pissing me off.

Todd was busy re-packing when an email from Gregor came through that evening. I'd emailed him earlier when I was all alone, letting him know I was out and about.

> *TO: meredith@meredithedits.com*
> *9:33 PM*
> *Subject: Re: Rodeo...*
> *Working out now after working in the yard most of the day.*
> *Workout is kicking my ass.*
> *Would rather be strapping yours... :)*

> *TO: bruisedassets@yahoo.com*
> *9:40 PM*
> *Subject: Belt...*
> *He did the same...yard work that is.*
> *He heads to the airport first thing.*
> *How did you know I've been missing your belt?*
> *Thinking about you all hot and sweaty...sigh.*

> *TO: meredith@meredithedits.com*
> *10:04 PM*
> *Subject: Re: Belt...*
> *Text or email when you're heading back from the airport.*
> *Getting ready to shower. I need release. Probably in bed as I fall asleep.*
> *Thinking about strapping your needing ass.*

> *TO: bruisedassets@yahoo.com*
> *10:07 PM*
> *Subject: Re: Belt...*
> *Glad I'm not the only one who masturbates while my spouse sleeps soundly next to me...*

> *TO: meredith@meredithedits.com*
> *10:45 PM*
> *Subject: Re: Belt...*
> *I do it frequently. Occasionally she wakes up and joins.*
> *What about that massage?*
> *We will have to save the strapping for later.*
> *I should be able to meet after my conference calls.*

> *TO: bruisedassets@yahoo.com*
> *10:49 PM*
> *Subject: Re: Belt...*

Mine sleeps like the dead...

I went to bed and woke earlier than I wanted to. Deciding to take advantage of the time, I got up and got dressed for the gym. As I left the bathroom, Todd looked at me confused.

"Can you get them ready for school? I'm going to head to the gym."

He just nodded, "Yeah, that's fine. Have a good workout."

When I was in my car, I emailed Gregor.

> *TO: bruisedassets@yahoo.com*
> *6:19 AM*
> *Subject: Re: Belt...*
> *Couldn't sleep. Ugh. Can't stop thinking about a certain someone and his sex drive. I'm heading to the gym now to take out my frustrations on the bike. Looking forward to getting my hands on you.*

After the gym, I headed home and walked into the usual chaos. Kids screaming, Todd yelling, while they all scrambled to get ready. Locking the door, I showered quickly in peace. Before Todd and I headed to the airport, I got a response from Gregor.

> *TO: meredith@meredithedits.com*
> *9:22 AM*
> *Subject: Re: Belt...*
> *Calls were rescheduled. Drastically frees me up today. :)*
> *Let me know when you get back...*

> *TO: bruisedassets@yahoo.com*
> *9:28 AM*
> *Subject: Re: Belt...*
> *Will do. I'll text when I'm headed home. Probably around 11am.*

Dropping Todd off at the airport, he kissed me goodbye. Nothing extravagant, but at least he'd done it. It was a cold weekend for us. The only intimacy we shared was when I attacked him Sunday morning. As usual, he made no attempts to pursue me. That shit could really fuck with a girl's head.

Turning my music back on, alone with my over-analytical self, I cranked it up. *Falling* by Adria was what I picked. Thinking about Gregor and me, Todd and me, Gregor and his wife... Ugh. It scared me how much I needed Gregor, Todd, both of them...for different reasons.

One thing became very clear to me. We were two very lonely people lost in the worlds we'd created. Hell, I knew enough to know that we were probably four very lonely people, but only two of us were willing to act on it—that we knew of.

I'd fallen into the abyss of motherhood and being a stay at home mom. I joined the PTA—needing to belong to something more—and never said no when asked to help because I was desperate to feel wanted, needed. But I was saying yes to all the wrong things. And why was it when Todd told me he needed me I felt like he was suffocating me? But when Gregor alluded to such things it was redeeming. Everything was so ass backwards.

When I was about halfway home, I texted Gregor. My phone startled me when it started ringing. We rarely spoke on the phone, but when we did it always began with my heart racing. What was it about him? Taking a deep breath, I answered the call on my dash.

His voice filtered through my speakers as I drove down the freeway. "How you doing?"

Smiling, "I'm good. You?"

"Good. What's your ETA?"

"I'm probably twenty minutes out."

"Ok. Meet me at Rodeo 1. I'll text if it's compromised."

"Sounds good."

"Everything else good?"

Sighing, "Yes. Is what it is. It was a rough weekend. What about you?"

"Ah, just the same old bullshit. I need to do a few things before I head out. Drive safe, stay focused on the road. I'll see you soon."

"Ok."

The call ended and I started the song over again. I almost missed my exit because I was focused on him and the fucking lyrics to the song. Everything felt impossible, yet doable. Desire was a tricky thing. It can make you lose all sense. It can make you feel invincible and vulnerable all at once.

It was almost interchangeable with poison or drugs. Again that analogy. Was it possible for a human to become a drug to another? The thought of it, of him, made my body throb and willing to do what I never imagined I would do. And all for just one more hit.

I was about five minutes out when the phone rang again.

"Hello?"

"Head to Rodeo 2. How far away are you?"

"Should be there in five minutes."

"Ok. See you soon."

"Ok. Bye."

Pulling into Rodeo 2 a few minutes later, I parked and started walking toward him. Hat on, his big grin beamed at me across the lot. Hands crossed as they usually were, they unfolded themselves once he was within arm's length.

He reached for me as he murmured, "I'm not feeling very dominant today."

Shrugging my shoulders and smiling, I let him pull me close and buried my face in his neck as he did the same. "I don't mind."

Snickering, he added, "Doesn't mean I won't take my belt to you."

"Mmmm."

I was already lost in him, my body molding itself to his as strong arms encircled my waist. I don't even recall if I said anything more. His lips were already trailing my neck and my eyes closed as I savored every second. When I was with him he owned me and the feeling was paramount. I never knew possession could be so freeing. In his presence I was safe, cherished, likely marked... And entirely owned. I didn't want it any other way.

Pressed up against his truck, I untucked his shirt, desperate for my hands to be on his skin. He didn't try to stop me. Running my hands along his chest and back, he nuzzled my neck and ear. I let the tremors wash over me and felt his lips smile against my skin. He held me tight for a long time while I continued caressing him. He almost fell asleep there against me, in the sunlight, my body held prisoner between him and his truck. It was nice having that kind of power over someone, knowing I could soothe him.

He whispered, "I want to lay in the grass, under the sun, with you all day."

It took me a few seconds for his words to register with me. Though, I wasn't even sure if he was aware that he'd said it, but I wanted the same thing too. "That would be amazing."

With him time stood still. Every kiss, glance, touch, and words exchanged with him were stolen ones. The only thing that mattered in those moments were him and I and taking advantage of every second. His hazy dark blue eyes pulled me in and

I wanted to know more of him. I wanted to run away and that's exactly what I did anytime he called or emailed... I ran away to him.

I had dreamed about summer days with him, napping under the sun while lying in a hammock or on a blanket in an overgrown field. The darkness of night enticed me too. I wanted to count the stars with him instead of the sunsets that would pass before I'd see him next. Things were a mix of uncontrollable lust and tender moments with us.

Pulling back, hand at my neck, he kissed me. It quickly turned into one of his signature kisses that had me weak in the knees. Hair pulling, throat holding, tongue fucking... Moaning into his mouth, my fingernails dug into the flesh of his back, harder than I had intended. Groaning, he pulled my hands away.

"No marking."

"Sorry, Sir. I wasn't trying to mark you, just get you closer." Ok, maybe I lied. I wanted to mark him and he knew it.

"I am closer." Smiling, he teased me as he almost pressed his lips to mine several times.

Groaning, I grabbed the collar of his sweater and tried pulling him closer. "Kiss me, dammit." I was now pleading, attempting to order him around.

Tugging on my hair, he snarled in my ear. "Someone's getting a little aggressive. Is that what you did with Todd before you made him fuck you?"

Oh, God. "Umm, we didn't fuck."

Eyes back in front of mine, he seemed confused. "But you said..."

Shaking my head, "I said he got me off. I didn't say he stuck it in."

His brow scrunched as he asked, "He's been gone for weeks. Did he fuck you at all this weekend?"

I just shook my head. Embarrassed at my admission, but I wasn't going to lie to him.

"What the hell?" I knew my eyes were about to betray me as Gregor studied my face.

I didn't even have time to answer Gregor or have a chance to try to defend Todd—though I wasn't sure I wanted to. Turning me around, he bent me over and pulled my skirt up. I loved when he just took control, took charge.

Trailing his hands over my bare ass—yes, I was commando, again—and between my legs. "You're soaked."

"Yes, Sir."

"What has you so turned on?"

"You, Sir. Only you." My mouth betrayed me.

Gripping my hips, he pressed his erection against me, making my breath stagger and reminding me of what I did to him. Closing my eyes, I concentrated on the feel of him and pressed back harder. His hand came down on my ass a few times as I mewled with desire. In those next moments the rest of the world faded away as I faded into him.

"Hold. Still."

Closing my eyes and biting my lip, I conceded. "Yes, Sir."

He spanked me a few times, before I heard the wood paddle being pulled from its hiding spot. So much for him not feeling very dominant. It didn't last long and his strikes were more for pleasure than for punishment. In between almost every slap of the paddle, his fingers or tongue would tease me.

The last few hits were harder and then he dropped the paddle on the floor of the truck. Kneeling behind me, his tongue attacked my pussy as a finger slid into my ass. Christ, I needed this so badly. Clenching around him viciously, I felt him stand back up. Both hands continued to tease me as he leaned over my back.

"Do you need to come?"

I was confused. He'd never allowed my release when we met. Only ever happening at our longer visits at the hotels.

"I asked you a question."

"Yes, yes Sir. Please make me come."

Pulling me up and turning me toward him, he moved me to the front seat. Both front and back doors were open, giving us a little bit more privacy. I was dazed and not sure what his plan was. Hands on my hips, he helped lift me to the seat and pulled my skirt back up.

His head buried itself between my legs. "Fuck!"

Leaning back, my head against the center console I let him do what he did best. But I needed more friction, craved it. Lifting my legs, uncaring if I left shoe prints on his seats and door walls, I grabbed the 'Oh, shit' handle, lifted my hips, and fucked his face.

It wasn't long before I was starting to show him the tell-tale signs of my impending release. "That's it. Come for me."

"Oh, Sir... Gregor." His name was barely a whisper as my body began to shake.

Biting my lips, trying to be quiet, I needed this release desperately. Claiming me, I released the 'oh, shit' bar as every nerve ending started the collision course of ecstasy through my body. Then, never ceasing to surprise me, he made me come again.

CHAPTER
Twenty-Seven

RUNAWAY

Smiling down at me, he grabbed the 'oh shit' bar and yanked vigorously. "Well, I think it's safe to call these 'oh fuck' bars now." He was mocking me and I laughed. "Did they help, give you that added friction?" His brow was arched at me, awaiting my reply.

Giggling, "Yes, the 'oh fuck' bar helped immensely."

Sitting up, I grabbed the waist of his jeans. Leaning down, he kissed me as he freed his cock for me. Smiling wickedly, I lowered myself, sitting on the step bars and let him fuck my face. It didn't take long. His arms braced against the door opening, he spilled down my throat.

Holding and kissing each other, we each worked our hands over one another until the tremors were gone. Not sure if we had time, I started massaging his neck. He groaned in response.

"Want that massage?"

Looking around, he was contemplating it. Spotting a picnic table, he motioned me to follow him. Closing his truck doors, we walked across the field to the picnic table and he sat down. Standing behind him, I started in on his neck and shoulders.

We talked about everything like we typically did while I massaged his back. Kneeling down to my knees, I worked his lower back as he lowered his head to his arms that were resting on the table. He grew quiet and I didn't mind. The weather was beautiful and I was enjoying my time with him.

After working over his back for quite some time, my hands were throbbing. They needed a break. Sitting down next to him, he turned to face me, one leg on each side of the seat. I had no idea how much time had passed and I didn't want to know.

Moving closer, he started kissing me again. His hands delicately moved over the side of my neck and into my hair. My hands were on his hips as he pulled my legs over his thigh. My roaming hands found a hole in the crotch of his jeans and wiggled a finger inside.

"Easy access hole?"

Laughing, "Almost every pair..."

Lowering my eyes, I smiled, "Even busted the patch. Hmmm..."

Pursing my lips together, he caught my innuendo and laughed some more. "I'm cheap."

"Clearly."

We kissed some more and held one another. My head on his shoulder his arms wrapped around me. Closing my eyes, I fantasized about being able to do this whenever I wanted. 'Reel it in!' Pushing Tami's warning from my thoughts, I started to nibble on his neck until soft moans left him.

"Let me see those eyes." Cupping my face, he stared at them and smiled. "Those deep eyes." He then shook his head and I felt the blush creep up my face. "Love those eyes."

"I love yours, too." He seemed a little taken aback. "They're beautiful. The blue is so unlike mine. I love looking at them."

A corner of his mouth turned up as he pulled my lips to his. My hands ran over his exposed forearms as he kissed me. Forehead to forehead, we stared into each other's eyes for a moment before I closed mine, unmoving. His hands played with the hair at the nape of my neck as I softly cooed.

Whispering against my parted lips, "I have to go."

My hands were now caressing his thighs, I responded, "I'm not stopping you." He continued kissing me as soft moans fell from both of us and we inched a little closer together.

We played that game for several minutes. It was a dangerous one. One where we couldn't get enough of each other, teetering on a line I wasn't sure if we were supposed to cross or not. Knowing we'd likely crossed it long ago. Were we breaking the rules set in place? I didn't know and like so many things with him, I didn't care. Or maybe I cared too much.

Finally, he moved to stand. Sighing, I followed suit. Starting the walk, he slapped my ass as we walked back toward our vehicles. Reaching his truck, I turned to face him and smiled. He pulled me into a hug, squeezed me tight and then released me.

"Hope the massage helped."

"It did. Thank you."

"You're welcome."

"I'll talk to you soon."

I nodded and headed toward my car as he climbed into his truck. He pulled out of the lot before I did. Looking to the clock I saw that almost two hours had passed. Closing my eyes, I turned on the one song that had been playing in my head almost the entire time I was with him. *Runaway* by Grace Mitchell. Lowering my head back, I sat there while the song played and recounted our visit.

Unable to resist. I emailed him.

> *TO: bruisedassets@yahoo.com*
> *2:35 PM*
> *Subject: Re: Belt...*
> *Thank you. As always, it was great to see you. I think you knocked something loose...I can't see straight. Course I may just need to eat food instead of your protein shot! Lol. Talk soon...*

Giving myself another moment, I pulled out of the lot and headed home. My email pinged. Was he even home yet? Probably. Smiling, I opened the email.

> *TO: meredith@meredithedits.com*
> *2:42 PM*
> *Subject: Re: Belt...*
> *I could let you do that for hours...*

I started the song over as I typed my reply when I pulled into my drive.

TO: bruisedassets@yahoo.com
2:47 PM
Subject: Re: Belt...
   Right back at ya. That tongue sucking of yours and hair pulling nearly had me on my knees. Ok, so I was on my knees, but... Of course anything you do has that ability. Do it again!
   Vision is back to normal...Ass is officially very sore. :) Can't wait to have you in a bed again...

A few more emails were exchanged as I ran a few more errands. We talked a little bit about our potential night away before the Holidays. I reached out to Tami and my babysitter, trying to figure something out.

Once the kids were in bed that night, I sat down to email him once again.

TO: bruisedassets@yahoo.com
9:39 PM
Subject: Sore bottom :)
   Hope you had a productive rest of the day. I'm sure you're still going!
   Just rubbed some of that cream onto my sore bottom. And I'm very wet... still. The things you do to me... :)
   I'll probably fall asleep rubbing said marks. There's nothing quite like it...except you rubbing them.
   Thinking of you...
   Talk soon.

I didn't hear back until later the next day.

TO: meredith@meredithedits.com
3:57 PM
Subject: Re: Sore bottom :)
   :) I like rubbing your marks...

TO: bruisedassets@yahoo.com
8:39 PM
Subject: Re: Sore bottom :)
   The coming weeks are going to suck as I count down to our night away.
   I'll be around rest of the week, getting shit done...unless I get a call from some perv wanting to spank my ass... :) Lol. Then I'll come running...

TO: meredith@meredithedits.com
8:57 PM
Subject: Re: Sore bottom :)
   Or crawling... :)

Shaking my head. I got caught up on some editing and other housely duties. In the morning, after the gym, I had an email.

> *TO: meredith@meredithedits.com*
> *10:30 AM*
> *Subject: Re: Sore bottom :)*
> *Did I sufficiently satiate you in your dreams last night or was I slacking...?*

> *TO: bruisedassets@yahoo.com*
> *10:36 AM*
> *Subject: Re: Sore bottom :)*
> *I would say it was enough for my dreams. Lol. I already warned you that I'll probably never get enough. Just seeing you always calms/satiates me for a few days. I'm going to be a hot mess until I see you again. Then I'll be a wet mess. I hate waiting.*
> *Just left the gym. Sweaty, needy, wet...*
> *How did you sleep?*

> *TO: meredith@meredithedits.com*
> *10:40 AM*
> *Subject: Re: Sore bottom :)*
> *Well, but short. Got to the hotel late and then had emails to respond to.*
> *Up early for meetings.*

Before I knew it, a couple of weeks had passed. Thanksgiving would be upon us soon. I was going away for a week with Tami to New Orleans. We both needed the time away which meant we'd be reading, drinking, eating, and sleeping! And when her cousin offered up his house *and* the air miles to fly us down, we couldn't pass it up.

Hoping to see each other before Thanksgiving was upon us, we were emailing, trying to work out a time before I was gone for the week. The late night emails were becoming another issue, but a good one when you're in bed alone.

> *TO: bruisedassets@yahoo.com*
> *12:25 AM*
> *Subject: Greedy bitch*
> *You around in the am? I need a fix. Greedy bitch!*

> *TO: meredith@meredithedits.com*
> *12:34 AM*
> *Subject: Re: Greedy bitch*
> *Not likely. I need to hit the road pretty early for some lunch meetings.*
> *What does the greedy bitch need now...? :)*

TO: bruisedassets@yahoo.com
12:43 AM
Subject: Whisky
Lol...just the arms of her Sir. Maybe a swat or two of his hand and a reminder of who owns her from time to time...
Can't stop listening to Tennessee Whiskey by Chris Stapleton. Makes me think about whisky kisses for some reason...
Sounds delicious...

TO: meredith@meredithedits.com
12:51 AM
Subject: Re: Whisky
I had some for the first time in a while tonight...hmmm
Need to taste it on your breath...

TO: bruisedassets@yahoo.com
12:54 AM
Subject: Re: Whisky
That a question or a statement...

TO: meredith@meredithedits.com
12:58 AM
Subject: Re: Whisky

Statement...but easily construed as a question.

TO: bruisedassets@yahoo.com
1:03 AM
Subject: Re: Whisky
It works either way for me... :) I'll lick every drop off your tongue and lips...
You're making me horny. I was planning to be good tonight...

TO: meredith@meredithedits.com
1:08 AM
Subject: Re: Whisky
Bad, bad pussy.

TO: bruisedassets@yahoo.com
1:10 AM
Subject: Re: Whisky
But bad, bad pussy is so good...

The emails stopped for the night and picked right back up in the morning.

TO: bruisedassets@yahoo.com
10:33 AM

Subject: Re: Good morning
18 miles down...

TO: meredith@meredithedits.com
10:36 AM
Subject: Re: Good morning
You need anything else to down...?

TO: bruisedassets@yahoo.com
10:37 AM
Subject: Re: Good morning
Always if it's you...
Need a blow n go before you leave? Or are you already gone?

TO: meredith@meredithedits.com
10:48 AM
Subject: Re: Good morning
Yes.
But today isn't looking promising. Hopefully tomorrow... :)

TO: bruisedassets@yahoo.com
10:51 AM
Subject: Re: Good morning
Ok.
Just drove by both Rodeos...sigh
Drive safe. Talk soon.

After dinner, I heard back from him.

TO: meredith@meredithedits.com
6:58 PM
Subject: Re: Good morning
Just finished working out and headed over to the bar to wait for my customer. Hot little local sat down next to me and chatted. Desperate housewife... :)

Agh! He knew what he was doing. I sat and stewed for a few minutes. How did I respond? Fuck it! I didn't give a shit what he thought of my response.

TO: bruisedassets@yahoo.com
7:08 PM
Subject: Step off MY Sir
Tell the hot little local to step off MY Sir. Lol.

TO: meredith@meredithedits.com

7:09 PM
Subject: Re: Step off MY Sir
LOL
You want to whip her little, intruding ass don't you...?

TO: bruisedassets@yahoo.com
7:10 PM
Subject: Re: Step off MY Sir
And yours. :)

TO: meredith@meredithedits.com
7:13 PM
Subject: Re: Step off MY Sir
Uh oh...

TO: bruisedassets@yahoo.com
7:15 PM
Subject: Re: Step off MY Sir
*She can't suck cock like I can. And that is NOT a challenge to find out. I
can reassure you tomorrow!*
    :)

TO: meredith@meredithedits.com
7:16 PM
Subject: Re: Step off MY Sir
How else can you substantiate that claim...?

TO: bruisedassets@yahoo.com
7:18 PM
Subject: Re: Step off MY Sir
I'm going to kick your ass. Not the reassurance I need...

TO: meredith@meredithedits.com
7:19 PM
Subject: Re: Step off MY Sir
How you going to kick my ass from there?
Good news if you can go second so you know what you're up against... :)

TO: bruisedassets@yahoo.com
7:22 PM
Subject: Re: Step off MY Sir
*I believe she'd be going second. I had you first, unless she's a hot local
you know.*
    Wrap it up! I don't want what the hot local barfly has. :) JERK! Lol

Then I waited. My mind was going crazy and I wanted to hurt someone. Why the hell was I so jealous? Fuck!

> *TO: meredith@meredithedits.com*
> *7:37 PM*
> *Subject: Re: Step off MY Sir*
> *Do you need someone to turn that bottom red and wipe away the pouty tears...?*

ASSHOLE!

> *TO: bruisedassets@yahoo.com*
> *7:43 PM*
> *Subject: Re: Step off MY Sir*
> *Maybe, yes. I enjoy spanking games, not jealousy and wondering if I'm one of a slew enjoying your talents.*
> *I'm crazy stressed. I warned you I don't share well. :)*

> *TO: meredith@meredithedits.com*
> *7:45 PM*
> *Subject: Re: Step off MY Sir*
> *Hmmm...she says as she is brandishing a drink and the flogger...*

> *TO: bruisedassets@yahoo.com*
> *7:50 PM*
> *Subject: Re: Step off MY Sir*
> *I'm going to take that flogger to you...or make one of my authors give you a nasty STD in their book! :)*

> *TO: meredith@meredithedits.com*
> *7:51 PM*
> *Subject: Re: Step off MY Sir*
> *Ahhh...resulting to the pen when the sword is week...*

> *TO: bruisedassets@yahoo.com*
> *7:53 PM*
> *Subject: Re: Step off MY Sir*
> *You enjoy riling me up.*
> *And it's 'weak', not week. Lol*

> *TO: meredith@meredithedits.com*
> *7:55 PM*
> *Subject: Re: Step off MY Sir*
> *Autocorrect.*
> *And possibly...*

> *TO: bruisedassets@yahoo.com*

7:57 PM
Subject: Re: Step off MY Sir
LOL
There's no 'possibly' about it... :)

TO: meredith@meredithedits.com
7:58 PM
Subject: Re: Step off MY Sir
Careful. You obviously need to be whipped for insolence...

TO: bruisedassets@yahoo.com
8:01 PM
Subject: Re: Step off MY Sir
:) Tongue whipped, finger whipped, dick whipped...I can go on and on...
And you also enjoy my insolence...keeps you on your toes. :)

TO: meredith@meredithedits.com
8:04 PM
Subject: Re: Step off MY Sir
Flogged and broken...
I'm going to thoroughly enjoy whipping it out of you...

TO: bruisedassets@yahoo.com
8:06 PM
Subject: Re: Step off MY Sir
Sigh...stupid pulsing clit and damn smile on my face. You suck...

TO: meredith@meredithedits.com
8:09 PM
Subject: Re: Step off MY Sir
No. You do...well.

TO: bruisedassets@yahoo.com
8:10 PM
Subject: Re: Step off MY Sir
Thank you. Can't wait to remind you...

TO: meredith@meredithedits.com
8:12 PM
Subject: Re: Step off MY Sir
While competing for first place...

TO: bruisedassets@yahoo.com
8:13 PM
Subject: Re: Step off MY Sir
Damn straight... :)
You're in first place too...

TO: meredith@meredithedits.com
8:15 PM
Subject: Re: Step off MY Sir
Is there a competitor waiting to unseat me?
Do we need to do a lick off...?

TO: bruisedassets@yahoo.com
8:18 PM
Subject: Re: Step off MY Sir
LMAO. No. There's no question...you're my #1 in more categories than I care to admit. Wouldn't want your ego to over-inflate!
I'm sure I'll wake up several times tonight due to thoughts of your #1 skills.

TO: meredith@meredithedits.com
8:19 PM
Subject: Re: Step off MY Sir
LOL
You know you need to be spanked and all holes properly stuffed.

TO: bruisedassets@yahoo.com
8:21 PM
Subject: Re: Step off MY Sir
There's no denying that. But can we get them all stuffed and ass spanked at the same time?!?! :)

TO: meredith@meredithedits.com
8:22 PM
Subject: Re: Step off MY Sir
That will take multiple toys or multiple partners...

TO: bruisedassets@yahoo.com
8:23 PM
Subject: Re: Step off MY Sir
Snort...I have multiple toys. Not sure my other 'partner' would be ok with that...the toys, toys in my ass, or multiple partners. Lmao. Shhh, don't tell him. OMG...what is wrong with me?!

TO: meredith@meredithedits.com
8:26 PM
Subject: Re: Step off MY Sir
Well...you know I will use toys, my tongue, and cock on and in your well spanked ass...

TO: bruisedassets@yahoo.com
8:28 PM
Subject: Re: Step off MY Sir
I know...and I'm very grateful. I've been working on getting my ass

prepared for your welcome intrusion.

We had yet to have anal sex, just unable to successfully get me to relax enough. But I wanted it, knew he wanted it, but he'd assured me he was patient and we'd keep trying.

> *TO: meredith@meredithedits.com*
> *8:31 PM*
> ***Subject: Re: Step off MY Sir***
> *And how have you been preparing...?*

> *TO: bruisedassets@yahoo.com*
> *8:33 PM*
> ***Subject: Re: Step off MY Sir***
> *I knew that'd get your attention. My new butt plug has been getting a workout...*

> *TO: meredith@meredithedits.com*
> *8:34 PM*
> ***Subject: Re: Step off MY Sir***
> *Is it ready to be stuffed and fucked to the hilt...?*
> *Does the butt plug have that setting...?*

> *TO: bruisedassets@yahoo.com*
> *8:36 PM*
> ***Subject: Re: Step off MY Sir***
> *It's been fully set in place, though it's not as big as you. I love and hate it...it's not you...*
> *How's your cock feeling?!*

> *TO: meredith@meredithedits.com*
> *8:40 PM*
> ***Subject: Re: Step off MY Sir***
> *Full. Taut. Needing release. Maybe tonight. Maybe tomorrow.*

> *TO: bruisedassets@yahoo.com*
> *8:36 PM*
> ***Subject: Re: Step off MY Sir***
> *That's a lot of maybes... Maybe both...*

> *TO: meredith@meredithedits.com*
> *8:42 PM*
> ***Subject: Re: Step off MY Sir***
> *Possibly*

TO: bruisedassets@yahoo.com
8:44 PM
Subject: Re: Step off MY Sir
 I'll be in bed tonight listening to music, imagining you whispering dirty words in my ear, denying me release, and all sorts of other things...

CHAPTER
Twenty-Eight

USE ME UP

Aᴎᴅ ᴊᴜꜱᴛ ʟɪᴋᴇ ᴛʜᴀᴛ, ʜᴇ was gone. He said he was waiting on his customer. Odds were that's what was occupying him, at least it better be.

> *TO: bruisedassets@yahoo.com*
> *11:37 PM*
> *Subject: Re: Step off MY Sir*
> *Eyes are getting heavy. Crawling into bed in a few. Hope your meeting is/went well.*

> *TO: meredith@meredithedits.com*
> *11:42 PM*
> *Subject: Re: Step off MY Sir*
> *Just got back to hotel. Should I come and drift off to sleep or save it all for you...?*

> *TO: bruisedassets@yahoo.com*
> *11:44 PM*
> *Subject: Re: Step off MY Sir*
> *You know the answer. I want it all. I'll behave too if you tell me to...*

Again, he went quiet. I didn't even know if he'd gotten my plea for him to save it for me. I fought sleep all night, dreams and thoughts consumed by him. And I told him as much when I woke in the morning, sending another email. He responded right away.

> *TO: meredith@meredithedits.com*
> *7:42 AM*
> **Subject: Re: Restless sleep**
> *Slept good. Fueled by a long day. Bourbon, thoughts of flogging your protruding ass, and an orgasm in which I almost gave myself a facial – I went to sleep quick and stayed asleep... :)*

I sighed. Jerk!

> *TO: bruisedassets@yahoo.com*
> *7:44 AM*
> **Subject: Re: Restless sleep**
> *I probably would've slept better had I not denied myself...*
> *Are you satiated or do you need to look in my deep eyes while I suck you off?*

His reply came through while I was getting the kids ready for school.

> *TO: meredith@meredithedits.com*
> *8:18 AM*
> **Subject: Re: Restless sleep**
> *LOL – I was too tired and had too much to drink to be satiated. I think I fell asleep before I finished coming...*
> *I prefer to watch you enjoy yourself as you are immersed with providing me pleasure. Maybe today... :)*

Better fucking be today! I replied when I got home from dropping the kids at the bus stop.

> *TO: bruisedassets@yahoo.com*
> *9:03 AM*
> **Subject: Re: Restless sleep**
> *If not today you're going to be waiting. I leave tomorrow morning for my week away with Tami.*
> *I'll be struggling with wanting to nap today. I'm exhausted.*

> *TO: meredith@meredithedits.com*
> *9:13 AM*
> **Subject: Re: Restless sleep**

You need some rodeo time...

TO: bruisedassets@yahoo.com
9:14 AM
Subject: Re: Restless sleep
But of course...that's up to you. :)

TO: meredith@meredithedits.com
9:17 AM
Subject: Re: Restless sleep
Let's see how well you convince me between now and when I get back that you deserve to be on your knees with my swollen cock in your mouth.

I about fell out of my chair. Pressing my lips together mischievously, I typed my reply.

TO: bruisedassets@yahoo.com
9:21 AM
Subject: Let me convince you...
Hmm...should I write you something dirty, play hard to get (that's a joke and we know it when it comes to you), ask for mercy and plead for one last blow n go before my long weekend, tell you that some time with you will help get me through the coming weeks...? All I thought about last night was you behind me, holding me, fucking me, spanking me, stroking me...

Bam! Inspiration hit and another poem flew off my fingertips.

TO: bruisedassets@yahoo.com
9:34 AM
Subject: Re: Let me convince you...
Mold me, hold me, fold me into you
Take me higher with your control
Cool my desire with your own fire
My lips are eager to feast on you
With your words that tempt
And hands that hurt
Pain so true
Pleasure through and through
No one else can do what you do

I waited over forty-five minutes for his response. And it was worth the wait.

TO: meredith@meredithedits.com
10:23 AM
Subject: Convinced

I will plan on meeting you on my way back. It will be brief. Bring the flogger. It will be used over the clothes. It will be woefully short of the punishment and discipline your bottom needs and craves, but will serve as a reminder of what you have had and what you will soon receive once we can be together again. While I will not get to see the individual strands strike your naked bottom or get to relish the sound only the flogger can make on bare skin – I can provide enough intensity to make you know more will be forthcoming without marking you. It will be fast and swift. You will then be placed on your knees to appropriately finish the task I started last night. When finished, you will look me in the eyes with those bright, beautiful eyes and satisfying smile and thank me. I will kiss you and send you on your way to finish prepping for your weekend away and then the coming holiday. While I will be wanting to hold you in my arms and kiss those lips for hours – I will not have time and that is simply not something that can be rushed or done satisfactory in 10 min.

I am now fully erect thinking about you being bent over and wanting the full brunt of the flogger and my cock knowing you will have to excruciatingly wait several more weeks. However, as you know, the wait will be well worth it.

I may have fainted, fallen from my chair, and struggled to get back in it. 'Several weeks'? Then it dawned on me. He was planning to make me wait until our night away. FUCK! No, no, no!!!!

> **TO:** *bruisedassets@yahoo.com*
> *11:18 AM*
> Subject: Re: Convinced
> *Thud.*
> *Yes, Sir.*

Inspiration hit again. Music playing, *Use Me Up* by Wanderhouse was put on repeat. I hated waiting for him. But knew once I did, it was always worth it. His words were indeed true.

> **TO:** *bruisedassets@yahoo.com*
> *11:43 AM*
> **Subject: Re: Convinced**
> *I wrote this one, too...*
> *Strung up and waiting for you*
> *Tied up and chained to you*
> *I await my punishment*
> *For your deliverance*
> *Your darkness a comfort*
> *Your touch my saving grace*

My demons dance with yours
Across the glass covered floors
Break me if you must
For it is you I wholly trust
You take me on and release my pain
Insurmountable pleasure what we gain

Later that afternoon I got an email and was told to start heading to Rodeo 1. Then he called.

"Head to Rodeo 2. 1 is compromised."

"Ok."

Heart racing, it dropped when I got to Rodeo 2. I texted him: *Compromised.*

Waiting he asked me to give him a few minutes. Then he called.

"Head east and then turn south at the first street. About a quarter mile down, there's a place to park. I'll be there."

"Ok. I'm glad I'm not directionally challenged."

His laugh vibrated through the phone as I drove, then he said, "I see you. Back it in."

I started giggling, "That's what she said."

Laughing, he replied, "Bye!"

"Bye!"

His strong arms greeted me as they always did, holding me tight as I instantly relaxed into him. I inhaled deeply, wanting to embed his scent into my memory. He didn't wear cologne, but he always smelled heavenly to me.

"You smell good."

Chortling, he said, "I'm not wearing anything."

Muffled, as I spoke into his neck, "I know, but you still smell good."

Moving us, I was soon leaning against the back seat as he held me close, his hips grinding against mine. One hand moved up my neck and cupped my jaw as he kissed me. His tongue stroked slowly, deeply, as if he, too, was savoring my taste. Hands on each bicep, I gripped them tightly through his sweater.

I moaned and he pulled his lips from mine. "You were pretty pissed last night. You wanted to paddle her didn't you?"

Smirking, I squeezed his ass and admitted, "I wanted to paddle your ass, too. Fucking mess with my Sir."

He was laughing whole-heartedly as he asked, "Jealous?"

"I told you I don't want to share your talents. Not yet."

His eyes searched mine before I pressed my lips back to his. Unzipping my pants, his hand moved in and sank between my soaked lips. Gasping, I kissed him harder, bit his lips, and sucked his tongue. It started building quicker than I thought it would. My arms moved to his neck and held fast to him.

Snarling in my ear, "You want to come?"

I couldn't even finish my reply as I started clenching around his fingers. "Yes..."

"That's it. My naughty girl." My lips were pressed together, face buried in his neck. When the shudders ceased, he stated, "That was quick."

Blushing, I whispered, "Sometimes I'm quick. Don't get used to it."

He laughed. And I knew we were short on time. Grabbing him through his jeans, he nipped at my lips as he freed himself for me. Dropping down, ass on the step bars, I took him deep in my mouth.

"Fuck."

Smiling around his girth, I sucked harder, and took him as deep as I could. Squeezing his ass, I held him closer as he fucked my mouth. Glancing up, one hand was braced on the truck, the other in my hair. I moaned against him as I felt his balls rise and the pulsing began. Before he was done, a car pulled by. He stilled as I continued to suck, my presence not visible to the passerby, and started to spill down my throat.

From the other side of the truck, I heard a voice ask, "You headed out soon?"

Gregor pried himself out of my mouth and moved a few feet down the side of his truck and said, "Yup, about twenty minutes."

"Right on." I heard a door close as the car drove off.

I burst into laughter at the sight of him standing behind the bed of his truck, dick still erect, and dripping. His smile overtook his face and we both started laughing. Putting his dick away, I openly pouted.

"I'm not done!"

Laughing, "Come here." Pulling me close, we kissed some more, and held each other for a few short minutes. "We should get going."

Grumbling, "I know."

"Enjoy your week away and Thanksgiving. I'll be in touch."

Trying to keep a brave face, not knowing when I'd see him again, touch him again, taste him again, I nodded. I kissed him one more time before he pushed me toward my SUV, slapping my ass like he typically did.

"Bye."

Smiling, he climbed up to the steps before sitting down and waved. "I'll email you."

"Ok." I got in my vehicle and drove away.

As I drove, I realized we'd never used the flogger like he said. Smiling, I ran my fingers over my swollen lips. Nobody knew how to use me like he used me. Glancing in the mirror, they were definitely looking used, too. I ran a quick errand to pick up milk and then headed home.

After the kids were home, I got an email.

> TO: meredith@meredithedits.com
> 4:56 PM
> Subject: You missed some.
> You didn't get it all. Had it running down my leg.
> Left me smirking... :)

> TO: bruisedassets@yahoo.com
> 5:02 PM
> Subject: Re: You missed some.
> Well, you moved on me. Damn hunters. I wasn't done!
> My lips looked thoroughly used after.
> I ran to get milk and panicked as I walked in: Hope I don't have mud smears on my ass! I didn't but that had me laughing.
> Thank you. I know it was too quick, but I really feel like a weight has been lifted getting to see you before the next couple weeks consume us. Thank you for grabbing on to me tight. It seriously releases tension for me.
> I can't stop giggling thinking about you standing there, still erect, talking to him...you should've just said, 'Dude, I'm getting blown, come back in 20!' LOL
> Talk soon...

The next morning, Tami and I headed to the airport. The flight was uneventful and I was ecstatic when we landed. Getting our luggage, we flagged a taxi and we were on our way.

"So your cousin is just offering up his house to you?"

"Well, we need to talk about that."

Glancing at her, I asked, "What did you do?"

Smiling, "He's not going out of town. I told you that because I knew Todd wouldn't agree to you staying with some dude, with or without me there."

I dropped my head and took a big breath. "Dammit, Tami."

"Sorry, not sorry. He was originally supposed to be out of town, but the trip got rescheduled. I didn't want to jeopardize our trip."

"What does it matter? It's fine." I just had to make sure Todd didn't find out.

The taxi pulled up in front of the house as I took it in. I'd never been to New Orleans and was excited to take in the sights and the city. We climbed out as the driver pulled our bags from the trunk. Paying him, Tami then led the way to the front door. Her cousin had a beautiful house. I'd never met him, this Jared, but Tami said he was super cool.

I was so looking forward to a week away from everything, returning the day before Thanksgiving. I'd seen Gregor for a few minutes before we headed to the airport. His schedule had opened up for a few minutes and he wanted to see me on my way out of town.

"Have fun!" His smile beamed at me before he pulled me in for a hug.

"I will. I promise to behave."

Pulling back, he scrunched his eyes together. "I don't want you to behave. Have fun. It's NOLA! Get that ass spanked, and not by Tami." I stared at him, mortified but smirking. "And I want proof."

"You're the devil. Ok, so I have homework for you."

"I'm listening."

Smiling, "I want an email. Every day. Just so I know you're thinking of me."

Pursing his lips, he smiled and agreed. "Have fun." He kissed me quickly and then swatted my ass before pushing me back toward my waiting car and Tami.

Walking through the front gate, we headed up the steps to the front porch. Tami rang the bell and shortly after the door was swung open. I paid no attention as the figure reached down to grab Tami's bags from her.

"Come on in. Did you have a good flight?'

Chirping, "Thank you again so much. Yes, the flight was great. No problems."

I followed up the steps as a hand touched mine and took my bag. "It's really heavy, I can manage."

"Nonsense."

My eyes darted up and then did a double take. *Holy fuck he was beautiful.* A brilliant smile greeted me as he motioned his arm to welcome me in. But it wasn't the smile that necessarily caught my attention. He had beautiful eyes. A blue, different from Gregor's, but just as striking. Looking back to my bag that he now carried, I spotted the wide black leather bracelet that donned his wrist.

"You must be Meredith?"

Nodding, "Yes. You must be Jared?"

"That's me."

Walking into his home, I took in the ambience. It was very well decorated and not true to his bachelor status. Nothing was out of place. Tami mentioned he traveled a lot so maybe that's why everything was so immaculately kept; he was never home to disturb it.

"Follow me."

He carried a suitcase in each hand up the stairs like it was nothing. It was then that I noticed the biceps and triceps bunching the fabric of his black t-shirt. *Fuck!* Tami looked back at me and followed my eyes and then gawked at me.

"Gross!" I just shook my head at her. Her cousin was hot, she had to know that.

"These two rooms share the bathroom; it's a Jack and Jill suite." We entered the same bedroom as he dropped the bags at the foot of the bed. "Here." He walked through a doorway that led to a bathroom and then through another door that led to another bedroom. "Hope this works for you two."

I chimed in, "It's more than adequate. Thank you. I figured I was cuddling with your cousin all weekend."

Tami, being the whore she was just deadpanned, "We both know I'm not the cousin you want to cuddle with."

I felt myself blush immediately. Unable to resist, I looked to him and caught him checking me out before his smile made me speechless. And then, he left the room without another word. Rushing over, I closed the door and then glared at her.

She was already laughing. "What the hell is wrong with you?"

"Um, clearly my cousin isn't offended by that idea."

"Christ, shut the hell up! There's no way that he's interested in me."

"Why not?"

"Um, I know he's your cousin, but have you seen him? That body..." I plopped down on the bed as something occurred to me. "This isn't a setup is it?"

She put her hands up in defense. "Promise, no cahoots." She sat down next at me and asked, "Which room do you want? Or do you want to check out his room first?"

"Oh my God. Stop it." Getting up, I walked to the other room. "I'll take this one." It was decorated in soft blues and whites, which appealed to me.

"Ok." She followed me in and took her suitcase back to her room.

Laying back on the bed, I dozed off.

CHAPTER
Twenty-Nine

NOT STRONG ENOUGH

A WHILE LATER I FELT A HAND on my shoulder and opened my eyes to see Tami standing over me.

"Sorry. How long have I been out?"

"Only an hour. Your phone is going crazy with alerts."

"Shit." Reaching to the night stand, I grabbed my phone. "I forgot to let him know I arrived."

"Todd or Gregor?"

Chortling, "Both." I sent Gregor a quick email and Todd a text reassuring them I was safe.

"That's it?"

"Yup. I'm on vacation. What's the plan?"

"Jared wants to know if we want to go out for dinner or if we want him to cook."

"If we're going out I need to change."

"I think we should hang here tonight. We can make a plan for tomorrow over dinner."

"Fine with me."

Heading downstairs, I followed Tami to the kitchen where we found Jared. He was leaning on the granite counters and typing away on his laptop. Tami gave me a quick tour of the house. He had a poker table in the dining room in lieu of a dinner table. Now that made more sense considering he was a bachelor.

"So, what's the plan ladies?" He had a big smile on his face and rubbed his hands together devilishly.

"You're cooking cuz."

Nodding, "Ok." Looking to me, he asked, "Any allergies I need to know about?" I shook my head. "I'm going to call a friend. Maybe we can get a Euchre game going." He laughed at the surprised expression on my face. "May be a NOLA boy now, but I was born and raised in the north. And I haven't played in forever."

Laughing, "Sounds like a plan to me."

Later that night, after dinner, we stood around the kitchen counter when the doorbell rang. He'd mentioned he invited his friend Sam over and that he would arrive after we ate. When this was mentioned, Tami had openly groaned at Jared. After a brief discussion, Tami agreed. I wasn't sure if Tami just didn't like this Sam person or if there was more to it.

Jared and I had exchanged pleasantries over dinner and I found him exceptionally easy to talk to. Though, he made me slightly nervous, too. There was something about him, but I couldn't quite put my finger on it.

As Jared walked away and to the door, I asked Tami, "You know this Sam guy?" She groaned. "Yes, we've met."

Guessing from her tone, she wasn't a fan, or she was trying to cover. "And?"

"Don't ask." I pressed my lips together and nodded, because time didn't allow for it.

I heard their voices as they moved through the house and back to us. He was taller than Jared and dreamy in a different sort of way. He wore all black, was more slender, and darker, but definitely in great shape. His eyes landed on Tami's and instantly you could feel the tension between the two of them. Then he smiled and it transformed his face. I liked him already.

His eyes moved from Tami's direction and over to mine. He offered his hand, "Sam."

"Meredith." I took his hand as I watched him and Jared exchange a peculiar look. *What was that about?*

Grinning, he added, "But you can call me Vice."

"Vice?" Tami groaned, I glanced at her and could tell she was visibly annoyed.

"Don't ask." Then he winked.

I didn't have time to think about it. "Alright. Who's ready for a drink and some cards?"

An hour later Jared and I were killing them at Euchre. I had decided to go alone with a hand full of hearts. "BOOM!" I took all five tricks and couldn't resist bragging.

"You whore!"

I took a dramatic bow and said, "You know it!"

"I need a cigarette." Tami pushed her chair from the table and headed out the patio door and Sam followed.

When they were gone, I inquired with Jared, "Do you know something I don't?" I motioned my head in their direction.

Smiling, he deflected. "They both smoke."

Rolling my eyes, I headed to the fridge for another wine cooler. When I turned around, he took the bottle from me and opened it before handing it back. I nodded and he started washing the dishes from dinner. I thought it only appropriate that I help.

"You don't need to do that."

"You cooked. I can help clean up." He smiled at me as his hands placed dishes in the sink full of water and added soap. "And you paid for us to come here, so."

"It was nothing. I have plenty of air miles to spare."

"Well, it was still very generous."

When the dishes were cleaned, dried and put away, we headed outside to find Tami and Sam deep in conversation. I stopped in my tracks, knowing I was intruding upon something I knew nothing about.

With his hand on the small of my back, Jared guided me to the other side of his back yard. We sat down on some beach loungers and he started talking, distracting me from Tami and Sam. He and Sam had joked about handcuffs while we were playing cards and I caught on right away. We'd all exchanged subtle remarks and I wondered if anything would be brought up again.

"So?" He just smiled at me, waiting for me to open dialogue.

"Ok. I'm just going to ask. Are you really into leather, spankings, et cetera?" His gaze became intense as he stared at me. Growing nervous, my eyes dropped to my lap as he chuckled. "If you're not, just forget I said anything."

"I am. Floggers, cuffs, blindfolds...you name it."

"Wooden paddles?" My eyes looked up to his curiously as I wrung my hands together in my lap.

Now that took him a little aback. Laughing, he admitted, "I haven't really explored with wood...yet."

"Oh." I tried to leave any hint of disappointment from my voice.

"You?" Pressing my lips together, I looked to the sky and felt myself blushing. I looked back to him and took him in. Could I trust him? How much did I tell him? "I'm going to assume you know plenty about wooden paddles."

Sighing, I said, "Truth. They don't mark the same way floggers to." Then I waited.

Leaning back, I could see the wheels turning in his head. "Care to divulge?"

"I don't know. Does this conversation stay here, between us?"

"Of course."

Something about him spoke to me, made me comfortable. I knew I could trust him. "So, clearly you're somewhat familiar with BDSM?" He nodded. "Would you like to take any guesses as to what I am?" I knew that if he was being honest, I didn't need to explain my question any further.

Scanning my body and then my face once more, he guessed wrong. "Domme."

Smiling wickedly, I shook my head. "Though I may have a touch of switch in me."

"Sub?" I nodded. "Nice."

"I'm presuming you're more Dom or Top."

"You'd be correct." I just shook my head. "What gave it away?"

"Just something you said when we played cards and the leather bracelet caught my attention."

He nodded and asked another question. "So, you and your husband?" I shook my head. "Ahh. Now I understand."

I let out an exaggerated breath. "Yeah."

"So, I'm listening. Who is he?"

I don't know what it was, but I felt completely at ease. I spilled *everything*. And he just sat and listened intently, for hours. A soft chuckle or comment from him came every now and then, but he'd insist I continue. When I was finally done, I looked around the yard to find Tami and Sam nowhere in sight.

"They went upstairs a while ago."

"Together?" He just laughed. "Ok. I didn't see that one coming." Lifting my hands, I started rubbing on my neck and moving it from side to side.

"Need a massage?" I froze and looked at him. That was a dumb question. Of course I needed one. "I'm good at it."

Smiling, I agreed. "Ok." He spread his legs and motioned me to sit down in front of him. "Oh, Jesus."

His hands dug in and I was almost immediately limp. His chuckle drifted over me as he started telling me his story. "Our stories are very parallel."

"How so?"

Then he spilled his story. He'd been divorced a few months, his sub was in the process of a divorce, and they'd been 'together' for several years. I could imagine his turmoil, and hers, since I myself knew I was standing at a crossroads of my own.

"You love her." It wasn't a question.

"Yes. We're way beyond what you and Gregor are."

I nodded. "Yes, clearly."

"Have you thought about telling him? He might be waiting on you."

I just shook my head. "No. I mean, I've thought about it, but—no." I paused and then added, "We agreed to no love."

"Well. Things change, people change, and he clearly cares about you."

Playing with my phone I put on *Not Strong Enough* by Shinedown. "I'm not sure I could handle either response from him if I told him." I knew he was listening to the lyrics of the song, digesting them like I was.

When the song was over he comforted me. "I get it. I've been there, walked the same path."

"I know he cares. I do." I said it more to myself, trying to rationalize his feelings.

"Well, I get it. This is really therapeutic having someone to talk to about all of this."

"I completely agree." His fingers moved into my hair, massaging my scalp. "You're going to put me to sleep."

He pulled me back a little closer. "So, go to sleep."

He eased me back, massaging my arms, shoulders and neck some more. And

I dozed off. I was bolted awake when Gregor's special tone went off. Pulling my phone from my pocket, I realized I was still leaning on Jared. Dropping my phone, while trying to move away from him quietly, he started chuckling.

"Gregor?"

Picking up my phone and looking to him, I smiled. "How'd you know?"

"I know that look."

"It's pitch black out here. You can't see my look."

"I don't need light to see you, Meredith." Insert *THUD*. I hypothetically fell to the ground at his remark. "So, is it him?"

"Yes." I confessed. "I gave him homework."

"Did you?"

Laughing, I nodded. "Yup. He gave me homework, too."

"That's pretty funny. Looks like both of our subs have been given homework." I met his eyes in the moonlight and gawked at him. "She's away on business and we both gave each other tasks. Maybe I can help you out with yours."

"This is insane. Though, I'm not sure you're what Gregor had in mind."

"So ask him. I'll ask Heather."

I ran my hands through my hair. "This is, just, yeah. I have to use the bathroom. I'll be right back." Then I played with the match I was holding. "Do you want a massage in return?"

"Yes. I'd love that. Let me know what Gregor says."

I opened my mouth and shut it right back. There was no point in denying what I was about to do. I was going to go use the bathroom *and* email Gregor.

Quickly, I emailed him back. He was talking about the weather and hoped I was having a good time. I just threw it out there in the email telling him about Jared and that he was a Dom and had homework of his own to complete. I left it at that, waiting to see what he said. His response was almost immediate.

> *TO: meredith@meredithedits.com*
> *11:56 PM*
> *Subject: Re: Homework*
> *It could be a nice start to misbehaving... :)*

I sighed. Vague, yet not. What did that mean?! Closing my email, I put my phone back in my pocket and headed back outside. Jared was still on the lounger, playing with his own phone. When he saw me coming, he put the phone away and smiled at me.

"She's intrigued."

I stopped short, before sitting and he laughed as I confessed. "Gregor told me it could be a nice start to misbehaving."

We both laughed as we took each other in. Moving forward, I took his cue and sat down behind him and got to work. Holy cow he was built. Gregor was built too, but not like this. Jared instantly relaxed as a few sighs left his mouth.

"Jesus. You're good."

"Mmm. Gregor has the same reaction. I can feel the tension leave him every time."

"He a good masseuse, too?"

"Hmph. That I wouldn't know. I have yet to get one from him."

"What? He doesn't rub you down before or after?"

"Not like this. We're usually fighting the clock when we see each other."

"But you rub him down."

Laughing, "Yes. Would you like his number? You can tell him that he's slacking in his duties."

"I may have to."

An hour later, I was getting another massage when he pulled my arm back. I instantly had a visual of getting handcuffed when he whispered in my ear.

"If I had my handcuffs with me this would be more fun."

Giggling, I turned my head back and said, "My safe word is 'keep going.'"

His reaction was priceless. Eyes bulged for a split second and then he belly laughed. We laughed about it for quite a few minutes before we were interrupted by a commotion coming from inside. I heard Tami yelling, but couldn't make out what she was saying. But she was clearly pissed.

"Oh, shit."

"You can say that again. I know my cousin and I know Sam. We should go intervene."

Getting up, we rushed inside to find Sam and Tami practically nose to nose arguing with one another. Holy shit there was definitely some kind of history there. Jared stepped between the two of them and walked out the front door with Sam.

Once they were gone, I moved to stand in front of Tami. Placing my hands on her shoulders to get her attention, I asked, "Tami, what's going on?"

She snapped at me. "Nothing. I fucking hate him."

I highly doubted that. "Ok. What happened?" I spotted a hickey on her neck, but chose to ignore it.

"I don't want to talk about it." Marching to the fridge, she pulled out another drink. "Fucking asshole!" She pulled out a beer and chugged half of it down then looked at me. "I'm surprised you're still up."

The mere mention of her words had me yawning. "We were outside talking."

"And?"

I caught her snippy tone and knew it wasn't in regards to Jared and me talking for hours, but it still hurt a little. "And nothing. We talked. But I am exhausted."

Jared walked over—alone—and said, "You should both get some rest. It's late."

Tami glared at him and demanded. "You and I need to talk."

Completely calm, he agreed. "That's fine."

"Ok then. I'm going to bed. I'll see you two in the morning." I headed for the stairs and as I started to climb them, I felt his hand on my wrist. Looking to my wrist and then his eyes, I froze, wondering what he wanted.

"We should talk again tomorrow. And I may want another massage."

Narrowing my eyes, I nodded. "Only if I get one, too."

"Deal. Get some rest."

"You too." Releasing my wrist, I finished climbing the stairs, the warmth of his hand still lingering on my skin.

> TO: bruisedassets@yahoo.com
> 2:33 AM
> Subject: Re: Homework
> We just talked for another two hours. He wants to talk more tomorrow. Just climbed into bed...alone. Thinking of you. :)

I didn't hear back from Gregor. Surprisingly, I slept quite well for being in a bed that wasn't my own. Waking several hours later, the sun was filtering through the curtains as I stretched out in bed. Checking my phone, still no email. I put some music on and recounted my conversation with Jared from the night before.

After a while I decided to get up and shower. Taking my belongings to the bathroom, I saw Tami still asleep and quietly closed the door as to not disturb her. After, when I was in my room getting dressed, I heard her in the bathroom. Already dressed, I headed out of my room. Passing by an open door, I heard heavy breathing and when I glanced inside I saw a shirtless Jared lifting weights.

I stopped briefly and as I was about to scuttle away, he caught my gaze.

"Hey. Did you sleep well?"

"I did. Thank you."

He continued lifting and said between reps, "Help yourself to anything you can find in the kitchen. I'll be down shortly."

Nodding, I did just that. Finding some oatmeal and juice, I sat down at the island and enjoyed the peace and quiet.

"Morning whore."

Smirking, I turned to Tami who looked worse for wear. "I could say the same to you."

She simply grunted and started rifling through the fridge and cabinets. "Seriously!"

"What?" She was agitated and I couldn't figure out what she was looking for. "What are you looking for?"

"I know my cousin. He has cereal here somewhere. He's just hiding it." She kept digging and then gasped, "Jackpot!"

She poured herself a bowl of the sugary cereal and sat down across from me. Tami was still in her pajamas and her hair was a wreck. We sat in silence, both eating, and then she headed outside for a smoke. I followed her.

"So. Sam." She glanced at me and I could see it all over her. "Spill it!"

"He's an ass."

Rolling my eyes, "So, tell me why."

"Ugh. We have a history. He was a friend of Jared's before Jared moved down here. Sam followed—business thing—and, well. Sam left me in Michigan."

"Wait. What? Left you how?" Tami and I were close, but I didn't know everything, clearly. "How long ago was this?"

"Long enough."

Then it dawned on me. "He's the guy." She narrowed her eyes at me. "It's all clear now. He's the one that got away."

She scoffed and took another puff of her cigarette. "More like I'm the one that got away. Thank fuck."

"Sure. Keep telling yourself that." She ignored me. "So, what happened last night? Clearly there's still an attraction."

Shrugging her shoulders, "We never could deny that. It's everything else that's a mess. Always has. Always will."

"Morning ladies."

Turning, we both acknowledged Jared, though Tami's greeting wasn't nearly as enthusiastic as mine was.

Rubbing his hands together, he smiled, "What's on the docket for today?"

Homework! I didn't say it, but it's the first thing that came to mind. I was going to hell. Hopefully Jared or Gregor—hell, they could both come—would be there to welcome me!

CHAPTER
Thirty

MY FAVOURITE FADED FANTASY

J ARED SHOWED US AROUND NOLA and filled us with more food than I'd ever admit to eating. We got home shortly after dinner time and when Jared asked if we were hungry, Tami and I both groaned.

"Please, God. No more food."

"Ditto. Coffee would be good though."

I seconded Tami's request. "Yes! Coffee please or I'm going to pass out from a food coma."

"Done. I'll put a pot on."

Tami was in a better mood and there'd been no mention of Sam. Deciding to watch a movie, Jared put on Interview with a Vampire. Tami was curled up on one end, with Jared on the other end on the chaise. I sat in the middle and held my cup of coffee in my lap. It'd been so long since I'd seen the movie that I became enthralled with it.

I'd sent Gregor a picture of Tami and me standing in front of a bakery in NOLA. He'd responded simply with 'It's beautiful there'. He also said that he hoped I was thoroughly enjoying myself. He hadn't inquired anymore about Jared, but I'd told Gregor that Jared was going to help me with my homework. I had to believe that had he not liked that idea, he would've said so.

Half way through the movie, I glanced over and found Tami asleep. Moving my eyes to the other end of the couch, Jared's eyes were already on me. Lifting his hands, he moved them as if he was already giving me a massage. Patting the space in front of him, I took the invitation and sat down after placing my empty cup on the coffee table.

Softly, he leaned in and said, "Heather gave me a thumbs up." A chill ran up my back and he caught it. "Is that a shiver of approval or...?"

"It's a shiver of 'What are the fucking odds?'."

He chuckled and continued working on my neck. "Nothing happens that you don't want to happen." He didn't say anything else.

Jared worked his magic on my neck, shoulders, back, arms, hands, and scalp until the movie ended. As if she sensed it was over, Tami woke, and didn't say anything at finding Jared and I on one end of the couch. She stepped outside and I followed her.

She lit her cigarette and said, "I think I'm going to crash. Are you going to be ok with him alone?"

Scrunching my face, "Of course. I'm not worried about him."

She giggled. "Yeah. I had a feeling you two would get along. Not *this* well, but..."

"He's really easy to talk to. I feel bad. He's your cousin and I feel like I'm stealing your time from him."

She waved it off. "Nonsense. We talk all the time. I'm just happy to be here with you both. Enjoy yourself."

"Ok." I pulled out my phone and refreshed my email. Nothing.

"Does *he* know what's going on here?"

I nodded, "He encouraged it."

Laughing, "Of course he did." I glanced at her. "No judgement from me. You know that. Have fun." She put out her cigarette and hugged me. "I'm crashing. See you in the morning."

Looking inside, I saw Jared talking on his phone. Sitting down on a lounger, I put some music on. I was missing Gregor terribly. More than I cared to admit. I put on *My Favourite Faded Fantasy* by Damien Rice and then perused old emails between him and me. Time got away from me and Jared scared me when he asked a simple question as I was looking over a poem I'd typed up the night before.

He laughed when I jumped. "Sorry, didn't mean to startle you. Email from Gregor?"

"No. Actually, a poem I wrote last night."

"Poem? Can I?"

I gawked at him, unsure I wanted to expose my thoughts to him. "Umm, it's not that good."

"Give it here. I'll be the judge." Hesitantly, I handed him my phone and he started reading it aloud.

> *"He was my darkness*
> *He was my dangerous*
> *He was my deadly*
> *He was my devil*
> *He was my demise*
> *I was his starlight*
> *I was his shelter*
> *I was his salvation*
> *I was his saint*
> *I was his sanity*
> *We were ensnared"*

I couldn't even look at him. It was worse than standing naked in front of a complete stranger.

"That's fucking deep." My eyes jerked up to his. "It's really good. Do you have any more?"

Nodding my head, "Yes, there's more but I'd have to siphon through a ton of emails to find them."

"It's ok. So, have you heard from him?"

Putting the phone in my lap, I shook my head. "Haven't heard from him since yesterday."

"Is that typical?"

I shrugged my shoulders. "It varies. He knows I'm on vacation. He usually emails at least once a day, but it's fine. I know he's busy."

He sat down next to me. "So, I have a work thing to attend tomorrow evening.

Sam will be there and we were hoping you and Tami would come with us." I looked at him slightly confused. "Strictly as friends. Low key, totally casual."

"I mean, sure. Though I'm not sure Tami will be ok with the Sam part."

"You let me worry about Tami."

"Be my guest!" We shared a laugh at that.

"You want to watch another movie? It's not that late." He seemed to pick up on my nervousness. "Meredith, what is it?"

I exhaled heavily. "I just. This," motioning between us, "is what Gregor and I were supposed to have."

Tilting his head, he asked, "What do you mean?"

Smiling, "The platonic, candid, no emotions, just friendship thing." He looked at me as if he was disappointed. "Hang on! I'm not saying I'm not attracted to you. I am. It's just...different."

"I get it. I do." Standing, he reached for my hand and I took his. Embracing me, "I still think you should tell him."

Squeezing him a little tighter, "I know. Let's go watch that movie."

The next afternoon, Tami and I were doing our hair and makeup. I hadn't heard from Gregor since the day before and let it go. He'd been sending an email every day like I'd requested so I couldn't complain. Of course, Jared was a good distraction. Jared and Sam had to make an appearance at some charity event and we were going with them. They assured us we could dress casual, but we both pulled out the nicest outfits we had with us. Both in maxi dresses, we headed downstairs complete with our hair and makeup done.

Both of the guys looked each of us up and down and whistled. I suddenly felt like I was headed to the prom, but way under dressed. Walking outside, Tami and I climbed in the back of Jared's car allowing the guys to have front.

Leaning over, I whispered, "You sure you're ok with this?"

"Its fine, I'll be fine. I can handle Sam... Or let him handle me."

I laughed at that and tried covering my mouth. Glancing up, Jared's eyes caught mine in the rearview mirror and he winked. Smiling, I averted my attention back to Tami.

"I'd let him handle me, too."

"Bitch, please. You have enough men in your life." Realizing how loud she'd been, she blushed and then busted up laughing. I didn't have to look in the rearview mirror to know Jared was watching me.

"You're dead to me." I tried to say it in all seriousness, but we both knew it was bullshit.

We arrived at the charity event and it ended up being a bust. Jared and Sam said hello to the people they needed to while Tami and I occupied ourselves at the bar. We were in a pretty swanky hotel and Tami had mentioned there was a nightclub upstairs on the roof. I hadn't been to a club in years and part of me wanted to go, though I wasn't sure I was ok with being the old lady in the crowd either.

"Alright ladies. The night is ours. Where to?" Sam had our attention.

But he lost mine when I felt Jared sidle up behind me. Sitting on a barstool, I glanced back to see him leaning against the bar. I could feel the heat of his body drifting onto my exposed shoulder blades and tried to hide the reaction my body had.

"Do you dance?" I could see the devilish gleam in his eyes.

I laughed. "Not well."

Tilting his chin up, he challenged me, "Prove it."

"Oh, Jesus. I think not." I turned back to Tami.

Then he whispered in my ear, "I just saw that little spark of Domme in you. Trying to convince me or yourself?"

What the hell was it with him and Gregor? How could two men so different have the same effect on me with their words? Shifting in my chair, I pursed my lips and stared at him. But he won the contest. His eyes said way too much in those few seconds. I didn't know whether to run or climb him like a tree.

"Meredith!"

Realizing she'd been trying to capture my attention, I turned to Tami. "Sorry. What's up?"

"We're going to the club. Come on."

Sighing, "Oh, shit. Ok." Looking at Sam I gave him a look of warning.

As if he knew what I was trying to say, he smiled and nodded.

Jared leaned in and said, "He'll keep an eye on her."

Once we entered the club, Jared and I found a corner and sat down to talk. Tami and Sam headed to the bar. It wasn't long before Tami was trying to drag us both to the dance floor. I tried to evade her, but Jared was no help. Taking my hand, he pulled me behind him, following Sam and Tami. Snagging a shot glass from

Sam, I threw it back as he and Jared both laughed at me.

Shrugging my shoulders, Tami and I began dancing. Tilting my neck, I tried to shake off the feeling of his eyes on me. There was no way I could sense that in such a short time. More than once that night—hell the couple days I'd been there—I could feel his eyes on me. There was no explanation for it, except maybe that different wiring that Gregor and I so often talked about.

After a couple songs, where Sam and Jared basically leaned against the wall and watched us, I surrendered. Tami cursed me and then dragged Sam to the floor with her as I traded spots with him against the wall.

Jared's fingers gently caressed my hip. Turning my head, I found his eyes transfixed on me and my pulse quickened as my breasts immediately ached. The look in his eyes held promises of what was to come. To anyone else he may have appeared agitated, but to me I knew it was hunger that lurked in his eyes. He was looking at me, his meal, and I was ready to be devoured by him. Standing straighter, my breath caught in my throat as I tried to take a deep breath.

Leaning into me, his breath fluttered over my ear as his fingers continued to secretly caress my hip. "Can we go? I need to touch you."

My panties were wet in an instant. Without a single word, I headed toward the exit knowing he was behind me. I walked to the elevator and was grateful we appeared to be alone. Stepping into the vacant space, the doors closed and the air grew thick. Leaning against the wall behind me, my eyes drifted to his. His expression was different, darker, and that's when it happened.

In a single stride he closed the distance between us. His hands grabbed my hips as they pulled me against his own. My eyes closed as I sought out his lips. I needed air, needed to breathe, and in that moment only his breath would do.

DING!

Shit!

The doors popped open as Jared quickly removed himself from my body and another couple entered the space with us. Avoiding eye contact with them, I glanced at Jared and he smirked. *Ass.* They exited before we did and again, he was on me instantly.

Pulling my arms above my head, he pressed his entire body into mine as I moaned in response. The kiss was heavy and too fucking short. It left me feeling famished, and not for food. The elevator stopped and we were at the main floor.

Motioning me out, I tried to keep myself composed. We headed toward the exit and that's when I grew concerned about Tami.

"Wait. What about Tami?"

Jared smirked, "Sam has a room here. She'll be fine."

Holy crap. Shit just got real! "Oh, ok."

Leaning into me again, he taunted me. "That means tonight, you're mine."

"Fuck."

Stopping, he looked at me and said, "It's up to you Meredith."

"No. I, yes." Blushing, I asked, "Can we go please?"

"I got a live one here, don't I?"

"Guess you'll have to find out."

I was going to follow through on my homework and I was going to enjoy myself. I knew that I was playing with fire—again—but I wanted Jared; wanted to experience another Dom and I already had Gregor's encouragement. Life was too short for regrets and what ifs. I'd rather be old and gray and be able to say, 'You know what, I lived, I learned, I loved, I broke hearts, and had my heart broken more than I had the right to. And I experienced things most people are never willing to try.' In my eyes that meant I won, I lived. The other option, having none of that or too little, wasn't ok with me.

"I have a request." We were in his car and he nodded for me to continue. "No anal." He looked at me funny. "Wait, let me clarify. No dick in my ass. Gregor and I haven't done it yet. We're working up to it." I paused as he waited, knowing I had more to say about it. "I'm saving that for him."

"I can respect that. No dick in your ass. Got it. Butt plugs, fingers, tongue are all a go, though?"

Giggling, I nodded. "Yes."

"Deal."

Then I grew nervous and paranoid. I *needed* Gregor's ok. I knew the hypocrisy involved, but feeling as if he owned me, there was no other option. I pulled out my phone and emailed him quickly, Jared more than likely aware of what I was doing. He remained silent, but gently rubbed my neck as we finished the drive and I typed my email.

TO: bruisedassets@yahoo.com
8:59 PM

Subject: Re: Homework

I'm freaking out. I know I shouldn't, but I am. We're headed back to his place, alone, and I feel like I'm cheating...and not on Todd. I'm attracted to him, I just. I don't know what I'm trying to say...

I wanted Jared, there was no denying it. As we pulled in the drive, my phone began to ring. I wasn't even sure the email had gone through yet and if he'd had time to read it. My heart immediately began to race.

Jared pulled my chin toward him. "Talk to him. I'll wait outside."

As he climbed out of the car, I answered Gregor's call.

"Hello?"

"How you doing?" I slapped my hand to my forehead. Always that same initial greeting.

Trying to sound calm, I confessed, "I'm freaking out. I know it's just sex, but..."

I heard his chuckle and it just turned me on more. "It's good to play with others. I gave you homework. If you like him, trust him to give you what you need, go with it. You'll get no judgement from me, except a pleased Sir."

"Ass!" I exhaled, a lone tear falling from my eye.

"Your ass needs a good paddling or flogging."

"Gregor..." my voice trailed off.

"Enjoy yourself. You deserve it."

I steal myself knowing he's really ok with it. Glancing over to Jared on his own phone as he sits on his porch steps, I know he's talking to Heather. "Ok. No looking back now."

"Good girl, that's the woman I know. Have fun. I'll talk to you tomorrow."

"Ok."

I put my phone on silent and shoved it into my purse before climbing out of the car. Jared slid his phone into his back pocket and smiled at me. I could tell he wasn't sure where I stood. Smacking his ass, I climbed the stairs and waited for him to open the front door.

"I guess that means we're completing our homework?"

"Not if you don't open this front door, right now!"

Laughing, he did just that.

CHAPTER
Thirty-One

BAD THINGS

ONCE THE DOOR WAS CLOSED, he took my hand and led me up the stairs to his room. Closing the door behind us then turning to face me, he cupped my face between the palms of his hands and kissed me. It wasn't Gregor's kiss, but it had the needed effect on me. Gripping his suit jacket, I pulled him closer.

Whispering against my lips, his hands pulled up on my dress. "This needs to come off." I lifted my arms willingly, allowing the removal of my dress. Turning me around, I felt his eyes all over me. His fingertips traced the lace of my bra between my shoulder blades. His voice was thick with lust, "This is so sexy."

A shiver ran over me as the heat from his hands singed me. "Thank you."

Turning me back around, he confessed, "I'm not thinking this through. I should've made you wait for me."

Smiling as he nipped at my lips, I offered, "We still can."

Hands on my shoulders, he nodded. "Put your music on and wait for me there." He pointed to the end of the bed before he walked to his closet. He returned and gave me further instructions. "I want you kneeling on the bed. Here," he dangled a blindfold and a leather collar between us. "Put your music on."

Pulling my phone from my purse, I pulled up my playlist. Since I was thoroughly being bad, I put on *Bad Things* by Meiko and set it down on the nightstand. Returning to stand in front of him, I turned so that he could put the blindfold on. Gregor had yet to use a blindfold on me and I was excited at this new experience.

Cupping my face between his hands, "Your safe word is unicorn, yes?" I nodded. "If things are going too fast or you need to stop, use your safe word. Understood?"

"Yes, Sir."

Gently, Jared placed it over my eyes. The soft material captured my sight as all my other senses immediately became more aware.

"Can I collar you?" He picked up on my apprehension. "I know you're his, but I prefer the collar on during play. I know it's different for everyone."

"Ok."

"Ok, what?"

"Yes, Sir. You can collar me. I'd like that very much, Sir."

I heard his moan of approval. "He's trained you well." Then his warm breath was in my ear, "Or it's just natural."

Smiling, his finger traced over my lips as I replied, "He says it's natural." Then I felt the cool silk wrap around my neck. I lifted my hair up as he secured it around my neck.

"I can see that." Cupping my face between his hands, "Your safe word is unicorn, yes?" I nodded. "If things are going too fast or you need to stop, use your safe word. Understood?"

"Yes, Sir."

Smiling, he said, "I'll be back. I expect you kneeling on the bed, waiting."

"Yes, Sir." I felt his presence leave the room.

Using my hands to feel the bed, I climbed up and got on my knees. I wasn't sure if he wanted me facing the head of the bed or not. Deciding to face the side of the bed, I assumed the position. On my knees I sat and relaxed, palms up and resting on my thighs.

I was growing warm and was well aware of the puddle forming in my panties. Several minutes passed as I wondered what we'd do together. What he'd do to me and likewise. Then I heard him. My ears perked up as I straightened my back a little more.

Then I felt the cool tip of a leather tool—flogger or crop, I wasn't sure yet—

drift over my shoulder. "Are you ready?"

"Yes, Sir."

SMACK!

It was a crop. Another new tool to experience.

When I woke, I was sprawled on his chest. My body and throat—and everywhere in between—both ached pleasantly. Glancing up, he was asleep. Rolling to the side of the bed, I sat up and let my feet dangle off the side. My music was no longer playing and when I checked my phone, I saw that the battery was entirely dead.

Feeling him stir, I looked over my shoulder at him. He had a smile on his face and I knew if I curled back into him, he'd welcome me. "You don't have to go."

Smiling, I acknowledged him. "I know. Do you have a charger?"

Nodding, he took my phone and plugged it in on his nightstand. "Do you want to talk? Are you ok?"

"I'm good. Really good."

Standing, I found my dress lying over a chair and threw it back on, skipping my bra and panties. Climbing back up on the bed, I crossed my legs as I sat facing him.

"Are you dying to email him?"

I giggled, "Maybe a little."

"Make sure you tell him I said he has a very obedient girl, who knows how to swallow cock like no other." I just nodded, blushing profusely, as he clasped my knee and gave it a reassuring squeeze.

"Have you talked to Heather, yet?"

"Not yet." Grinning wickedly, he said, "I was a little preoccupied and then pinned to the bed by a sleeping sub who was thoroughly exhausted." He winked.

"Sorry. You wore me out...in a good way."

Laughing, he leaned up and kissed me. "I'm going to shower. You're welcome to join me."

"I probably shouldn't, but that doesn't mean I won't watch."

I watched as his ripped body climbed from the bed and headed to the shower. I couldn't help but let my eyes wander over his chiseled body, but tried to be discreet about it. As he disappeared into the bathroom, I picked up my phone and turned it on, hoping it'd charged enough to power up. Unable to resist any longer, I typed up an email to Gregor.

> *TO: bruisedassets@yahoo.com*
> *7:47 AM*
> **Subject: Greetings...**
> *I really hope you were serious about me misbehaving. :)*
> *Jared told me to tell you that you've got a very obedient girl that you've trained well...and who knows how to swallow cock very well.*
> *Hope all is well.*

Placing the phone in my lap, I listened to the water turn on. I was about to ask Jared something when Gregor's email came through. With a big smile, the nerves ate me as I opened his response.

> *TO: meredith@meredithedits.com*
> *7:49 AM*
> **Subject: Re: Greetings...**
> *I'm glad to hear you have been obediently naughty and thoroughly enjoying it! I just hope your Sir doesn't get pissed...*
> *Speaking of cock...how was his?*

I couldn't control the burst of laughter that came from me. I loved how we teased each other. Of course it just made me ache for him that much more.

> *TO: bruisedassets@yahoo.com*
> *7:50 AM*
> **Subject: Re: Greetings...**
> *Lmao. I'll be getting proof for you...my job here done! Lol*
> *I'm craving you badly...*
> *Not yours...*

Jared's voice filtered through the bathroom and into the bedroom. "What's so funny?" I started to reply when he yelled, "Get in here girl and talk to me."

Smiling, I walked to the bathroom doorway to find him lathering his body in soap, shower curtain open. Sweet Jesus I wanted nothing more than to climb in there with him.

"He emailed. And?"

Smiling at him, I nodded. "Yes. He asked how your cock was."

Jared laughed, "And, how was it?"

Knowing I could be absolutely candid, I confessed, "Great, but not his."

A big grin stretched across his face. "You've got it bad. I really enjoyed myself, too."

Another email came through. I could feel Jared watching intently as my eyes scanned Gregor's message.

> *TO: meredith@meredithedits.com*
> *7:53 AM*
> *Subject: Re: Greetings...*
> *LOL...you running for office...?*

I snorted and told Jared what he said. He laughed as I responded, telling him every word I was typing.

> *TO: bruisedassets@yahoo.com*
> *7:54 AM*
> *Subject: Re: Greetings...*
> *Only for yours. No one will compare to you.*

Jared and I waited.

> *TO: meredith@meredithedits.com*
> *7:56 AM*
> *Subject: Re: Greetings...*
> *You sound like you're 14 telling your mother about your first crush... :)*
> *I'm good at many things and maybe even brilliant at some – but I'm rather sure there are many, brilliantly sufficient cocks out there that would make mine pale in comparison. Nevertheless – I will take the compliment accordingly and let you have said cock on your sexually triumphant return to the Great White North.*

> *TO: bruisedassets@yahoo.com*
> *7:57 AM*
> *Subject: Re: Greetings...*
> *Can't wait...*

I sent my reply knowing I likely wouldn't see him for a few weeks. But I held on to the thoughts of knowing what was to come. Tami and I were flying home later in the day and while I was eager to see my kids, I was going to miss this connection with Jared. Having him to talk to the past few days had been the best kind of therapy. The sex was pretty great, too.

The water turned off as I watched him dry off. "So, can we exchange phone numbers?"

Smiling, he agreed. "I would love that. We need to stay in touch."

I programmed his number into my phone and sent him a text. He got dressed and then walked me to my room. I needed to pack and shower myself. He sat on the bed as we talked some more while I packed my suitcase. When I was about to jump in the shower, someone began banging on the front door downstairs.

Grinning, he said, "I think Tami's back. Take your shower. I'll be downstairs."

Nodding, I did just that.

A few hours later we were headed to the airport. Jared drove us and we talked, trying to get info out of Tami, but she remained silent most of the time which was so unlike her. Pulling our bags from the trunk of his car, he hugged Tami. They exchanged some words, but I didn't hear them. Then he turned to me and gave me a big hug.

"Stay in touch. I mean it."

"You, too. Thank you again for everything."

"Anytime." Smiling at us, we grabbed our bags and headed into the terminal.

Once we checked our bags and made it through security, I hammered out a quick email to Gregor. He replied almost immediately.

> *TO: meredith@meredithedits.com*
> *4:54 PM*
> *Subject: Re: Greetings...*
> *Have a good flight...*

I tried poking and prodding Tami for info about what happened with Sam and she just wouldn't confide in me. I tried to not be hurt, knowing I rarely hid anything from her. But, she wasn't me and if she wanted to tell me I knew she would in her own time.

My phone alerted me of a text.

JARED: You were AMAZING this week! Thank you for feeling comfortable enough to talk with me. It's opened the door to a great friendship! I'll definitely keep in touch, please do the same... And I wouldn't mind kinky updates from time to time, maybe they'll inspire some new activities on my end! :)

Smiling, I started my response and included a picture I'd taken when I was alone from earlier that morning. My shoulders had bruises on them, just like the bruises Gregor had left on me in Casper. Gregor already had a copy of it and I figured Jared deserved to see his handiwork.

MEREDITH: *Attached is a pic of your handiwork. :)*

JARED: *Omg! I wish I was responsible for those... I would've changed the location though! I knew you had to go home to Todd so I didn't spend as much time spanking/ marking you as I wanted!*

Giggling, I replied. Tami was nose deep into her e-reader as we sat at our gate.

MEREDITH: *Those ARE from you! Lol. There are a few on my shoulder blades, too. You and Gregor both leave marks there from doing doggie.*

JARED: *That's hot as fuck!*

MEREDITH: *Yup. Drip, drip. I should've kissed you goodbye. Looking for my halo... lol*

JARED: *I would love another chance with you! This time I'll bring my girl and we can both play with you for hours!*

The tingles were present everywhere. The thought of Jared and Heather, Jared and Gregor, hell, all four of us... My mind went crazy at the thoughts running amuck in my head.

MEREDITH: *Sigh. Yeah, don't get me started on the thought of having you and Gregor both at the same time...*

JARED: *That would be so fun taking both your holes at the same time... I can hear your moans/screams now!*

If I wasn't already sitting down, I would've fallen over.

MEREDITH: *Jesus...I mean 'Yes, please!'*

JARED: *Good girl! Your approval makes me happy!*

MEREDITH: *Happy to oblige. I'm freaking wet and raw...you suck.*

JARED: *You got me rock hard right now, girl... Well played, well played!*

MEREDITH: *Lol. Again, drip, drip, puddle. My breasts ache. You fucking Sirs and your power over us. So, can I ask your favorite moment?*

JARED: I'd have to say... Hearing you request permission to come! I didn't even have to say anything... You're an obedient sub! HUGE TURN ON!

Grinning like a fool, I replied.

MEREDITH: Yes. I do take pride in it and it's something Gregor praises me for. For me, the elevator kisses because that's when I knew 100% 'Game On.' Well, and you saying 'I need to touch you.' Instant wet panties.

JARED: Confession: During the first massage I desperately wanted you to lay back on me, wrap my legs around your waist so I could kiss/lick the nape of your neck! I wanted you so bad!

MEREDITH: Omg. Did you suspect? Confession: I admit, the minute I saw you I was VERY intrigued and thought 'He's Mine' not thinking anything would come from it.

JARED: I didn't sense sub, but when I want something... I won't stop until I GET IT! Your confession is hot as fuck! #claimed

MEREDITH: Now I know what that look was that you gave Sam! I have magic pussy. Lol

JARED: Yes. That look told him you were off limits. I want to taste your tight pussy again! I'm getting VERY hungry!

I still couldn't wrap my brain around Jared being hot for me, but clearly it had been mutual.

MEREDITH: I'm starving! Could go for some protein!

JARED: Yes! That mouth of yours! I really enjoyed hanging your head off the bed and fucking your face. You took me so deep! Goddamn, I'm so fucking horny right now!

MEREDITH: Sigh. Boarding soon. I'm sad. Thank you again. Talk soon.

JARED: Safe travels babe! I had a blast kissing, tasting, fucking, spanking you! I hope we get to do that many more times in the future!

I knew there was a chance I'd see him again with him being Tami's cousin, but who really knew? He lived so far away. Thank God for technology! At least I knew I had someone I could talk to besides Tami and Gregor. And now Jared had someone to talk to as well.

The flight was uneventful and when we landed we both groaned. It wasn't even Thanksgiving yet, but the snow was covering the ground. As the other passengers got off the plane, we waited. I emailed Gregor and his reply came through when were at the baggage claim.

TO: meredith@meredithedits.com
4:54 PM
Subject: Re: I'm back...
Welcome back to the snow and frigid temps! :)

No shit! Some warning would've been nice!

The next couple weeks passed dreadfully slow. I have no problem admitting that I was counting down the days till my night away with Gregor. His schedule with work kept him insanely busy and the big school fundraiser that was coming up did the same to me. Even the emails had become limited.

He'd gone silent, into work mode. It was as if he'd vanished, never existed. I couldn't feel him, hear him, or touch him. I was all alone with my thoughts and memories. I wasn't used to him being so quiet. I knew I was probably overthinking—what else was new—but I missed his snarky, dirty emails and wondered if he missed mine.

I was desperate to feel his touch; like a junkie and her drug. My world went silent when he was around, silencing the tidal waves of thoughts that overlapped each other. Around him all I could do was feel. I popped a Jolly Rancher in my mouth, needing the distraction—and something to suck on—and wondered if we'd be able to control ourselves when we saw each other again. I knew control was his game, not mine, and I rather enjoyed playing knowing I'd gladly lose.

Looking back, I now understood why he'd planned a night away so far in advance. The Holidays and everything else entailed with that time of the year made it increasingly difficult to see one another at a moment's notice. This was when my thoughts became dangerous ones. Dangerous in the sense that I began to doubt him, and not knowing if those thoughts were valid or not.

Every time I told myself I was going to pull back and not reach out to him right away or respond to his emails immediately, he'd screw with my plans by emailing me first. And I couldn't resist replying. It was a high I couldn't fight, just making it more evident that he owned me, whether he knew it or not. Who was I kidding? He probably knew it.

CHAPTER
Thirty-Two

MISSING YOU

IT TOOK ME A LONG TIME to stop feeling that every time I saw him, it'd be the last time. I still had moments of self-doubt, but they were greatly improved. All I had to do was recount his emails in my head. He wasn't going anywhere. Lying in bed reading over an email I'd sent Gregor on Thanksgiving morning, I spent the time reminding myself of his constant presence.

> *TO: bruisedassets@yahoo.com*
> *7:07 AM*
> *Subject: Thankful*
> *Running my hands over the defined contours of my body, I yearn for you. Patiently I wait for the moment you unwrap me and claim me once more... over and over. I want to kneel at your feet, feel your hands mark my body as yours and then have your tools do the same. I need to lie on your lap, sit naked with you face to face with our arms and legs encircling each other. I need to lie down wrapped in your arms, kiss you until my lips grow numb and then start all over again.*
> *You're one of many things I'm thankful for this year...*

Todd was on the road again. December was almost upon us. Thanksgiving had been good...better than I expected. Todd had been more loving toward me than he had been in quite a while. Shit like that really fucked with a girl torn between two so different people and two different lifestyles.

Until you've stood in my shoes, there's no way to understand loving two totally different people in two totally different ways. Some say it's impossible to love more than one person and I'd always disagreed with that. I just didn't expect to experience it myself. One had given me the world while the other had become my world. And I didn't know what the fuck I was going to do. In that moment I truly believed I couldn't survive without either of them.

In bed alone that night, I was trying to distract myself and continued reading emails from the previous weeks since I'd returned from NOLA. I'd sent him a quote I'd found that made me think of him.

> *TO: bruisedassets@yahoo.com*
> *10:07 PM*
> *Subject: Mmmm*
> *Something that made me think of you...*
> *'Can we play a game where I put my hand between your legs and see how long I can spank you with my other hand till you're wet?'*

> *TO: meredith@meredithedits.com*
> *10:09 PM*
> *Subject: Re: Mmmm*
> *0 seconds*

I started cracking up, again. It was the same response I'd had when I'd originally read it.

> *TO: bruisedassets@yahoo.com*
> *10:10 PM*
> *Subject: Re: Mmmm*
> *Shut your face! We can pretend...*

> *TO: meredith@meredithedits.com*
> *10:12 PM*
> *Subject: Re: Mmmm*
> *Ok. 0.25*

> *TO: bruisedassets@yahoo.com*
> *10:13 PM*
> *Subject: Re: Mmmm*
> *I deny you have that power over me (drip, drip, drip)...*

TO: meredith@meredithedits.com
10:15 PM
Subject: Re: Mmmm
Do you need that drive by sucking tomorrow?

TO: bruisedassets@yahoo.com
10:16 PM
Subject: Re: Mmmm
Do I need it or do you? :)
Maximus miss me?

His reply gutted me that night, in a good way. It still did.

TO: meredith@meredithedits.com
10:18 PM
Subject: Re: Mmmm
Maximus isn't the only one missing you...

TO: bruisedassets@yahoo.com
10:19 PM
Subject: Re: Mmmm
I miss you, too...
*I'm going to try to sleep since it's eluded me the past two nights. I'm sure
I'll wake with you on the brain...frequently. Get some rest and have naughty
dreams. Talk soon.*

Then the tears overtook me once again. He'd said the words I didn't realize I'd
been dying to hear. I read those words over and over again, just like I did when the
email had come through days prior.

Pulling up my playlist I put on the song that had been plaguing me. *Missing You*
by Betty Who. It'd played that night we had our first overnight, but I had no idea
how much the words would mean to me over a month later.

He'd sent me a picture of the hotel we would be staying at for our upcoming
night away. It was beautiful and I'd never stayed at a nicer place. I continued reading
the old emails remembering how my dreams were filled with the things to come,
then and now.

TO: bruisedassets@yahoo.com
9:07 AM
Subject: Re: Mmmm
Dreams of being pressed against those floor to ceiling windows with you

fucking me from behind...
 Morning... :)

His reply had come later that morning.

TO: meredith@meredithedits.com
11:38 AM
Subject: Re: Mmmm
Oh, I would be lying if I said I hadn't been thinking the SAME thing ever since our first meeting... :)

My jaw dropped and my body throbbed. I giggled and shook my head reading it again.

TO: bruisedassets@yahoo.com
11:39 AM
Subject: Re: Mmmm
Be careful, I could go off at any moment. You're speaking my language...
First hotel meeting in Casper or sitting on that park bench?! Tsk tsk... :)

He hadn't answered the question, but I knew he was most likely referring to the park bench. Devil! I continued reading on.

TO: bruisedassets@yahoo.com
3:07 PM
Subject: Re: Mmmm
The thoughts of the pain and pleasure to be had is all consuming. Steals my breath and sends tremors through me. It's been too long...

TO: meredith@meredithedits.com
7:10 PM
Subject: Re: Mmmm
You need some rodeo time...

TO: bruisedassets@yahoo.com
7:15 PM
Subject: Re: Mmmm
Yes. Hopefully soon. I imagine you do, too...

TO: meredith@meredithedits.com
7:16 PM
Subject: Re: Mmmm
Always.
Getting ready to go out and plow the drive.
Global warming my ass...

I scrolled through several more and then came across another one that made me smile, as short as it was.

> *TO: meredith@meredithedits.com*
> *7:49 AM*
> *Subject: Morning*
> *Good morning sexy!*

> *TO: bruisedassets@yahoo.com*
> *7:51 AM*
> *Subject: Re: Morning*
> *Omg...keep talking like that. I'll do whatever you want. Ok, I'd do that anyway. Need a blow n go or a fondling?!*

> *TO: meredith@meredithedits.com*
> *7:54 AM*
> *Subject: Re: Morning*
> *Always...*

> *TO: bruisedassets@yahoo.com*
> *7:55 AM*
> *Subject: Re: Morning*
> *What does that mean? Lol. I'm offering my services!*
> *P.S. I want your dick in my mouth.*

> *TO: meredith@meredithedits.com*
> *7:59 AM*
> *Subject: Re: Morning*
> *Hmm...since you put it that way...*

> *TO: bruisedassets@yahoo.com*
> *8:05 AM*
> *Subject: Re: Morning*
> *You're a damn tease. Happy driving with that hard-on. Miss me...I'm craving you...*

> *TO: meredith@meredithedits.com*
> *8:12 AM*
> *Subject: Re: Morning*
> *You are rather lippy. Sounds like you need a round with the big paddle and then have that sore bottom stuffed with a swollen cock.*

> *TO: bruisedassets@yahoo.com*
> *8:15 AM*
> *Subject: Re: Morning*
> *Is that a threat or a promise...? :)*
> *A sub has needs...*

TO: meredith@meredithedits.com
8:18 AM
Subject: Re: Morning
This sub is going to wait till our night away to be properly paddled and fucked if she isn't careful.

TO: bruisedassets@yahoo.com
8:20 AM
Subject: Re: Morning
This sub is impatient to be properly paddled and fucked. I wonder what new paddle/s she will present to her Sir on said day?! Lol
Say it again with me on my knees in front of you... :)

TO: meredith@meredithedits.com
8:22 AM
Subject: Re: Morning
You wouldn't be able to reply then. Your mouth would be full...

TO: bruisedassets@yahoo.com
8:23 AM
Subject: Re: Morning
Oh, I can still reply... with sucking, licking, teasing, ass squeezing, etc.

TO: meredith@meredithedits.com
8:27 AM
Subject: Re: Morning
You really do like my ass... :)

TO: bruisedassets@yahoo.com
8:30 AM
Subject: Re: Morning
It's great to hold onto while I'm sucking you off and something nice to smack! :)

TO: meredith@meredithedits.com
8:31 AM
Subject: Re: Morning
Oh, I certainly can't argue with that...

I smiled and fell asleep. The paddles I'd ordered for him would be arriving any day. I couldn't wait to see them or to give them to him.

Several more days passed. My night away with Gregor was just over a week away. That particular morning my daughter woke with a very high fever. Keeping her home, I sent the other kids to school. I started to get concerned when her fever continued to spike even with fever reducing medication in her system. She wasn't eating, but managed to keep some liquids down.

After becoming more and more lethargic as the day went on, I called the doctor. Upon speaking with the office staff over the phone, they suggested I take her right to the ER after listing her symptoms and with the height her temp was at. I'd called Todd to let him know what was going on, but there wasn't much he could do from the other side of the country.

"Please keep me posted, Mer. I'll come home if I need to."

"Ok. I'll call you back when I know more."

Putting my cell back in my pocket, the scariest moment as a parent happened to me. My sweet girl started convulsing as we waited on the gurney in the ER. I'd had enough CPR training to know that I needed to stabilize her as best I could. Before I could even start screaming for help, medical personnel took over.

I called Tami in a panic and she was off work and said she'd get the other kids off the bus. I didn't have anyone else to call. Then I called Todd to tell him what was going on.

"She had a seizure. It's probably from the fever, but they're admitting her. I don't know what to do."

"Calm down. Let me make some phone calls. I'm coming home."

"I'm sorry..."

"Don't be sorry, Mer. She's sick and needs us both home. I'll try to find a flight home tonight."

"Thank you."

A couple hours later, my baby girl was asleep in her hospital bed. One of the neighbors was sitting with the kids and Tami brought me my laptop and a bag of clothes. Todd had managed to catch a flight and would be home around midnight to watch the kids.

Tami walked in and hugged me. "Are you ok? How is she?"

"I'm ok. She's stable now."

"Do they know what caused the seizure?"

I shook my head, "Everything is coming back negative. It could just be from the fever."

We sat down and talked for a while.

"Have you told Gregor?"

"No. In all the commotion, I haven't had a chance."

"You go away next week right?"

"Yes. We're supposed to. But now... I mean I can't if she's still in the hospital."

"She won't be. Think positive."

Like he sensed it in the force, my phone alerted me to an email from Gregor.

> TO: meredith@meredithedits.com
> 10:36 PM
> Subject: What's going on?
> I heard rumors at school pickup that one of your kids is in the hospital, or you are. Are you ok?

I snorted. Tami looked at me wondering what was going on.

"He heard that either I or one of the kids was in the hospital. He's checking in."

"Isn't that a good thing?"

Sighing, "Yes, I'm just exhausted."

"You should email him back so he's not worried."

Smiling devilishly, I joked, "I shouldn't and make him sweat it out."

She shook her head at me. "That's just vile."

"I know." I started typing my reply.

> TO: bruisedassets@yahoo.com
> 10:42 PM
> Subject: I'm ok
> It's my daughter. We've been admitted. They've already warned me she'll probably be here tonight and tomorrow night. High fever and she ended up having a seizure. They've run a battery of tests and so far everything comes back normal.
> Todd is on a flight home to stay with the other kids.

> TO: meredith@meredithedits.com
> 10:45 PM
> Subject: Re: I'm ok
> Keep me posted. Hope you can get some rest.

Tami left shortly after and I put the blankets and pillow on the 'parent bed'. This 'bed' was a fucking joke. It was a recliner that lay flat, but it was horribly uncomfortable. When I finally found a comfortable position, with my music playing softly, I tried to relax. That was until a nurse would come in to check vitals.

Eventually, curled up in the hospital recliner, I drifted off to sleep. My thoughts were a jumbled mess, worried about my daughter and thinking about Gregor...and Todd. Sighing, I threw my arm over my eyes and concentrated on the sound of my child's breathing.

Fingers were gently caressing my face. I knew that stroke, those fingers, and the gentleness behind the man who could be fierce when warranted. I had to be dreaming so I refused my eyes' plea to open so that they could gaze at him. Then warm lips came down on my forehead.

"Get some rest. I'm thinking of you."

Smiling, I bolted upright in the recliner as my eyes adjusted to the dark. The machines beeped their normal rhythm as my eyes darted toward the door. It was closed and nothing seemed out of place. Had he really been there or was my subconscious aching for him again? I didn't dare ask the nurses. Getting up, I checked on my little girl who looked so innocent, sleeping soundly. Looking at her this way you'd have no idea she was so sick.

> *TO: bruisedassets@yahoo.com*
> *8:48 AM*
> *Subject: Re: I'm ok*
> *Doc came in this am and told us we're staying another night. I already knew that. Right now it's a waiting game. Her fever is still high and meds don't seem to be helping much. Todd got home around midnight and is with the kids today.*
> *Anyway.*
> *I got maybe a few hours shut eye, but not much. If the nurses weren't waking me with checking vitals, I had thoughts of you waking me. Lol*
> *Hope you have a productive day.*

> *TO: meredith@meredithedits.com*
> *8:54 AM*
> *Subject: Re: I'm ok*
> *Is she ok though? Staying another night for monitoring?*

> *TO: bruisedassets@yahoo.com*
> *9:02 AM*
> *Subject: Re: I'm ok*
> *She finally ate something early this morning. Her fever needs to be under control before they'll release her. Doc said it's a waiting game.*
> *My head is pounding, but I'll survive.*

Todd was a real blessing during that stressful time, caring for the other kids at home and tending to home matters. My daughter ended up coming home two days later. She was eager to get back to school and I wasn't going to stop her. Gregor and I emailed each other during her entire stay, though he never admitted if he'd come up to see me or if it was just my imagination.

Back at home the next day, the kids gone, I sat and stared at the mountain of work I needed to get done. I was so tired and sore. Being back in my own bed was nice, but it was going to take time to work out my sore muscles.

Closing my eyes, I tried remembering the sound of his voice and then the video reels would just play over and over in my mind. I had to force myself to stop so that I could get work done. It'd be too easy to lay in bed all day and just daydream about our time together.

An email popped up as if on cue. He was responding to an email in which I mentioned that my back and neck were stiff, which was in response to his email asking how I was. I laughed at his reply.

> *TO: meredith@meredithedits.com*
> *10:54 AM*
> *Subject: Re: Glad you're home*
> *You're projecting. You just want something stiff. Stiff drink. Stiff cock up your ass.*

> *TO: bruisedassets@yahoo.com*
> *10:57 AM*
> *Subject: Re: Glad you're home*
> *LOL. Just be gentle when you bend me over. My back hurts. Maybe on my back is better so you can finger fuck me at the same time...*
> *Thinking I'm going to run out for some lunch or at least some caffeine and fresh air.*

> *TO: meredith@meredithedits.com*
> *11:04 AM*
> *Subject: Re: Glad you're home*
> *Where? I can meet for a few after I finish my errands.*

I immediately perked up. I wasn't expecting there to be any chance that he would be able to meet.

> *TO: bruisedassets@yahoo.com*
> *11:07 AM*
> *Subject: Re: Glad you're home*
> *I'm easy. The fast food joint at the corner of M-32 and Middlebury road is fine with me.*

TO: meredith@meredithedits.com
11:09 AM
Subject: Re: Glad you're home
I can do that. I'll text you with an ETA. Probably be an hour or so.

Like clockwork, an hour later his text came through that he was ten minutes away. I got in my SUV and headed to the fast food joint. When I pulled in, he was already there. Heading inside I ordered my food and sat down at a corner booth and waited.

A few minutes later he walked in and sat down across from me.

"How are you?"

Smiling, "I'm good. Glad to be home."

That devious smile and his gorgeous blue eyes were devouring me. I could almost feel him stripping me naked and we weren't even touching.

Glaring at him with a smile, I chastised him, "Stop it!"

Laughing, he braced his hands behind his head as he leaned back and asked innocently, "What?"

"Looking at me like I'm your next meal." I couldn't even look at him. Turning my face, I ran my hand over my forehead, biting my lip, as his laugh echoed in my ears. Glancing back to him, I whispered, "I hate you."

CHAPTER
Thirty-Three

SENSUAL

I WAS GRATEFUL FOR EVERY second with him, even though we couldn't touch each other. I kept catching myself staring at various parts of his body, knowing full well the pleasure and pain they were capable of.

His mouth and the words that flowed from them had the ability to drop me to my knees and set my body on fire. His hands spoke to me, too. Every time he touched me, gripped me, caressed me, fingered me, spanked me, and pulled me closer, those potent hands left remnants of a language on me that only my body could interpret. And his eyes. Eyes that still saw right through me and to the devious cravings that hid inside me.

I had to keep my hands busy, afraid I'd launch across the table just to touch him. Then when it was almost time to go, he stretched his leg out below the table, placing it next to my thigh where I sat. If he thought I'd keep my hands to myself he was sorely mistaken. I knew he wanted my touch as much as I needed his. If this was a test I wasn't sure if I'd pass or fail, and I didn't care.

Immediately I pushed my hand under the cuff of his jeans and ran my nails over his lower calf. His speech momentarily halted as we stared at one another. I just smiled and continued running delicate swirls over his skin.

"I'm going to fall asleep if you keep that up."

I just looked into his eyes, smirked, and shrugged my shoulders.

A few minutes later he walked me to my vehicle. Hugging me, his hand snuck down and grabbed my ass as he leaned in and pecked my lips quickly. I loved that he'd done it and hated that the quick peck was all it could be. I glanced at his truck and he caught my gaze.

"No. Not in the light of day."

Scrunching my brows, I argued, "That hasn't stopped us at either Rodeo."

Grinning, "That's different, secluded, and you know it. I'll talk to you soon. Just a couple more days." He hugged me again and said, "Keep me posted on her recovery."

Nodding and pursing my lips, I climbed in my car and watched as he walked away and climbed into his truck.

> *TO: bruisedassets@yahoo.com*
> *3:17 PM*
> *Subject: Lunch*
> *Thank you for lunch... I'm all smiles.*

> *TO: meredith@meredithedits.com*
> *3:19 PM*
> *Subject: Re: Lunch*
> *I was trying very hard not to drag you out to the truck for a backseat spanking...*

> *TO: bruisedassets@yahoo.com*
> *3:20 PM*
> *Subject: Re: Lunch*
> *Lol...I could sense it in you and I would've let you.*

> *TO: meredith@meredithedits.com*
> *3:23 PM*
> *Subject: Re: Lunch*
> *And THAT'S why I had to show restraint...prudence and all :)*

> *TO: bruisedassets@yahoo.com*
> *3:25 PM*
> *Subject: Re: Lunch*
> *Fuck that bitch! :)*
> *I could use some deep kissing and petting. Lol. So could you! :)*

TO: meredith@meredithedits.com
3:27 PM
Subject: Re: Lunch
You're in dire need of a long, slow round with the crop followed by a slow, deep face fucking...
Got anyone in mind?

TO: bruisedassets@yahoo.com
3:28 PM
Subject: Re: Lunch
Hmmm...only one person I can think of. Blue eyes, smile of the devil when he sees me, magic fingers...

I didn't hear back until later that night as I was walking out of the grocery store.

TO: meredith@meredithedits.com
8:03 PM
Subject: Re: Lunch
I'm at Joplin's. Dark parking lot.

I froze and looked around. I didn't spot his truck right away, but there it was.

TO: bruisedassets@yahoo.com
8:05 PM
Subject: Re: Lunch
I'm here, too. Loading my groceries into my car. Should I wait?

TO: meredith@meredithedits.com
8:08 PM
Subject: Re: Lunch
Go back inside, I'll swing around and pick you up. There won't be any spanking, tonight.

Groaning, I didn't care. I just wanted to be in his presence.

TO: bruisedassets@yahoo.com
8:09 PM
Subject: Re: Lunch
Ok. I'll be good. I'll keep my hands to myself.

I walked back inside and a moment later he walked right past me like I didn't exist. Watching as he climbed in his truck, he swung around the back of the building. When his truck pulled back by the entrance, he stopped and I climbed in the back seat. He smiled at me wickedly and then proceeded to park his truck off in a dark corner.

He climbed into the back of his truck where I awaited him. I sat there and kept my hands to myself like I said I'd do. But he didn't. The lights hadn't even fully dimmed and he was pulling me toward him. My eyes closed as I reveled in the feel of him. A month was too long to go without his intoxicating touch and that's almost how long it'd been since I really felt him.

His deep voice penetrated my ears. "That sweater looks good on you."

My eyes opened and stared back at his as he admired me. A small smile formed on my lips as his hands roamed my hips. My left hand went to his side as my right began caressing his leg.

On my knees next to him, we kissed and touched. The windows were already fully fogged over. His hand made no hesitation in touching me through my clothes. My thighs opened for his hand and immediately clamped down around his wrist. Gripping the back of his neck, I deepened our kiss. My right hand drifted down to the ever-present bulge in his track pants and squeezed as a small groan escaped from his mouth.

Not long after, he released his cock for me. Licking the sweet pre-cum off the tip, I then took him in my mouth. His hand gently massaged my scalp as he thrust into me deeper and didn't release me. He'd warned me that this deep throat fucking was coming and I'd only encouraged it. My eyes began to water as I relaxed my throat around his girth. His hands continued to fondle me more diligently, making it hard to concentrate. I couldn't help the sounds I made as his fingers touched me just the right way.

"Someone's having trouble focusing on her task." I simply moaned in response. "My naughty little slut...so obedient."

I was already close to my own release from him only touching and spanking me over my clothes. A month apart becoming easier and harder to handle for so many different reasons. Just when I thought he was about to spill down my throat, he pulled me back up to him.

His hot breath fanned over the side of my face and down my neck. "I can smell you." Lowering his voice he taunted me. "You smell like pussy." I knew the blush crept up my cheeks. How could I possibly deny that I was aroused? "Do you need to come?"

I tried keeping eye contact, but I was drunk and dizzy, barely able to focus. Two Gregors swayed in my vision. "Yes, Sir. Please, Sir."

Smiling, he groaned into my ear, "Not until I tell you. Understood?"

"Yes, Sir."

I needed to be closer and moved from his side to straddle his thigh. Once there, I began grinding against him as his hands captured the back of my neck. He pulled on my hair and angled my face so that his tongue could fuck my mouth deeper. Lifting me slightly, so that I no longer sat on his thigh, his hands resumed their torture upon my pussy.

I couldn't hold back the cries as I clasped my arms around him.

"Not yet," he reminded me of my instructions.

I moaned out in frustration, but it quickly turned to pleasure as he continued his pursuit. His right hand came down on my clothed ass again and again, each strike harder than the last. This continued as his left hand pushed up my sweater.

Freeing my breasts, he proceeded to mark my nipples once his hand returned to my throbbing clit. I was drunk—at least that's how I felt. My legs were beginning to shake and I couldn't hold my head upright anymore. Dropping my head to his chest, my hands gripped his shoulders fiercely.

"Come for me."

I took a relieved breath and let go of the restraint. Relaxing against him I let him work his magic, knowing he now wanted my release as much as I did.

Crying out, "Sir..." he held me tightly as I clung to him, the convulsions claiming me. My whole body trembled against his as he whispered naughty words in my ear.

"You've soaked through your pants. Anyone could smell you right now and know what you've been doing."

Smiling, I panted against his neck as he fondled every last tremor out of me. I didn't want to come down from his high, ever, but knew I had to. He pulled my lips back to his and kissed me deeply, slowly. I'd come to recognize his kisses. This was his 'until next time' kiss.

"I need to get home. I'll email you. Things are crazy at work. Our night away might be compromised."

The emotions flooded me before I could even try to rein them in. Pleading with him, I choked out, "Please don't cancel. I need to get away desperately."

His eyes searched mine and he nodded. Leaning in, he held my chin as he kissed me. "Ok. I'll talk to you soon."

"Thank you." I kissed him back.

Straightening my clothes with his help, I smiled as he then climbed back behind the driver's seat. Swinging by my car, he dropped me off and we both headed toward our separate homes.

Turning my playlist on, *Sensual* by TVA came on and I listened to it all the way home. When I got home and climbed out of my SUV, my legs almost gave out on me as they hit the garage floor. I steadied myself against the door; closing my eyes I replayed our encounter once more. Fuck, he was good.

The next afternoon he sent one of his snarky emails that I loved so much.

> *TO: meredith@meredithedits.com*
> *1:15 PM*
> **Subject: What do you think?**
> *According to my spam email, I need a longer penis and a firmer erection. What do you think?*

> *TO: bruisedassets@yahoo.com*
> *1:19 PM*
> **Subject: Re: What do you think?**
> *Disagree... but you do need to let me stroke and suck the perfectly long and firm cock you already have.*
> *I'm here when you need me. Wink.*

> *TO: meredith@meredithedits.com*
> *1:21 PM*
> **Subject: Re: What do you think?**
> *Good plan... :)*
> *Need you or use you..?*
> *I was thinking of sending you to Rodeo and when I get there you tell me 'please use my ass Sir', you obediently turn around, pull your pants down/skirt up, assume the position, and then let me fuck you hard and fast in the pussy/ass. I pull out, come in your panties, pull them up, gift your ass a hard slap, turn you around, kiss you on the forehead, you say 'thank you, Sir' and then I send you on your way. Nothing else spoken. Quick. Raw. Service.*

> *TO: bruisedassets@yahoo.com*
> *1:23 PM*
> **Subject: Re: What do you think?**
> *Jesus Christ...*
> *Tell me when...*
> *Though I don't know if I believe you wouldn't kiss me... :)*
> *My dreams were filled with you last night. Even woke fondling myself, but denied my release.*

TO: meredith@meredithedits.com
1:27 PM
Subject: Re: What do you think?
You building it up for next week..?

TO: bruisedassets@yahoo.com
1:29 PM
Subject: Re: What do you think?
Maybe :)
Or if you decide to use me between now and then...

TO: meredith@meredithedits.com
1:33 PM
Subject: Re: What do you think?
I certainly may. But then you may be instructed to refrain until then so that I may properly tease you and exploit your swollen clit.

TO: bruisedassets@yahoo.com
1:35 PM
Subject: Re: What do you think?
Can't wait for you to instruct, tease, exploit and so on... :)

TO: meredith@meredithedits.com
1:38 PM
Subject: Re: What do you think?
Maybe I should just give you a quick paddling today or tomorrow...

I just shook my head and didn't respond. He knew how to reach me and knew my availability.

Two days before our night away, we were able to squeeze in a quick meet at Rodeo 3. The second he climbed into the backseat of his truck with me and shut the door, we were on each other. Yanking my coat off, his hands thrust under my shirt and tugged my breasts free from my bra. My hand pressed against his erection as his fingers pinched my nipples roughly while he tongue fucked my mouth. Groaning, my hands clutched at his biceps and then he quickly bent me over his lap.

"Time to get that bottom warmed up. Get you primed and ready for what's to come."

I became putty as he pulled my sweats down and spanked my bare ass repeatedly. Rubbing my tender ass, once he was done, I reached under and back to his dick as it pressed into my side.

"Please, Sir."

Lifting me up, he opened his pants and gave me what I wanted. I happily took him into my mouth as he started spanking me again and teasing my clit and asshole.

"I want to bend you over and lick that tight hole of yours. Would you like that?"

His hands gripped the meaty part of my ass as I bobbed my head up and down his shaft. My only response was a guttural moan that was partly caused by the joy of having him in my mouth, but mostly due to the influence his words had on me. I wanted nothing more than his tongue in my ass, and his cock too.

The chemical reaction my body went through when I was near him would never get old. I could feel him under my skin, in my bones, pumping through my veins, and in my very being. I couldn't get enough. Was it supposed to be like this? Were we more than just chemical or was the chemical reaction just the tip of what we had? Logic told me it was more, but I was terrified to admit it, especially to him.

Just before I was sure he'd come, he stopped me and pulled me up. Moaning in disapproval, I dropped my head to his shoulder as he chuckled.

Whispering against his neck, "I want you to come, Sir."

"I know you do. Soon enough." He held me tight, hands running over my back and buttocks. "I need to go. Pushing me back, he cupped my face, "Drive safe. I have a vested interest in you arriving in one piece." I nodded. Kissing me once more, he praised me. "Good girl."

Pulling my panties and sweats back up, he then put his erect dick back in his pants as I openly frowned at him. One last signature kiss and we were both headed back to our normal lives.

I spent the next day wrapping his gifts and packing. Todd was out of town and Tami was going to watch the kids for me.

TO: bruisedassets@yahoo.com
2:54 PM
Subject: Requests
Any other requests? I have the toys, flogger, and your gift. I'll bring your whisky and may just drink what you're drinking. :)

He responded a couple of hours later.

TO: meredith@meredithedits.com
4:49 PM
Subject: Re: Requests
Massage oil.

Assortment of butter plugs.
Endurance.

I was cracking up. I knew it was autocorrect but I had to tease him about it.

> *TO: bruisedassets@yahoo.com*
> *4:52 PM*
> *Subject: Re: Requests*
> *I can bring an assortment of massage oil.*
> *Butter plugs... not so sure.*

> *TO: meredith@meredithedits.com*
> *4:59 PM*
> *Subject: Re: Requests*
> *Yes. Autocorrect wants butter plugs. And, now I'm curious. Google here*
> *I come...*

We exchanged a few more emails, but nothing noteworthy. But, I emailed him first thing. It was the day and my heart was already racing.

> *TO: bruisedassets@yahoo.com*
> *7:16 AM*
> *Subject: Re: Requests*
> *Good morning, Sir.*

I got the kids off to school, having made pancakes—their favorite—and started getting ready. I was going to miss them, I had tried to be with them as much as possible before my trip. But I wasn't going to cancel because I really needed this time for me. Tami was due to arrive shortly after lunch so I could begin the two hour drive to Gregor's hotel.

> *TO: meredith@meredithedits.com*
> *9:05 AM*
> *Subject: Re: Requests*
> *Good morning.*
> *It will be an even better evening... :)*

We emailed a few more times before I jumped in the shower and got ready. Fully packed, I waited for Tami. When she walked in the door, I emailed Gregor.

> *TO: bruisedassets@yahoo.com*
> *1:04 PM*
> *Subject: Re: Requests*

Leaving in 5 unless you're not ready for me. :)

His reply was instant.

> **TO: meredith@meredithedits.com**
> **1:05 PM**
> **Subject: Re: Requests**
> *Cum cum...I'm always ready for you.*

> **TO: bruisedassets@yahoo.com**
> **1:06 PM**
> **Subject: Re: Requests**
> *Good to know you're eager too...*

I put my suitcase in my SUV and pulled out of the drive. Pulling onto the freeway, I got another email.

> **TO: meredith@meredithedits.com**
> **1:15 PM**
> **Subject: Re: Requests**
> *Have to warn you though – I am in work mode. You may have to put up with it/ease me out of it for a while...lol*
> *Been a hectic week.*
> *Would love some dark chocolate. Your Dom will be grateful.*

> **TO: bruiseassets@yahoo.com**
> **1:41 PM**
> **Subject: Re: Requests**
> *Mission accomplished. Goodies have been purchased. Back on the road. This could be fun. I could crawl around on all 4s, tempting and teasing to get you out of work mode.*

> **TO: meredith@meredithedits.com**
> **1:45 PM**
> **Subject: Re: Requests**
> *Drive safe and stay focused on the road!*
> *ETA?*
> *I'm going to go work out in a few.*

> **TO: bruisedassets@yahoo.com**
> **1:50 PM**
> **Subject: Re: Requests**
> *GPS says no later than 3:30pm.*

He became quiet and I put my music back on and tried to relax and enjoy the drive!

CHAPTER
Thirty-Four

WANT MY LOVE

TO: meredith@meredithedits.com
2:49 PM
Subject: Re: Requests
Ok. Probably have to add some time on there for traffic. I'll meet you in the lobby and give you a key. There are cameras everywhere so it needs to be somewhat inconspicuous. I'll join you after. It will give you some time to get situated and unwind from the drive. :)

I didn't respond right away, just focused on the road. *Want My Love* by Cathedrals was playing, images of him and me floating in and out of my mind. As I got closer and off the freeway, I messaged him.

TO: bruisedassets@yahoo.com
3:13 PM
Subject: Re: Requests
10 min out.

TO: meredith@meredithedits.com
3:19 PM
Subject: Re: Requests

You must have been flying...
Sit in the lobby by the gift shop. Catch up on emails and such. :)

Parking my car, I got my suitcase and headed into the hotel. Sitting down I began playing on my phone and waited. Fifteen minutes later I started growing anxious. Maybe I was in the wrong lobby, I mean, it was a big hotel.

> **TO: bruisedassets@yahoo.com**
> **3:35 PM**
> **Subject: Re: Requests**
> *I'm in front of the coffee shop by the valet.*

Then I felt it, that familiar presence as I stared at my phone. I knew I had a ridiculous smile on my face and so I didn't dare look up. I knew I'd looked like a kid in a candy shop if I dared expose my face to anyone. Taking a couple deep breaths, I finally looked up. My heart leapt.

In a sweaty t-shirt, shorts, with a towel in his hand, he was walking down the staircase. And of course, that fucking wicked grin on his face. Making eye contact and trying to contain my smile, I shook my head at him as I clutched my phone in my lap.

Descending the last step he asked, "Were you flying?"

Chuckling, I admitted, "I may have had cruise set at minimum 75 and traffic was great until I approached downtown."

His hand stretched out and handed me a key card. Tucking it in my hand, I blushed as his eyes traveled my body. I wore a black skirt and a red blouse—his favorite color, and black knee high boots.

"Head on up. I'm going to go finish working out."

"Ok." Grabbing my suitcase, I turned with him grinning after me and headed for the elevators.

Walking into the room a weight was lifted. Everything was in pristine condition. Walking to the floor to ceiling windows, I took in the view. The bed was made and his jacket hung on the desk chair. I removed my coat and placed it on the same chair and put my suitcase on a different chair. I unzipped my suitcase and carried my shower bag to the bathroom. A full size tub and a separate shower greeted me. I set my bag down and headed back to the room.

I put our drinks in the fridge and laid out the chocolate and fruit I'd purchased.

Then I put the toys, flogger, oils, lubes, etc. in one of the dresser drawers. Staring at his wrapped present, I pondered what to do with it. Then I heard a key in the door. He sure didn't waste any time. I was debating putting something else on and now that plan was thwarted.

Standing still, I waited as me walked toward me. Once I was within arm's reach, he took my hand and tugged me to him, kissing my lips. How was it that in his presence alone, I felt like the most beautiful and treasured thing? While I struggled to take a compliment, I believed any he gave me.

"You look great." His arms pulled me tighter against him as he continued to kiss me sweetly. Fingering the low cut neckline of my blouse he admitted, "I like the red."

"I wore the red for you, Sir. Lots and lots of red." The smile never leaving my face.

Peaking in my blouse, he eyed the red bra and stated, "I'll enjoy taking it off later."

"Me, too." My hands moved over the dampness of his shirt as it clung to his shoulders.

"I'm all sweaty."

I kissed him again, deeper, and confessed what he should have already known, "I don't mind. I like you all sweaty."

That spurred him onward as his hands pulled my body closer to him and he moved his hips against my own. Soft moans fell from my mouth as they always did when he kissed me, touched me. The heat of his hands penetrated my blouse before he lifted it and ran his hands underneath to my waist.

I let him mold me to his body before he walked to the end of the bed. Sitting down, he pulled me between his legs and wrapped his arms around my waist as he buried his face in my belly. I ran my hands over his drenched shirt, not caring that he was all sweaty from his workout as he ran his hands over my hips, thighs, and butt. Massaging his neck and shoulders, I enjoyed the soft groans that fell from his mouth.

We stayed that way for a long time as I continued manipulating his muscles. Then I asked sweetly, "You going to fall asleep on me?"

"Mmm, I could."

Hands moved over the bare flesh of my thighs and travelled upward. His fingers moved to cup my ass, sliding over my hips, and then slipped into my panties. The only sounds that could be heard were my mewlings as he fondled me. Thighs and ass clenching, I lifted one leg and placed it on top of his knee as his fingers slid into me. Tugging at the back of his shirt, I wanted it off. But it didn't happen.

He stood back up and held me tight. Ever so softly his lips brushed against my neck, "I missed you."

My throat constricted as my heart sped up. "I missed you."

He pulled his head back and claimed my lips with renewed energy. There he was, my Dom, my Sir, my lover, my play partner. His hand gripped my neck as his tongue invaded my waiting mouth. We took our time kissing and touching, knowing we had plenty of time.

Lips thoroughly swollen, I pulled back. I was dying to give him his gifts. Looking at me, he smiled like he knew I was up to something.

"Would you like your gift?"

His grin got even bigger as he nodded. "Yes."

"Ok."

I pulled the box out of my suitcase. It was wrapped in shiny red paper. He sat on the bed and waited for me to hand it to him. His smile got bigger as he looked to me and then back to the box. I sat down and watched with apprehension as he opened it. He pulled the two plastic wrapped paddles out of the box and yanked the plastic off.

He examined them closely as I watched, even inhaling their intoxicating scent deeply. "You said you wanted a heavy duty leather slapper. And, well, I couldn't decide. So, I got both!"

I'd gotten a large leather paddle that had red fleece on one side, while the other paddle was actually a three layer leather slapper. Smacking them both in turn against his hand, he now looked like the kid in the candy shop.

Then his eyes, thick with lust, looked to me and asked, "You ready to play?"

Biting my lip, I nodded. "Yes, Sir."

Rising from the bed, he motioned me to where he wanted me. Still fully clothed, I got on my knees on the end of the bed. He guided me to the exact location and spread my knees. Lifting my skirt, he slowly pulled my panties down and discarded them.

I knew that I had some fading marks and I cooed when his teeth nipped at them. Instinctively my hips pushed back further, aching to be closer to him. Then the smack of his hand came down and I pressed my lips together in a smile.

"Don't move." His tone was serious and I smiled even more.

He used both of the new paddles; placing special attention to the fleece lined one. Slapping and then caressing with the opposing sides it featured. Over my buttocks, down the outside of my thighs, back up the delicate skin of my inner thighs, and then gently over my clit. Then his hands would do the same. Fingers soaked, he reached around to put them in my mouth as I cleaned them off.

"Where's the butt plug?" His tone was soft.

Out of breath, I panted, "In the dresser." I pointed in its direction, "The top drawer."

I heard him rifling through the drawer, then heard the lube being squeezed out before he returned to me. My face was buried in the comforter as anticipation had me nearly delirious. Gripping my ass and spreading my cheeks, I felt his thumb gently press into me. Then, slowly, he replaced his thumb with the butt plug.

There was no accurate way to describe the way it made me feel. Full didn't do it justice. All I knew was I really, really liked it. Then the spanking and paddling resumed. After a few minutes I heard the wood of the 'significant damage' paddle being lifted off the desk. *Shit!* When I was on the brink of sobbing, he ceased.

Sitting in front of me, he lifted me up so that he could kiss me and wiped away the few stray tears as he did so. Then he lowered my mouth to his waiting cock. Eager as always, I sucked on him while his hands moved over my back and slapped my ass.

After a few minutes, he raised my face back to his and kissed me. On my knees in front of him, his fingers sank into me as I held onto him tightly.

"Please, Sir. I need you."

"What do you need? Tell me."

Blushing, but feeling no shame I confessed. "I want your cock inside me, fucking me."

Grinning, he kissed my cheek. "Get back on your knees."

I did as he bid. Hearing the tear of the wrapper, I waited for his invasion. Hands on my hips, he slid in as my eyes closed with pleasure. He fucked me while manipulating the butt plug to further my enjoyment.

"Come for me, sweet girl."

"Thank you, Sir."

Letting myself fall into the waves of pleasure, my orgasm quickly flooded me. Before the tremors were done, he rolled me over and buried his face between my legs. Soon, I was coming undone again with his fingers and tongue fully exploiting me.

When I was done, he moved to lie down next to me and pulled me close. Once my breathing returned to normal, we began kissing and touching once more. With his erection in my hand, I stroked him as he smiled against my lips. Rolling me over, his body covered mine as we lay face to face.

"I want to please you, Sir."

Grinning, "Don't move."

Climbing off the bed, he grabbed the bottle of lube. Returning to me, he slowly licked my clit and then removed the butt plug. With lube in hand, he covered his cock. On his knees, he lifted my hips with one hand; he began the process of claiming my ass. Finally, we'd be joined the way we both wanted for so long.

He took his time and was rewarded when I fully relaxed, letting him slide all the way inside. Stilling, his smile beamed down at me as I moaned. Proving his talents, fingers glided into my pussy, filling me completely.

"Oh, God." My eyes closed and reopened, joining his gaze.

His gruff voice had me pulsing in response. "I want to feel every part of you clench around me."

Reaching up, he took my hand and then placed my fingers over my clit as his own pumped in and out of my pussy. His cock slid out to the tip and then back in my ass at a restrained pace. I was nearly delusional with pleasure and struggled to concentrate.

"Look at me. I want to see those deep eyes." I did as he asked, though my eyes tried to flutter shut. "Does it feel good?"

Panting, I murmured, "Yes, Sir." He pushed in a little harder as I moaned in response.

"Tell me how it feels."

"Full, so much good pressure."

"How long has it been since someone's been in your tight ass?"

He knew the answer to that. We'd discussed it numerous times, but I answered him anyway.

Struggling to speak, my words broken, I answered him. "Too long, over a decade."

With that smirk on his face, he declared, "This ass belongs to me now."

Smiling, with the blush covering my cheeks, I admitted, "I don't want anyone else there."

He simply growled his response and continued fucking my ass. After a few minutes I could feel him losing control, wanting his release while still seeking another of mine. Finally, after all that time, we were joined the way we both wanted and all I wanted was his release.

"I want you to come, Sir." I didn't care if I came again, not now.

Groaning, he asked, "Where?"

Smiling, I pressed up to meet his thrusts and cooed, "Anywhere you want."

A small chuckle escaped his lips. I wrapped my hands around him as he came closer and caressed the taut muscles of his back. Then the guttural moans took over as he emptied himself inside my ass. The ass that was now his. Lowering himself fully, he kissed me slowly as the last of his orgasm rushed through him. Hands on his back, I took great pleasure in the tremors that my touch brought him.

A few minutes later, after kissing me and stroking my face, he excused himself to the restroom. Sated—for the moment—I remained on my back and waited for him. Climbing back on the bed, he lay down next to me and pulled me close. On my back, he lay on his side and tangled his legs with mine. He didn't stop touching me, caressing my face and body, and kept kissing my forehead.

We watched the sunset through the floor to ceiling windows. The colors transitioned from oranges, to pinks, and then reds and it was beautiful. Though I couldn't decide if I was enjoying the beauty in the colors of the sunset or in the beauty of the person I was sharing the moment with. Everything felt so right when I was with him. I closed my eyes and reveled in his touch, trying to take it all in so I'd never forget. His aftercare skills may have lacked when our visits were short, but when we had time, he made up for it in spades.

We talked some and it was a struggle for me to not doze off. Body, heart, and soul were completely at peace with him near. His warmth surrounded me, his tenderness consumed me, and his presence dominated me. His fingers twined themselves with mine while I listened to him describe the beauty of the sunset. I felt like it was a secret part of him that he was exposing to me.

Closing my eyes I finally admitted what I'd known long ago. I loved him. He taught me to embrace my own darkness, nurtured it, and treated me like I was the light in his night sky.

My emotions were becoming harder and harder to mask. If he knew, he didn't say anything. Even Jared had said he knew how Heather felt long before they revealed it to one another. I knew Gregor cared, but didn't know to what extent.

I wanted nothing more than for him to find happiness and yes, part of me hoped I was part of that. Full well knowing that he was a huge part of mine, even if it was only going to be for a short time. He could've had anyone, but he chose me. That had to mean something about our connection, compatibility. Of course I wouldn't be the first to let my emotions go overboard.

Part of me knew we'd both crossed a line long ago and I wondered who would break first. Or was it possible that he was just the most attentive Dom on the planet and I was the worst sub to interpret his attentiveness as love? His job was to know what I needed and wanted. I wanted the touching and his loving and naughty words whispered in my ear. All I needed was him.

There was just one problem. I loved him and I couldn't have him. I never predicted that I would feel this way and I had to shut it off before I ruined our night away. 'One day, one moment, one experience at a time, Mer.'

CHAPTER
Thirty-Five

DROP BY DROP

WE LAY ON THE BED, CURLED IN one another for close to an hour. Slowly, his fingers began to tease me once again. My body automatically reacted to him. Hips twitched, clit throbbed, heartrate picked up, and my breath caught in my throat.

Turning my face toward his, his full lips greeted my own. Soon, he moved down my body and took me to the brink once more. Panting on the bed, my arm over my face, he straddled me with a big smile on his face.

Removing my arm, I smiled. "Thank you."

Kissing me quickly, he said, "I'm going to shower. Then we can go to dinner."

"Ok."

Fingering my skirt that was still on me and underneath me, he declared. "You're going to need to change." His eyes met mine and said wickedly, "It's covered in cum."

Laughing, I said, "Sure am glad I brought a change of clothes."

Lifting my hip, he swatted my ass and then disappeared into the bathroom. Once the water was running, I sat up. Walking, I grabbed my phone and hit play on my Gregor playlist. *Drop by Drop* by The Sweeplings came on. The lyrics hooked me. Sitting down, I listened as a few tears fell. I was so happy, but so stuck.

I played it once more and changed into some jeans. Moving to the mirror, I attempted to fix my makeup, licking my finger to remove the smeared eye liner and mascara that was under my eyes. I finger brushed my tousled hair and then waited for him to exit the bathroom.

I was standing in front of the windows staring out when I heard the bathroom door open. Deciding not to move, I heard him stalk closer. Arms wrapped around me and kissed my neck.

"You ready?"

"Yes, just need a minute."

Heading to the bathroom, I quickly ran my brush through my hair and touched up my makeup. When I stepped back out he had his jacket on and held out my coat for me. Slipping it up my arms and over my shoulders, I thanked him.

"There are several restaurants just a few blocks down."

"Great." Slipping my phone into my purse, I walked through the hotel door that he held open for me.

Walking down the street, it wasn't lost on me the stance he took as we walked. He took the outer lane, by traffic. Most wouldn't think anything of this, but it was the spot a gentleman took, the spot of protection. Stepping into the restaurant, they weren't very busy and we were seated immediately.

The waitress took our drink order; whisky for him and a mixed drink for me. We ordered an appetizer and decided to split a pizza. The conversation flew easily between us. Nothing seemed to be off limits as we talked about our childhood, adolescence, and college years. Halfway through, my belly ached with all the laughter we shared.

"So, Judith sure likes to give you a hard time."

I groaned and nodded, "Yes. We have a history."

He was referring to the PTA meeting from a couple weeks ago. Judith had been unrelenting about the upcoming fundraiser, doing anything she could to get under my skin. Gregor had been at the meeting, but we hadn't exchanged any pleasantries, for discretion sake.

"Care to divulge?" His head was tilted and his eyes were warm.

"Not really. I shouldn't let her bother me."

"Well, I have my own history with her." This caught my attention. "Not like that." He chuckled. "I'm friends with her ex-husband. He was really torn up about the divorce."

"I can't imagine why? I figured he was happy to get away from her." We both laughed.

"Well, he's definitely better off."

Then out of nowhere a chunk of meat flew through my line of sight and landed on the table between us. Gregor was red from laughing so hard. I was still trying to figure out what happened and where the meat had come from. He finally pointed behind me and I turned cautiously.

"Oh, my God. Did that hit you guys?" A bubbly blonde was sitting in the booth behind me and was all apologies. "I'm so sorry."

Laughing, I assured her it was ok. "No harm, no foul."

The man she was with was clearly embarrassed and made a remark about her having too much to drink. That didn't appear to be the case to me, but what did I know. Turning back to Gregor, he was still red and snickering. Seeing him that way had me laughing all over again.

Holding my stomach, I pleaded, "Please, stop. It hurts."

Narrowing his eyes at me he said, "That's not the only thing that's going to hurt when I'm done with you."

Shaking my head, I wiggled from side to side. "Oh, how I've missed sitting on a sore ass!"

"Want me to make it more so?"

Licking my lips, I replied, "Don't threaten me with a good time."

He started cracking up again and pulled another slice of pizza onto his plate. Soon after, he paid the bill and we walked down the street to a local bar. I was thoroughly enjoying spending time with him in that way, but I was also growing anxious to return to our room. I couldn't help it!

Once in the bar, he helped me with my coat once more and then pulled out the stool as we sidled up to the bar. We each ordered a drink and began talking some more. I was turned toward him and struggled not to touch him.

An hour later, I put my hand on his leg and leaned into his ear. "If you don't take me back to the room, I'm going to get all grabby here, in public."

Grinning wickedly, he flagged down the bartender. "We're ready to check out."

Walking back into the hotel, we waited in the elevator with other couples who leaned on one another while we kept our distance. Heading into the room, I took my coat off and then sat on the bed. Stalking closer, he pushed me back and flipped me to my stomach. Slapping my jean covered ass several times, he then released me, just as I was completely wanton.

"I'll be back." Dumbfounded, I watched as he left the room.

Groaning, I lay there for a minute before getting up. I took my boots off and checked my phone. No calls or texts to worry about. Todd rarely reached out to me when he was on the road. Tonight no different. Scrolling through my newsfeed, Gregor re-entered the room a few minutes later. Probably calling his wife, or his harem of women, to check in. I inwardly snickered and set my phone down.

He began removing his clothes as I watched intently. He'd given me no instructions so I just waited patiently. Grabbing the remote, he put on one of the adult channels as I smirked. Such a guy. I didn't mind, I just found it humorous. Sprawling out on the bed in just his underwear he assumed the position. Face down, he pointed to his back.

Giggling, I agreed. "Yes, Sir."

Pulling out my massage oil, I set it on the nightstand and removed my jeans. Straddling his hips, I let the oil overflow in my hands and began working on his neck and shoulders. I worked him over for almost an hour. I slipped my fingers into his boxers and removed them before massaging his ass. He was almost completely asleep. This made me happy but wasn't a good sign for someone wanting to have sex with him again.

Slapping his ass, I requested for him to roll to his back. With a soft smile on his face he closed his eyes as I straddled his hips once more. Massaging his chest, I continued down until the only thing left to massage was his dick. I began teasing his inner thighs and his hips and watched as he grew more and more aroused.

When his hips rose a few times in response to my touch, I took him in my mouth. He didn't take long. And I sealed my fate. After the blow job he was out cold. I managed to get him to crawl up the bed and under the covers. Turning the television off, I put on my music and then slipped into my nightgown. Crawling into bed with him, I wrapped myself around his back and listened to his soft, even breathing as my music played gently.

It took me a long time to get to sleep, my craving for him growing with each passing minute. I knew what a long week and day he'd had and knew he needed his sleep. Eventually I dozed off. Waking a few hours later, I had to use the bathroom. When I returned to the bed he was still asleep and hadn't moved. I didn't want to disturb him so I crawled in and put my back close enough to his so that his body heat warmed me. A moment later his body flipped and pulled me to his chest. His warm breath against my ear, he tucked his arm around me. Smiling, I curled back into him as he held me tight and we both drifted back to sleep.

When I woke, his hand was sliding down my hip, removing my panties. I turned my face toward his and fresh, minty breath lingered over my lips. He must've brushed his teeth while I was sleeping. I welcomed his kiss as his hand reached up to hold my chin. Rolling to my back, I welcomed the weight of his body against mine.

Hungry lips moved from my lips to my ear and neck and continued moving down. My breasts were already marked by his mouth and he proceeded to mark them further. Arching, I pressed them higher up into him, his hands and mouth branding both breasts equally.

"Oh, Gregor... Sir..." Nearly thrashing on the bed, I needed more of him, all of him.

I needed his possession. The way he swallowed me up, letting me drown in the domination he had over my body. Two fingers slid into my pussy and he hooked them up, hitting that sweet spot that stilled my breath. Unmoving, except for my heaving breasts, I focused on his fingers. Then that thumb pressed down on my clit hard and he waited.

Glancing down, his eyes no longer heavy with sleep met mine as we both waited for my clit to respond. Just his eyes penetrating my own did it. The slow beat of my clit coming to life under his thumb began and we both felt it. It felt like a bass drum as the vibrations echoed through my body.

Begging, I panted, "Please, Sir." He was taking great pleasure in the torture he was bestowing upon me. "Please..."

"What do you want?"

"You, just you. Anything you want to give me, just give it to me. Please."

I swore I heard him growl before his face sank down between my trembling legs. It was quick, powerful, and almost violent. Gregor, as hard as he tried, as strong as he was, couldn't keep my hips pinned to the bed as my orgasm flooded me. He wasted no time placing the condom over his erection and slammed into my still trembling pussy. He fucked me good and hard, just how I liked it. Hands in my hair, holding me steady as I clung to him.

Struggling for the words, I spoke true. "I want you to cum."

Lifting his head, he shook his head and kissed me. Whispering against my lips, "This is about you." He sucked my lower lip between his teeth, his pelvis grinding against me.

"Oh, Jesus." My nails dug into his back as he warned me.

"No marks, Meredith."

I loosened my hold on him, hands flexing. I wanted to mark him desperately, but knew I couldn't. Lifting up, he raised my legs, never relenting. I was crying out, panting, mewling, begging for more.

Leaning down, he panted in my ear, "You got one more in there? I think you do." I couldn't form words as his body hovered over mine, pumping in and out of me. All I did was moan and smile. "You want to come all over your Sirs face again or should I fuck it out of you?"

Giggling and gasping, I replied, "Both, but your face will do, too."

Smiling, he fucked me for a few more seconds before climbing off me and burying his face between my legs once more. He didn't get just one more orgasm out of me, but two. I was on my knees immediately after, rolling the condom off his cock. Taking him in my mouth, his hands tangled in my hair. He fucked my face and it wasn't long before he flooded my mouth.

Rolling over to my back, his body hovered over mine, his image upside down. He lowered his face to mine and kissed me. Even misaligned, his kisses stole another part of me. His hands found my tender nipples and tweaked them as we continued kissing.

"Come on. Shower time."

Closing my eyes, I nodded. Helping me from the bed, I followed him into the bathroom, my nightie discarded. The warm water flowed over us just like our hands did. Slowly, delicately, no spot was left untouched. He showered quickly and left me to finish my routine. He'd mentioned he had a morning meeting and I tried to smile. Finishing up, when I emerged from the bathroom he was already fully dressed.

"I got late checkout if you want to stay and hang out. But I need to get going."

I felt that tickle in my nose and then the pressure behind my eyes. *No fucking crying, Meredith.* Smiling, I sucked back the emotions threatening to ruin everything and just nodded.

"I doubt I'll stay. I have things to do, too." He held up the leather paddles and I knew what he was asking. Shaking my head, I said, "I got them for you... To use on me."

Grinning, he confirmed, "I know that."

"You take them. They're yours."

Smiling, he walked over to me and kissed me. "I had a great time. Drive safe."

"Me, too. I will. Please do the same."

Placing the paddles in his suitcase, he then picked it up and headed for the door. Turning to smile at me, he said, "I'll email you." I just nodded.

The door slammed and my heart left with him. Gutted, I sat on the bed as the tears fell. What the hell was I doing? Why was I so upset? I knew full well what this was and that in the morning it'd be over... until the next time. Would there be a next time? Why could I never stop thinking every time would end up being the last?

I seriously contemplated crawling into the bed and letting the sobs take over. There was time if I wanted it. *NO!* I wouldn't do it. Slapping the tears away, I got up and packed my bag. After getting dressed, I did another sweep of the room to make sure neither of us forgot anything. And there it was. His jacket. Pulling it from the chair, I clutched in between my hands and then raised it to my face.

Inhaling deeply, it smelled like him. Not that I expected it to smell like anyone else. Looking to the clock, I knew he was long gone. The pockets were empty so I knew he had everything he needed. Shoving it into my suitcase, I decided to email him that I had it.

> *TO: bruisedassets@yahoo.com*
> *10:38 AM*
> **Subject: Jacket**
> *You forgot your jacket. I'll take it and give it you when I see you again.*
> *Thank you again for a wonderful night.*

> *TO: meredith@meredithedits.com*
> *10:40 AM*
> **Subject: Re: Jacket**
> *Shit! Ok. I'll figure something out.*
> *Thank you.*
> *Drive safe! :)*

I sighed. I don't know that I expected him to say anything more, but it was clear when we were in the shower that he'd gone back into work mode. Grabbing my purse and suitcase, I made my way out. Sliding the key card into my purse, I walked to my car.

Before I pulled into traffic, I called Tami to check in.

"Hey. I'm heading home."

"That's sooner than I figured."

Sighing, "He has a meeting, or so he says."

She caught on and asked, "You ok?"

"Yes. It's silly. I know." I took a deep breath. "Just the usual feelings of loss and wonder. If that makes any sense."

"Yes, it makes sense. Drive safe. The kids are all at school and I just got home."

"Ok. Thank you again."

"No problem. Call me if you need me!"

"Will do."

CHAPTER
Thirty-Six

FEEL ME

About twenty minutes after I was on the freeway, a song I'd never heard before came on. The lyrics were like a punch to the gut. *Feel Me* by Mecca Kalani sang her melancholy song as I digested the words. It *was* all just a fairytale, Gregor and I. But one thing I knew he did well was feel me. I added the song to my Gregor playlist and listened to it over and over.

I decided to stop and do some shopping on the drive home. I'd spent the first half of the drive, wiping at tears, laughing, and smiling. I was a hot fucking mess. I knew he'd be checking in to make sure I got home safe, so I took a preemptive strike and emailed him.

> *TO: bruisedassets@yahoo.com*
> *12:49 PM*
> *Subject: Re: Jacket*
> *Stopping to do some Christmas shopping. Then home.*
>
> *TO: meredith@meredithedits.com*
> *12:55 PM*
> *Subject: Re: Jacket*
> *Do they have red furry, thick leather paddles there...? :)*

Thanks again for the presents even if they were self-predicated...

TO: *bruisedassets@yahoo.com*
12:59 PM
Subject: Re: Jacket
  Lol. Thinking not. I'm glad you liked them. I enjoyed the smile on your face when you opened them and can imagine the smile upon using them...

No response came. I finished my shopping and then headed home. Unpacking, I changed my clothes and hung his jacket up under some of mine. I took a mental note to put it in my car so I could give it back to him when I saw him next. Of course, we both knew and had discussed that we may not see each other until after the New Year. Groaning, I did not want to think about that.

I didn't hear from him the rest of the day, but in typical fashion he emailed as I crawled into bed. I was beginning to really wonder if he had some mystical powers that told him when I was in bed and thinking of him.

TO: *meredith@meredithedits.com*
11:27 PM
Subject: Re: Jacket
Hope you sleep well tonight... :)

Smiling, I started my reply and hoped he was right.

TO: *bruisedassets@yahoo.com*
11:30 PM
Subject: Re: Jacket
  Right back at you. Body aches in a good way, like I was riding a horse or something. LOL. And I think my tits are hickey marked worse than my ass! :)

Later the next day I emailed him, not having heard back from him.

TO: *bruisedassets@yahoo.com*
2:17 PM
Subject: Re: Jacket
  Thought you'd like to know that every time I sit down my thighs, ass, and hips holler at me!

No reply came until that night after the kids were in bed.

TO: meredith@meredithedits.com
9:36 PM
Subject: Re: Jacket
Hope you are still getting nice reminders every time you sit. :)

TO: bruisedassets@yahoo.com
9:39 PM
Subject: Re: Jacket
Reminders are ever constant. I have a drink in hand and heating pad on
my back. Hope you have some reminders, too.

Almost a week passed. The emails continued, but I had yet to see him. His jacket still hung underneath mine on my side of the closet. I was always good after seeing him...for about a day or two. Then the craving started to build again. I'd never been a drug user until him, Gregor now my drug of choice. He was an addiction I didn't know I'd ever be able to kick. When the craving peaked, I'd grow irritable and start searching for something to curb it, but nothing worked. Chocolate, snacks both salty and sweet, masturbating, alcohol, coffee, hell, I'd tried cigarettes, too. Nothing helped.

The big school fundraiser was this coming weekend. My stress level was almost at max capacity. Todd was able to come home on Thursday, knowing the fundraiser would need my complete attention on Friday. Something I hadn't relayed to Gregor.

That morning, I packed a small bag, grabbed my dress, and headed to the banquet hall for final preparations. Todd was going to get the kids off the bus and then we had a sitter coming to watch them so he could join me. I told him he didn't need to come knowing I'd be unable to pay him much attention, but he'd insisted on coming.

I knew that Gregor would be there and the odds were pretty high that we'd run into one another. He'd said he wasn't sure if his wife would be there or not, as she was always tied up with hospital politics.

I spent the day running around, making sure everything was perfectly done to my specifications. An hour before the event was due to start, I rushed into the bathroom and started to get ready. Emerging twenty minutes later in a dress with my hair and makeup done, I started greeting fellow parents.

I was distracted with friends, laughing and drinking when a chill ran up my back. Slowly, I turned and discreetly ran my eyes over the surrounding throngs of people. His dark blue eyes met my light ones and he smiled at me. I couldn't help but let my lips turn up and then they immediately dropped. Reality hit me like a punch to the gut. A petite woman sidled up next to him and slid her hand in his. The wife. Amy. Closing my eyes, I looked away, but not before I saw him turn and whisper something in her ear.

My stomach churned.

I'd already gotten a phone number for a divorce attorney, unbeknownst to Gregor and Todd. I wasn't naive. I wasn't seeking advice from an attorney about divorce with the expectation that Gregor would leave his wife. I was doing it because I couldn't pretend with Todd anymore. I had no idea what was going to happen, but I needed to know my options. Gregor might be content to pretend with his life, but I wasn't built that way. And there was a good chance that if I divorced Todd, Gregor might pull away from me too. It was a big mess, but I had to do what was right for me and my kids.

"Excuse me." Trying to put on a happy face and hurried off to the bathroom.

I found it empty and locked myself in a stall. Fanning my eyes, I refused to let myself cry. I felt like I was hiding a mountain of shit. And while that was true in regards to Todd, and for obvious reasons, I felt guilty about Gregor and that he didn't know I was contemplating divorce. It was ridiculous.

After a moment, I checked my makeup, and left the restroom. When I opened the door I saw him immediately. He was standing in the corner across the hall and nodded toward me. He wanted to talk. He was pushing it and I didn't care. When he saw that I was heading his way he continued walking so that I would follow him.

"Mer, there you are." Todd.

My fists clenched in response to his intervention. "Hey. Just had to use the restroom."

Todd stepped between Gregor and me, unknowing, and escorted me back to the party. My eyes drifted back to Gregor, who now stood no more than ten feet away, eyes staring after me. What did he expect me to do? Then Todd's hand came over the small of my back and I swear I saw Gregor's own fists clench. He looked angry. What the hell did *he* have to be angry about?

As the night progressed, the auction was over and music played. Some couples danced, but most socialized over drinks. His eyes met mine from across the room, that devilish smile occupying his face as he gazed at me. I smiled and let out a breath before pulling my eyes away from his. In a room full of so many people—people we knew—we couldn't afford for the wrong person to witness our exchange.

The last thing we needed was to draw attention to ourselves. Of course, we were adults and had conducted ourselves as such. People would think what they wanted no matter how well we behaved in public. And how we behaved in private was for us to know and them to wonder.

Later that night I found myself alone in the banquet hall kitchen. I needed a moment of silence. But I wasn't alone for long.

"What is he doing here? You told me he wasn't coming." His voice was laced with contempt.

I was annoyed and relieved at the same time. Turning to Gregor, I kept my voice low and said, "He got home early. What do you care?"

He took a step closer and spit out, "You said you were barely even on speaking terms. Looked different to me."

I shook my head and looked to the ceiling before returning my eyes to his. "He's my husband, Gregor. I'm not sure what you want me to say here."

He grumbled something under his breath as his hand ran over his face. This wasn't like him. He was always cool, calm, and collected.

Stress got the better of me as I pushed for a reaction and I knew I was overstepping. "Don't you dare give me shit! I'm not the only couple in this place putting on a happy face. You may be content to lie to yourself, your wife, and the world that you're the perfect happy couple, but I—we—know differently."

His tone said it all. It was a warning to tread lightly. "Meredith."

I may be submissive in the bedroom, but I wasn't going to take his shit or anyone else's. "I'm moving forward with my life. I have no other choice."

I turned to leave as he barked, "We are *all* lying." What the hell did that mean? I didn't have a chance to ask before he spoke again. "And what does that mean... 'Moving forward'?"

Looking at him over my shoulder I planned to tell him that I was planning to meet with a divorce attorney when Judith walked through the door. Surprised at my quick thinking, I looked to Gregor and said, "Thank you for the donation. It's greatly appreciated." Ignoring the looks from them both, I made my exit.

A couple hours later, I was finally at home. Todd got home before I did as I had things to wrap up at the venue. I walked into the bedroom, already pulling the zipper down on my dress. Walking into the closet, I froze. He stood there holding

Gregor's jacket. *Shit! Think, Mer, think.*

"Whose is this?"

My heart was racing as I made up my lie. "Someone left it at the PTA meeting this week. No one claimed it, so I brought it home."

He was eyeing me suspiciously. "Who is he?"

Gulping, I laughed. "Really? You think if I was having an affair I'd bring him back here?" Moving past him, I pulled my dress off and grabbed a hanger to put it on. "Dream on, Todd."

His hands gripped my shoulders and turned me to face him. "Goddammit, Mer. This isn't funny."

Jerking out of his hold, I walked back out of the closet. "I know it's not funny." Sitting on the bed, I removed my stockings and the pins holding my hair up. Feeling his eyes on me, I looked back up to him. "Todd. Relax. I'll send out another email and see if anyone is missing the jacket. You need to relax."

"Don't think that I don't know things aren't right with us."

Scoffing, I agreed. "Yes, they haven't been right for a very long time."

He stood there a while, watching me. That was until I grabbed my pajamas and closed the bathroom door on his face. I didn't lock it, but there was no need. He didn't attempt to come in.

Leaving the bedroom, I found him on the couch. I walked to my office and shut down my laptop as a precaution. Grabbing my phone, I headed back to the bedroom and went to bed.

I spent the next week cleaning and decluttering the house. Christmas was upon us and I needed all the distraction I could get. Todd and I continued to fight. Sleeping next to him at night was almost unbearable and he refused to sleep anywhere but his bed. More than once I slept on the couch or curled into bed with my youngest. Gregor tried to encourage that I work on things, still not knowing how seriously I was contemplating divorce. Our schedules also had yet to work out to see each other.

A few days after the New Year, we had a PTA meeting. I was dreading it. There was already talk about the upcoming elections and everyone presumed I was going to stay on board as President. I didn't have the heart to tell anyone that it wasn't going to happen. I was done with it and had way too much going on in my personal life to take it on for another year. I needed to focus on my kids and myself. It was too draining.

The day of the meeting, I was out running errands. When I came home I swore I saw Judith pulling out of my subdivision as I pulled in. *That was odd.* When I pulled in the drive, I saw that Todd was home. That, too, was odd.

Walking in, I headed to the bedroom to find Todd making the bed. *What the fuck?* The bed was made when I left the house that morning. I saw red. I know, I was a hypocrite. But I'd never brought Gregor into my home, let alone my bed. I knew immediately what had happened.

"Are you fucking kidding me right now?" He had yet to see me and turned and stared at me blank faced. "Did you think I wouldn't find out?"

He made a move toward me and I stepped back. "Mer. Let me explain."

I started laughing. "Nope. There's no need." I walked into our bathroom and started looking around. I wasn't sure what I was looking for or if I'd even find it. "You fucked her in our bed!"

"It won't happen again." I shoved him away from me.

"You fucking pig. Did it ever stop?" He just stared at me. "Jesus. I'm an idiot." I didn't realize I was crying until I tasted the salty tears. "Get out."

"Meredith..."

I was surprised how calm my voice was. "Todd, I said to get out. Pack your shit and go."

"I'm not leaving."

Grinning I said, "Oh, but you are. You're going to pack your shit and you can go stay with her for all I care. Or sleep in the fucking street."

He made a move for me and I slapped him in the face. "I'm sorry. I, it's just..."

"I don't want to hear it. This has gone on long enough. How long I've gone on thinking it was over is beyond me."

He packed his bag and when he left he was continuing to plead with me that we needed to talk. He tried bringing the kids into it and the look on my face shut him down. He left. It was then that I started shaking. My hands were trembling. I called Tami.

"Are you home?"

"Yes."

"Can you come over?"

"Is everything ok?"

"No. It's not. Please just come over. I need you."

"Ok. I'll be there as soon as I can."

His continued infidelity with Judith was just proof that our marriage was over long ago. And, yes, I said continued. I'd forgiven him once, long ago, and was foolish enough to believe it wouldn't happen again. I'd done it, convincing myself that we needed to stay together for the kids.

Then I was reminded of something my therapist had told me a couple days prior.

"*Listen. People, typically, don't wake up one day and decide to throw a grenade on their life, their marriage. You were in the desert dying of thirst. Todd wasn't there—or was unwilling—to give you the water you needed. Then someone, Gregor, came along and he gave you the water you so desperately needed.*" He paused and nodded. "*Stop beating yourself up.*"

Then I realized, while the situations were different, Todd himself was also dying of thirst.

Looking at the clock, I panicked. The bus would be arriving at the bus stop any minute. Getting myself together, I climbed in my SUV and headed to pick up the kids.

When we arrived back at the house, Tami was in the driveway waiting. She looked at me funny and then devoted her attention to the kids as they swarmed her. We all headed inside and I put a movie on for the kids. Tami followed me into the bedroom as I started stripping the bed.

"Mer, what's going on?"

"It's over. He fucked her in MY bed. I caught him red-handed."

"What?"

"Judith. I saw her leaving the subdivision and when I got home he was making the bed. And, he didn't deny it."

"Jesus Christ."

She helped me put fresh sheets on the bed, though I contemplated dragging the mattress to the curb and setting it on fire. She remained quiet, knowing me well enough to know that I was thinking, though probably too much.

"Shit!" I sat down and she waited. "She'll probably be at the PTA meeting tonight."

"So don't go."

"I have to. I'm the President."

"Then I'll come with you. Want me to throat punch her?"

I laughed. "Yes, but no. I'd have to take the kids and I don't need them witnessing that." Crap, the kids.

Like she knew. "I can watch them. I'm off until tomorrow."

"Thank you."

She and the kids kept me occupied until it was time to head to the PTA meeting. I had an email from Gregor, but I hadn't even read it yet with everything that was going on. Todd hadn't called or texted and for me, that just confirmed it even more. Todd and I were more than likely over.

Pulling into the school parking lot I spotted Gregor's truck and Judith's monster SUV. *Fuck me. Please Lord, let me not go to prison tonight.*

CHAPTER
Thirty-Seven

LIFT ME UP

Closing my eyes, I took a deep breath before getting out of my SUV and walking inside. I was greeted by the usual smiling faces, just nodding and smiling back at them, I headed to the PTA office. Standing behind the desk, my arms braced the edge, fully extended as I dropped my head between them. My heart was racing and it hurt to breathe.

A knock came to the door. "You got a minute?"

My head and neck tilted in response to his voice, almost as if I could feel his breath on my neck. "Not really." Raising my eyes, I tried to smile.

His eyes narrowed on me and he knew immediately something was off. "What's going on?"

I shook my head, "I can't. Not now."

Marcy poked her head in the door and chirped, "We're ready when you are." Then she left.

"Can you talk after?"

Smiling and squinting at him, confused, I asked, "Here? Umm..."

Lowering his voice, he directed me. "Meet me at Joplin's. I'll pick you up and we can talk."

I blew out a breath. I couldn't say no and I needed him. "Yeah. Ok."

Stepping closer, he smirked, "I can't wait to see you. Spank you." And then like his shoes were on fire, he bolted out the door.

Several minutes later the meeting was underway. Admittedly, I struggled to focus. He leaned against the back wall, alone, and I had a puddle in my panties knowing his eyes were on me. I pushed the sleeves of my sweater up my arms and pressed my water to my face. Glancing his way, he smirked at me. He knew exactly what was going on with me.

Chugging some of my water, I tried to remain focused. "Meredith, do we have the final tally from the auction?"

Her voice was like listening to nails on a chalkboard. She sat in the front row, right in front of me. That was probably part of my problem, too. The fucking balls this bitch had were unbelievable. Hell, maybe she was a dude. That would make everything so much more tolerable. Yup. I decided then and there she was a dude and Todd was gay. I started laughing.

"I'm sorry. Is something funny?"

That brought me back to the question at hand. "Judith." I smiled, though it didn't touch my eyes. I shuffled through my papers. "We raised over seven grand."

She sighed, "You don't have an exact number?" I caught her tone and she's lucky I didn't launch myself, or my bottle of water, at her.

"No, actually I don't. I must've forgotten my spreadsheet at home." I tilted my head at her. "You know where I live, right?" Her face began to pale. "I mean, with all those kids, and no maid to help me out, and a husband who's always gone, it's easy to understand that I misplaced it."

She sat her ass down and shut up. If she thought I was going to leave her unscathed in all of this, I just let her know that I wouldn't if pushed hard enough. Gregor, who'd been playing on his phone the whole time, now wasn't. His hands still clutched his phone, but his eyes were on me. He was probably wondering if he was going to have to break up a cat fight and if so, why with Judith.

Gregor knew I didn't like her, but never knew why. And it was a conversation I didn't want to have with him. Ok, maybe that was a lie. *Fuck.* I just wanted out of that school and in the back of his truck. Damn him!

The meeting was almost over when one of the parents, one of Judith's minions, asked a question about elections. She was prying and wanted to know if any of the positions would even be open. Typically we all ran unopposed. Just further evidence that no one wanted these jobs bad enough to compete for them.

Fuck it. I didn't care anymore. "I have no intention of running for President, if that's what you're asking."

The room grew silent. Marcy chimed in, "But you've done an amazing job. You're not running?"

Marcy was sweet, but there was no way I was running again. Then Todd's cross-dresser opened her mouth and I lost it.

"Well, that's a relief."

I saw Gregor push himself off the back wall out of the corner of my eye, but I ignored him. Eyes narrowed at Judith, I spit out, "I'm sorry Judith. Is there something you want to say, want to confess to?" She just balked at me, but her minion opened her mouth.

"I nominate Judith Miller for President." The room was still silent, all eyes on me and Judith. While I wasn't popular like Judith, I was respected.

"You know what? I think that's a fan-fucking-tastic idea!" I started gathering all my PTA paperwork, placed it in my hands and then walked over to Judith. Dropping the stack of papers at her feet, she jumped and leaned back in her chair. Towering over her, I gleamed. "I quit! You can have it." Then I lowered my voice so only her and her minion could hear it. "You can have him, too. He's all yours." Then I walked out the door.

I bee-lined it for the PTA office, grabbing an empty box that sat in the hallway on my way. I heard footsteps following behind me, but didn't know or care who it was. If that bitch said one more word to me, I wouldn't hesitate to expose her.

Throwing the few personal items I kept at the school in a box, I heard the door close. I almost said his name, presuming it was Gregor, and was glad I didn't when I saw who it was. It was Principal Patterson.

"I hope you weren't serious, Meredith. This school needs you."

I shook my head as tears threatened. She was a kind and fair woman and was a great leader at the school, but there was no way I could do this again. "I can't do it. I'm sorry. This isn't like me, but please understand that I have no other choice."

She sighed. "Ok. I won't pry, but know I'm here if you need anyone to talk to."

"Thank you."

She opened the door and as I headed toward the exit, I saw Gregor pacing the front hall. As I approached him, more people flocked toward the exit, the meeting officially over. I couldn't bear the thought of running into Judith once more, so I left, not saying a word to him. Once in my car, my phone alerted me to a text.

He still wanted to meet, but suggested we try Rodeo 1 first. I replied that I'd be there in ten minutes. I made it there before he did, *Lift Me Up* by Mree playing. I texted him that it was all clear, knowing I'd left the school before he did.

The lights of his truck pulled in a few minutes later. Waiting for him to climb out of his truck, I then followed. We hadn't been to Rodeo 1 in so long. It was nice to be back there, at our original spot. He stood by his truck waiting for me.

When I was within touching distance, he pulled me close like he always did. Unable to fight it, I dropped my head and clung to him.

"You doing ok? You were pretty emotional in your emails this week." I raised my eyes to his unsure how much I should tell him.

It was like kismet. My emails *had* been emotional, almost as if I saw something horrible coming before it'd even happened.

Looking away, I nodded and lied. Even when I tried to hide my emotions from him, I couldn't do it. Not even in email. "I'm better."

"No you're not." He clasped his hands around my arms, whispering, "You need a good cry." He had no idea.

It was a statement, not a question and I simply nodded though I knew there was no time for crying now.

Cupping my face, he pulled me closer. "Soon, this week. We'll get you back in balance."

Whispering against his lips, which lingered in front of mine, I consented. "Ok."

"So, what was that with Judith?"

"Can we not talk about her? Please."

Leaning back, it almost fueled him on. "Now I know we need to talk. What's going on?"

I felt sick. "Can we sit?"

"Sure." He took my hand. He'd never done that, not like this, and led me to the picnic table where we sat down. "Talk."

"There's just no easy way around it. And I'm well aware of all the hypocrisy, all things considered."

"Ok."

"Todd and Judith are sleeping together." His lack of shock shocked me. He had almost no reaction. He didn't say anything so I continued. "He didn't deny it when I confronted him. Turnabout is fair play or something like that."

"I have to tell you something." I narrowed my eyes at him as he removed his hat. "I knew."

My bones ached and my face felt like it was on fire and I slid back a few inches. "Excuse me?" He just stared back at me. "What do you mean 'you knew'?"

He explained that he found out the night of the auction. But he didn't realize Todd was my husband until I walked out of the bathroom and Todd stole me away from him. Then he told me that was the reason he found me in the kitchen and what he meant when he said 'we are all lying'. Now it made sense. But it didn't make me feel any better.

"I'm sorry. I really didn't know he was your husband." And why would he? Todd was rarely ever at the school, always on the road. "I spotted him and Judith talking privately, and, well, it doesn't take a genius to figure it out."

I laughed and said sarcastically, "Yes, and you're a genius so...jokes on them, or me? I'm not sure anymore."

Then unwillingly, the floodgates opened. My husband was having an affair and my own lover knew. So, Gregor had only known a couple weeks, but in those couple of weeks he'd urged me to make things work with Todd, or at least try to.

"Why did you encourage me to work on things with Todd if you knew he was cheating?"

"Because I of all people know how complicated it all is. Maybe this is the gateway for you to stay together but also get the outlet you both clearly need."

I lunged back. "Fuck you! No. That's not what he's doing." I jumped to my feet and began to pace. Turning on him, I unleashed. "It wasn't up to you to decide if I was Todd's consolation prize." Turning again I screamed into the cold night air, "Mother Fuck!" Sobs started to tear through me. "I'm sick of being a consolation prize or sloppy seconds."

Gregor tried touching me and I pushed him off, but he was a fighter too. "Meredith..." He said my name, it wasn't lost on me, and he probably did it on purpose. It distracted me just long enough for him to wrap me in his embrace from behind. His voice whispered in my ear, "You're not a consolation prize or sloppy seconds."

"Yes, I am. You don't know everything." Sniffling, he turned me and held my head to his chest. I clung to him, trying to get closer than I possibly could.

"Then tell me."

Fuck. He knew almost all of my secrets. What was one more?

"Judith and Todd have a history. They were college sweethearts." I felt him still before I continued. "I caught him and Judith in bed and we broke-up. But, I was pregnant and didn't know it yet. Long story short, we had a shot-gun wedding and he swore it'd never happen again." I started chuckling, "Hell, maybe they never stopped. Her kid could very well be his. I just don't know anymore."

A long time passed as I cried and he held me, never saying a word. Just let me be. Pain ripped through me like never before. I had my own transgressions to answer for; I knew that I wasn't innocent. My world was spinning out of control and I felt like I couldn't move; helpless to watch it disintegrate. Slowly, I pulled myself out of his arms, his hands still stroking me and gently rubbing my neck.

"I should go."

"Stay."

Baffled, I looked at him. Looking at our surroundings, I knew that wasn't possible. "Where?" Looking at his truck, I began to shiver from the cold, and then I stated the obvious. "You know I can't, you can't. We both have to go home. You have nothing to offer me."

He flinched, like I'd slapped him, but never lost eye contact with me.

"Gregor, we're doing the same thing they're doing. The only difference is they've been found out and it's been going on a lot longer."

"It's not the same thing."

Scoffing, "Isn't it? I'm not your first choice, I wasn't his first choice. But I'll be *my* first choice. I'm going home."

"It's more complicated than that and you know it."

Nodding, I agreed. "Yes, it is. But *I* can't change anything. I know what this is," I motioned between our bodies, "and what it's become and what it can never be. I can't change it no matter how I may want to."

"What do you want to change?"

The tears threatened again. "Don't. You're not stupid." I fumbled with my keys and turned to leave, but stopped in my tracks. "What happens next is up to you, not me."

His voice was calm, yet stern as he said, "You can't tell Todd about us."

Glaring at him over my shoulder, I spit out, "Yes, I know that Gregor. No one can know."

I pulled away before he could try to stop me. Whether he wanted to or not, I didn't know. The song resumed and I started it over. I just had my first real disagreement with Gregor since all of this had begun. It hurt worse than finding out about Todd and Judith.

God! I was an idiot to think either of them cared for me the way I needed and deserved. Before I realized what I was doing, but knowing who I needed, I took a chance and texted Jared. I pulled into a parking lot near home and waited a minute.

He didn't respond, but my phone rang a few seconds later.

"Hey babe, you ok?"

I started crying again. "No. I'm not."

"Did you tell him?"

"I was planning on it, but I found out that Todd's been having an affair."

"Meredith, I'm sorry. You weren't happy with him."

"It's not that. It's with Judith and it's been going on since before we got married. I thought it ended when we got married. How have I been this blind for so long?"

"Jesus. I don't, fuck. What can I do?"

"That's not the worst part... Well maybe it is."

"What is it?"

"Gregor knew."

Silence, he didn't speak.

"Jared?"

"I'm here." He took a deep breath and exhaled it loudly. "You know that I believe he loves you. But he's got to hear it from you, too."

"I just don't know if I can take that risk. I don't know if I'm strong enough."

"You're strong enough."

"I wish I believed in me—in Gregor and me—like you do."

"Neither of us can make him choose you. It's so complicated. What do you want from him?"

"I want to ride off into the sunset." We both started laughing. "Ok, that's a far stretch. I understand so many more of the complexities of this lifestyle...since being with you. Ugh. I just..."

"What is it?"

"I just want to know that he loves me, too. It'd be enough...for now. Living in limbo, wondering how he truly feels is killing me."

"I know it is. It took me a long time to admit it to myself, let alone Heather. I'm lucky she stuck around as long as she did."

I smiled at that. I could picture his face light up at the mention of her name. "He's stated over and over that he won't let this control or complicate his life. Family and home first. I'm probably not even in his top ten. He won't hesitate to drop me like a bad habit."

"Bad habits are hard to break, not easy."

"Jared..."

"Meredith..."

"Wait...did Heather tell you how she felt or..." I didn't need to finish asking the question.

"She didn't need to. A Dom knows his sub. I knew how she felt."

"Goddammit, Jared! That's not helping."

He was suppressing his laughter. "Well, and *your* emotions are written all over your face. He knows."

"I'm going to jump off the bridge now."

"No you're not. Take a few days. A connection like you two have won't be severed in a day or two. He may surprise you and reach out to you first."

"And if he doesn't?"

"Call me. And don't reach out to him. Give him a few days. You both have a lot on your plate."

I was shaking my head. "We've gone over a month without being able to be together. You think a few days will change anything?"

"It's different now."

"How?"

"Don't ask. It just is. I know. But be prepared for him to walk away from you. Men are just as unpredictable as women. I think he needs you, maybe more than you need him, and that probably scares him to death. But that doesn't mean he's going to leave her either."

Pinching the bridge of my nose, "I know. I need a drink."

"So go home and have one, or two, but don't get drunk or do anything stupid. I'm too far away to bail you out of jail."

Laughing, "Ok. Got it. Thanks for talking. I appreciate it."

"Anytime. And the offer is still open. Heather and I would love to have you... for a few days."

He and Heather had both told me that they wanted me to be their third. And I wanted that, too, but just didn't know when or if it would ever happen.

"Mmmm. The offer is enticing, especially now. You'll be the first to know should my schedule open up and I can fly out for a few days."

"You need a break."

"Jared, don't make this any harder than it is. I'd drive to the airport now if my life wasn't in complete shambles. Todd and I still need to talk."

"Ok. Well, might be smart to keep Gregor out of this. Clearly Todd's not happy in the relationship, but there's no need to rub your happiness in his face."

"I know."

"Ok, babe. Stay in touch."

"Will do. Give Heather my love."

"Night."

"Night."

CHAPTER
Thirty-Eight

DARK IN MY IMAGINATION

Idrove home knowing that most of what I said to Jared was true. I just wanted one night away with Gregor and for him to tell me he loved me while he held me in his arms. Was that too much to ask? I knew the love was different, but it was unique and it was ours. Even if it was just one time and I never saw him again. At least I'd know it had been real for him, too. I'd rather know we loved and lost than to wonder the rest of my life if it'd been real.

Of course, if he didn't love me... Well, I didn't know if that was a hurt I'd ever be able to get over. If I exposed my true feelings to him I could very well lose him, lose the most exciting and potent thing to ever happen to me. Part of me was willing to live with the secret if it meant I could keep him a little longer.

I pulled into the driveway and actually felt better. Tami was asleep on the couch and I didn't want to disturb her. Walking to the bedroom, I grabbed my pajamas and headed to the bathroom. The counter was littered with Todd's toiletries and my own.

My phone alerted me to an email. I didn't know whether to be happy or annoyed that he was emailing. He was reaching out. I hadn't done it first. *Fuck.* He was annoying and I wasn't sure if I was referring to Jared or to Gregor.

> **TO: meredith@meredithedits.com**
> *10:31 PM*
> **Subject: Home**
> *Did you make it home?*

> **TO: bruisedassets@yahoo.com**
> *10:33 PM*
> **Subject: Re: Home**
> *Yes, I'm home.*

I left it brief on purpose. I was trying to be strong.

> **TO: meredith@meredithedits.com**
> *10:35 PM*
> **Subject: Re: Home**
> *I've been where you're at, life and marriage at a crossroads. I'm here if you need to talk. Just take it one day at a time.*
> *Try to get some rest.*

Grief flooded me. I screamed at my phone and dropped to the bed.

Tami found me sobbing into my pillows. "Honey. Are you ok?"

Shaking, my voice cracked as I admitted what was already obvious. "No. I'm not."

"Is this about Todd? I mean, I feel like I saw this coming long before Gregor came into the picture."

"That's not it. I'm not crying because of Todd." I looked to her and quickly looked away. "I'm crying because I'm afraid I might lose Gregor in the process."

"Oh, shit. Meredith." She wrapped her arms around me. "What can I do?"

"I don't know. I want off this fucked up ride."

Sighing, she said, "Don't regret anything, Mer. All of this is part of who you are and who you'll become. I know it hurts."

I chuckled, "You almost sound like him."

She grinned at me as we lay face to face in my bed. "I should go. I have to work in the morning. Will you be ok?"

I nodded. "Yes. I'll be ok. Thank you for everything."

"You're welcome."

I walked her to her car and then went to bed.

The next morning after the kids were at school, I headed to the store. I was wandering aimlessly and decided to look at the home décor. A painting caught my attention. I stood there staring at it for quite some time. I'd been looking for something to hang over my bed for a long time, never seeming to find anything that spoke to me. But this, this painting spoke to me. I put it in my cart and grabbed some more items that we needed.

That night it finally happened. Sitting outside my son's karate class in my SUV, I saw his truck driving down the road. As it came closer, the figure that dominated the driver's seat was all the confirmation I needed. I'd recognize his form anywhere. Both of us attending to duties in our regular life, almost colliding with our secret life.

He'd sent an email earlier in the day to check on me and I told him I was managing as best I could. He still wanted to work out time to see me and I wanted that, too. I pulled up my email.

> *TO: bruisedassets@yahoo.com*
> *5:39 PM*
> *Subject: I wonder...*
> *Running errands are you? I see/saw you...*

> *TO: meredith@meredithedits.com*
> *5:43 PM*
> *Subject: Re: I wonder...*
> *Maybe :)*

Always so vague. After the kids were in bed that night, I hung up the new picture above my bed. Admiring my handiwork, I took a picture of it. Then, sitting at my desk, inspiration hit. I attached a picture of the painting.

> *TO: bruisedassets@yahoo.com*
> *9:21 PM*
> *Subject: Dark Imagination*
> *My imagination is dark and my fantasies darker. Like the dark winter forest of the painting I'd purchased, its depths were unknown and waiting to be explored. I felt one with that painting, like I was staring at a part of myself. It was full of mystery, intrigue, and innocence, places untouched, dangerous landscapes, dark corners, and most of all, hope.*

> *TO: meredith@meredithedits.com*
> *9:23 PM*

Subject: Re: Dark Imagination
I'm thinking a swift, firm paddling to help release all of that stored up emotional energy and help rebalance the system that I didn't get to do last night.
With it being so cold – can't have your bottom exposed too long anyways...
:)

No matter how bad things were with Todd, Gregor could always put a smile on my face. Todd had texted and tried to call. I agreed and told him we needed to talk, but I needed some time.

TO: bruisedassets@yahoo.com
9:24 PM
Subject: Re: Dark Imagination
Guess you'll have to bring it quick and hard...

TO: meredith@meredithedits.com
9:23 PM
Subject: Re: Dark Imagination
You talking about your paddling or my cock...?

TO: bruisedassets@yahoo.com
9:24 PM
Subject: Re: Dark Imagination
Both! Do you know someone who can train me and my naughty bottom?!

TO: meredith@meredithedits.com
9:27 PM
Subject: Re: Dark Imagination
I will ask around...

TO: bruisedassets@yahoo.com
9:29 PM
Subject: Re: Dark Imagination
His words should be able to bend my will, his touch bring me pleasure and pain, his kiss set me on fire, and his gaze make me weak...
Not too much to ask...

TO: meredith@meredithedits.com
9:30 PM
Subject: Re: Dark Imagination
Want. Want. Want.

TO: bruisedassets@yahoo.com
9:31 PM

Subject: Re: Dark Imagination
You. You. You.

TO: meredith@meredithedits.com
9:32 PM
Subject: Re: Dark Imagination
Beg. Beg. Beg.

TO: bruisedassets@yahoo.com
9:33 PM
Subject: Re: Dark Imagination
On my knees, Sir...deep eyes pleading...

Adrenaline was running rampant at our exchange. I loved email sparring with him.

TO: meredith@meredithedits.com
9:39 PM
Subject: Re: Dark Imagination
I have some interesting thoughts running through my head for the future...

TO: bruisedassets@yahoo.com
9:41 PM
Subject: Re: Dark Imagination
Mmm...dare I ask or will I be surprised?

TO: meredith@meredithedits.com
9:45 PM
Subject: Re: Dark Imagination
:) Tomorrow.
Be prepared for instructions in the morning.

Good grief. I didn't hear from him the rest of the night and focused on editing for a couple hours before I crashed for the night. I fell asleep listening to *Dark In My Imagination* by of Verona thinking about him and the painting. He possessed me, captivated me, and so many other things. I was under Gregor's spell, my imagination becoming darker and darker with each encounter, email, and embrace. And as to the spell he had me under, I'd probably be under it for a very long time.

Once the kids were at school and I showered, I emailed him.

TO: bruisedassets@yahoo.com
9:19 AM
Subject: Re: Dark Imagination

Woke with soaked panties this morning. Just got out of the shower. It's fucking cold out. Come warm me up!
Any direct orders?

> **TO: meredith@meredithedits.com**
> **9:21 AM**
> **Subject: Re: Dark Imagination**
> *Later and your ass will be warmed...*
> *Plug time. Masturbate, but do NOT come.*

> **TO: bruisedassets@yahoo.com**
> **9:22 AM**
> **Subject: Re: Dark Imagination**
> *(Covers face with hands and sighs) Yes, Sir.*

I did as he directed. Sitting back down at my desk, butt plug in place, I sent him an email.

> **TO: bruisedassets@yahoo.com**
> **9:39 AM**
> **Subject: Re: Dark Imagination**
> *Lil bit of lube and that plug slipped right in. I'm so wet and achy. I can feel the blood pulsing in every part of me...arms, legs, toes, fingers, chest... My breasts haven't ached like they do now in so long...*

That was bound to get a response out of him. Of course I waited over an hour for it. And all he sent was a dick pic.

> **TO: bruisedassets@yahoo.com**
> **10:54 AM**
> **Subject: Re: Dark Imagination**
> *Mine! Gimme! My legs are already fucking trembling. This should be interesting!*

I was ready to burst I was so horny. And he made me wait, and wait, and wait some more.

> **TO: meredith@meredithedits.com**
> **12:30 PM**
> **Subject: Re: Dark Imagination**
> *It's been too long since this has been used... time to get your ass paddled and relieve the built up stress. You will be paddled to tears. Don't fight them. Meet me at the party store by Joplin's in 15 min. I will pick you up and*

drop you back off.
   Leave the plug IN.

I stared at the paddle. It had tiny holes throughout and I knew that it was most likely one he'd made himself. *FUCK!* I couldn't wait!

> ***TO:** bruisedassets@yahoo.com*
> ***12:33 PM***
> ***Subject: Re: Dark Imagination***
> *Take away my pain with your paddle; heal my soul with your belt. I will submit to your cross.*
>   *Yes, Sir...*

He picked me up at the local party store and I climbed in the backseat of his truck. It was then that I wondered where exactly he was taking me. I wasn't worried about my safety; I was worried about the line we were crossing. I knew what street he lived on, but I'd never sought his house out, and didn't know what it looked like. Soon we were on that very street.

My heartrate increased and it became hard to breathe.

He pulled down a dark paved drive and I knew instantly that he *was* taking me to his house. It was crazy, yet reassuring that he trusted me this way. My eyes couldn't help but scan the house and property, like I was gawking at a freak car accident on the freeway. I didn't want to look, but I couldn't stop myself from staring.

My heart was still racing as he pulled into the attached garage and closed the door behind us. I stayed in the truck, paralyzed, and unsure if I should get out or stay put. I decided to stay put. When and if he wanted me out of the truck he'd get me. He secured the garage doors, an entry door, and then walked to his tool bench. In the empty space next to where he parked I watched as he set up a stool and set the paddle from the email down on it. Fuck if he wasn't always prepared.

I had joked with him about hiding him in my SUV and pulling into my own garage a few days prior, telling him no one would know and we could screw in there. Well, now he was turning the tables on me and admitted to just that when he opened the door to let me out.

"You mentioned your garage and I thought 'shit, I have a garage, too.'" I just smiled, nerves stealing my words. "This should be warmer than the freezing winter air on your skin, but I don't have a lot of time."

He took my hand as I nodded my approval and helped me down from the truck. "Ok."

There was no hesitation as he yanked my hips against his and kissed me. Pulling away, I removed my coat and then let him pull me close again. I loved how his hands held me like he owned me. Of course, in that moment he did own me.

"Are you ready to get rebalanced, get the stress out?" His voice was soft and reassuring.

He stared into my eyes and I slowly closed mine and placed my forehead on the bridge of his nose. "I think so. Yes."

I knew what was coming, what I needed, what I consented to, what I asked for. Emotions had been flooding me all day just thinking about it. I was scared of losing him, falling for him, missing him, needing him... and terrified of confessing just that. Ok, let's be honest. I'd fallen for him long ago.

He maneuvered me to where he wanted me. "Bend over."

I did as he asked, placing my forearms on the stool. Hiking up my skirt he ran his hands over the red satin thong I wore. We both knew I wore them specifically for him and his caress was his approval and appreciation.

The paddle was removed from in front of my eyes and I smiled for many reasons. He'd never used this paddle before and I didn't even know he had one like it until the earlier email. It was a good thing I'd chosen another paddle as his birthday gift because I'd almost purchased one similar to the one he was about to use...

'SMACK'.

I tensed with the force of it and hardly had time to recover when the next strike came down.

"Don't hold it back, Mer. Let it out."

Those same emotions came to the surface again. I wanted to let everything out, but I'd conditioned myself to keep it in or to keep it private. How many times in the recent weeks had I gone to bed with tears silently falling from my eyes as I stopped the sobs from taking over? I didn't want to know because it was too many.

Years of crying in the shower, where no one knew my pain, wanted to come barreling out. I was warring with myself and with Gregor's paddle. Knowing that only Gregor and his paddle had been able to get me to sob like I needed in the last few months.

I didn't even try to keep count of the strikes. My watering eyes were making a mess of my makeup as my hands clutched back in my hair. My shoulders were beginning to slowly shake as his free hand moved over my back.

"Stop holding back!" He stepped away from me as I silently chastised myself.

I was a glutton for punishment. I was so wrapped up in my own head, screaming at myself to let it out, that I wasn't sure if he grabbed a different paddle or not.

"Spread your legs and put them straight." That stern voice, my only focus, I did as he ordered, as he continued trying to break me.

The strikes resumed and I focused on the thought of losing him. As it always was with him, everything went silent, only my winces of pain and the sound of the paddle against my delicate flesh echoing in my ears. I was ready to cry out for mercy when he ceased.

Guiding me to the back seat of the truck, we climbed in and he pulled me onto his lap. I straddled him and grew limp as my tears soaked the collar of his jacket. This was it, my safe haven, tucked in his arms as he cradled me like a child.

"Get it out."

We'd done this before, but it was different. My guard was still slightly up, but in a different way. While before I was worried he wasn't truly invested in me and couldn't handle my emotions, now I was worried about how invested *I* was.

"You have more in there don't you?" *Fuck!* I'd never stop being surprised at how well he read me. "Get out. Back to the stool."

I couldn't even look at him. He was right to scold me like a child. I was being disobedient. I took my place as soft sobs continued, not the sobs we both knew I was holding onto. I heard him undo his belt and pull it from his jeans and hell if I didn't sigh in response. I loved his belt and he knew it. It left a different and more potent sting, but didn't leave a lasting mark like the paddles did.

I focused on the thought of losing him, losing us. After doing that, the sobs broke entirely free. I couldn't imagine him not being in my life in some form or fashion. The thought of him out of my life was unbearable. The sobs stole my breath and it was all I could do to breathe.

I love you. I don't want to, but I do.

He stopped and I wondered if my silent confession hadn't been silent. Tears were pouring down my face as my shoulders shook. Pulling me to stand in front of him, he lowered my skirt and wrapped his arms around me. He held me tight and soothed me while I cried. It was a good thing his hold was so strong because I don't think my legs could've held me up on their own.

"Let it out. I have you." Yes, he certainly had me. "I know how hard everything seems right now. But you'll be ok."

"Please tell me you won't abandon me." Squeezing me even harder, till it hurt to breathe, I melted into him.

"There's no need to rush a story like ours." Softly he whispered, "I'm not going anywhere." My sobs broke free again as he soothed me.

A few minutes passed as we stood there clinging to one another. Warm, strong hands moved under my sweater and caressed my bare flesh. Pain was returning to desire as his other hand ran through my hair and over my neck.

"Feel better?" Cupping my face, he looked into my eyes and ran the pad of his thumb over my cheek.

"Yes, Sir. Thank you, Sir." I was his to continue to do with as he saw fit.

The feeling of his hands delicately moving across my bare flesh ran through my bloodstream like waves, awakening every nerve. I could feel him all over me, running through me like the tide. The need to drown in him would never fade.

Kissing me softly, he guided me back to the backseat of his truck. Gently, he laid me down. His hands moved up and over my legs, removing the red thong I still wore. Moving over me, he put them in my purse and kissed his way back down my torso. He pushed my sweater up and unclasped the front closure of my bra. He paid special attention to my breasts for several minutes.

My cheeks were still damp with tears when his tongue began to devour me. We kept eye contact for some time until I couldn't take it anymore and let my head drop back. He teased every part of me, pressing on the butt plug, fingers pumping my pussy and tongue suckling on my clit.

"Come for me." He made eye contact with me once more.

As if he knew I needed more of him, he clasped my hand in his, threading our fingers. The feeling of his hand in mine almost had me in tears again. It took longer than I expected for me to reach my release, but when I did, it was worth it.

I was cradled in his arms again after we were both satiated. I was running my hands over his bare chest as he murmured, "You're going to put me to sleep."

"I could fall asleep, too." Nibbling on his neck I reveled in the small moans that fell from him.

"I have to go soon."

"I know." Moving my lips to his, I thanked him again. "Thank you."

Smiling, he kissed me while holding my face. "You're welcome."

I climbed off his lap and got myself resituated as he did the same. Then I watched as he put the stool and paddles away. Soon we were driving back to my SUV. As we got closer, he reached his hand back and held my own. Caught off guard by the intimate act, I took his fingers into my mouth. I devilishly sucked on them until that smile of his spread across his face. Pulling to a stop, he reached around and swatted my ass as I climbed out of his backseat.

"Be good." The devil's smirk on his face.

Grinning sardonically, I proclaimed, "Never."

His laugh filled my ears as I closed the door and walked to my vehicle.

CHAPTER
Thirty-Nine

BURNING HOUSE

D RIVING HOME, I WAS ALMOST in shock. He took me to his house. What the fuck? I mean, not into his house, but to his garage. I needed music to distract me. Putting on my playlist, I decided that was a bad idea and put on a channel that played Top 40 Pop music.

> *TO: meredith@meredithedits.com*
> *2:32 PM*
> *Subject: Re: Dark Imagination*
> *My boxers have cum smeared everywhere...lol. Between pre and post cum – they are sticky. I am sure you don't want to hear about it from an inconvenience standpoint, but I thought you would enjoy knowing what you do/did.*
> *I hope that restored your balance... :)*

I'd been home for a few minutes when his email came through. I was taking a picture of my freshly paddled ass for him. When I captured a picture I was happy with, I sat down—gingerly—to email him back.

> *TO: bruisedassets@yahoo.com*

2:51 PM
Subject: Transformation
I swallowed every drop you gave me in the moment. I love knowing what I do to you. It's mutual.
Thank you for your time. It means a lot... Thank you for trusting me. That means a lot, too.
Legs are still trembling. Balance is coming and something I'm getting better at. I feel much better, lighter... it helps a lot. I have a fear of losing you, but I think I already said that. Sigh.
Can't decide if I'm hungry or tired. Lol
Enjoy the pictures and the transformation of the marks.

TO: meredith@meredithedits.com
2:54 PM
Subject: Re: Transformation
Damn...looks like someone was very naughty... :) Is she a good girl now?

TO: bruisedassets@yahoo.com
2:56 PM
Subject: Re: Transformation
It fucking hurts to sit, Sir! I'm always a good girl! :)

I didn't hear from him the rest of the day. Emailing as I crawled into bed with my music on, I attached another image of my welted and bruised ass.

TO: bruisedassets@yahoo.com
11:11 PM
Subject: Re: Transformation
Only thing I missed today was your dick in my ass. :) Probably masturbate and pass out while caressing my marks. Sweet dreams...

Then of course, I couldn't sleep. Brain wide awake, I scrolled through my newsfeed. A while later his reply came through.

TO: meredith@meredithedits.com
11:49 PM
Subject: Re: Transformation
I was going to fuck your ass, but you seemed to need the emotional release more than the fucking and I was limited on time... :)
Sleep well.

TO: bruisedassets@yahoo.com
11:55 PM
Subject: Re: Transformation
You read me well. Until next time...

Wrapped around my pillows post masturbating. Thinking about today just resumes the trembling. Thank you for holding me like I crave and letting me know I'm safe without having to say a word.
    Good night. :)

I found myself listening to Burning House by Cam a lot during those weeks. All the dreams and the life Todd and I had built together had been a sham.

Gregor was in touch through email, but I didn't see him. Work, family visits, and everything else had him swamped. We knew and expected this, but it didn't ease the ache. The only thing that did that was the emails. He could email me to tell me the sky was blue and it'd help. Just hearing from him calmed me.

A couple weeks after the Judith confrontation, Todd and I sat down to talk. We sat and stared at each other, not really knowing where to start.

Gregor was in touch through email, but I didn't see him. Work, family visits, and everything else had him swamped. We knew and expected this, but it didn't ease the ache. The only thing that did that was the emails. He could email me to tell me the sky was blue and it'd help. Just hearing from him calmed me.

A couple days after Christmas, Todd and I sat down to talk. We sat and stared at each other, not really knowing where to start.

Having enough of the silence, I was honest. "I don't want this to be an ugly divorce, Todd. I have no plans to rake you over the coals."

Scrubbing his hands through his hair, he nodded. "I'm really sorry it came to this."

I shook my head, "Please don't. Not unless you really want to discuss the façade you've put on for all these years. I'll try to let it go if you stop making excuses."

His face crunched up, "Excuses?"

I closed my eyes and sighed. "Ok. Fine. How long?"

"What?"

"How long have you been fucking her?" I glared at him from across the table. "Did it ever stop? Are you the father of her kid?"

"Jesus!"

"Well, I think I have a right to ask that considering she's the reason we broke up all those years ago."

He dropped his face into his hands. "It would stop for a few months here, a year there." I was going to vomit. "Her kid isn't mine. We checked."

I pushed my chair away from the table. "Unbelievable."

"I'm sorry."

"You're sorry? Really? You've lied to me for the last ten years. For ten years you've ached for her, wanted her, been sleeping with her. All the while I was here, trying to bridge the gap, raising your kids, paying bills, playing housewife. And for what?"

He just stared at me blank faced. Then he asked me what I didn't want to face. "In all these years, you've never strayed?"

I debated about telling him everything, but I just didn't know how he'd react. "Let's say I have strayed. Would it change anything?" Tilting his head at me, he processed my question and then shook his head. "I just want us both to be happy. Does she make you happy?"

"Yes."

"I feel sorry for you both." His eyes narrowed at me. "I just mean how many years have the two of you fought this? It's sad, really. Of course you had your cake and ate it, too, so it doesn't really matter."

There was no point in telling him about Gregor. Did Todd deserve a reason to be angry with me? Maybe, but I just looked at it as an unnecessary obstacle that we didn't need. It wouldn't change anything. He wanted Judith, I wanted my freedom.

My only regret in my whole life was that I'd never truly stood on my own two feet. I always believed myself to be a strong and independent woman. Hell, maybe that was my downfall in all of this. I had a fierce desire to be my own person, my own woman, answering to no one but myself.

Now I was going to get just that.

"I don't expect you to understand."

Oh the temptation to tell him after that statement, but I refrained. "No, probably not." I lied. It wasn't worth the argument. He had no idea and probably wouldn't be able to comprehend how well I actually did understand.

"Did, or do you have any remorse at all? I mean, I feel like I've wasted the last ten years of my life. I gave up really pursuing my career because you insisted I should stay home with the kids. It's all been a lie. This whole time you've wanted someone else." I could feel the heat of the tears as they fell down my cheeks.

"You have your editing. It hasn't all been bad. We have the kids."

"Don't bring them into this. They're the only thing I don't regret right now. I had an internship waiting for me in New York. Do you remember that at all?"

"You got pregnant."

Anger filled me. "That's not the point!" I took a few deep breaths. Anger and resentment would get us nowhere. I truly didn't want this to be a long drawn out process. "I have the number for an attorney. I think we should try to make this as civil and quick as possible."

"You have a number?"

"For God's sake, Todd. Please. Don't try to convince me for one second that you don't have names and contacts. I don't know how long you expected this to go on or to continue to do this, but ten years is long enough." I chuckled and he looked at me funny. "I give her credit for waiting this long."

He didn't say anything.

"We need to tell the kids. Do you have somewhere to go?"

"I'll be moving in with her." There was no guilt in his voice.

"Of course you are." I looked at him and informed him, "You know I could make this very difficult, refuse her any contact with MY kids."

"Mer?"

"Don't. I won't. But I'm not happy about it either. If I catch one iota of a hint that she's treating the kids badly, this will get ugly."

"She won't."

"Todd, I don't want to hear 'she won't', I want to hear an agreement."

He agreed.

Soon after that talk we met with a mediator. Everything was pretty cut and dry. I was going to have to cut back on some expenses, but I'd survive. He wasn't taking on any added expense moving in with Judith and he was very generous with alimony and child support. Since we were staying in the same town we agreed that the kids would spend the weekends with him and we'd try alternating weeks, but I assured him he could see them whenever he wanted. Of course we still had to wait for a judge to sign off on everything.

Sitting the kids down was the hardest part. They cried, though our youngest didn't fully understand the gravity of it all. There wasn't much in the house that he wanted. Most of the furniture was staying except for some family heirlooms of his. The weekend he moved out was rough. His parents took the kids for the day, trying to ease the hurt for them.

Tami kept me company, but kept to herself while he was there. Gregor had been emailing, just reinforcing how important it was for Todd and I to remain friends and a united front for the kids. I was grateful for his support, but it was also annoying on some level. And yes, I wasn't sure what level that was.

That night I got an email from him as Tami and I sat on the couch watching TV.

> *TO: meredith@meredithedits.com*
> *10:38 PM*
> *Subject: Re: He's out*
> *How did today/this evening go?*

> *TO: bruisedassets@yahoo.com*
> *10:44 PM*
> *Subject: Re: He's out*
> *Things are good. Watching a movie with Tami. Kids are in bed. We have a new normal to get used to.*
> *Will email more in the morning.*

Another week passed. We were still email sparring like we typically did. While I didn't necessarily have appearances to keep, he did. All of our friends and neighbors, that Todd and I were relatively close with, knew that we were divorcing. Most were shocked and when they inquired I'd just say it'd been a long time coming, but that it was a mutual decision.

That morning I'd sent Gregor a selfie. We'd been trying to work something out to see one another and I was doing everything I could to make it harder for him to say no.

> *TO: meredith@meredithedits.com*
> *6:08 PM*
> *Subject: Re: Temptation*
> *Love those deep blue eyes... :)*

I smiled.

> *TO: bruisedassets@yahoo.com*
> *6:12 PM*
> *Subject: Re: Temptation*
> *I know you do... They need to be looking up at you while I'm on my knees...*

I didn't hear back for a few hours.

> *TO: meredith@meredithedits.com*
> *10:45 PM*
> *Subject: Re: Temptation*
> *:) Really was just thinking lunch...*

> *TO: bruisedassets@yahoo.com*
> *10:49 PM*
> *Subject: Re: Temptation*
> *Lunch sounds good...*

And it didn't happen. Schedules and conflicts always popping up and ruining our plans. Another week passed. That morning after the gym, I sent him a picture of me in my bra and panties. It wasn't long before he replied.

> *TO: meredith@meredithedits.com*
> *10:49 AM*
> *Subject: Re: Pretty in pink...*
> *Trying to get me to skip my errands tonight? I should be out and about. Do you have the kids?*

> *TO: bruisedassets@yahoo.com*
> *10:51 AM*
> *Subject: Re: Pretty in pink...*
> *No, they're staying with Todd tonight since he'll be out of town this weekend. I'll be waiting, mouth open...*

> *TO: meredith@meredithedits.com*
> *10:55 AM*
> *Subject: Re: Pretty in pink...*
> *May just bring the small paddle and send you quickly home with a very sore bottom and a watering mouth...*

> *TO: bruisedassets@yahoo.com*
> *10:57 AM*
> *Subject: Re: Pretty in pink...*
> *Watering from your cum or lack thereof?!*

> *TO: meredith@meredithedits.com*
> *11:05 AM*
> *Subject: Re: Pretty in pink...*
> *Lack thereof. Might make you wait until next time.*

> *TO: bruisedassets@yahoo.com*

11:07 AM
Subject: Re: Pretty in pink...
Yes, Sir...

I waited to hear from him. He let me know when he was headed to Joplin's and I made the drive to meet him there. As we'd done before, I stood by the exit and waited for him to swing by to pick me up. Jumping in the back seat, he parked in a dark corner and then hopped in the backseat with me.

Like it so often was, barely any words were spoken. I wasn't sure if he pulled me into his lap or if I climbed into it. Taking his hat off, we began kissing like long lost lovers typically did. No restraint, just primal, carnal passion consuming us.

Separating our mouths, he laid me across his lap after pulling my leggings down. Before his paddle struck my skin, his teeth nipped and sucked on the sensitive skin of my bottom. One hand circled over my lower back and the other began to paddle me. He'd pause every now and then, fingering me when he did.

Makeup thoroughly smeared, he pulled me up to face him. Bringing his fingers to my lips, he gently ran his fingers over them and then kissed me. God, he was filthy and I absolutely loved it. Finding the waist of his pants, I unzipped them and pulled his cock out for my attention.

Lowering myself, knees on the floor of his truck, I took my time. I missed having him in my mouth and I wanted him to know it with my actions.

"Christ. I missed that mouth."

Smiling around him, I continued. Waiting for him to pry me off him, he didn't. Flooding my mouth and down my throat, I sucked with vigor. When he was done, tucking himself back in his pants, he pulled me into his lap and kissed me.

I hadn't gotten off and I didn't care. Slowly we kissed each other and held one another close before we parted ways. Dropping me off at the front doors, I climbed out.

"I'll try to work something out for this week."

Smiling, "I'd love that." Then he drove off.

When I pulled in the drive that night, Todd's car was there. *What the hell?* When I got out of my SUV he climbed out of his car and headed toward me.

"Is everything ok?"

He looked pissed. "You changed the locks?"

Sighing, "Yes, I changed the locks."

Growling, he asked, "Where were you?"

I know he didn't think it was any of his business. "Um, really? You don't get to ask me that anymore, Todd."

"You have someone, don't you?"

I just sighed and shook my head. "Todd. I'm not doing this with you. Now, is everything ok?"

Our youngest had left her teddy and had refused to go to bed without it. He told her he'd swing by and pick it up.

"Todd, it's late. She should be in bed."

"She is. I've been sitting here waiting." I looked at him confused. "Judith texted a while ago that she fell asleep."

He'd been waiting almost an hour. We probably just missed each other as I headed to Joplin's. I just sighed. "Let me go grab it. I'll be right back."

Running upstairs, he waited in the garage. Walking to him, I handed it over and he left without another word. Groaning, I closed the garage door and headed to my laptop.

Of course, I had an email.

> **TO: meredith@meredithedits.com**
> **11:19 PM**
> **Subject: Re: Pretty in pink...**
> *I smelled my fingers all the way home... :)*
> *Hopefully your ass received enough attention to get you by this week...*

> **TO: bruisedassets@yahoo.com**
> **11:28 PM**
> **Subject: Re: Pretty in pink...**
> *Agh! Pervert. You're supposed to let me lick and suck it all off! :)*
> *Ass stings, come rub it! It might get me through to Wednesday! Though the marks will probably last into next week. :)*

> **TO: meredith@meredithedits.com**
> **11:31 PM**
> **Subject: Re: Pretty in pink...**
> *I could have let you suck like that for hours. Felt amazing.*

Mission accomplished. I went to bed with a smile on my face, hands rubbing my ass.

CHAPTER
Forty

UNDER YOUR SPELL

T HE SORDID EMAIL SPARRING continued the whole next week. After running errands and going to the gym, I got home and sat down and emailed him that I was home. We were still trying to find time to see one another. His response came shortly after and had me laughing, as well as wanting.

> *TO: meredith@meredithedits.com*
> *1:37 PM*
> *Subject: Re: Running errands*
> *Good – Now you can get back to focusing on my cock*
>
> *TO: bruisedassets@yahoo.com*
> *1:38 PM*
> *Subject: Re: Running errands*
> *When and where? Everything aches to feel it! :)*
> *How would you like me to focus on it?*
> *Suck it.*
> *Fuck it.*
> *Lick it.*
> *Stroke it.*
> *Fondle it.*
> *Squeeze it.*

Rub it.
Blow it.
The options are endless...just like my need... :)

He simply replied with 'LOL' *Jerk!* Later that night, the kids in bed, I couldn't stop thinking about him.

> **TO: bruisedassets@yahoo.com**
> **9:00 PM**
> **Subject: Re: Running errands**
> *How fitting that I'm hungry and nothing sounds good but you. I guess I'll just enjoy licking some peanut butter off a really big spoon!*

> **TO: meredith@meredithedits.com**
> **9:01 PM**
> **Subject: Re: Running errands**
> *:)*

Seriously? Just a smiley face. Ugh!

> **TO: bruisedassets@yahoo.com**
> **9:03 PM**
> **Subject: Re: Running errands**
> *You and that damn smiley face. I'm trying to be patient while wanting to be demanding! :)*

Again, silence. I knew he was on the road and probably out with customers. Listening to *Under Your Spell* by The Sweeplings—one of my new favorite artists—I nearly choked on my water when I read his next email that night.

> **TO: meredith@meredithedits.com**
> **10:41 PM**
> **Subject: Re: Running errands**
> *I just read SPAM mail asking if I want to make women squirt with my mouth....should I ask for more information...?*

> **TO: bruisedassets@yahoo.com**
> **10:44 PM**
> **Subject: Re: Running errands**
> *No, but I'll let you experiment on me all you want! :) If anyone will get me to, it'll be you.*

> **TO: meredith@meredithedits.com**

10:47PM
Subject: Re: Running errands
Maybe tomorrow...

AGH!

TO: bruisedassets@yahoo.com
10:49 PM
Subject: Re: Running errands
Don't tease...
Your place or mine? :) I'm free.

TO: meredith@meredithedits.com
10:52PM
Subject: Re: Running errands
I need that hour massage...

TO: bruisedassets@yahoo.com
10:53 PM
Subject: Re: Running errands
I know you do. We could meet for lunch first?! :)

TO: meredith@meredithedits.com
10:55PM
Subject: Re: Running errands
Depends on timing. Your lips will be too worn out to speak...

TO: bruisedassets@yahoo.com
10:56 PM
Subject: Re: Running errands
Worn from what? Pray tell! :)

TO: meredith@meredithedits.com
10:58PM
Subject: Re: Running errands
Sucking cock out of submissive obedience

TO: bruisedassets@yahoo.com
11:01 PM
Subject: Re: Running errands
As you wish... So, is that a no to lunch then? Lol.
Why must you make me so horny when I'm conveniently lying in bed...
alone?

TO: meredith@meredithedits.com
11:02PM

Subject: Re: Running errands
Because I'm out with customers and my cock is about to pierce this denim layer of secrecy.

TO: bruisedassets@yahoo.com
11:04 PM
Subject: Re: Running errands
Groaning. When do you get home? Fucking thoughts of your hard dick... sliding into me...

TO: meredith@meredithedits.com
11:07PM
Subject: Re: Running errands
Sometime tomorrow...

Vague, vague, vague. Sigh.

TO: bruisedassets@yahoo.com
11:09 PM
Subject: Re: Running errands
Guess sometime will depend on how badly you need that massage and sucking. Heehee.
To masturbate or abstain...

TO: meredith@meredithedits.com
11:10PM
Subject: Re: Running errands
No. You should. Repeatedly.

Uh. This was a first.

TO: bruisedassets@yahoo.com
11:12 PM
Subject: Re: Running errands
Hmm...do you want me extra sensitive?

TO: meredith@meredithedits.com
11:13PM
Subject: Re: Running errands
I want you fucking raw

Jesus H Christ. I felt the blush creep up my cheeks and over my whole body.

TO: bruisedassets@yahoo.com

11:14 PM
Subject: Re: Running errands
Jesus Christ...moaning...I'm in the middle of something. Hold please...

TO: meredith@meredithedits.com
11:15PM
Subject: Re: Running errands
Fuck that. Tell them to leave a fucking VM.

His response made me laugh. Did he really think I was on the phone? How could my attention be anywhere but on him at that moment? I did as he ordered.

TO: bruisedassets@yahoo.com
11:21 PM
Subject: Re: Running errands
I need to be filled with you when I come...
Orgasm one done. Now I'm all sweaty and still panting...

TO: meredith@meredithedits.com
11:23PM
Subject: Re: Running errands
You need two more tonight at least.

The man was trying to kill me!

TO: bruisedassets@yahoo.com
11:24 PM
Subject: Re: Running errands
Yes Sir! Little hard to swipe with cum covered fingers...

TO: bruisedassets@yahoo.com
11:35 PM
Subject: Re: Running errands
Two done. I'm fucking trembling and not from being cold. Fingers got a good workout.

TO: meredith@meredithedits.com
11:37PM
Subject: Re: Running errands
Make them fucking weak in the knuckles...

TO: bruisedassets@yahoo.com
11:53 PM
Subject: Three down...
Yeah, I'm struggling to make a fist at the moment. I may or may not be

sticking to the bedsheets.

I was struggling to stay awake. Three orgasms, self-inflicted ones at that, were bound to take a lot out of a girl.

> **TO: meredith@meredithedits.com**
> **11:58PM**
> **Subject: Re: Three down...**
> *Don't fucking stop.*

> **TO: bruisedassets@yahoo.com**
> **12:33 AM**
> **Subject: Re: Three down...**
> *Vibrator over my panties and legs instantly started to shake...which turned into the butt plug joining in the fun and no more panties. Holy crap, I need you. Heart is pounding, abs are hurting, legs are quivering. Clit – still pulsing...*

I passed out and emailed him in the morning.

> **TO: bruisedassets@yahoo.com**
> **8:29 AM**
> **Subject: Re: Three down...**
> *Good morning, Sir. Hope you got some rest. Mine was intermittent and filled with ordered orgasms and naughty thoughts. Getting ready to take the kids to school. What to do next?! :)*

When I got home from the gym, an email waited for me.

> **TO: meredith@meredithedits.com**
> **10:48 AM**
> **Subject: Re: Three down...**
> *Sounds like your bottom needs a refresher...*

> **TO: bruisedassets@yahoo.com**
> **10:52 AM**
> **Subject: Re: Three down...**
> *My bottom needs you... :)*

Emails continued throughout the day and night. We got on the topic of bringing in a third. He wanted another woman—shocking—and I wanted another man. The shocking part for me was how open he was to my idea. And, open to me inviting Jared in on it. Like that would happen with him being so far away. And, I wasn't sure I'd know what to do with myself if they were ever in the same room together. The thought enticed and scared me to death at the same time. I could only imagine the shit the two of them would come up with. Gregor and I emailed until way past midnight and then were back at it first thing in the morning.

> *TO: bruisedassets@yahoo.com*
> *6:54 AM*
> *Subject: Re: Three down...*
> *Sigh. So. Damn. Horny.*
> *Yes, my mind has been reeling all night, asleep and awake. Thoughts of being face to face with you and Jared behind me...or vice versa...everything is throbbing.*
> *Oh, I meant to say 'Good morning.' :)*

> *TO: meredith@meredithedits.com*
> *6:55 AM*
> *Subject: Re: Three down...*
> *So the vibrator didn't help...?*
> *Maybe the paddle will later.*

> *TO: bruisedassets@yahoo.com*
> *6:57 AM*
> *Subject: Re: Three down...*
> *It helped put me to sleep...for a short while.*
> *I want you and your paddle in my bed now! (Stomps foot!) Lol.*

> *TO: meredith@meredithedits.com*
> *6:55 AM*
> *Subject: Re: Three down...*
> *When and where are you sucking this today?*

He'd sent another dick pic and my mouth watered. God, I missed him. A few more emails went back and forth. We decided to meet for an early lunch and 'negotiate', or so he said. I was convinced he just wanted to make me squirm. Grabbing his jacket before I left, he'd had yet to get it back from me.

We decided on a small 'hole in the wall' joint in town. I arrived before he did and sat down in a booth and placed his jacket down beside me. A few minutes later he walked in and sat down, that fucking grin that undid me plastered on his face.

"How you doing?" His eyes were electric.

Pursing my lips, I smiled. "I'm good. You?"

"Better now."

I just shook my head at him. Handing him his jacket, "Here you go."

"Thank you."

"No problem."

"So. Are we really eating or are you going to get your ass paddled?"

Huffing, I chastised him, "I believe lunch was your idea, not mine." He started laughing at me. "I'm going to choke you. I knew you were just doing everything you could to rile me up."

"Maybe. And I'm the one who's supposed to administer the choking."

My face was hot and I knew he could see it. "Yes, well, I'm ready to go when you are."

"We can't leave now."

Just then the waitress came over and asked for our drink order. I put my acting skills to work and groaned, "I'm not feeling very well. My throat is killing me. Something warm and creamy should help. Do you have any soup on the menu?" I knew full well that they didn't serve soup and I watched as Gregor's expression changed.

"We don't have soup, but I can get you coffee or some hot chocolate." She was clueless to my innuendo, but Gregor was shifting uncomfortably.

"Hot chocolate sounds great! Thank you." Turning my eyes to him, I smiled brightly.

"I'll have the same." When the waitress walked away, he smirked. "That just earned you five extra strikes."

Beaming, I replied, "Thank you, Sir. May I have another?"

"Six." I raised my eyes, thinking. Lifting my leg under the table, I brushed my boot along his thigh. "Seven."

I started chuckling.

"Keep it up and I'll start taking them away." I dropped my foot and clasped my hands in front of me. "Someone's in love with my belt. Or is it my paddle?"

"You tell me."

It was then that the bell to the front door rang and her voice grated through me. *Shit!* What the hell was she doing in this place? Gregor heard it, too, and when I looked to him, his eyes were on the door. I'd left the dominant spot of the booth for him, knowing he'd prefer to see who was coming and going. Something else, or someone else, was with Judith.

Shit!

Calmly, he whispered, "Remain calm."

It was all he had to say to confirm what I already knew. Todd was with her. I was momentarily pissed. He'd never gone to lunch with me in the middle of the day, let alone a work day. The restaurant was tiny. There was no way they wouldn't see us. Watching Gregor's eyes as they rose, I knew one or both of them were walking over.

"Meredith?" He was surprised to see me here, let alone with another man.

Smiling, I turned. "Hey." His eyes looked to Gregor and I was about to introduce them when he beat me to it.

"Gregor." He stretched out his hand. He'd given him his preferred name, not his given name, William.

From what I could gather, Todd didn't recognize him from the school, but Judith knew who he was. I could feel my palms sweating and my heart hammering. The waitress came over and dropped off our cups of hot chocolate as Todd moved to stand at Gregor's side of the booth to make room for her. I watched his eyes as they lingered over Gregor's jacket sitting on the seat next to him.

Gregor had no idea that Todd had seen that jacket. *Fuck, fuck, fuck! Let it go, Todd. Please.* Glancing back at Gregor and then to me, again, I knew he knew. Maybe not everything, but he knew something.

Looking to Gregor, he grunted, "Nice jacket." I couldn't look at him and then he just walked away. I heard him exchange some words with Judith and then heard the bell of the door.

"They left. What was that about the jacket?" He waited, but only a moment. "The jacket." My eyes, glassy and stinging looked up to him. He sighed heavily. "What does he know?"

Shaking my head, "He found it and I told him I brought it home from a PTA meeting. That's it."

"Did he believe you?"

"Wha, I don't know? He never brought it up again." I knew what was going through his head. His exposure. Our exposure. I had no idea what was coming next, but it wasn't what I expected.

"Go to Rodeo 1. I'll be there in ten minutes. If it's not clear, move to Rodeo 2."

I didn't have to ask if he meant now. His expression said it for him. Calmly as

I could, I got up from the booth and headed for the door. Scanning the parking lot, I didn't see Todd's car or Judith's massive SUV anywhere. Hopping in my own, I buckled up and headed toward Rodeo 1. I was trying not to panic, but it was hard. I had no idea what Todd would do, what he'd figured out, and I knew Gregor was going into protection mode as I drove. And that protection wasn't in regards to me.

Rodeo 1 had cars and so did Rodeo 2. I sent him another text and he said Rodeo 3 was also compromised. *Shit!* Then an email came through and my heart raced as I read it.

> *TO: meredith@meredithedits.com*
> *12:03 PM*
> *Subject: Tonight*
> *Can you meet tonight? I need to think about this. I can't have Todd exposing us. Emotions can go haywire in a heartbeat.*

The stinging behind my eyes and the tickle in my nose happened immediately. *No, no, no, no...* I had no way to control Todd and if I tried to confront him about it, it'd just make things worse.

> *TO: bruisedassets@yahoo.com*
> *12:05 PM*
> *Subject: Re: Tonight*
> *Yes, the kids are with him tonight, unless he changes his mind. I'm really sorry. I will not reveal anything about you, us, to him.*

> *TO: meredith@meredithedits.com*
> *12:06 PM*
> *Subject: Re: Tonight*
> *I'll be in touch...*

I sat there for a few minutes in shock. Everything was going so well and now I didn't know what was going on. Tears rolled down my cheeks as I drove home. I wasn't home for five minutes when someone knocked on the front door. Nearly sprinting, I flung the door open and I know my jaw dropped.

"Can we talk?"

Closing my eyes, I shook my head in disbelief. She was the last person I wanted to talk to. I knew she had a history with Gregor—her ex-husband being a good friend of his. What could she possibly want to talk about? I couldn't reveal anything to her because she'd just tell Todd.

"I guess." I didn't want her in my house, but I wasn't going to stand out in the cold with her either.

We stood in my entryway and I moved to my office. Sitting behind my desk, she took the chair across from me. Spotting the email from Gregor, I closed my laptop—not that she could see it anyway. I stared at her and realized she was nervous. This was a side to her I wasn't used to.

"Judith, you came here. What do you want?"

"All I've ever wanted is him." Her voice was broken and I tried to be sympathetic while on the inside I was gagging.

"You have him. You've always had him."

Her doe brown eyes lifted to mine and she shook her head. "You're the mother of his kids, it's different."

I sighed. "Judith, listen. I don't want Todd back. You may feel like he chose me, but he never let go of you. So, honestly, I feel like we both got screwed over by him. But, I can promise you. He will never be back in my bed or in my heart like he was. I've moved on and need to keep doing so for my own sanity and for the sake of my kids."

"Is there something going on with you and Gregor?"

This was none of her business. "He's a friend."

Her eyes scrutinized me and that statement. "He and my ex are really close." I tried to look like I didn't already know this information. "He has dirt on me and could've really screwed me over." She paused, "He didn't and I'm not sure why."

I exhaled. "Well, based on what I know about him. If the information was just going to make things worse for both of you during the divorce, that's why Gregor didn't use it. He's a peacekeeper and protector."

She met my eyes again and then looked out the window. Nodding her head, she agreed. "You're probably right. Had he shared that info, I'd have had nothing after the divorce."

"Judith, I don't want to know anymore. Whether it's about Todd or not, I just... I can't know anymore."

"I understand. I know I'm the last person who should be giving any kind of advice, but I hope you know what you're doing."

Standing, I just smiled and said, "Thank you."

"You know he's not going to leave his wife for you, right? They never leave their wives."

I laughed and snorted. "Um, really? He left me for you didn't he?"

Shrugging her shoulders, she said, "Like you said, we're different."

I walked to my front door and opened it for her. "Yes, we're *all* different."

She didn't say another word and neither did I. After closing the door and sitting back at my desk, I had no idea what the hell had just happened. Did she know Gregor and I were fucking? Did Todd? My head was pounding. Taking my phone with me, I laid down in my bed.

Startled, I woke an hour later. No email awaited. It was still early and he'd said 'tonight'. I tried to remain calm. His email didn't come until dinner time.

> *TO: meredith@meredithedits.com*
> *6:13 PM*
> *Subject: Re: Tonight*
> *Can't meet tonight. Something came up.*
> *I'll be in touch.*

My heart dropped into the pit of my stomach. I had a horrible feeling that everything had just gotten royally screwed up. I couldn't lose him, not like this. Losing him needed to be on my terms. If it wasn't, I knew there was a possibility I'd never recover.

CHAPTER
Forty-One

SALVATION

A WEEK PASSED. THE EMAILS WEREN'T like they'd been. He was pulling back and it was taking everything I had to keep it together and not scream at him in email. I had enough sense and sanity not to call him, but that didn't mean the urge wasn't there. He exercised control in all things. I knew this. Even when he was being irrational—which wasn't often, that I knew of—he was in control.

Salvation by Gabrielle Aplin was playing. The lyrics—like so many—spoke to me. It touched on all parts of him; his eyes, his effect over me, him walking into my life when I needed him most—even when I didn't know it myself. We were worlds away from one another and when we collided, we never expected that in the wreckage, we'd find something so wonderful.

The utter despair I could let myself sink into, if I let myself, was constantly present. He wasn't my White Knight or my Prince Charming. And Lord knows I didn't need or expect him to rescue me. If anything, he was my Dark Prince.

Staring at the beauty of the snowfall, my thoughts were heavy on him. The snow represented innocence, purity, and looked like a blank canvas begging to be painted on. The complete opposite of me. I was no longer innocent, or pure, and my body and heart had clearly been colored upon. If you looked close enough you could see his marks, both inside and out.

And then, more poetry came.

Standing at the riverbed of your love
Waiting for your hands to pull me under
Slowly, I step closer to your tide
Hands, like the waves, wash over me
Drifting in and out of your current
Impossible to quell the desire
Unbearable to turn back, I fall
I succumb, floating closer to you
Looking above, the rain falls down
Unlike my tears, cooling my fevered face
Sinking, I feel you all around me
Underwater, bathed in every part of you
Your touch is like a siren's call
Willingly, I drown again and again

I sent him an email, missing his quick wit like never before.

> **TO: bruisedassets@yahoo.com**
> **12:35 PM**
> **Subject: Hey**
> *I know you're swamped with work and other bullshit…me included. Hope all is well.*
> *Thinking of you.*

He responded later that afternoon.

> **TO: meredith@meredithedits.com**
> **3:17 PM**
> **Subject: Re: Hey**
> *You're special bullshit though… :)*
> *I will try to find a time to meet soon.*

Sighing, I replied. He was always vague enough to leave me wondering, yet hopeful enough to keep me hanging on.

TO: bruisedassets@yahoo.com
3:20 PM
Subject: Re: Hey
Glad you still feel I'm special. My sentiments are the same.
The kids are with Todd rest of this week.

Yes, I threw in my availability because I just never knew if he was talking about meeting today or in two months. I laughed at that and got back to work on editing. I was up to my knees in editing when his email came through.

TO: meredith@meredithedits.com
6:11 PM
Subject: Re: Hey
Running to the store and some other errands after the kids are in bed.
Can you meet at Rodeo 1 around 9pm?

TO: bruisedassets@yahoo.com
6:13 PM
Subject: Re: Hey
Yes. Shouldn't be a problem.

He didn't respond, but I knew he would as it got closer. He texted me close to 9 and said he was on his way to Rodeo 1. Fear and anxiety tore through me. Part of me didn't want to go, but I also wanted, no needed, to see him. Even if it was for the last time.

Pulling into the lot, the only other vehicle there was his truck. Every memory we'd shared in that backseat flashed through me like an electric shock. The night he'd asked me to stay, I should've said yes. I still didn't know what he'd meant, whether he wanted me to stay for an hour or all night, and I would've done either had he persisted.

I parked my SUV as dread continued to creep up my spine. I couldn't do it. I couldn't get out of my vehicle and face him. I had a bad feeling and I wasn't ready to let him go. He was sitting in the dark at our picnic table, waiting, and I wondered how long he would wait. The tears, unlawfully, began falling from my eyes as I pressed the palms of my hands over them.

I became distracted by the song playing and was startled when the door opened. I inhaled a sharp breath, trying to compose myself. "Mer, come here. We need to talk."

He took my hand and led me to the table where we both sat down. My body was trembling and he was well aware of it. I tried closing myself off to him, but his power over me was still prevalent, and I feared it always would be. He stroked my face as I leaned into his hand, his other arm wrapping around me as his warmth cocooned me.

Turning my face to his, he whispered, "I'm going to miss those deep eyes." I covered my face as the tears started flowing again and he wrapped his arms around me. "We have to end this Meredith. We agreed to 'no falling in love'. Let alone everything else that's happened."

"Why would I ever admit that I love you?" My voice cracked as I avoided his eyes. "It's the one thing you said not to do, the one thing I knew if I admitted to..." I stopped talking as my body began to shake.

"When, how long?" He pulled my face to his and stroked it the way only he could. I knew then that he had come to see me that night as I lay asleep in the hospital. "This wasn't supposed to break up your marriage. You're getting a divorce."

"Todd and I had problems long before you came in the picture. You know that. Are you telling me that if you found out Amy was having an ongoing affair, since before you married, you'd be ok with that?"

He ignored my last question as he so often ignored many of my questions. "This was supposed to help us both find balance and peace. Not find love."

"Sometimes we find what we least expect when we need it most."

"Mer..."

I was growing angry. I knew he felt it and I was going to deny it until he admitted it. I'd never even said it to him and he was acting like I made some big proclamation. "I'm not in love with you. Don't flatter yourself." I was fighting my emotions with everything I had so that I could keep him. And he knew how stubborn I was.

I saw him fight the smirk as he floored me with his comment. "I didn't say *you* were." I looked in his eyes and my heart cracked in half. I know what I saw in his eyes, I'd seen it for a while and he could deny it all he wanted, but maybe he'd just admitted it. "You said you were."

I took in a shaky breath and denied it. "No, no I didn't."

Shaking his head softly, he reaffirmed, "But you did. In my garage." He took a deep breath. "I should've ended it then and there."

I knew the exact moment he was referring to. I thought it'd been just a thought, but I must've said it out loud. Covering my face, I began to choke on my own sobs. He pulled me close and let me bury my face in his chest. When I was calm enough to breathe, I lifted my head and struggled to make eye contact with him.

Pressing his forehead to mine he confessed, "I'm going to miss you."

Greif and anger tore through me. "Tell me. Tell me it was at least real, that I'm not crazy." He searched my eyes. "It became more than just sex for you, too. Please give me at least that much."

Sighing, "It did, it is. That's why we can't continue." He ran his hand over his forehead, "And now Todd and Judith might know."

I just shook my head. "You know how unhappy I am, was, at home and in that marriage. You wouldn't be here with me if you were happy, too." I suddenly lost my words, unsure of what I wanted to say next. "Ugh, this is wrong. It's all wrong."

"But for a while it was beautiful and so right, Mer."

"Then why are you ending it? It can still be beautiful and right. We make each other happy; fulfill needs and desires that no one else can." He didn't say anything. Then I confessed what I was pretty sure he already knew. Crying out, "Nobody knows me like you do. I can love you from afar." I was pathetic, but I didn't care.

"Mer, you'll find another person to meet your needs. It just can't be me. I can't just walk away from her and the kids."

And there it was. I never expected him to walk away from his kids. They were his world. I just thought his happiness would mean more to him. I said from the beginning that I wasn't naive and knew he'd never leave her for me. But somewhere along the way as feelings grew and our relationship blossomed, hope planted itself inside me that we'd become more than just play partners, confidants, and lovers.

I was a fool. I wasn't going to argue with him. Only he could change his mind, I couldn't do that for him.

Cupping my face between his hands, he forced me to look at him. "I'm releasing you. We're no longer tied to one another."

I couldn't leave without one more kiss. I pressed my lips to his and he reveled in it as much as I did. He kissed the tears as they fell to our joined mouths, never letting go of my face.

Breathless, I pulled away. "That's where you're wrong. We'll always be tied to one another. It'd be impossible not to be given the world you opened up to me. Whether you know it or not, you saved my life."

I got up and he growled, "Don't walk away from me."

Turning on him I cried, "I'm not walking away from you. All I want is you. Even if it's just a small piece on rare occasions. You're the one walking away." He didn't say a word. He sank back down to the bench of the table. And being the prideful bitch I could be, I stuck the knife in further. "I may enjoy kneeling in front of you and submitting to you, but I will not give you my pride and dignity."

With that I got back in my SUV. I restarted the song that had been blasting when I first pulled up. *For You* by Rae Morris started over as the tears poured down my cheeks. It took everything I had to drive away from him that night. If, and that was a big if, he wanted to talk to me he knew where to find me.

I borrowed someone who didn't belong to me. It was magical and everything I never expected. It was everything I needed. But our ruse was over. Never to be forgotten or regretted.

Not even aware of what I was doing until I did it, I stopped at the local party store and picked up a pack of cigarettes. Sitting in the parking lot, I smoked a couple, which was enough to curb the hurt, but made me nauseous in return.

I debated about calling Tami or Jared, but decided against it. They'd dealt with enough of my problems and had their own issues to deal with. I was a big girl and I had to get through this on my own, as much as it hurt. Picking up a third cigarette, I smoked it down, nearly gagging halfway through.

"Stupid." I threw the remaining pack out the window and drove home.

Walking into the house, the quiet that I normally craved, confounded me. Tears still rolled down my cheeks as I walked through to my bedroom. I put on my pajamas, grabbed a bottle of wine—no, I didn't get a cup—and the ice cream. Sitting down on the couch, I turned the TV on and searched for something to watch. Nothing sounded good.

Picking up my phone, I had an email waiting from him.

"Fuck you!"

I didn't even read it and seriously debated about deleting my email account and creating a new one. Clutching my phone, the sobs broke free once more. Pulling my knees up to my chest, I hugged my legs and cried the way only Gregor had seen me cry.

An hour later my phone pinged again.

"Jesus Christ."

TO: meredith@meredithedits.com
10:29 PM
Subject: Home
Did you make it home?

TO: meredith@meredithedits.com
11:37 PM
Subject: Re: Home
Don't ignore me.

Asshole. He had no right anymore to order me around.

TO: bruisedassets@yahoo.com
11:41 PM
Subject: Re: Home
I'm home. You released me, remember?

I didn't hear back from him. Belly completely full of crap and aching, I crawled into bed that night, his playlist serenading me to sleep. I found myself smiling and crying as I recounted the memories each of those songs represented.

I woke several hours later, in the same position and the music still playing. Turning it off, I checked to see that there were no more emails. Rolling to my stomach, I clutched my pillow and fell back to sleep.

Several weeks passed. It got easier, yet more difficult. I didn't run into him at school and wasn't sure if he was avoiding me. Again, it was a big school and I didn't even know who he was until all of this started all those months ago.

That Saturday I ran into Joplin's to pick up some groceries. Grabbing a bottle of water, it was then that I saw him. He was at another register and I froze. I couldn't not look at him. My eyes quickly looked at the throngs of people near him. I didn't see his wife, but then I saw his kids. I certainly couldn't just walk over and say 'hey'. I probably would've broken down.

His eyes met mine as he walked by and the slight falter in his step wasn't lost on me. I felt it too. I let my lips curl up to a half smile and watched as he walked out the door. He didn't look back and that's when the 'hard' part of all of this came to the surface. We'd discussed early on the problems that could arise from being in the same town. This would be one of the problems. I would have to get used to running into him from time to time.

I didn't cry. Though I wanted to. I called Tami.

"Just breathe, girl."

"I am. I just, I wasn't expecting to see him. I nearly fell over when I spotted him."

"Are you home this evening?"

"Yes. Headed home now with no plans."

"Ok. I'll be in touch. Maybe we can hang out."

"That sounds lovely."

Walking into my house, I had a moment of panic thinking about cleaning since Tami was thinking of coming over. Then it dawned on me that the house was clean, the kids with Todd and Judith.

Part of me loved that Todd and Judith were together. As long as she treated my kids well and they fucked up her house like they did mine, we'd all get along just fine! I could just picture her in tears as one of my hooligans smeared their dirty boots on one of her Persian rugs. It brought me way more pleasure than I'd ever admit.

I was on the phone when the doorbell rang a couple hours later. Opening the door, he was the last person I expected to find on my doorstep. His blues eyes shone at me and his big grin took my breath away. Without caring, I disconnected the call and threw my arms around his neck.

CHAPTER
Forty-Two

BAD INTENTIONS

THE EMOTION IN MY VOICE WAS evident. "What are you doing here?"

His arms held me tight as he spoke softly, "A little bird told me you could use a friend."

Squeezing each other tighter, I praised 'little bird', "I love Tami." Pulling back from him, he wiped the lone tear rolling down my cheek. "Is Heather with you?"

Shaking his head, "No. I figured this was a trip I should make solo." I nodded as he asked, "You going to invite me in?"

"Yes! Sorry. Come on in." He had a suitcase with him and I smiled. Apparently he was staying and I didn't mind. "I can't believe you're here!"

Shrugging his shoulders, "We might have been planning this for a couple weeks. With everything going on, we wanted to make sure you didn't have the kids, etc."

"Yes, that'd be hard to explain."

We laughed. "So, you've been quiet the past few weeks. What's going on?" I hadn't told him about Gregor ending things. "When did he end it, what happened?"

Chin starting to tremble, I folded my arms across my chest. He walked over and pulled me to him. "I screwed everything up. I knew I shouldn't have told him I loved him."

"So you did tell him?"

"Not like you think. It slipped out during a scene."

I heard him sigh. "Ok. That's not uncommon. Scenes can be very emotional. Was he paddling you?"

I nodded against his chest, "To the point of tears."

"Did he end it then or?"

"No, he waited. Todd and Judith saw us at a restaurant together. He ended it shortly after that."

He blew out a breath. "Wow, did he fuck things up."

I pulled back and leered at him. "What?"

"If it was the 'love' thing, he would've, should've, ended it the minute you said it. Or at least stopped the scene, gotten you out of subspace and then talked to you about it." Moving us to the couch, he pulled me to his side. "What happened with the rest of the scene?"

"Umm. He didn't paddle me anymore after I said it, though I thought I just said it in my head. Whatever, doesn't matter now. He went down on me, but didn't fuck me like he planned. He later said he knew that I needed the emotional release, not the fucking."

He chuckled as I looked at him. "He's got it bad."

"Ugh." I dropped my head back to his shoulder. "No, he doesn't."

"Whatever."

"Yes, whatever. It's over and is what it is."

"Has he emailed?"

I shook my head. "Not since that night to make sure I got home ok."

"This isn't over." He stopped me from looking at him, holding me tight. "Don't argue with me. Just trust me. He's not finished with you." I started crying again at his words. "What can I do, Mer?"

"You're doing it. I just want someone to hold me."

Pulling me to my feet, he took my hand. "Come on."

He led me to my bedroom and crawled on the bed. He opened his arms and I crawled in next to him and let him hold me. Jared held me in his arms for over an hour and it helped. I really did just need someone to hold onto and he knew that. A small giggle left my mouth and he laughed.

"You want something. What is it?"

"Massage!"

"Done. On one condition." I looked at him and he gave me his condition. "You massage me first."

"Done!"

Sitting up, he moved forward and climbed behind him on the bed. Without asking, he yanked his sweater over his head.

Sighing, "You trying to distract me?"

"Yes, yes I am." Grinning back at me he asked, "Is it working?"

"Maybe." I started in on his shoulders as he groaned. "So, how are things with you?"

"They're good."

His tone was slightly somber. "You sure about that?"

Shrugging, he mumbled, "Heather is pulling back. The divorce is getting ugly, exactly what she didn't want."

"Is she pulling away or just really stressed? I know that the process is really just beginning for Todd and me. We've agreed on most everything, but now we wait for a judge to sign off."

"Her ex is being nasty. Bringing up the infidelity on her part."

Sighing, "Well even my attorney said there's really no point in bringing that up because a judge will typically discount it. Unless there's some reason to believe the kids are in jeopardy." He looked back at me as I laughed. "I know you're not a threat to her kids. Sounds like he's just on a power trip."

"Yeah. Something like that."

My hands worked lower down his back. "Does she know you're here?"

"She knows I'm in Michigan. She knows you're here."

"Jared?"

Reaching back, he put his hand on my knee. "Don't worry about it. We're fine. We'll be fine. I think I needed the time away and a friend as much as you do."

"You can say that again. Every girl needs a friend like you."

He laughed at that. "I've missed your humor."

"I should go on tour."

When my hands were thoroughly sore we switched spots. The first thing he did was pull my hair aside and kissed the nape of my neck. It was enough to send tingles through me. Tingles I hadn't felt in a long time. Since the 'break up', if you could call it that, with Gregor it was like my libido had been turned off.

His fingers dug in and I instantly relaxed. "Oh, God. I almost forgot how good you are at this."

"You need a full body massage."

"Hmm. I wouldn't turn it down."

Leaning in, he whispered, "Maybe later."

The chill ran over my entire body as he continued working on my sore muscles. He always managed to find things that were sore on me that I didn't even know existed.

I couldn't resist asking. "Did you bring your goodies with you?"

His voice was low and tempting. "Maybe."

"Handcuffs?"

"Guess you'll have to wait and find out."

And... Puddle in my panties. Thank God. I wasn't broken.

A long while later he said, "So what now?"

I leaned back into him as he wrapped his arms around me. "Honest?" He nodded. "I'm starving."

"Eat in or out?"

"Um, takeout maybe?"

"Perfect."

He put his sweater back on and I threw on a hoodie. We got in his rental and headed up to the closest plaza. Deciding on Chinese, we went in while he looked over the menu. We placed our order and then sat down at the window booth and waited. We were laughing, I was laughing, and it felt so good. I hadn't laughed like this in such a long time.

Following his gaze, he was looking at something in the parking lot. "See something?"

He shook his head. "Thought I saw something. Just someone staring at us."

My eyes scoured the parking lot through the window. My first thought was Gregor and then Todd. I guess it didn't really matter. I was a free woman and could be seen with whomever I wanted. Our food was ready and he paid for it and then we climbed back into his rental. I climbed in before he did. When he sat down he asked what I wasn't expecting.

"Gregor drive a truck?"

"Umm, yes. Why?"

"Just curious." I glared at him and he laughed. "Sorry. I don't even know what he looks like so I'm sure I'm just being paranoid."

I sighed, "Can we go eat please? I just... Yeah. I can't even."

"What is it? Him seeing you with me or the thought of both of us."

I started cracking up. "Well, both." I immediately got very hot. "Roll down the windows. Shit!"

Laughing, he put the window lock on before I could get my window down. "You ass!"

"I like you all hot and bothered."

"I know you do! But you're still an ass."

After eating, which I didn't do very much of, we were on the couch and he was rubbing my shoulders again. *Bad Intentions* by Niykee Heaton was playing. My imagination started going crazy at the prospect of both of them at the same time. Jared and Gregor at the same time... I might die. Gregor and I had discussed adding a third, male and female had both been options, but I didn't think there was any way I could handle a second Dom in the room and had said as much to Gregor.

Now that I'd experienced Jared, all I wanted was him in the same room with Gregor and me. I wanted them both to manipulate me. Knowing now it would likely never happen. I thought about the two of them collaborating as to what would happen before the time came. I wanted to know that they discussed me in the dirtiest of ways, about how to get the most pleasure from using me as their sex slave.

I shook the thought away as I felt Jared's breath against my ear. His lips started kissing my neck as he pulled me back to him. "Jared..."

"Tell me what you want, Meredith."

Cooing, "This. Turn it all off. Please."

Turning my chin, he looked in my eyes. "I'm not Gregor."

Somberly, I replied. "I know that."

"Ok." He kissed me then made his demands. "Get undressed and wait for me. I want you kneeling on the floor."

"Yes, Sir."

"Good girl."

We walked to the bedroom and I started to undress. Before he left the room, he pulled a blindfold out of his bag and handed it to me.

"Put this on." He laid it on the bed and walked out the door.

The next morning, I showered and ran my hands over my sore ass. Jared didn't mark me the way Gregor typically did, but it was something. As I was stepping out, Jared climbed in. He swatted my ass as I put the towel over my head, wrapping my hair.

"I'm going to put coffee on." He smiled and then I left the bathroom after putting my robe on.

Coffee now brewing, I was headed back to my bedroom. I heard the water turn off and then there was a knock on the front door. That was weird. Pulling the towel off my head, I dropped it to the floor. Securing my robe, I opened the front door.

I was paralyzed with fear. Why was he here? What was he doing? He was risking so much to be seen here in the daylight. His truck was parked in front of the house. I couldn't breathe and I was probably as white as a ghost.

Gregor stepped inside and closed the door behind him. His hand reached out and touched my cheek. My lungs remembered to work as I took in a deep and shaky breath. He stepped in closer and was about to kiss me, I was sure of it.

"Mer! Where you at, babe?"

Jared. My eyes moved to my bedroom door and then back to Gregor. *Holy shit!* Gregor's eyes searched my own, wondering who this man was in my house, knowing it wasn't Todd.

"Gregor, this..." I couldn't speak. My heart was working so hard, I thought for sure I might hyperventilate.

Jared walked over and stuck his hand out. "Jared. You must be Gregor." Gregor accepted his hand and I nearly blacked out.

I envisioned myself straddling Jared, his cock fully embedded in my pussy. Tingles ran up my spine as I felt Gregor's hands on my body from behind. His deep, throaty words trickled against my neck and ear. Words of possession, reminding me of who I belonged to as Jared pumped his hips against me.

Cooing in approval, Gregor's hand clenched my jaw, turning my lips to his. His mouth obliterated my own as his other hand slid down to my ass. Working the hole with his fingers, we slowly leaned forward. Jared's moans growing louder as Gregor started to prod his dick against my anus, which opened for him with ease.

Slowly, Gregor buried himself all the way inside me. Sweat glazing my body as I trembled against them both, Gregor's chest pressed against my back, his warmth soothing me.

"That's my good girl. Relax and tell me how good it feels."

My tongue, barely able to work, as I started mumbling, "It feels ah...amazing. I," Jared's fingers moved to my clit as I clenched tighter around both of them, eliciting groans from them both.

"You were saying?" Gregor continued to taunt me, pulling my ear between his teeth, sucking the sensitive flesh into his mouth.

"I need to come, Sir."

Chuckling, they both denied my plea, "Not yet."

They continued to fuck me, manipulate me, and use me until I was seeing stars. Gregor's arm was wrapped around my chest as my fingers dug into his forearm, the only thing for me to hold onto. His other hand taking turns from silencing my cries by covering my mouth and then eliciting more by tugging on my hair. Sucking on his fingers, I bit down gently trying to distract myself from the need to come.

"She's ready. Her clit is ready to burst." Jared's words interrupted, but rang true. I moaned in agreement, not knowing if Gregor would concede.

"Is he right? Are you ready?"

"Yes, Sir. Please." I immediately became silent for the split moment he pinched my nipples. "Please..."

His words, directed at Jared, not me, agreed, "She's ready." Then he whispered in my ear. "Take every last drop of me like a good little slut." Turning my face toward his, he knew what I wanted. Needed. Pressing his lips to mine, he growled in my mouth, "Come for us, Princess."

Relaxing once more, I let my body fully enjoy the fullness of them after fighting the sensations for so long. Jared pulled my right hand down to my clit and then gripped my hips, Gregor's lips and teeth never leaving my neck and shoulders, hands cupping my breasts.

"Oh, fuck. Sir! Gregor! Jared!" In my hysteria I wasn't sure whose name to cry out, knowing they were both responsible for my current state.

My fingers worked my clit harder. I wanted to slow down and speed up. I couldn't decide if I wanted to come or not. I just knew one thing, I didn't want it to end.

"Open your eyes!" This time it was Jared's command and I did as I was told. He smiled, "He's right. Your eyes are intoxicating, especially when you're about to cum."

I couldn't hold back anymore. Gregor's hand circled my throat as he bit my neck.

"Relax."

I did as he ordered. Crying out, "I'm going to come..." It started in my fingers and toes as waves of euphoria moved up and through my body.

"That's it."

They touched and teased me until the tremors from my first orgasm ceased, knowing full well if they kept it up they'd just push me into another orgasm and maybe that's what they had in mind. I was limp, lying back in Gregor's arms, catching my breath, still straddling Jared. He was still pumping me and then his release claimed him, fingers digging into my hips as I moved mine over his ripped torso to pinch his nipples. A small smile fell upon my lips as I watched his face start to relax in the aftermath of his orgasm. Turning my face toward Gregor, I clenched around him, still rock hard in my ass. He slipped a finger into my mouth and I sucked it happily.

"Every last drop, Sir. Please."

Groaning, he squeezed his arms around me tighter and proceeded to empty himself inside me. His release brought a peace over me like nothing else. All I wanted was his pleasure and satisfaction, knowing I was the one giving it to him in the moment. Closing my eyes, gentle kisses were placed over my shoulders as I fully relaxed against him.

I was barely coherent as they moved me and cleaned me. Gregor's scent infiltrated my senses as he pulled me to his chest. There was no way I could stay awake any longer. Then I remembered Jared and raised my head. As if they both sensed it, Jared's hands ran over my back, soothing me as Gregor shushed me.

"Shh, you need to rest."

Drowning in the feel and scent of them both, I let sleep claim me.

I shook the fantasy away, realizing my arousal was dripping down my thighs. If they wanted me to be a dirty little slut, they'd accomplished it!

CHAPTER
Forty-Three

I CAN'T STAY AWAY

"Meredith."

Shaking the fantasy away, I looked to each of them in turn. "Sorry." Jared caught on, but Gregor was on edge.

"I'll go. You two should talk."

Gregor interjected. "I can't stay. I just need a minute."

"Ok." Jared walked back to my bedroom and closed the door. It was then I realized he only had a towel around his waist.

"I can explain."

He managed a smile. "It's fine. Now that I know it's Jared. It makes sense." I didn't know what to say to that. He wiped at his brow and I noticed he was sweating. He was nervous. "I wanted to talk to you. I just..."

I couldn't help myself. I wrapped my arms around his neck and his hands grabbed my hips and then held me close as he squeezed me tighter. He didn't show up here to tell me to fuck off. I knew that much.

"I miss you."

Choking out, my lips against his neck, I whispered, "I miss you, too."

Pulling back, he cupped my face and kissed me. I nearly cried in agony when he pulled away a moment later. I needed more. "Here." Looking down, he'd pulled a folded piece of paper out of his pocket. "Read this. Please. I really can't stay."

"Ok." Before I could say anything more, he was out the door.

A few seconds later, Jared was standing in front of me, now fully clothed. He pulled my trembling body to his before taking me back to the bedroom. Sitting down on the edge of the bed, he waited.

My shaking hands managed to unfold the piece of paper and began to scan over the letter. I couldn't see the words through my tears. I handed it to Jared and he scanned over it. Then he read it aloud.

> *"Dear Meredith,*
>
> *These past few weeks have been some of the hardest I've had in a long time. While conflict and complications are the last thing I want in either of our lives... You're a complication I never saw coming and one I can't let go of. While I'll never be able to provide for you the way you deserve and the way you may need from me, I still want you.*
>
> *I'll be staying in Casper tonight and tomorrow night, at the same hotel. There will be a key waiting for you at the front desk. I'd love to see you, even just to talk in private where we can talk more in depth. I know that you deserve at least that much from me.*
>
> *Your Sir"*

Jared handed the note back to me and sat silent. He wiped at my tears and I put my head on his shoulder.

He whispered, "I told you he had it bad. And he's clearly not finished with you." I groaned. "Now you need to decide if you're finished with him."

"Seriously? Will you ever be finished with Heather?"

"Nope. Probably not."

"Fuck. I don't know what to do."

Grinning, he said, "Yes you do. You need to at least go talk to him. Does Todd have the kids?"

I thought about what day it was. "Yes. Conveniently so for the next three nights, then he's out of town for a couple of weeks."

"Well, sounds like you need to pack."

I was smiling through the tears when I asked, "Am I crazy?"

He pulled me in and kissed my forehead. "Nope. Just in love. His effect on you is immense and it's the same for him. I could feel it radiating off the both of you. How the two of you get away with being in public together is beyond me."

I laughed at that. "Not easily." I sat a moment and then worried about Jared. "What about you? Where will you go?"

"Vice is in town, too. We have a room."

My eyes got big. "Vice is here?" He nodded. "Oh, shit. Do I need to check in on Tami?"

"Probably, but not now. I'd give them a few days." We both laughed at his comment and the lingering innuendo in it.

We parted ways a couple hours later. Jared said he'd be in town all week and wanted an update from me. I thought about making Gregor wait, but knew that he was more patient than me. I had no idea what time he was planning to arrive in Casper, but I didn't want to alert him that I was coming either.

I headed out around dinnertime. And as if mocking me, *I Can't Stay Away* by The Veronicas came on. I arrived around eight p.m. His truck was in the parking lot, but I parked quite a ways away, not wanting my vehicle visible in case he was out. Grabbing my suitcase, I walked into the hotel and headed for the front desk. I was greeted with a smile.

"I should have an envelope waiting. Meredith Nichols."

Smiling, she opened a drawer and then pulled out an envelope and handed it to me. "Enjoy your stay."

"Thank you."

I headed to the elevator and opened the envelope on my way. Sitting inside was a smaller envelope with the key card inside. Staring at the number written down on the key envelope, my heart fluttered. 315 was the same room he was in when I came here that first morning all those months ago. Yes, I had a thing for remembering numbers, always had.

Making it up the elevator I now stood in front of the hotel door. Not bothering to knock, I inserted my key and then opened it when the light flashed green. With apprehension, I opened the door and found the room quiet and empty.

"Gregor?"

I wasn't expecting a response and none came. I debated about emailing him or texting him, but if he was indeed with customers, I didn't want to interfere. Rolling my suitcase to the corner, I debated about unpacking it, but decided not to. Yes, I'd packed our goodies, but we needed to talk. That was paramount.

Looking to the desk, I remembered him propped back in the chair, legs kicked up on the desk as he lounged when I walked in that morning all those months ago. It put a smile on my face. His suitcase sat by the bed, not a single item of his strewn about the room. His OCD rivaled my own.

Pulling out my phone, I texted Jared—who was with Tami—and told them I'd arrived and was waiting for him to get back to the room. I sat on the couch and remembered myself draped across his lap as he spanked me. Looking to the clock, I knew I could possibly be waiting a few hours for him to return.

A yawn stifled me. I wanted to crawl in that bed, but I wasn't going to play that easy to get. Getting up, I grabbed the ice bucket and went out to the hall to fill it. I put our drinks in the small fridge and then sat back down on the couch.

Putting my music on, I curled up in the corner of the couch and dozed off. I dreamed of him, his hands on my face and in my hair, whispering those sentiments about my eyes, how natural my submission was, and everything else in between.

I bolted upright a while later and saw that I'd been asleep for almost an hour. Checking my phone, no messages or emails awaited, my music still playing. I used the bathroom and checked my makeup. Moving to the window, I glanced out and admired the stars and full moon. Sighing, I moved back toward the couch when I heard a key slide into the door.

I froze.

Standing between him and the bed, I waited for him to see me. Halting, his eyes met mine and that grin spread across his face and touched those hazy blue eyes of his I loved. Moving forward, he let the door close and then turned the lock.

"You came." I just nodded. "How long have you been here?"

"Just over an hour."

"You should've texted."

I shook my head, "No, I didn't want to interfere if you were with customers."

Stepping closer, he apologized. "I'm sorry I kept you waiting."

"It's ok."

Removing his hat and glasses, he set them on the desk along with his jacket. My hands were playing with the hem of my sweater, nerves eating away at me. Now standing in front of me, his nearness had me trembling. Pressing my lips together and closing my eyes, I remained still.

"Let me see those deep eyes." His finger traced down the side of my cheek as I opened my eyes. He sighed, "So beautiful."

My heart was racing and I could feel the heat building in my chest, on my lower back, and between my legs. Leaning in, I pulled back for the first time ever. He looked back to my eyes and examined them.

"We need to talk, Gregor."

Nodding, "You're right."

Motioning to the couch, I moved to sit down and he sat down in the desk chair, turning it to face me. I smirked, he put himself in the spot of dominance. We were both sitting, but his chair was higher as he looked down at me. It didn't matter, really. I knew that it was more likely instinct with him, not him trying to usurp his authority.

"I don't know where to start, Gregor. You need to tell me what you want."

"You need to tell me that as well. You said a lot that night at Rodeo 1." He exhaled, "This should be easy, but given the circumstances, it won't always be."

"I know that." Meeting his eyes, as my hands continued to play with the hem of my sweater, I confessed, "I meant what I said. I'm fine with our arrangement and the little pieces of you that I get."

Then he did what I never thought I'd see him do. He knelt down in front of me and took my hands into his. "I'll never be able to provide for you the way you may want and the way you deserve." His eyes searched mine. "I need to know that you can handle that."

"I'm not asking for another husband, Gregor. That's not what I want or what I need. But I do need you to be a little more transparent with me."

I knew that was going to be hard for him. He had to know what I needed from him was a confession of his feelings. "Meredith..."

"Just once. Sometimes words need to be spoken even though actions speak louder. Tell me I'm not crazy, not imagining things. I know I'm not your only one. I'm not asking to be." He wiped at the tears as they rolled down my cheek.

"We agreed to no love."

"We agreed to a lot of things. Pretty sure I'm not supposed to know where you live and vice versa. Or know the names of your family, where you work, what you do, and so on." We both took a big breath. "We also agreed that it's possible to have deep bonds with more than one person. I have a bond with Jared, but it's nothing like what I feel for you. Does my bond with him bother you?"

There was no hesitation. "No. I might've been a little jealous when I saw you out with him last night and then saw him in his underwear this morning at your house. But once I knew it was Jared, it made sense. And, I thought I worked out."

I chuckled. "Yes, he's pretty ripped. Lucky me." He didn't say anything. I could see his wheels turning. It was obvious to me now that Jared had spotted Gregor the night before, he just didn't know it was Gregor. "I don't love him Gregor, not in that way. I care for him deeply, probably always will, but he doesn't own me." Our eyes met, "Not like you do."

Lowering his eyes, he sighed. "I don't own you. Never have."

I leaned back, that was not what I wanted to hear.

Squeezing my hands between one of his, the other came up under my chin. "You own me. Have since that first day at lunch. I should've run for the hills. You intoxicated me immediately." We were now face to face, "I'm still trying to figure out if it's your eyes that did me in or something else."

My voice shaking, I pleaded with him. "Please shut up."

Grinning, "I thought you wanted to hear the words?"

First I nodded, then I shook my head, "I do, but I want you to kiss me, too."

Eyes narrowing, lips turned up, he asked, "How badly?"

Searching his eyes, I smiled. "Please, Sir. Please kiss me."

That smile came again as he whispered against my lips, "As you wish."

My breath faltering, I replied, "I think that's my line."

His hand moved to the nape of my neck as his lips pressed against mine. His full lips mingled with mine as his scent infiltrated my senses. Moaning, I gripped the collar of his shirt, trying to get closer to him. His hands grabbed each hip and yanked my ass to the edge of the couch as he kissed me deeper.

Then he slowed down, his tongue gliding across mine and every part of my mouth. No kiss would ever compare to his. Squeezing my ass, he pressed his groin against my own. My legs wrapped around his waist as his hands slid under the back of my sweater.

"Oh." I couldn't contain the gasp as my body reacted to his hot hands on my bare flesh.

Then, slowly, he began to run his hands all over me. Torturing me, knowing exactly what he was doing to me. Leaning back, head resting on the back of the couch, our eyes glued to one another as his hands traveled my body. Little shivers would tickle my skin as he hit nerves just the right way.

Without warning, he grabbed me and turned me over. One hard strike with his bare hand came down on my jeans and then another. His hands pushed my sweater up and left it over my head, my sight taken from me. My knees now on the floor in front of the couch, he pressed his chest against my back. Pulling me upright, the sweater falling back down, his fingers worked my jeans open after removing my boots. Sliding them down my hips, he left the red satin cheeky panties in place.

He growled, "Red. You're a good girl."

Panting, I acknowledged him, "Thank you, Sir."

Slowly, his hands examined the seam of my panties, pulling them aside once my jeans were discarded. "He marked you."

"Yes, Sir." His teeth came down and bit one of Jared's welts. "Oh."

Gripping my neck he pulled me back to him. "Does that hurt?"

"Yes, Sir. Please do it again."

He sucked my ear into his mouth before pushing me facedown onto the couch. Tucking the panties further into my crack, he continued teasing and torturing me, paying special attention to the marks Jared had left on me. His fingers slid over the wet center of my panties and I pushed back against him harder. Slapping my ass, I did it again.

"Someone's missed me."

"Yes, Sir."

CHAPTER
Forty-Four

WRITING'S ON THE WALL

SLIDING MY PANTIES DOWN and off me, his fingers slid in and started fingering me. My nails curled into the cushions on the couch as I tried to remain still. Then the thumb on his other hand began to tease my ass. His erection was pushed tight against me, pressing harder and harder against me.

"You're dripping."

Kneeling down behind me, his tongue slid over my clit and left my legs trembling. Holding my hips, he tongue fucked me until I was ready to burst.

"Please, Sir. I need permission."

Growling, he ordered, "You are NOT to come yet." Turning me over, he crushed his lips against mine.

Kissing his lips, that smelled and tasted like me, I sucked his bottom lip between my teeth. I whispered, "You taste good."

He brought his finger up to my lips. "You taste good, too." I hungrily sucked on it as he watched me closely.

That smile of his turned up his lips as I smiled back at him before pulling his lips back to mine.

Whispering against my mouth, his words surprised me. "I have something for you."

Standing, he took my hand and had me sit on the bed. I had no idea what to expect. He'd never gotten me gifts and I'd never expected them. Opening the safe in the hotel closet, he walked over and handed me a thin square box. It was about the size of a box of chocolates and I giggled knowing there was no way he got me chocolates.

I grew nervous as he urged me on. "Open it."

Glancing back to him and then the box, I unwrapped it. Lifting the lid a red leather collar stared back at me. I couldn't take my eyes off it. He'd never collared anyone, had told me so himself. It didn't bother me and wasn't ever going to press the issue. I knew how monumental this was.

It was barely a whisper. "Gregor?" I struggled to meet his eyes.

"Do you like it?"

Fingering the leather, I told him my true thoughts. "It's beautiful. I just, you don't have to do this."

Fingering my chin and lifting my eyes to his, he smiled, "I want to do this. As long as you agree."

Nodding, "Yes. I agree."

That big grin on his face, he motioned me to turn and lift my hair. "Anytime we're alone like this, you'll wear the collar. It represents our bond. I am yours and you are mine." He fastened it around my neck and then turned me back to face him. "Red suits you."

"That's because it suits you."

"Did you bring any other toys with you?" I nodded and pointed toward my suitcase. Lifting it to the bed, he opened it up. Holding up the wrist restraints, he gleamed, "We haven't used these yet."

"No, Sir."

"Come here."

I stood and walked over to him. Eyes on mine, he pulled the sweater over my head and then removed the red bra. A finger softly glided over my collar bone and between my breasts before he teased my clit upon reaching it.

"You've been a naughty girl."

Bending me over the desk, he began belting me. Already sore from Jared, it wasn't long before my legs almost gave out on me. Quickly, he moved us to the bed and comforted me. I was entirely naked and he was still clothed. Moving to our sides, we were face to face as he wiped my tears and kissed me softly.

"You know I care for you." I nodded. "Now I'm going to fuck you like I hate you... because I love you." My heart leapt and my eyes closed. I started to speak and he put his finger over my lips, my eyes popped back open to look into his. "I don't want to hear you say it until you're ready to come. Let it fall from your lips like a plea for air, as if you're drowning and saying the words will save you." He kissed me and asked, "Understood?"

"Yes, Sir."

"And when I say it back, and only then, are you allowed to come." I bit my lip and he smiled. "Give me your wrists."

I did as he asked. Putting the restraints over my wrists, he rolled me to my back and then climbed off the bed. He grabbed the 'significant damage' paddle and wedged it between the mattress and the headboard. Yanking on it, he smiled down at me.

"This should hold, but be good and remain still."

"Yes, Sir."

Lifting my wrists, he slid the short chain over the paddle. Testing the strength, he said, "I don't know why we didn't try this sooner."

Smiling, I purred, "Now we know."

I watched as he undressed. Then sliding the condom down his length, he climbed the bed and lifted my leg. His hot lips lowered to my inner thigh as he worked his way up my leg and to my hip, avoiding the spot my body needed him most.

Moving up my belly, he then sucked longingly on each nipple while rolling the other with his finger and thumb. My moans filled the room along with my music. Sam Smith's *Writing's On The Wall*. Then, he began to slide into me and watched my eyes as he fully buried himself within me. His breath fanned over my face, still smiling, as he lowered his lips to mine.

Pressing up into him, it was my way of asking him to move, to give me more of him.

"Wanton little hussy."

"Only for you."

He started fucking me hard and slow, making me feel every inch of him. As the sensations began to build, he removed himself from my body, and with his help he repositioned me. On my knees, wrists back around the paddle, he fingered my ass and then reclaimed it with his cock.

Fingers in my pussy and teasing my clit, his dick slid in and out of my ass. It wasn't long until I was tensing.

"Sir!"

Groaning, he commanded me, "Say it!"

"I love you! I love you!"

Hand in my hair, he growled, "I love you, too."

My orgasm claimed me just as the tears claimed my eyes. No longer able to hold myself up, my body sank to the bed with him still inside of me. Pulling out, he released the restraints with fervor.

Rolling me to my back, he put a new condom on as he confessed, "I need your hands on me. I love your hands on me."

Smiling at his confession, I happily grabbed onto him once my wrists were free as he fucked me with a new determination. His mouth reclaimed mine. Legs and arms wrapped around him, face to face, his hazy eyes stared into mine. Every emotion that had been building for months and that had been expressed between us in the last hour were present there in those eyes of his I loved. And I know that the reflection in my own was the same.

Both of his hands gripped the back of my head, tangled in my hair as he kissed me. I thought that I knew what his possession felt like, but in that moment I knew what I'd felt before had paled in comparison to what I felt in that moment.

Panting he asked, "You going to come again? You sound like you're close."

Nodding, I moaned, "Yes. God I've missed you. I love you fucking me like this."

My eyes met his once more as the smile I wore reflected back at me in those hazy blue eyes of his. His hand reached up and pulled back on my hair again, exposing my neck for his love bites.

"Don't forget my rule." He pounded into me harder and then sucked and nipped my neck and ears.

"It was in Roosevelt."

He never stopped moving inside me, but raised his eyes to mine. "Roosevelt?"

Struggling to speak, gasping, I confessed, "You asked when, how long." He hit my sweet spot as my nails dug into his back. "It was in Roosevelt when I fell for you."

Smiling, he understood. "I know. I just wanted to hear you say it."

Grinning, I pulled his mouth down to mine and then pleaded with him again. "I love you."

Moving down my body, he said, "I love you, too. Now come on your Sir's face."

The End

I did it. It was done. My Secret Submission had come to an end. I'd finished my first book. The smile consumed me and emotions flooded me. Months and months of hard work had finally paid off. Taking a deep breath, I attached the file to email and sent it to my editor.

My divorce had been finalized and we were all surviving better than I ever thought we would. The kids were coping with the changes well and their father was more present in their lives than he had been before. He'd actually been promoted and wasn't traveling as much which worked out great for all of us.

A couple months later I sat at my local bookstore for my first signing. I signed another book and when I lifted my eyes for the next one, his hazy blue eyes paralyzed me. What was he doing here? He was breaking the rules, again. I fingered the delicate anchor charm that rested against my neck.

Pursing my lips, I shook my head and then asked, "So, who am I making it out to?"

Leaning down, voice lowered, he said, "Sir."

I smiled and tried to contain my giggle. Biting my upper lip, I then released it and confirmed, "Sir it is." I scribbled in the book and handed it back to him.

"That was quite a dramatic ending."

I narrowed my eyes at him, "You've read it?" He nodded and I shrugged my shoulders. "I have a penchant for it, or so I'm told."

"Do you think she regrets any of her choices?"

Smiling, I shook my head. "Not one. She chose herself and her own happiness in the end and that's what we all have to do sometimes."

Nodding, with that grin on his face, he commented on the necklace. "That's nice. Gift?"

Smiling, "Yes, from my Sir."

"He has good taste." I wasn't sure if he was referring to me or the necklace. "Thank you."

"No, thank you. See you around." Then he winked before walking away.

That night I walked into his hotel room like I'd done so many times before. He was waiting for me and immediately put me in the corner. His hands traveled my body as I relaxed into his touch. Tension rolled off me like it always did.

"I'm proud of you. Do you think anyone suspects?"

Laughter in my voice, I replied, "I think they all suspect, yet are clueless. Good thing we changed your name."

Tugging on my hair and pulling my face toward his, he whispered in my ear, "Are you ready for your punishment?"

"Yes, Sir. I'm ready."

My book had long since ended, but our story was just beginning. But like he'd said so many times, "There's no need to rush a story like ours."

PLAYLIST

Lost - Liza Anne
R-Evolve - Thirty Second To Mars
Blue Blood - Laurel
I'm on Fire - Bruce Springsteen
In for the Kill - Billie Marten
All the King's Horses - Karmina
Blue Eyes Blind - ZZ Ward
Girl Crush - Little Big Town
Fingerprints - Kita Klane
Poison - Vaults
Secret - Angel Snow
Shaped Like a Gun - Tailor
Pull Me Under - Adria
Beautiful Undone - Laura Doggett
Until We Go Down - Ruelle
Raise the Dead - Rachel Rabin
Pieces - Rob Thomas
Hypnotic - Zella Day
Under the Influence - Elle King
I Feel A Sin Comin' On - Pistol Annies
Desire - Meg Myers
Together - The xx
Rescue My Heart - Liz Longley
All I Want - Daniella Mason
I Forget Where We Were - Ben Howard
Falling - Adria
Runaway - Grace Mitchell
Tennessee Whiskey - Chris Stapleton
Use Me Up - Wanderhouse

Not Strong Enough - Apocalyptica, Brent Smith
My Favourite Faded Fantasy - Damien Rice
Bad Things - Meiko
Missing You - Betty Who
Sensual - TVA
Want My Love - Cathedrals
Drop by Drop - The Sweeplings
Feel Me - Mecca Kalani
Lift Me Up - Mree
Dark in My Imagination - of Verona
Burning House - Cam
Under Your Spell - The Sweeplings
Salvation - Gabrielle Aplin
For You - Rae Morris
Bad Intentions - Niykee Heaton
I Can't Stay Away - The Veronicas
Writing's On The Wall - Sam Smith

ACKNOWLEDGMENTS

I don't even know where to begin with this. So many people have held my hand during the writing of this book. They never stopped encouraging me, praising what little tid bits I'd reluctantly show them, and so on. This is for all of you. Here are just a few.

My muse/s: Thank you. You know who you are.

Tami: You've been such a blessing to my life. Knowing I can cry on your shoulder and then laugh my ass off within seconds... Who needs any more than that in a true friend?

Skye & Tyf: Sigh. I just can't. I would not be here without you two and never would've finished this book without your unconditional support.

Jaime & Stacey: Thank you. You two have become such blessings in my life.

Gabbie, Jess, Elaine, Betsy, Tracey, & Rebecca: Thank you for always offering to help and able to make me laugh. Can't wait to see you all again!

Drue & Deanndra: You've both been more supportive of me during this process than I deserve. Words will never be enough...

Letty: You never cease to fail me. Pulling me back from the ledge and guiding me back to the path and pushing for more from me. Thank you.

Cassy: Thank you for this beautiful cover and formatting!

To my children: Your dreams are valid and worth pursuing. Never forget that.

MORE FROM J.M. WITT

ABOUT THE AUTHOR

I'm a stay-at-home mom with four young children residing in Metro Detroit, Michigan.

I've dreamed of writing romance novels since I was little. After having baby #4, who may or may not have been fathered by Christian Grey, I decided it was time to pursue my dreams.

I love music and believe that books and music can't exist without the other. My goal is for you to read more than a good book, but for you to have an experience!

Facebook: www.facebook.com/jmwittbooks

Twitter: @WittyMomAuthor

www.jmwittbooks.com